STARBOUND

S.E. ANDERSON

BOLIDE
PUBLISHING LIMITED

STARBOUND

First published in 2019 by Bolide Publishing Limited

http://bolidepublishing.com

ISBN NUMBER: 978-1-912996-17-9

In a saga, the author inevitably
dedicates one of their books
to the readers,
to you.
I shouldn't have waited
this long
to do this,
but you are worth the wait,
and I hope this book is half as worthy
as you are.

TITLES BY S.E. ANDERSON:

Starstruck Saga

Starstruck

Alienation

Traveler

Celestial

Novellas

Miss Planet Earth

The Horrible Habits of Humans (Pew! Pew! - Bite My
Shiny Metal Pew!)

Miss Planet Earth and the Amulet of Beb-Sheb-Na
(Pew! Pew! Volume 4: Bad versus Worse)

Dark Star (From the Stars, Torment Publishing)

CONTENTS

PROLOGUE
PROLOGUES DON'T NEED A NAME BUT I'LL CALL THIS ONE STEVE   1

CHAPTER ONE
I RUIN SOME PERFECTLY GOOD TEA   25

CHAPTER TWO
INTERPLANETARY SIBLING RIVALRY, NOW IN TECHNICOLOR   39

CHAPTER THREE
RETURN TO NOR-MARCY   51

CHAPTER FOUR
CAREER OPTIONS FOR THE HARDENED SPACE CRIMINAL   65

CHAPTER FIVE
SWAT TEAMS MAKE TERRIBLE ALARM CLOCKS   76

CHAPTER SIX
THE WONDERS OF PYRINIAN ADMINISTRATION   87

CHAPTER SEVEN
DRUNKENLY STUMBLING ON EARTH-SHATTERING SECRETS   103

CHAPTER EIGHT
A SHIP IS BORN   117

CHAPTER NINE
BOOK FIVE, IT'S TIME FOR A WEDDING!   129

CHAPTER TEN
CRISIS-PROOFING YOUR TEENAGE SPACESHIP   142

CHAPTER ELEVEN
I GET MYSELF AN ISLAND   156

CHAPTER TWELVE
COMING FACE-TO-FACE WITH THE CLONES OF OUR PAST   168

CHAPTER THIRTEEN
RETURNING TO THE LAND OF THE LOST   180

CHAPTER FOURTEEN
HAVING FUN ISN'T HARD WHEN YOU'VE GOT A LIBRARY CARD   196

CHAPTER FIFTEEN
WORST CONTACT   213

CHAPTER SIXTEEN
CAUGHT READING MY SISTER'S DIARY   227

CHAPTER SEVENTEEN
SALLY WEBBER GOES TO WASHINGTON   242

CHAPTER EIGHTEEN
THE ABSOLUTELY UNEXPECTED TERRIBLE DAY   261

CHAPTER NINETEEN
THIS ISN'T AN ACTION MOVIE, IT'S THE END OF THE WORLD   275

CHAPTER TWENTY
THE SIBLING TRAP   284

CHAPTER TWENTY–ONE
SAVING THE WORLD IN ALL THE WRONG PLACES   296

CHAPTER TWENTY–TWO
PRETTY BADASS RESCUE, IF I DO SAY SO MYSELF   309

CHAPTER TWENTY–THREE
TOTALLY NOT A ZOMBIE ROMANCE   322

CHAPTER TWENTY–FOUR
HERE'S TO THE NICEST GUY I KNOW   334

CHAPTER TWENTY–FIVE
SALLY'S CHOICE   348

CHAPTER TWENTY–SIX
A GOOD OLD-FASHIONED FIGHT SCENE   359

CHAPTER TWENTY–SEVEN
TROUBLE IN PARADOX   373

CHAPTER TWENTY–EIGHT
ALL THE JOYS OF TIME TRAVEL, NONE OF THE MILES   387

CHAPTER TWENTY-NINE
I HATE MAKING TERRIBLE DECISIONS 398

CHAPTER THIRTY
I USED TO THINK BEING TRAPPED IN A LIBRARY WAS A DREAM 412

CHAPTER THIRTY -ONE
I DIDN'T BRING THE RIGHT DRESS FOR THIS HOMECOMING 425

STARBOUND

BOOK 5 OF THE STARSTRUCK SAGA

PROLOGUE

PROLOGUES DON'T NEED A NAME,
BUT I'LL CALL THIS ONE STEVE

The first time I died, it was a doozy of a death, and I didn't even get to see it.

The second time, my life flashed before my eyes in the form of an '80s movie flashback sequence—record scratch, freeze frame, and all. So, that was a nice change.

Now, you're probably wondering how I got here: lying under an overpass in a pool of my own blood, wearing the most hideous dress you've ever seen. I know, awful, isn't it? As for the how-I-got-here part, well, it's a long story. As I said, flashback sequence. It's gonna explain everything.

I'm stating it for the record: I hate flashbacks. Start in the middle of the action, confuse the viewer, and then, bam! Send them back to two weeks earlier when their life gets turned upside down. Really makes them hang in there. Or makes them really hate the narrator, whichever comes first.

So why this was how I was going to live my last moments on Earth, I didn't know. My mind was flickering back to all the moments in my life that led to my demise to being, well, lying here, *thinking* about these moments that led to my demise. All the little bits that added up to me being shot in the stomach.

Yeah. That.

Did I mention it was painful, too? The most pain I had ever experienced, and I'd had all my atoms spliced and chucked halfway across the galaxy several times, so I've got a pretty reliable scale here. Not to mention I had died before, though I really hadn't noticed it at the time.

My hand clutched the gaping wound in my abdomen, and I couldn't help but think how sticky all this blood was. I couldn't tell which was the part that hurt the most: the wound in my stomach, slowly killing me as my blood rushed out, free at last, or the thought of never making things right between us, of never seeing their faces again, of never telling them everything I had intended to.

So, how did I end up here? Well, how much time do you have, and how far back should we go? Personally, I'm reliving my greatest hits. Like when I almost got to sleep with a starship captain, but he ended up having the same name as my ex, the same one who had been brutally blown up by my boss and my roommate. It's a long story.

Or maybe I should go all the way back to that stupid hot-air balloon that cost me my job and started me on the most insane course my life could ever have taken. It had been fun, for a little while, but now that I was dying, I found a lot of it regrettable.

Blinding light filled what was left of my vision, and all I could think was that people were right when they said how annoying it was in their own near-death experiences. It seemed so far away, yet still somehow within reach, as if it hung in the air before me, just waiting for me to grab it.

Or maybe that was just the spaceship circling overhead.

The light shut off. I had won.

I had also been shot, which sucked. And I was dying, which sucked even more.

Anyway, the end of my life. End of the road. You missed quite a bit, but I think that's my fault. I have to tell you how I ended up here. I have to tell someone. I can't just die here; I hadn't offended the stripper yet.

Well, I guess I can. Since I am.

I thought dying was supposed to be a calm process of numbness and transition.

I was dead wrong, then I was just plain dead.

Until I wasn't.

One Year Ago

"5, 4, 3, 2, 1…. Happy new year!"

The club erupted into cheer, brimming glasses of colorful drinks held high as they started a warm round of "Auld Lang Syne," which quickly dropped the beat and moved on to something with a little more oomph. The DJ was having the time of his life up there, clutching half his headphones to his ear and shouting something I couldn't hear, and soon could not see as the balloons fell from the ceiling and a very affectionate drag queen threw confetti in my face.

I sputtered as the small pieces of paper hit my eyes and stuck to my lips, and I brushed them away with my wrist. I shouldn't have been looking up like that; I shouldn't have…

Not everything is an emergency, I told myself, taking a deep breath. *This is nothing, why are you beating yourself up about it?*

The problem was that I *was* beating myself up about this. About everything. Maybe I deserved it because here I was on New Year's Day, and there were two people who hadn't come into 2018 with me. Zander and Matt were not the only things I would miss from last year, though; having a job and being happy were ranked quite high on the list.

So far, this new year didn't look any more promising than the last. I had missed celebrating the last one since I had been in the hospital because of the Incident. One year down, and so far, no Zander in sight. Not a trace of him. It was, to say the least, very frustrating. He had promised he would come back, and clinging to the idea, to his promise, was probably the last thing keeping me from completely falling overboard.

I eyed one of the pretty drinks, suddenly very aware of my dry mouth, and shook my head. *Snap out of it, Sally Webber.* But I wanted it. I needed it. I needed something sweet to fog up my thoughts and push the bad memories under the rug for a little while.

I forced a smile on my face and looked up again.

The sweet drag queen with the confetti watched me sadly, her face growing with recognition as she took me in. I had been getting a lot of looks like that, lately. Perks of having graced the national news after the Incident. She gave me an apologetic smile, probably having to do with how unnerved I looked.

I turned to find Marcy, the only reason I had come out here tonight. But her face wasn't her face anymore. No. Instead, latched on to her bright red lips were bright purple lips belonging to the pirate queen herself, Dany. The woman's many golden earrings caught the light from the club and were blinding. She had lifted my small friend into the air, holding her up in a passionate embrace.

My face turned hot, burning from the pure awkwardness of it all. My hands were shaking again, though I didn't know if that came from watching the very PDA make-out session or from forcing back my urge to drink copious amounts of alcohol. I stuffed them into my pockets and tripped as I realized my leggings didn't have any.

What the hell was I even doing here? What was I doing with makeup caked on my face, wearing a sequined shirt and shoes so high my knees were going to snap? I felt the unease growing in the pit of my stomach, the signals in my head blaring—I was about to break.

"Sally?" Marcy's hand was suddenly on my shoulder, her voice calm and soothing, but her face was a bright red, even in this blue lighting. I turned to face her and noticed her 2018 glasses were slightly askew on her giddy face.

"You all right?" she asked, a hint of worry sneaking into her voice.

"I'm fine," I lied, smiling back in a way I hoped looked convincing as I shoved everything down as deep as I could into my stomach. "Why?"

"You're not singing or anything. That's not like you. Have you had too much? Should I be—"

"It's just a bit crowded in here." I shook her off with a wave of my hand. "I swear I haven't had anything, Marcy. I'm just going to step outside for a few minutes. Or maybe I'll go home."

"We can come with you if you want," said Dany, with that stoic voice of hers. It always sounded like she was making decrees when she spoke.

"Nah, don't let me bring down your evening."

"Promise me you'll call an Uber?" begged Marcy.

"I'm fine, Marcy. Really, I am."

"Okay, if you say so." She didn't have time to finish her sentence. Dany scooped her up, wheeling her off into a dance. She laughed as she flew across the club, people making room for the two of them to waltz past. I watched them go, happy to see her so exuberant, yet my mind flashed back to the months before when I had flown across that very floor, on the arm of Zander, the most incredible dancer I had ever had the chance of knowing. That night, I had literally been swept off my feet.

I had to get out of here.

I made a run for it, if you could call what I did in those shoes running. I found the back exit and threw myself out the door, breathing heavily as I leaned against the brick wall. Anxiety attack? Panic attack? One of them was coming for me if I didn't get myself calm.

Breathing fast.

Heart pounding.

Weight on my chest.

Here it came.

I closed my eyes, counted the seconds as I breathed in, held the breath, and let it out again. I lost track of time as I did this, focusing only on the breath, on the calming voice of Dr. Shuman teaching me the technique ages ago.

In. Hold. Out. In. Hold. Out.

When I finally opened my eyes, I realized that I was cold. I had forgotten my coat, and, of course, this door was exit only. White, fluffy snow covered the ground, my shoes crunching as I made my way down the thin strip of an alley. I shivered, watching my breath rise in front of my eyes. The steam rose in the night air, swirling mist in the dark evening. I watched it dance in a daze, my eyes unable to focus.

Shit. It was freezing out here.

I glanced up and down the alley, trying to remember my way out. But I was assaulted by yet another memory, this time of Matt taking my face in his hands and kissing me softly. My hands reached up and clutched my head. No, no, no. I did not need a replay.

That was the night he had told me to stop being friends with Zander. Why? The thought of our conversation made me feel weird. It hadn't before. But I didn't want to remember Matt as being possessive; I wanted to remember him as the sweet, gentle guy I knew he was. I shoved those feelings back down where they belonged.

7

I saw movement out of the corner of my eye and straightened. A few feet back into the alley, near the dumpster, a crouched form was half concealed by shadow. It sounded like they were retching—another casualty of the party.

"Have a bit too much to drink?" I called out, stepping in their direction.

They didn't answer. Whoever they were, they were dressed better for the weather than I was, with a heavy winter coat obscuring all their features. I couldn't tell anything about them from this angle.

"You all right?" I crossed my arms over my chest against the cold. It wasn't helping much.

This time, the person heard me. They snapped upright like a jack-in-the-box. Pop goes the weasel. Now that they were upright, they towered over me, a meter taller than anyone I had ever met before. A bundle lay on the ground before him, where I had expected to find barf.

The realization hit me like a brick in the face, a sharp, sudden thwack that stopped my heart for a beat and forced me back. The form at his feet was oozing, emitting a rotten smell I could not place and didn't want to.

Because I knew. Even before the form turned to show me way too many teeth. I knew that the coat wasn't a winter coat but dirty black rags, the kind the reaper would wear. I knew that the smell wasn't puke.

A shudder rippled through me. This had to be some cosmic joke. I had just gotten myself through a panic attack, and *now* there were actual dementors? Where was chocolate when you needed it?

Oh, and magic wands. Please, universe, if you're going to send me dementors, send me a magic wand, too.

The creature dropped its hood, and the dementor-type creature *poofed* out of existence. Pale, sickly white skin and a mouth completely round, hundreds upon hundreds of razor-sharp teeth protruding from the orifice.

Well, *that's* not human.

"What did you do to him?" I asked. Shit, I probably should have said something a little more intimidating. Having met more than one alien before, I knew not to jump to conclusions, but it was a little hard to misread *this*.

Could I outrun them? No, not in these shoes; I could barely walk. Could I fight them? What were two fists against a thousand teeth?

Crap. I was trapped.

The creature, of course, gave no answer, except for a sound somewhere between a hiss and a snarl. I wondered if my clutch could be a weapon, then frowned at the idea.

"We're on Earth. Learn to speak the language," I snapped. "My translator doesn't have a setting for 'asshole.'"

The creature hissed again as if they had understood the insult. Oops. Or, maybe they were just mad I had interrupted dinner.

Shit! I was dessert!

Oh, hell no. I had just survived an exploding power plant, seen a friend die, and lost another one to interstellar travel and the annoying side effect of time dilation. I wasn't going to get eaten in a dark alley *now!*

I gathered my wits, balling my hands into fists, and with a shout, I lashed my foot forward, kicking where I expected to find a groin. No such luck—my foot went straight through, and I toppled forward into the snow, my face smothered in the putrid fabric.

Okay, so floating alien murder guy. Happy new year, Sally Webber!

The creature swooped back, pulling the fabric out from under me. The snow was cold through my sequined top, and my fingers were starting to get numb, not to mention soaking wet. I pushed myself up on my feet just in time to dodge the thing as it swooped down low.

Yank. Even though they had missed me, I was now somehow flying backward in the air. The chain of my clutch had gotten tangled in their arm, and now I was soaring backward while the alien struggled to shake me loose. I dug my feet into the freezing snow and tugged my clutch, but the alien was strong, pulling against me the other way.

"Let go, dammit!" I screamed. "It doesn't go with your outfit!"

They let out a gurgling hiss again, somehow sounding angrier now. They swooped forward, knocking me back on the ground with an *oomph.* Winded, I tried to push myself up, but they were already on top of me, gliding through the air like it was nothing.

Sharp, razor-sharp shark's teeth. With a long tongue, they licked their upper lip, which I guess could be considered their forehead.

I scrambled back, my hands burning in the fiery cold

of the snow, but the creature followed easily, one long, slender hand still wrapped in the chain of my purse. I couldn't get up; I couldn't run. All I could smell was the odor of the beast's putrid breath, a metallic scent coating it all.

It was ravenous, hungry, fully intent on me. But I had no intention of being its next meal. I grabbed a handful of snow and threw it at the monster's face, but it did nothing, only sliding into its mouth like I had given them pop rocks.

And then it was over me, on me, its leech-like mouth edging closer to my face—

Bang.

The creature fell on my chest, dead. I pushed it off me and crawled back, panting heavily. Its body had barely made any sound as it hit the fluffy snow. The hole through its chest was wide, wider than my arm, a clean cut right through its body. I scrambled to my feet, trying to calm my breathing, my overwhelming shock. Someone had saved me. Someone had known what to do.

Silhouetted in the alleyway was a man, gun in hand, silent. My heart skipped a beat: the build, the height, the gun—it was Zander.

He had come back for me.

But as I gathered my breath and my eyes adjusted to the gloom, I saw that I could not have been more wrong. It wasn't a man standing there. They were less muscular than Zander but still tall, and the hairstyle was so similar it had caught me off guard.

And, then, I realized I recognized them.

"Taylor? What are you doing here?"

They smiled as they lowered the gun.

"Saving your ass, of course," they said, smirking. "Now come on. You're soaked. We need to get you warm. How do you feel about pie?"

Taylor looked exactly the same as the last time I had seen them, except maybe for the beautiful blue trench coat and the lack of terror in their eyes. They bent over the alien corpse, patting around the neck and chest, making sure the creature really was dead, before going through the pockets of its long, black robe. Finding nothing, Taylor slung the body over their shoulders with a low grunt, walked it over to the dumpster, and threw it in, slamming the lid shut. Then they were at the side of the victim, checking his pulse. They must have found one because they pulled out their phone and made a few frantic calls while speaking encouragement to the man on the ground. I thought I heard my name thrown in there.

And I, like a dumbass, just stood there shaking in the snow.

"So, pie?" asked Taylor, slipping the phone back into their pocket. They took my arms and scanned them over, turning my hands up and down a few times until Taylor was content. Their touch was warm, even through the gloves.

"Um, sure, I guess," I stammered, taking my hands back. "I thought you were never coming back here! Aren't you supposed to be changing identities? Aren't you supposed to be in hiding?"

Taylor gave me a knowing smile, a very Zander-like smirk. They leaned down, picked up my clutch, and handed it to me. I took it with shaking fingers.

"I'm fine. Thanks for asking," they said. "Things have changed lately. You'll see in a few. I've made an ally who's been really remarkable in all this; she'll meet us inside. And you? Are you all right? Last I heard, you and that Zander dude blew up a power plant."

"I didn't…" I shuddered. That was exactly what we had done, though I hadn't been the one to press the self-destruct button.

"You're not in shock, are you?" they asked. "Near-death encounters can cause you humans to go into shock."

"I'm fine, really." I shook my head. "I haven't been back to the hospital since that other interview with death. Late-night talk show, so I didn't stay long."

Taylor chuckled quietly under their breath before giving me a warm smile.

"So, pie?" they asked, grinning. And before I knew what I was doing, I nodded quickly.

The great thing about small university towns is just how close things are to each other. Across from Scintillance, or at least a short half-block down, was the Jitterbug, my favorite coffee place. And, apparently, Taylor's favorite pie place. And, miracle of miracles, they were open in the middle of the night on New Year's.

We sat in one of the cozy booths as Mona, the only staff here tonight, came over with the menus. Taylor got apple pie; I got cherry. We ordered three coffees. Mona brought us the order then went back to playing Candy Crush on her cell phone, giving us a little privacy.

"I keep expecting you to start sobbing or something, but you seem fine," Taylor remarked casually enough between ravenous bites of pie. "That *interview* with death, so to speak, must have been pretty bad for you to be so calm right now."

"It was." I nodded. "Surviving explosions does that to you. But I think it's the fact I'm soaking wet and exhausted that makes me realize there's nothing left to panic about anymore. I mean, this is my life now. Aliens in alleyways. Aliens coming to my rescue. Everywhere I look, extraterrestrials are trying to screw up my day."

"Or buy you pie." Taylor slurped at their coffee.

"Why are you back here, Taylor? Not that I'm not happy to see you again. I am. But I thought you had left for good."

"I had." They put the mug back on the table. "But I've had an interesting few months. And I honestly just wanted to check up on you."

"You did?" My eyes went wide. "Why?"

"You made international news for not dying. I had to see what was up."

"That was weeks ago."

"I have a lot on my plate," they sighed heavily. They waved Mona over and got a second slice of pie, this time peach cobbler. "Anyway, lucky escape."

"It was. I'm not sure how or why I survived; I'm just glad I did."

I returned to my pie, unable to really taste it, as Taylor tucked into the cobbler. A long awkward silence went by, neither of us wanting to say anything.

Finally, with my pie done, I felt like I had to do something. This was Taylor, for heaven's sakes. Taylor was back. And aliens were still as real as they were last month or last year.

"You said you have a friend coming." I pointed to

the extra mug, and Taylor nodded.

"Just stay cool, okay?" they said, a weak smile on their face. "She doesn't know I'm... not from here. We've been helping each other with things. She can help you, too."

"Help with what?" I asked, but at that moment the door opened, and speak of the devil, in stepped the stranger.

She was beautiful. Tall and slender, she wore a smart navy blue pantsuit that made her seem taller than she already was. Her hair sprang out in every direction, a burst of magnificent black, perfect curls surrounding her gorgeous face. Her bright brown eyes were alert, on fire even, locking onto mine as a smile grew on her face.

"Ah! Sally Webber, I take it?" she said, marching toward me, her hand already outstretched to shake mine. I stood, feeling quite suddenly like I was at a job interview.

"Sally, this is James Felling," said Taylor. "Felling, this is Sally."

"You look quite calm for having just met a leechin," said Felling, suspicion crossing the dark features of her face. "Are you all right?"

"It's just shock, Felling," said Taylor. "Sit down. Your coffee's getting cold."

Felling slid into the booth, taking the spot that had previously been Taylor's. She picked up the coffee with relish, smiling as she breathed in the scent. As she moved her arm, I caught the bulge of a sidearm holstered under her breast. I shuddered.

"James?" I asked.

"Yes?"

"It's a bit of an... odd name, isn't it?"

"It's complicated. Have you given her the talk yet?" she asked Taylor, who shook their head.

"No, I thought you'd want to do the honors." Taylor then glanced at me and gave a quick wink.

"Okay." Felling put down the coffee and crossed her hands on the table before her. She leaned forward, drawing me in. "I'm going to be perfectly honest with you. I think you deserve the truth after what you've been through, and Taylor here vouches for you."

"O... kay?" I replied, confused as ever. This was starting to become my default setting.

"It's pretty big," she warned. "Life changing. Your world will never be the same."

"You sure you want to do that to me?" I asked, and Taylor rolled their eyes. I hoped this wasn't going where I thought it was.

"You deserve it," Felling insisted. "Anyway... the creature that tried to kill you tonight? We call them leechins. And they're...they're aliens."

My eyes went wide. Taylor was barely containing their laughter at this point. They grabbed their mug and made a fuss of drinking the coffee.

"Aliens...?" I muttered, feeling my eyebrows ascending my forehead like they were a part of an alien abduction themselves. Or maybe because they wanted to be anywhere but here.

"I've seen them myself." Felling nodded slowly. "I know it sounds preposterous. But after what you've seen tonight, you can't deny that that creature was not of this world."

"Right, so taking what you're saying is true," I said, feigning ignorance, "what did this so-called leechin want with me?"

"We call them leechins because they're so much like leeches," she explained. "Leechins are pretty common and are always nasty. They're scavengers, you see, much like vultures. Wouldn't go back to their home planet, even if they had the chance. Anyway, it probably found the victim passed out and went in for an easy meal. You threatened it."

"It started it!"

"I'm amazed you lasted long enough for Taylor to show up," said Felling. "I'm glad you're all right."

"Yeah, thanks," I muttered and picked up my coffee mug. This was really awkward. "So, you do… what, exactly? Shoot down aliens from outer space?"

"Leechins are pests." Her tone turned solemn. "Incredibly dangerous to the human population but dumb as hell. No longer any intelligence, no full brain capacity. Of course, we try to keep them under wraps, but the taste of human blood makes them dangerous, almost insane. If they do take a human being as a snack, we have to put them down."

"Oh, wait, don't say it!" I wanted to laugh. Holy hell, my night was weird. "You and Taylor are part of a shady government conspiracy to keep humans safe from aliens. Am I right? I have to be right; this is just like on TV. The way you're dressed—it's too perfect! So, who do you work for? FBI? CIA? Secret government task force?"

"Wait, I know you," said James. "You're that girl! The one from the Grisham case!"

I groaned internally. Or maybe out loud, judging by the looks I got.

"Yeah," I said, "sorry."

"Shit." Felling leaned back, taking her arms off the table and angling herself over to Taylor. "You didn't tell me your friend was *her.*"

"I wasn't exactly planning on calling you over here tonight, James," they said. "I didn't want you turning her into another one of your cases."

"But she's already a case," Felling insisted, glancing over in my direction. "She became a case when she recovered from third-degree burns overnight."

"I said I was sorry about that," I muttered. I started planning my escape route. How fast and how far could I run before this agent pulled her gun on me?

"She's my friend," said Taylor, blankly. "She saved my life."

"And you just saved hers."

"Now we're even!" I said. "Mazeltov! Felling, are you going to take me in or something?"

"Why would I do that?" she asked, finally turning back to face me.

"You just said that—"

"Look"—Felling rolled her eyes—"right now you're being hailed as a medical miracle. I'm sure someone has already told you they want to monitor your health to see if the explosion did any lasting damage to your body."

"Yeah." I nodded. "And something about subterranean radiation bullcrap. Monthly blood tests and all that."

"Well, that's the extent of their interest." She

shrugged. "Your case landed on my desk. I thought nothing of it. There's nothing to it, is there?"

"No." I shook my head. "Nothing to it. How do you know all this? What do you mean by 'cases?'"

"I'm not at liberty to say."

"Tell James about your friend," Taylor said, making urgent motions with their face. "Please?"

"What friend?" asked James.

I shrugged. "Some of my friends are aliens. Well, one of them. Both of them are aliens, but his sister doesn't seem to like me very much. So, not exactly a friend."

"You're kidding." James whistled, glancing at Taylor nervously. "You're just making fun of me, aren't you?"

"I'm serious!" I nodded, and Taylor nodded too. "Though I don't know why I'm telling you this. Taylor?"

"Trust me," Taylor said, "the two of you need to be on the same page."

I swallowed the concerns. If Taylor thought the James chick was to be trusted, then I was going to take the chance. Taylor had saved my life, after all.

There was a tap on my foot—Taylor. I met their gaze, and they gave me a halting glare. Now, this was getting confusing. So, I was meant to tell Felling about Zander... but not everything. I guess? How much could you really tell from a foot tap?

"Fine, then. He came from outer space, and I promptly ran him over with my car," I explained. "He lived in my spare room for two months, correcting sci-fi movies and books. He integrated into our culture, and I found him an office job. Then his sister came, they blew up the plant, yada-yada-yada, and now, now he's gone."

"Dead?"

"Just… away."

"You've got a serious problem," she said, leaning back and crossing her arms over her chest. I could only shrug. "Taylor, what is this shit?"

"Why would I make that up?" I sputtered. "To impress you? To make fun of you? We just met. I've got no reason to lie. This is the truth."

I slammed my hand on the table, making our dishes jump with a loud *clang*. My hand tingled from the collision. Not a smart idea.

"I don't believe you."

"Well, Zander and Blayde were pretty unbelievable in the flesh as well."

At the sound of their names, she froze, petrified, as if she had, in fact, turned to stone. She stared at me, her eyes wide with shock. Unable to speak, she glanced at Taylor, who nodded, then she looked back at me.

"Zander and Blayde?" she urged, her face a dazzling smile. "You said Zander and Blayde?"

"Yeah."

"And you knew them? And Zander lived at your house for two months? This is impossible! I'm actually speaking with someone who has met Zander and Blayde!" She looked uneasy, excited, nervous, all at once, and she kept glancing at Taylor for support. Her face ran hot and red, her hands trembling slightly.

Taylor looked quite smug in all this. "You see? Told you."

I pulled out my phone, scrolling through the camera roll as Felling waited. I picked a good selfie, one Zander had taken accidentally as he was trying to use my phone as a mirror. First day of work and hating on ties and Terran culture. My heart tightened as I looked at it. I wasn't ready to see his smile just yet.

Breathe. Just breathe.

"That's him, right there," I said, and Felling stared, her eyes somehow becoming wider.

"It's him… it's really him," she muttered, almost a whisper. Almost a prayer. Taylor shot me a wink. I didn't think my night could get any weirder than this, and now… now, I apparently met one of Zander's fans.

"So," I said, clearing some pie from my throat, "how's this connected to Zander? You know him or something?"

"We've noticed him," said James, leaning in conspiratorially. "As we looked through old frescoes and paintings and such. Always the same man, accompanied by the same woman. Always. There are representations of him scattered throughout human history. We even found a written record of him in the original tale of Sir Arthur."

"He mentioned meeting him," I agreed as if that was the most casual thing in the world. It was odd, the things I had gotten used to with him as my roommate.

"We discovered their names in the journal of Maria Theresa, Queen of Hungary. Marie Antoinette's mother. She called him Zander. Then Blayde showed up in the records of Louis the XIV of France's court. They called her "*La Lame,*" which technically means Blade in French. Totally different meaning in English. For years, we've been calculating the probabilities of him appearing in certain locations, gathering information from different sightings of him."

"Wait, you can predict where he'll jump to?" I sat up taller in my chair. My heart pounded; this time from excitement, not fear. "How does it work? And has it worked?"

"Not yet." She grinned, as if slightly embarrassed, combing her hand through her thick black hair. "I had to teach myself statistical physics to try and interpret the data, but he seems to appear in places at random. It's like we're missing something: jumps that weren't recorded or an extra dimension to our math."

"So, it hasn't actually worked yet."

"Urm, no."

"Ah."

"But you've met him!" she exclaimed. "There's so much you can tell me about him!"

"I don't know how much I should say." I glanced at Taylor for support, but this time, they only shrugged. I guess Zander's identity was up to me. "He is a real person, a friend. He deserves some privacy."

"Think about it," she said, reaching into her pocket and pulling out her card. She scribbled a number on the back before handing it to me. "Here's my number. Call me day or night. I just want to know a little more about him. Why he pops up throughout history. Why he never changes. I just… I just want to know his deal." She stood now, nodding to both Taylor and me. "I have to go. I've got to be in Alexandria in the morning. Taylor, you have her from here?"

"Don't worry about us," said Taylor.

"Great," she said. "Sally, please do think about calling me. Or texting. Whatever. I can be a formidable ally if you want me to be."

And with that, she turned into a whirlwind and flew out the door. Taylor scooted to take their empty seat, eyeing me fully. "So, what do you think?"

"Of her?" I wanted to laugh. "Taylor, what's going on? You're helping a human deal with alien cases? It's adorable!"

"Stop it," Taylor insisted. "Cut it out! I'm not a child."

I let out a giggle. My evening could not get any weirder, but here I was, in a coffee shop, chatting about crushes with an alien I hadn't seen since we'd escaped abduction together.

"Sorry I dragged you into this," they said. "I needed to give Felling something she wanted. Now she owes me."

"But who is she? What is she? Like… FBI? Are you her lone gunman?"

"Is that an *X-Files* reference?"

"Yeah? Taylor, is she Mulder?"

"I'm not allowed to say," Taylor replied, grinning conspiratorially.

"Where are you headed?" I asked, getting up. "It's the middle of the night. You have a place to stay?"

"I was heading for a motel." They shrugged. "Spotted a nice one on the way into town."

"You could stay with me. "I've gotten in the habit of inviting aliens into my spare room."

"Or maybe," said Taylor, "maybe it doesn't have to be your *spare* room."

And that's the story of how I took Taylor home on New Year's Day.

CHAPTER ONE

I RUIN SOME PERFECTLY GOOD TEA

You never really get to know your friends until they abandon you in the living room with an out-of-control vintage robot.

Picture this: You just came from a harrowing trip where you were lost pretty much up until the last minute. Finally home, riding off the high of making it back not just in the right century but the right day of all things—which still made no sense—you promise them all tea.

You leave the kitchen with steaming cups, and instead of seeing your alien best friend and his sister, the room is empty. You catch a breath. And, then, in their place, a robot in full *Terminator*
mode comes bursting out of the bathroom, shattering the door into little white splinters, and your first thought isn't "*Oh crap, there's a robot on a killing streak in*

my home," or "*How am I going to explain this to my landlord,*" but this: "*They had left.*"

Again.

And this time there was nothing for them to return for. They were gone, and they weren't coming back.

This was when I stopped speaking in the hypothetical and realize that, shit, this was really happening. This wasn't a cute interlude but was actually happening to me as I stood, dumbstruck, in front of my couch with a tray of three steaming mugs and a killer robot traipsing all over my rug.

It was exactly how I imagined a killer robot would look, if, say, I were living in the 1950s. While human-shaped, every form was boxy and squat, though the arms ended in a slick point, a tentacle of shiny, deadly metal. It waved the arms around like a wacky inflatable balloon man, either trying to kill me or sell me used cars. What really tuned me into the whole wanting-me-dead bit was the glowing red of its eyes. They meant business—they meant death.

No Zander in sight. No trace of Blayde, save for the muddy boot prints on my couch I would inevitably spend an hour scrubbing off without her help.

"Stay where you are," said the robot, its digital teeth lighting up as it spoke. Whatever movie it had crawled out of, it had terrible production value. "Prepare to be arrested. Please do not move. An agent of the law shall be with you shortly."

An agent of the law? Whose law? And which agent? Was someone else coming, or ...

That's when I saw the shiny, gold badge pinned to the robot's chest. Oh, this was the agent.

For a split second I thought, *"Hey, maybe this is a prank. Or maybe a test, to see if I was made for better things, ready to take on the universe in a whole new light. Maybe the siblings had just stepped out to the balcony for a quick look at the stars and trusted that I could handle any mess there was in here."*

I glanced over. Nope. It was true: Zander had left. He had brought me back to Earth, as promised, and jumped away without a second thought. I should have been happy: he had fulfilled his oath and brought me home safely. But leaving me alone like this? It felt like a betrayal of everything our friendship had ever stood for.

I truly believed it was more than ... this. Everything we had been through together, the places we'd been, the people we had saved—the *worlds* we had saved— that had to count for something. There was a moment, back on the beach, when I thought we might even have had something more. Even though we both knew it would have been impossible, we were dipping our toes into a new depth to our friendship. For a moment, maybe just a second, I thought he might feel something for me. In that second, I had known I felt something back.

I did not want to go through the pain again, but the pain of this loss was ten times worse already. Losing Nim, losing my friends, losing a connection to the universe I could never forge again.

"Please, do not move," the robot repeated. "An agent will be with you shortly to arrest you. To save time, please read your rights now."

All this pondering had taken up a surprising amount

of time. The robot—which walked painfully slow, taking ten tiny steps to cross a meter and had to take the long way around the couch—was now at my coffee table. I couldn't care less. With Zander and Blayde now light-years away, never to come back, I half-wanted the robot to be done with it, and quick. To take what was left of my gutted soul and end the pain right then and there.

But that wasn't who I was anymore. Even Blayde had said as much. That I was more than just a tagalong. That I brought some value to the team, that I was useful. Pretty much as good as I could get with her. But now the fog had lifted, and I knew the truth. I was nothing more than a third wheel, that annoying, useless limb that needed to be severed. And, so, they had.

I was Sally-freaking-Selena Webber, Goddess of the Moon, savior of the *Traveler*, assistant-to-the-liberator of Da-Duhui. I was fire. I was flame.

I was a tiny, little human with three cups of tea.

So, I did the only thing I could think of: I flung the tray at the robot, partially in self-defense but mostly in anger, showering its shiny blue buttons and lights with a dose of good ol' Lipton Earl Grey tea.

My voice was a siren that would not be shut off. The sounds that came from my throat were not words, not even human. The water flew out of the mugs, dousing the robot's chest, droplets cascading down and staining my favorite rug. Sparks flew out of the buttons as the robot roared, a cassette being thrown into a waste disposal.

"How do you like that, huh?" I snapped, wielding the tray above my head like a baseball bat. "Serves you right for breaking into my home!"

"You ... are ... arrested..." The robot shuddered, the lights in its mouth flickering, flickering, dead. I swung at it with the tray, and it fell into my couch, landing in a seat as if it were a friend.

Lovely. Now I had new furniture.

How it had gotten into my apartment, I didn't know. It was too large for any of the doors, evidenced by the pile of wooden shards now sitting in front of my bathroom. And I certainly didn't know what it wanted, in the early hours of the morning, from me, a little nobody from Earth.

Now if it had come for Zander, that would make a whole lot more sense. Maybe he had realized it was there and had run out before having to deal with it. But that made no sense, especially if he was supposed to be protecting me.

Maybe that deal ran out the second we came home.

But I didn't need anyone protecting me. I had handled this robot intruder pretty well on my own, if I did say so myself.

Still ... a goodbye would have been nice.

The searing tea was the last of my problems. It had splashed up my legs, scalding the exposed skin, leaving red blotches. I stared at the robot, hands trembling with rage.

"Welcome to the party, agent," I muttered, as I reached down to grab the remains of my once-favorite mugs. So much for sharing those with my alien besties.

I dropped the remnants in the trash then slid onto the couch beside the non-functioning robot, my mind spiraling out of control. Idiot, idiot, idiot. Stupid idiot.

I had been so dumb to have thought I meant anything to these people. Immortals with the entire universe on their shoulders would never have seen anything of value in me.

Maybe they were right to leave me. It was better than ending up like Nim: dead and buried light-years from his home, forgotten by his family, remembered only by his kidnappers. And sure, I might have been one of said kidnappers, but the hole in my heart for him was real. Losing this kid, so full of promise, so wild and brilliant, the universe would be missing him as well.

I glanced over at the spare room, still sitting open. Taylor was really gone, too. Off to the middle of the ocean on a quest for more space. I guess they needed it. I grabbed the note I had left for them on my coffee table and tore it into a million pieces. They would never see it. They would never know.

I could go, too, now that I wasn't keeping an apartment on the off-chance the man I thought had been my best friend would come back and keep his promise. Now that I wasn't waiting anymore.

Now that I was free of him.

Zander had made it evidently clear this was the end, so I would move on. I would stop waiting for him to come back, as I had for those dull two years, my life on standstill as I waited for something impossible to happen. I had kept my apartment so he'd know where to find me, even though the place brought back so many painful memories. I had avoided moving on with my life so I would have nothing to drop when he was ready to show me the universe. I had been living my life based on a gamble.

How naive I had been.

Even so, clinging to the memory of Zander had been my rock, my tether to sanity. Losing Matt set me adrift; knowing Zander could return was an anchor. I might have been an idiot for making my life revolve around a guy who wasn't even on the planet, but it had brought me through the worst of times.

And now that he was gone, for good, I felt odd. I felt ... better. And I saw in myself something I had never noticed before: completeness. I had gotten myself through those two years of hell. I had, no one else.

I didn't need him. I completed myself.

I watched the sun rise from my comfy seat on the couch, an arm against the hunk of metal that had once been a threat. The sky changed from inky blue to red, to orange, and finally the chilly gray of a crisp winter morning. I needed to clean, to focus my mind on something else. Because it was something I could do to reclaim this space, this life, as my own. I would figure out tossing the creepy robot, but, hey, one thing at a time. First came the floor, the puddle of cold tea, and the smaller shards of mugs. Then, the muddy couch where Blayde had propped her feet. Boot prints covered the arms, and I wondered how much of the dirt had come from the park, and how much of it from worlds beyond my own. Part of it was now covered up by the robot's posterior, but I'd just have to wait to deal with him before finishing the job entirely.

I had left the trash there for over a week; no, not a week. Though I had lost track at the end, the worlds buzzing past me like channels flying by on the television, I knew it was much longer than the four hours I

31

had missed here on Earth. Impossible, yet here I was. I needed to get used to the fact that we had somehow broken the laws of physics to get me home.

Still, it felt disgusting to keep the trash here any longer. I wrapped it up and took it outside.

I was once again—more like constantly, at this point—overwhelmed with the sensation of being home. Of seeing *my* sky above my head, of breathing *my* air, tasting the cold of February on Earth on my lips. The sun was wonderful on the cold winter street, even more so because it was my sun, my solar system. Hello, sun! Hello, clouds! Hello, Virginian winter! Being home had never felt so—

Empty.

It was odd, bouncing between the feeling of wholeness and loss. Zander the person might not have been a part of me, but my image of him, my experiences with him, they were part of what defined me. I had lost a friend but gained a life.

At least it didn't hurt. Not like it had last time. Not like the pain of returning to an empty apartment with a friend dead and your roommate maybe dead along with him. I shuddered at the memory. I hated remembering.

When I returned to the living room, the robot was still sitting there, dead as a deadbolt, the only thing out of place in my little home. I turned around, returning to my room, breathing in deeply all the smells I didn't even think I'd miss until they were gone. It was time to get through the hard stuff.

It was time to make a promise. I would not let this hurt me like it had once before. I would chop it down before depression reached me. I wouldn't stagnate, oh no. I would go to the pharmacy, refill my prescription, and get back into my routine. I felt stronger after my off-Earth experiences. My time in the Cave of Ordeals on that unknown, ferocious planet had changed me more than anything could have. I felt stronger, both physically and emotionally.

But that didn't stop me from being sad.

Sad, but not depressed. Not yet. But being sad shouldn't stop me from living my life. Better get through the big stuff first and get it over with. Get the giant robot thing out of my house and find a safe place to dispose of it where it wouldn't raise too many questions.

Then, I'll deal with Nim.

I wouldn't even think about him right now, though. I didn't want to remember how the boy in my care was brutally murdered as a thank you for saving a planet. Remember the look on his face as he died the first time and the betrayal when he died again, killed to free him from a human form that was rightfully his to begin with. That look in his eyes would haunt me for eternity. I could never forget what came after—how the siblings and I drifted aimlessly through space, place after place, trying to cope with the loss of such a bright, young kid. A friend.

I high-tailed it to my bathroom, grabbed my medicine from the cabinet, and took my daily dose, flushing the pills down with water. Getting back into the rhythm of my life was a good first step. Healthy.

It was time to clear through the clutter of my life. Sitting on the kitchen island was my trusty duffel bag, surprisingly in one piece after having joined me across half the galaxy. So many places I couldn't even count. I had stopped paying attention when my friend died.

Unceremoniously, I dumped its contents on my coffee table. Like the TARDIS, it seemed to have been larger on the inside, carrying far more than I ever thought possible.

Purge time.

Out of the bag first was my scruffy UPAF uniform. The last time I had seen it, the world around me had been in flames, the sky red with fire, the ground gray with ash. The last I had seen it was when I was being carried up a pyramid on Zander's shoulder as Nimien died, alone, on a foreign world. Even if I hated it, it was like Nim was still attached to it somehow.

But it had other memories, too. Good ones. From when I was gifted it from the captain of the *Traveler*, who had been impersonating Captain Kork for years and had gotten the universe to love him; the crew, forced into action but unable to fulfill their duties; the ship the Alliance broadly proclaimed as the best in the fleet, the flag bearer, which was no more than a fancy team of dressed-up nobodies and poor excuses for role models.

I remembered the other Matt Daniels and how he left Earth so quickly with no word to his parents. If I could just reassure his parents that he was fine where he was now ...

Should I? Was that my responsibility? I didn't want to tell Matt Daniels's parents that he's not coming back. I had done that once before, and the memory still haunted me.

Next out of the bag was the small handful of random doodads Zander had handed me on Da-Duhui. Dozens of small figurines and knickknacks from who knew where, a random assortment that had lost its meaning or purpose. Zander wanted a place to keep his things, and now he was gone without them.

I should have tossed them, I know. But maybe a part of me hoped he would come back for them, the way he had once come back for his jacket.

Maybe.

Probably not. Throw them out, Sally Webber.

I kept them anyway.

I pulled out my dress from Da-Duhui, the gift Zander had intended to give me as a thank you and as a goodbye. He had told me then, hadn't he? He had made it clear that he'd never be able to stay. That on Earth, he technically was dead. That he would have to continue on with his search for his home, just as I was supposed to carry on with my life.

Why couldn't it be that easy?

The duffel bag, however sturdy and reliable, however much adventure it had followed us through, was just too dirty to put away without a good wash. Back on the coffee table it went, as I fell back on the couch.

Things had tumbled out of the bag during my examination. Small pieces of ripped fabric, a damp pair of jeans, and as a small piece of paper.

The photo.

The amazing photo of Zander and me, leaning over the rail of Da-Duhui's tallest building, the lights of the city around us, a small moment caught on camera of both of us, together, seeing the sights of an alien world. The last time we had even talked about what would happen when I got home.

The anger I felt at Zander—the pain, the loss— wasn't going to heal overnight. Maybe it was my fault all along. I had pushed him away out of fear of getting too close, and he had done the same. And when Nim died, it had cemented the fact that mortals and immortals don't quite have the same life expectancies.

Depression doesn't just go away if you will it hard enough. I had learned this time and time again, and every time, I refused to believe it. Like I could somehow fight it before it took hold.

Maybe I could. But I was just so damn tired.

"Location!"

The shout wasn't so much a shout but an extremely loud and belligerent robot waking from slumber. The air fizzled with steam as the water evaporated from its buttons, drying off as quickly and efficiently as the last round on my dishwasher.

I flew to my feet. This time, no water in reach, no tea tray to thwack it with, nothing but old photos and a muddy uniform.

"Location!" It repeated. It wasn't angry. No. Was I mad, or did it sound ... confused?

I stood, figuring I had the time. The robot wasn't going anywhere, wasn't trying anything. Its metal tentacle arms folded neatly upon its lap. It sat on the couch drying off, a lonely, lost robot with no idea of where it was.

Nope, nope, I was projecting now. I knew what it was like to have no idea where you were. That was over now, in the literal sense; in the figurative sense, though, things were just getting started.

Talk about a great time for an identity crisis.

I picked up my baseball bat and poised in front of the robot. It looked up at me, and, for a moment, I thought its eyes had connected with mine. But then its monotonous voice asked for a location again, and the spell was broken.

"You're in my apartment," I spat, "and I don't know if anyone told you, but on this planet, it's called 'breaking and entering.' Though since I'm pretty sure you didn't use the front door, I'd just call that entering, even if you did break a totally inoffensive bathroom door. Now, what the hell do you want with me?"

"Is this the residence of the one who calls themselves Taylor?"

My heart did a pitiful flop in my chest. Taylor. Of course, when I'm down and lingering on the loss of my best friend, I get reminded about how my roommate up and left me just when I needed them most. They were the only one I had ever told about Zander, what he was, all my secrets. Apparently, this made me impossible to live with. Way to go self-confidence after that one.

Figures the robot would be here for Taylor and not, say, the girl who was hanging out with the Alliance's most wanted.

"It was," I answered honestly. "Up until about a week ago. Then they up and left. And no, I do not know where they are. Or why you are looking for them."

"I am an agent of the Ordran," it said, still refusing to move. Which I guess was a good thing since I no longer had the element of surprise. "The one you know as Taylor desecrated Ordran territory. I have been tasked to retrieve them."

I could hardly believe my ears. When I first met Taylor two years ago, we had both been taken by mercenaries for bounties on our respective heads. Them, for flying through Ordran territory; me, for associating with Zander, whose bounty I am told could buy Earth a few times over. Taylor had been lying low on Earth ever since, for a few months as my roommate and then significant other. That was before they blew up at me and ran out to find space.

"Wow, you're like, what? Half a decade late? On top of the whole week thing."

"Thank you for your help. I will inform my superiors of your cooperation."

"Yeah, whatever. I'm owed compensation for the mugs and the door."

And with that, the robot, too, faded out of existence.

I guess that's what everyone did in my life. Taylor. Zander. Blayde. Matt. John. Everyone would just, inevitably, leave.

My door opened suddenly, keys jangling in the lock. Marcy stood in the entrance, keychain in hand, and I jumped up and hugged her as hard as I could, sobbing on her familiar shoulder.

For once, I was so glad to be wrong.

CHAPTER TWO

INTERPLANETARY SIBLING RIVALRY, NOW IN TECHNICOLOR

ZANDER

Sisters.

You love them. You hate them. They love you, support you, and then, just sometimes, they twist you up in knots and stab you repeatedly with every trick they know, not limited to those in the book. And sometimes that knife is quite literal. It's the cost of having family. Of having someone who will stick by you for no reason other than she shares some genes with you.

Or someone who will destroy you for no *farshing* reason.

Case in point: Just when I was feeling happy, ready to have a nice cup of tea and, I don't know, enjoy the feeling of being clean for the first time in days, my sister disintegrated me. Well, technically, she teleported me to who knew where, just when I was going to ask about the flower-scented soap in the bathroom and if it was okay that I had finished the bottle. In that case, it was a good thing Blayde got me out of there because things could have deteriorated fast.

But jumping me again so I couldn't get back? That was stone cold. A jerk move if I had ever seen one, and boy, had I seen jerk moves.

The second my cells started stitching themselves back together, they were ripped apart again, and I reeled through the vast emptiness of the universe. I couldn't see where I was going, I couldn't see where I had come from, and I couldn't see anything at all since my eyes technically did not exist.

It was at times like these I seriously considered buying myself a spaceship. Nothing fancy. Just something with a good faster-than-light engine or a warp drive, a place to keep my stuff and make my travels through the universe more scenic. And maybe, just maybe, having my own keys would stop Blayde from *farshing* kidnapping me.

But, then again, parking's terrible. And I hear the gas prices are worse than ever.

Suddenly, I was back in one piece, the ground firm beneath my feet. Instinct kicked in before I had gathered my wits about me, making sure all my limbs were still attached to my body, counting off the arms and the legs, fingers and toes, even as they spread into a pounce.

My roar rang in my ears as I flew through the air,

arms outstretched and hands ready to go for her jugular. My fingers wrapped around her neck before the neurons had fired from my brain. Fury burned through my veins like a poison, corrosive acid in my blood.

Blayde sidestepped easily, letting me crumple on the ground beside her. I felt the heat as my face slammed into the metal floor, my nose snapping from the collision.

But she did not return the attack. Flipping myself over, I brought a leg spinning under her. I used my own momentum to jump to my feet, dropping my center of gravity and swinging around to lash out with a right hook. She caught it square in the jaw, a tooth flying off in the air and lodging itself in a nearby wall. She scowled, blood pouring out of her lip, but I could already see the white enamel growing back to fill in the gap in her mouth. A bruise blossomed and wilted on her cheek.

I swung to hit her again, but her arm flew out to grab mine, holding it easily in midair. I struggled to break loose from her grip, but her fingers were clasped firmly around my wrist, and I could barely move it. Effortlessly, she gave it a twist, ripping my arm from the socket and effectively reducing the number of punching elements by half.

She said nothing, cocking an eyebrow, as if waiting for me to start. So, I did.

"What the *veesh* do you think you're doing?" I shouted as I struggled to break free from the titanium grip. She blinked then wasn't there, and suddenly I was face down on the ground, hands pinned behind my back, a knee on the back of my head.

"Weak," she snapped, anger dripping from her lips. "Look at you, you've grown weak."

She had underestimated me. I threw her off my back and pinned her down, my elbow pressing on her windpipe. My useless arm dangled by my side, but I hardly felt it. She smirked, unperturbed by the decrease in air flowing to her lungs.

"I'm not weak," I snapped back. "You've grown paranoid. Look at you!"

"We held up our end of the deal," she hissed. "We were free to go. Nothing left for us to do on that dull excuse of a planet."

"But you jumped us *twice*!" I pressed down harder, but she only rolled her eyes. She motioned as if to say there was no way she could reply if she had no air. I hopped on my feet, watching her get back up gingerly. I tried to cross my arms but failed with the dangler.

"I thought you might jump right back," she replied with a shrug, oblivious to what I meant. I shook my head. I mean, screw her; that's the part I was furious about in the first place.

"What if I wasn't ready to leave yet?" I snapped. "She was making us tea!"

"Can you even hear the words spilling out of your mouth?" She leaned back against a shelf casually. "Oh, tea, yes, let's all sit around and drink tea with the Earthling. When would you be ready to leave? Huh? A day? A month? Next year?"

"I—" I sputtered. But I couldn't reply. There was nothing I could say.

Out of nowhere, she sprung at me, her fist somehow flying up from below, colliding with my kidney. I reached over with my good arm and found her wrist, twisting it backwards until she couldn't move anymore. Or so I thought.

She pulled her arm downwards, into the grip. On anyone else, this would have been insanely painful, enough for a human to pass out. But not Blayde. She wasn't human, after all—or mortal, for that matter.

Blayde used my own weight to flip herself into the air, lock her legs around my neck, and squeeze until the air stopped flowing. A quick twist and she had floored me once again, leaving me out of breath, pinned beneath her boot, still with a dangling arm.

"Face it, Zander. You're becoming—" she paused, searching for a word, but unable to find it. She continued, nonetheless. "You're slowing down. No, you're settling down."

"So what if I want a bit of a break?" I said, furious. I knew what I was saying would hit a nerve, but I didn't care. I wanted it to hurt. Her hands rose slowly to her face, poorly concealing a gasp of horror. Good. Let her be horrified.

"I'm tired, Blayde," I continued, my breathing coming out heavier. "I'm physically and emotionally *tired*. So maybe I want to stay in one place for a little while. Not forever, just enough to—"

"What about me?"

"What about you? You're free to do what you want. We're siblings, not conjoined twins."

"But we're a team," said Blayde. "Me and you."

"Then why haven't I had a say in what we do? If we're a team, then why are you the boss?"

"Because," she said, coolly, "maybe I have my

priorities straight."

"And what are those, exactly?" I grabbed my arm and popped it back into the socket, feeling the oddly pleasant tingle of nerves coming back online. I could live for the endorphin rush. "Because they don't seem to take into account the fact that we need to live, every once in a while."

"We'll have time for that once we find home," she said. "Once we find out where we came from. When we've found home, everything will make sense. We'll have our families. Our home planet. A place to call ours."

"We can already have that! Anywhere in the entire universe! Face it, Blayde, our home planet no longer exists. Our families are long dead and gone."

"How can you say that?"

I might have gone too far. If Blayde had looked broken earlier, now she was shattered.

"How can you, of all people, say that? After all this time!" She stared at me.

"Exactly!" I said sharply. "Don't you think we'd have more to go on at this point?"

"But our families ... they'd be like us. They would still be here."

"And yet, we haven't seen a single other immortal out here," I insisted, watching as she shrunk away from me. "Not even a clue. Every lead has been a dead end. It's time to call it as it is—the end of the line."

"What happened to you there?" she shuddered. "What happened to you on that awful planet that's making you say these things? Was it Sally? Was it Nim?"

"Don't you breathe his name." I shook my head and

lowered myself to the ground. I could not stop the words once they started to spill. "I'm tired of jumping everywhere, no end in sight. We're always running, Blayde; the longest marathon in the universe. I need to stop and catch my breath."

"But you *did* catch your breath!" she sputtered; her eyes wide as planets. "You spent *months* on that planet! Months! And look what they've done to you!"

"Those months were the greatest things that happened to me in a long, long time. It was nice to sleep in the same bed every night, to know that I'd find food the next day, to have options to choose from for once. And, might I add, that in those two months, I didn't die once. Not one time, Blayde; not one single *farshing* time."

"You were *normal,* Zander. You were"—she choked on the next word, gagging as she forced it to exit her mouth. The words left her in a weak whisper—"*mortal.* You were acting *mortal.*"

I could see those days clearly. I could still smell the heavenly scent of pizza as Sally brought it through the door on Friday nights. I could hear the canned laughter on the television as a sitcom ran in the living room. I could feel the delight of waking up at noon on a Sunday, knowing I could stay in bed for as long as I wanted.

Putting a book down on my nightstand, knowing I could pick it right up the next day.

The smell of sizzling bacon on the stove.

Cheeseburgers.

Scented shampoos.

Coffee. Earth must have been the only place in the universe with a drink so divine.

"Is there a problem with that?" I asked, trying to

cling onto those sights and smells for as long as I could. Keeping them close. Keeping them real.

"Yes." Blayde was quick to reply, her face and voice sharp like the blades of her knives. She glared at me as if she were trying to roast me alive.

"What kind of problem?" I hissed. "I'd really like to know."

"If you were mortal—"

"Yes."

"Then you wouldn't be my brother!" She flung all her fury in my face, the spittle flying across the room and spraying me on the chin. She began to gag, hands rising to her throat, trying to calm herself, but it was no use. Her trembling knees led to trembling legs, and she toppled over, no longer restraining herself. And suddenly, there she was, sobbing alone on the floor, knees pulled up to her chin as she cried for the first time I could remember.

All anger toward her was put on a shelf. I was at her side in seconds, wrapping an arm around her, trying to soothe her, but it was no use. She wasn't making any sense, but this wasn't the time to judge.

"Of course I would be, Blayde." I rubbed a hand over her back. "Nothing will ever change that."

"You'd get a house." She hiccuped. "You'd get a job. Maybe even a pet—snake, is it? You'd become one of *them*."

"Blayde, I wasn't planning on any of that. Don't jump to worst-case scenarios. I'm here for you. I love you."

"Well, I'm not tired of traveling, Zander." She pushed herself back up to a seating position, glaring at me. "I want to keep trying. I want to keep looking."

"Even if it's pointless?"

"Zander," she said, slowly, "I can't remember doing anything else. I'm nothing if I'm not searching, hunting, for home."

I didn't say anything. She was right, the way she always was. My oldest memories were of the need to find home, to find a way back to the people like us. But none of them were of home itself. I didn't know where I came from, even though I'd been searching so long. Who had I been before? *What* had I been?

"Maybe it's time to let go. Maybe the past is staying where it's meant to be. In the past."

"I refuse to think that," she said defiantly, looking at me with that fire I knew so well. "Don't sprout motivational nonsense at me. I refuse to believe that, ever. After all I've done to keep this universe in one piece, maybe I deserve some peace of mind myself."

"Maybe." I nodded. "Maybe you do. But I don't. Not anymore."

She took a deep breath, in, out. Then another one.

"Did Earth do this to you?" she asked. "Did Sally?"

"No."

"Tell me this," she continued, "if you had stayed on Earth, alone, what would have happened to me?"

"You could do what you like," I said, squeezing her hand. "I would never push you away, Blayde. Ever. You're my sister."

"Well, you're pushing me away right now," she snarled, ripping her hand from my grasp. "I haven't had a real conversation with you since we let Sally come along. Sally this, Sally that. Sally-freaking-Sally."

"Don't be petty, Blayde," I said quickly. So, this was what this was all about—Sally. "She was *stuck* with us, and that was my fault, I give you that. We had to take care of her. To keep her safe."

"Make sure she didn't die, yes, but we didn't have to coddle her," she snapped. "You left me on my own, Zander. You were stuck to *her* like glue. She was doing perfectly fine on her own."

"I didn't want her to get hurt!" I sputtered. "She's not like us, Blayde. She'd break if we dropped her."

"There! You said it!" She was on her feet once more, backed up against the wall, trying to calm her rage. The tears were still coming, and she hadn't stopped sobbing yet. "She's not like us; she's mortal. You saw what happened ... to Nim."

I said nothing. I didn't want to think about Nim, the boy so full of promise and ... life. He was dead because of us. Because of our negligence. And Sally could have ended up just like him. It was selfish of me to think she could keep up with us just because I wanted her there, with me.

"She's *not* like us, yet you treat her like—ugh, I can't tell if it's a pet, or if she were made of glass, or if she were something else entirely."

"I thought you liked her," I said. "The two of you were starting to, I don't know, bond."

"I do like her. And it's because I like her that I split you up. She's strong, Zander, but not like us. She deserves to live the life she was born to lead. You can't stay with someone like her. It changes you, Zander. It changed you."

"And it changed you, too, Blayde," I said with a

shake of my head. "You didn't used to be like this. Selfish. Self-centered. And I'm not sure I like the new you."

"Where did all this come from? You didn't used to think this. We were fine before Sally came along."

"I keep telling you, it wasn't Sally!" My voice raised a few levels higher than I would have liked. "This isn't new. You're just not listening. I told you, Blayde, I'm tired. I feel like I ran a lap around the universe. My body is weary. My mind is full. I have seen everything over and over again, and we haven't made progress for years. Having a break, calmness, showers, a bed—it cemented it for me. I'm done searching. I'm ready for something new."

"What, then? There's nothing you haven't done in this universe. Nothing is new to you."

I did a double-take. That, I didn't know. I was tired of running, but what would I do once I dropped out of the race? Rest, sure, and then what?

Maybe Blayde was right. Maybe we were nothing without the search. Our life had no finish line, no glooming ending in the distance. We had to find our own meaning in life, and, well, this was it.

"Everything," I said. "I'm done searching for a past that's long gone. I want to have a future. I want to explore for the thrill of it. I want to see the universe anew. I just want to be, without reason. I want to be *me*."

"*You!*" Blayde scowled. "Hello, you're right here."

"Am I?"

"Yeah. I don't get it, Zander. You've had quite a lot of time to find yourself."

"Understatement of the millennium," I pointed out. "But I'm always changing. You're always changing. And—"

"And stop," said Blayde. "I'm tired of this psycho-babble. If you're done with me, be done with me. Say it, and don't be a coward."

"Blayde, come on, it's not like that. You know it. I'm not going to deal with you when you're like this."

"Neither am I."

I got up and turned around, trying to figure out where we were and if it was worth staying. We were in a laundry room, it seemed, with large wooden shelves towering up the walls and vacuum chambers in the corners. The lighting was poor, not that that was a problem for either of us. I found the door with ease, slipped the knife from my sleeve, and began to jimmy the lock.

"Answer me one question, Zander. Just one."

I felt her hand on my shoulder, warm, trembling slightly. Not like Blayde to ever tremble. I didn't reply, simply continued to work the lock.

"Zander," she asked, solemn-like, Blayde-like, "did you love her?"

"Why would that change how I feel about you?"

"You're not answering the question."

I put my knife back in my pocket and pulled open the door. Without a word, I walked away, striding down the empty hallway, my ears ringing from her sobs as I left her alone once again.

CHAPTER THREE

RETURN TO NOR-MARCY

SALLY

A week after my alien best friend abandoned me on Earth, my human bestie tried to make things better by faking a wedding disaster.

She didn't actually need last-minute alterations to her wedding dress. It fit her beautifully, and I should hope so, what with the exorbitant fee it cost her. All part of the massive event she had planned with Dany: renting the Casa Italia so they could have that old observatory all to themselves; buying every flower grown by this sweet Amish farm for all the arrangements; flying over all of Marcy's extended family from China, so everyone could be a part of their big day. There was only a week left before the wedding, so the rush was palpable.

Marcy never said why she needed such an elaborate wedding, and I knew she would have been happy with everyone crammed into her back yard. This seemed to be Dany's deal, despite her only inviting a handful of people. I didn't know what she did for a living, but Marcy insisted she was living off some family inheritance and it was all legit. The mystery was probably the only hesitation I had with this woman marrying my best friend.

But Marcy didn't bring me here to see her in such a beautiful dress, looking more regal than a queen in front of the three mirrors. No, she brought me here for the distraction and the bottomless champagne.

"Are you sure we can't bring in the bustle a little bit more?" she asked the seamstress, who had more pins pinched between her lips than any human should have allowed. "I've got a glorious booty to show off, you understand."

The woman let out a sound that could have been agreement as she hurried to place the last pins.

I sipped at the champagne, enjoying the sweet fizz on my tongue. God, I had missed Earth food. In space, I had eaten nothing but food that tried to eat me from inside or punch that made me drunk from only one glass. Nothing out there off-planet could be trusted. If anything good came from returning to Earth, it would be the good ol' reliable food.

This was the time when life returned to normal. Only it's not normal anymore, and there will never be a normal for Sally Webber. You could only be a goddess one so many times before it turned you into a completely different person.

The meds were working. The fog ebbed and flowed over my consciousness like a tide in short succession as my mind stabilized. I was going to be okay, and I knew it. I just needed time. But Marcy could tell something was wrong, which meant she was concocting an elaborate plan to get me out of my shell.

"Sally?" She tried to maneuver herself to see me better without moving the body of the dress. "What do you think?"

"Um, yeah, more booty," I said, keenly aware that my glass was already empty. Oops. It took only two minutes for someone to notice and refill the flute.

"So, what's been bothering you lately?" she asked oh-so-casually. I loved her for how normal she made me feel about my breakdowns. They had been frequent after the GrishamCorp incident, after Matt had died, and after Zander had gone. While they had slowed considerably in the past few months, they had not stopped for good, meaning it wasn't too unusual for her to walk in on me sobbing in my apartment for apparently no reason.

But could I tell her everything I had been through—the wonders of the universe and the weirdness of alien life? How could I tell her anything about Zander, a man she believed was a dead human? As much as she loved me, trusted me, I think this would have crossed the line. I would be institutionalized tomorrow.

"Taylor and I had a fight," I stammered. It wasn't a lie, just a deflection. "They're gone."

"Oh, Sally ..." Still sitting, she reached for me.

I placed my now-empty glass on the little tray beside

me—holy cow, wasn't that my second refill?—and reached for her outstretched hand. Like that first day on the playground when we'd promised we'd be friends forever. Now she stood here in a white dress, radiant and glorious, pure perfection. Promise kept.

I, however, had been so close to breaking it. I was an absolutely terrible friend. Marcy was supposed to be focusing on her wedding, not on my itty bitty other-worldly problems. Not to mention I took off with an alien in the middle of the night a week before her wedding, exploring worlds without even leaving her a goodbye note in case something went wrong.

And they *had* gone wrong. Many times over.

"Are you going to be okay?" she asked. "I swear, after this, we can get ice cream and put on a rom com and—"

"Mmmmerrrreeee!"

The seamstress let out an angry groan, glaring at us. She ripped the pins from her mouth.

"No ice cream! We want this bustle to work, you can't—"

"Don't be so dramatic," Marcy said, a smile growing on her face. "It's just a dress."

"Just a *wedding* dress!" I said. "Come on. You have a future wife to impress. If there aren't any tears, then I haven't done my job properly."

"*Your* job? I'm the one stitching here," muttered the woman, placing her pins in the cushion on her wrist.

"And you're doing amazing, Susan," I added. "Marcy will be the world's prettiest bride in the prettiest dress, thanks to you."

Before my brain had time to process what it was

seeing, my hand struck out and grabbed the bottle midair, seconds before it would have spilled over the blushing bride-to-be. I turned, dumbstruck, to see the shop assistant picking herself off the ground, visibly shaken.

"Spiderman moment?" Marcy muttered. "That was badass!"

"You okay?" I asked the assistant—Margot, I think, though I had only met her once or twice—as I handed her the bottle. The relief on her face was like that of a woman spared from execution. An expression I had seen in the flesh, so trust me on that one. I pushed Angee's face from my mind.

"Yeah, yeah, I'm good, thanks," she said, taking the champagne from me. "I cannot believe how clumsy I am today!"

"Mmmph!" No words from the seamstress were needed to make Margot straighten and dash out of the room.

"What are we doing tonight?" asked Marcy. "Before Jenn's dual bachelorette party, I mean?"

"Well, first, I have to stop by the hospital for one of those monthly blood test things. I know, terrible timing. My usual doctor caught a flu, and the only other guy in the know could only do today. Sorry about that."

"Jeez, still going on about the plant explosion? Two years down the line?"

"Hey, it's not a big secret that my recovery was borderline miraculous. They'll keep monitoring me until, I don't know, until I die from latent radiation poisoning or something."

"Don't say that!"

"Marcy, I'm not dying. I don't even know if that's a thing."

"Well, in any case, I have a suggestion for the evening," she said. "I was hoping we could ... catch a movie. Like we used to. Like I'm not getting married in the morning and you're not dealing with your room-mate-slash-ex moving out on you."

"Taylor and I were *just* roommates." Was that a lie? Even I didn't know what we were. The night they had left, it had sure felt like a breakup. The accusations ran wild, the *it's not you, it's me*, though in their case more like *it's not me, it's your stupid fixation on Zander coming back for you.*

Well, look at me now, Taylor! He came back, exactly as you said he never would. And then he left, just as you always predicted.

"I mean what I said," Marcy continued, dragging me back to Earth. "I want us to spend the afternoon remembering what it means to be besties. So we never forget. So we never close the door on that."

"That sounds perfect." Dang, this girl knew how to pull on my heartstrings. "But you have to swear this isn't like your birthday. I don't want your bachelorette party to turn into a Sally pity party."

"Pinky swear. I hear there's a new Alejandro Vasquez movie, and I've been dying to see it. It's a terrible rip-off of *Planet of the Apes* where highly evolved baboons battle against cybernetically enhanced pigs in a far-future post-apocalyptic epic. I think it's called *Squeal* or *When Pigs Fly* or something dumb that has to do with pigs."

"Sounds perfect," I said, and I meant it. Even if it had Vasquez in it, his handsome face a two-hour long reminder of how I let the Zoesh trick me with his puppet emperor. I needed to stop seeing reminders like that everywhere I went and face the truth of my reality.

Maybe I could live with this. I went on my big adventure, and Zander had fulfilled his promises, both by taking me to space and bringing me back. Now I just had to move on. I could finally get out of that apartment, figure out what I wanted to do with my life. Nothing was holding me back anymore.

It was odd, this feeling of doors being opened around me. This sense my world held endless possibilities. Did I miss the wide, infinite universe? A little. But I no longer felt trapped by Earth. Quite the opposite.

It was surreal, admitting it to myself. The voice in my head that usually told me, *"No, no, you don't deserve this,"* was oddly silent. I sat there, mad at Zander, mad at Taylor, heck, even mad at Matt, and I was just mad. Angry, furious even, but there was no sign of the cold chill of depression that usually lurked. It was like looking around the corner, wondering where your creepy stalker went. You were thrilled they was gone, unsure of where they were, and nervous they would show up again.

I smiled at Marcy and she smiled back, and it hit me once more how amazing a friend she was. Maybe that would be my goal now: to give it all back.

To be a better friend to her than I had been to Zander.

A few hours later, after a fantastically god-awful movie and a trip back home to change into something more bachelorette-party appropriate, I rang Marcy and Dany's doorbell, wine bottle in hand. I felt like a queen in my Da-Duhuian dress, a little over-the-top for the evening, perhaps, but dressed down with simple black heels and a faux-leather jacket.

"Sally!" Dany threw open the door, her ears laden with more gold loops and chains than I'd ever seen on them before. She was dripping in gold, so much so I wondered how they didn't pull her ears off her head. She scooped me up in a hug, lifting me high into the air. "You doing all right?"

The room behind her was packed with people, friends of Marcy I could tell at a glance, wearing silly party hats and drinking cocktails in varying shades of pink.

"You know it!"

"You seem ... different, somehow," she said, as she put me back down on the floor. I could have been imagining it, but it seemed she was staring more at my dress than my face. Maybe I had overdressed, then.

"Good way? Bad way?"

"I hardly even recognize you. You have life in your eyes now."

"Life? In my eyes?" I scoffed, though deep down my heart fluttered with the compliment. "I don't know."

"Planet to Sally," said Dany, as she ushered me inside and grabbed me a drink. "Bring that spark of life to the party?"

"Oh, sorry!" I accepted the glass and made a big show of being fancy with it, grabbing a passing Jenn and clinking it to hers.

"Jenn!" I cried out, probably too enthusiastically. "It's been ages since I saw you last! How are you? I can't believe you managed to get everyone here in one place!"

"Me neither!" She laughed, fist bumping Dany before the latter slipped back into the crowd. "Though nothing but the best for our best gals!"

"I thought we were going to do the small party thing. You know, with silly games and stuff?"

"Oh, we're doing silly games, all right. And I found the perfect stripper! There are just more people than is customary. You know Marcy!"

"Are you the ones they call '*bridesmaids?*'"

Behind Jenn appeared a woman so tall her beehive hair brushed the ceiling, and she wore the most bewildering trench coat I had ever seen, covered in photographs of bees in rain booties. If you had asked me to describe her face, I wouldn't have been able to. Every time I looked too close, someone shouted "telegram" in the back of my head, and I found myself overcome with the urge to hunt the room in case the message was for me.

Jenn ran off in a flash, leaving me standing with half a drink in front of the mountain of telegram-loving flesh before me.

"Um, yeah, maid of honor right here," I said, reaching out my hand to shake. "And you're here for Dany, right?"

"Dany. Yes." Instead of grasping my hand, she reached into her pocket to hand me a tissue. I took it gingerly, wiping the condensation from my glass with it. As if this conversation was completely normal.

"Have you known her long?"

"Since before she was her!" She grinned. "I travelled far to see her get wed. Her father would not be too pleased knowing what is going on."

"Oh?" I knew next to nothing about Dany's parents, except they weren't in the picture. Marcy had made it sound as if they simply didn't approve of the wedding, but I could tell she was seething every time they came up in conversation. "Do you know them well?"

"As well as one can *know* them."

"Cousin Glinda!" Marcy appeared from the kitchen with a martini in hand, wearing a *Bride #1* sash over her pink princess dress. "Don't be bothering Sally. Go socialize with Cousin Becky."

Marcy gave her a none-too-painful shove, and Glinda practically flew across the room to get away from her. She collided with a stout-looking woman wearing a bathing suit and a grass skirt.

"Having a good night?" asked Marce, grinning as if nothing had just happened, spinning me away from the trench coat and grass skirt.

"She was—"

"She's foreign," she said quickly. "How are you holding up?"

"I can't believe you're finally getting married," I stammered, trying to follow her lead and ignore the strange women. "*Married.* And while I'm super thrilled to see you hitched, I mean, I literally just replaced the dryer last week and was impressed with myself." That, and impersonated a goddess, but that was neither here nor there. "And here you are—getting married. Changing your names. Getting a joint bank account!"

"Yes, all things that married people do," said Marcy.

"And that doesn't freak you out? Even a little?"

She shrugged, but the smile on her face grew larger by the instant. "I guess it should, but it doesn't. I'm excited. I'm so ready to move forward, I don't want to wait for the wedding to call myself Dany's wife. We've lived together for two years now: I know everything about her, and she about me. The ceremony is just for family to feel involved; we're already a pair as far as I'm concerned. And, plus, the unreliable status of LGBT rights in this country means I should probably hustle and make it official. Oh, look, a stripper!"

"Huh?" I was tearing up at her speech, but the tears sucked right back up into their ducts as the door opened to reveal a girl in a boxy robot costume. Her chest was covered by a silver control panel, revealing only the slender legs poking out below. She adjusted the welding goggles on her forehead with a gloved hand.

"Who's the blushing bride to be?" the robot girl asked, as she stepped into the living room. She flicked her fishnets with an oversized wrench. "Either one, so long as the other isn't the jealous type. Or maybe that's better."

The girls hooted and laughed, pushing Marcy forward. My bestie blushed a shade of pink that matched her dress. She awkwardly took a seat as the stripper hit the music and began her routine. It was to a somehow-sexy version of "Mr. Roboto," and the girl strutted around the floor, adjusting her buttons and acting confused. This must have been some kind of inside joke for the couple, and I couldn't for the life of me get the reference.

Off came the first glove, which flew into the audience, caught by none other than Dany herself. The woman laughed, making a show of slipping it on.

If I hadn't been watching her so intently, I probably would have noticed the other glove coming right for me. Instead, I felt its cold slap across my face, the rubber bouncing off and landing limply in my hands.

I looked up at the stripper, and she froze.

"You!" she snapped, planting a foot firmly in the ground. "You… asshole!" My heart started pounding as everyone's eyes bore into me. She kicked her boombox, knocking the music off.

"Do I know you?" I squeaked.

"Seriously? Sally Webber, you ruined my life."

I stared at her. Taller than me, red-headed, incredibly cute, and dressed like a robot, but nothing in her features was familiar.

"You seriously don't know who I am? Seriously? Ms. Who? Esheim-Oun Medical GM-BH Corporate Hospital? You frigging gave me radiation necrosis!"

And with that, she ripped off her entire arm and threw it in my face.

My reflexes were in high alert, and I somehow grabbed it out of midair before it reached my face, but it was only a distraction. With a roar, the girl tackled me, still wearing her fake control panel, which surprisingly heavy as it rammed into my chest, knocking the wind out of me. Without thinking I swung the free arm at her, knocking her square in the jaw, feeling my hand explode with pain as it connected with something far stronger than bone.

Dany was the one wrangling the wild stripper off me before I had the chance to strike again. I took in a deep breath as her body weight was lifted off me, and I panted through the stars that flickered in my vision.

There was another roar as the stripper broke free from Dany's grasp and dashed for the front door, shoving the guests away from her as she disappeared into the dark, slamming it behind her.

"What the ever-loving vegan pancakes?" Marcy flew to her feet, her eyes wider than I'd ever seen them before. "Sally! Are you all right? Who was that? What happened?"

"Drugs!" shouted Dany, shooting me a look. A cover-for-me look. She tossed me the abandoned arm, which I tossed back to her, which she promptly threw out of the window.

"Drugs!" I agreed. "Drugs are a terrible thing."

"Don't do drugs!" Dany insisted, nodding intently. "But let's do shots!"

"Is this usual of a bachelorette party in"—Cousin Becky, the one in the grass skirt, held up a hand to read something from her palm—"Internet Unavailable?"

"She's from Tibet," Marcy announced.

"I am from Tibet," Cousin Becky repeated. "Internet Unavailable bachelorette party is fun!"

I tried looking at her face but kept getting distracted by the whine of a mosquito I could never find. I gave up looking, but I was still pretty sure she didn't have the look of someone from Asia. Not when her skin was that milky white.

"Shots! Shots!" shouted Dany, grabbing shot glasses

seemingly out of thin air, filling them with a bottle of something orange and mildly fluorescent. And, for an instant, I was sure her eyes met mine, and familiarity flooded through me.

That wasn't the look of someone just covering for a friend.

That was the look of a girl who had something to hide.

CHAPTER FOUR

CAREER OPTIONS FOR THE HARDENED SPACE CRIMINAL

ZANDER

Is it possible to both love and hate someone to this extent?

I sat alone at the bar, sipping the exotic drink before me. I never knew what I was ordering, but I had hit the jackpot with this one: bright green and insanely acidic. It was just what I needed to numb my thoughts. And quite literally every time something drifted up into my conscious mind, little tiny lemons sprang up to punch them back into the depths of my brain. Little, yellow alcohol buddies.

"You seem down, son," said the bartender. I had to admit I was amused by the thing: an android, shaped to look like one of the Tanady settlers of old.

It seemed this was a themed cruise. The entire bar was decked out to look like one of the Tanady parlors that had been so popular with the settlers of that small colony, before it became the gorgeously terraformed planet we knew today. Oxygen jugs were used as light fixtures, a nod to the days when pure air was better than booze. The barkeep himself was dressed in the skin-tight white jumpsuit that had been the fashion, more out of necessity than style, his poisonous spikes carefully sealed under their own individual little helmets.

It didn't seem too bothered that a humanoid was here. I wondered how much a bartending android was programmed to pick up on and made a face at it.

"It's nothing." I wanted no part in this odd historical reenactment, especially since I'd been there and lost friends to the Blue Lung. It seemed inappropriate to romanticize this past that never truly existed.

"Are you talking to me?" it grunted, slamming fifteen of its hands on the counter, the other three making seemingly rude gestures at the ceiling.

"Sorry," I said. "I thought a settler like yourself would be able to tell when a guy was into him."

"I'm sorry." The bartender went quiet. "My programming does not allow for this sort of interaction. Please restrict yourself to the following parameters of conversation: orders, insults, deep emotional turmoil, and the contemplation of the end of days."

"Fine, I'll do that," I muttered. He was no fun. I took what was left of my drink to a booth next to the large windows, glad the entire bar cabin was empty so I could be alone with my thoughts.

I pressed myself against the large window overlooking the beautiful planet our ship was orbiting. The bright red continents drew a sharp contrast with the silvery oceans. The quiet rotation of the ship was soothing, the only way to calm my nerves after losing it with Blayde.

Well, that and the drink.

Why would she do something like that? Why would she rip me away from Earth without talking to me? Why was she being so selfish?

Maybe she was right, a small voice whispered in the back of my mind. *Maybe I haven't paid enough attention to her lately. It's just been like going through the motions, like routine. And she had been hurt by our separation; there was no doubt about that.*

It didn't used to be like that.

Distant memories told another story of Blayde and I jumping from planet to planet, seeing the sights, constant bewilderment everywhere we went. Memories of us having fun, of us enjoying the ride. Enjoying life. Images in my mind of her smiling because she was truly happy.

But were they real memories or my subconscious trying to fill in the blanks? Her journal told of our earlier adventures, but how far back did you have to reach to find a moment when we were enthusiastic about jumping around the universe? So much of my memories were missing. Even the earliest ones looked like us going through the motions. Jump. Save the planet. Jump. Save the universe. Jump. Repeat.

Now, it was more like a job than anything else. It was boring most of the time and always repetitive. Every place we went, every single time, we had to face off with something bigger, save someone or some people, make things right. And every single planet felt old, like I had been there before. While there was room for wonder, I always felt a vague sense of *déjà vu*. Had I seen it all before?

Or maybe that was just me feeling old. *Getting* old. *Being* old. How old was I, anyway? Was it wrong to think I was too old to jump around the universe playing heroes with my sister? Or was it right to think I wasn't old enough to stop?

But that was all before I met *her*. Before I reached Earth, before I met Sally. Those months were bliss. Being able to shut my mind off, focusing on assimilation alone. Playing at integration. I lived without being on edge every second of every day. With her, everything was new again, as if the universe had rebooted and was showing me the wonders it had forgotten to show me before. Like everything was redesigned, exciting again.

Like, what the heck is ice cream? How can you make cream so good just by making it cold? Or Earth's pizza. Pizza was basically magic to me.

Who was I to blame? Was Blayde slipping away? Was Sally just naturally thrilling? Or was I that desperate to stop and catch my breath, I had been blind as well?

This is confusing. I need a stronger drink.

"Can I sit here?" Blayde said calmly. Her voice sounded empty, drained. As if having read my mind she held out a cup of some vibrant green drink, even more vibrant than mine, which I took from her hand as I nodded for her to join me. Her eyes were fixed on the planet below as well, neither one of us willing to make eye contact.

"Seems as though anywhere we go, we get our fair

share of problems," she said, distant, as if she spoke from the end of a very long tunnel. "Though, usually, they're not actually ours. Can't we ever get a break?"

"I guess not." I downed the drink she had given me in one gulp. Huge mistake. It was as if someone had taken my mind out of my head, ran it through salt and lemon, given it to a *blitcheen* to poke, then put back in, jamming the gray matter into my skull and fixing the scalp back on, poorly.

Excellent.

The little lemon buddies that had been sitting in my brain since my first drink back at the bar were now scattered through every part of my mind, punching thoughts left and right, allowing me to stare at the planet in a dizzy bliss.

"Zander"—Blayde crossed her arms in front of her chest and leaned forward on the table; straight to business, as always—"I'm stuck with you, whether you like it or not. I'm sorry to say this, but you *have* to snap out of it."

She wasn't being judgmental; she was just stating a fact. I remained silent.

"So how long is this going to go on?" she continued. "You can't give me the cold shoulder forever."

"I just need to figure some stuff out for myself, that's all." The little lemon figures were now going to war against a new faction that had popped up in my hypothalamus. Bright figures danced behind my eyeballs, all reds and blues swimming in my field of vision. "Is this stuff even legal?"

"I dunno. Do you care?"

"What's it called?"

She let out a sound like black hole going through a trash compactor then shrugged again. "But you're right, Zander, we need to figure some stuff out."

"Wait, you think I'm right?" I almost snorted the drink on her. "Well, that's new. " I slammed the glass on the table. Her mind was too far ahead, and she didn't give her mouth time to catch up, leaving me trying to fill in the gaps in her argument. "What are you talking about?"

"I'm saying that the universe has been giving us a sign."

"What kind of sign?"

"Don't tell me you didn't notice it, Zander," she said, a smile creeping up her lips. She had my attention now, and she knew it. "Everywhere we go, someone brings up the Berbabsywell monks. Everywhere."

"You call that a sign?" I rolled my eyes. "The last time you said you spotted a sign, you saw the sun reflecting off a lake and told me you spoke to a burning ram."

"Because I did. It told me I needed to listen to myself more. Or something like that. It was very empowering. I wasn't going to ignore a ram that was on fire and not burning!"

"It had red hair. Made eye contact *once*."

"Anyway," she continued, shaking her head, "this is different. You must have noticed it, Zan. The monks. Everywhere we go, every planet. I think they hold the answers."

"Which ones?"

"The ones we're looking for."

"So, let's just say the universe is being clement and is giving us a sign. The monks are still only legend. A myth. Is it really worth checking out?"

"Who knows?" She grinned. "But what's there to lose? Should I remind you that *we* sorta kinda fall into the myth category?"

I paused for a second, staring back down at the planet. I had to admit she was right. When the universe is signaling you, you don't just keep going on your merry way. You have to stop and hear it out.

"But it's been weirder than that," I said, leaning closer to her. "Didn't you notice Sally?"

My sister's face turned cold. "What about her?"

"There's just so much that doesn't add up," I said, trying to push the conversation toward something that would keep her interested. "All the events that led up to us meeting. The hot-air balloon, for example."

"What hot-air balloon?"

"The one that was draped over her window the morning of the day we met." That caught her attention. I watched her eyes widen before me, a surefire sign for me to continue talking. "The hot-air balloon cost Sally her job, which led to her getting in a fight with her best friend Marcy, which led to her leaving the party early and running me over with her car."

"Ignoring those banal details that I don't care about, a hot-air balloon led to our separation?"

"Weird, right?" I let it sink in a little bit, but I didn't stop there. "That, and her friend Marcy is engaged to Danirsh'ni'ah. Only now, she's a woman."

"Veesh, that's unexpected."

"And remember when we were on the *Traveler*?" I added. "Kork, it turns out, is not only from Earth impersonating one of Sally's favorite TV characters, but his Earth-name was Matthew Daniels."

"So?" She raised an eyebrow inquisitively, but I could tell she was engrossed.

"So, that's the name of her boyfriend, the one who died when we took Grisham down." I felt a pang in my heart at the thought of the man. He had hated me, which had been unsettling, but he had been a hero at the very end.

"Oh, that boy with the flowers?" Blayde nodded. "Okay, that's weird. But you realize there's nothing we can do about it, right? Sally's gone, Zander. She's home, on Earth, where she belongs. She'll live a long, happy human life. Find a human mate. Pop out babies. Grandbabies. Grow a garden and hunt for leprechauns or whatever humans do for fun. Get that pet snake. I know she was interesting to you. She was a good person. But she's gone."

I stared out at the planet, trying to drown out her words. I needed another one of those brain-wringing drinks. Something to keep my mind off her. To keep me distracted from all the could-have-beens.

"So where can we find these"—I turned my attention back to my sister—"Berbabsywell monks?"

Blayde grinned, lifting her eyebrows. "I have absolutely no idea. But I can tell you where we could start."

She grinned, showing off her shining teeth. I waited for her to continue, but it was as if she were stuck, waiting for a cut scene where we would miraculously pop up right at the next interesting point in the story.

"Um, where do we start?"

She frowned. Something she had wanted to happen wasn't happening, and it was frustrating her. She looked back at me and continued as if none of this had happened.

"So, I think I know who holds the answers," she said. "If anyone has access to the monks, it would be the Alliance. I heard rumors that they send the child hires who age out of their program there as some sort of tribute, so they can continue having access to the information stored there. Even Kork mentioned that the monks are mainly child hires who'd outgrown their usefulness."

"Let me guess…we need to go to the Islands?"

She nodded. "Won't be too difficult. They always up their security after we visit, but we're not interested in the president or any of the ministers, not this time anyway. It's just an easy in-and-out near their child hire offices. Nothing we'd be remotely interested in—usually."

"Right, simple," I agreed. "We just need to find a planet connected to the Alliance, find a ship to take us to Pyrina, then get on a shuttle to the Islands without raising the alarm. Easy peasy."

"Don't be a *glicker*, Zan." She grinned, downing a glug of her green drink. While it's always better to go into a heist clear-headed, the best ideas usually came to someone who's mind had just been twisted by lemons. The ones in my mind had finally achieved mind-world peace, and their civilization was beginning to stagnate over petty squabbles. *I might need a refill.*

"When the hell have you ever called me Zan?" I asked. "That sounds really weird."

"Sally called you Zan."

"Did she really?" I stiffened at the mention of her name. Sally—the two syllables that brought home a boatload of pain. A betrayal. Why Blayde would even mention her was beyond me. I gritted my teeth, trying to put the memories of her behind me, and focused on the plan ahead.

Being within the Alliance's core system, the shuttle would have to be a small, interplanetary ship, probably not fit for interstellar space. Interstellar ships would require too large a crew, and we didn't want that many people involved. So, we'd have to rig it for a quick getaway.

We had been to Pyrina a few times before, and it never ceased to amaze me how many people could live on that one giant rock. Billions, even trillions, of people lived in the Alliance's capital, in an incredibly dense city, one stacked above the other. The average building was more than a few hundred stories high, all the way across the planet, beautifully planned, and by far the most high-tech city in this arm of the galaxy. It even had oceans, albeit small ones.

That was where we would be headed: the Suspended Islands of the blue valley. Well, it was much classier in Pyrinian, which called the entire place *Puchana;* although, that could also translate as "really blue business center; enter at your own risk." This was, for all intents and purposes, the capital of the capital: the president of the Alliance himself lived there, along with other important diplomats and ambassadors. Away from the metropolis, the center of Alliance government was a floating city.

"Any idea how we should get in?" Blayde asked as she stretched out in the booth. For a split second, I saw her just as she was, yet it was on another sofa, planets away, as she ranted on about my need for a shower. Had she told Sally what she was planning on doing while I was out of the room? Had they said goodbye while I was gone?

Come back, lemons. Keep these memories at bay.

"You're asking me?" I said quickly, pushing the image out of my head. "I thought you already had a plan."

"I guess we should have talked more, huh?" She sneered. "Discussed plans? For the future?"

"Says the girl who kidnapped me from Earth," I snapped. I bit my tongue, but it didn't manage to stop me from saying what I wanted. She, however, had apparently turned on her selective hearing and completely ignored this.

"Right, options?" she said.

"Should we go crim or faux-legal?"

She grinned, happy to be planning once more.

"Faux-legal. More freedom that way."

Her smile brought me back to the last time we pulled a heist like this, which was a pretty long time ago from what I could remember. It was always fun to set up a plan and see it through, to work out the tendrils of interconnecting backup plans. She was giddy now, excited, like me, to be on a case once more.

It would be so much easier than when we had hacked the great radiator at the center of the great bank of Alcamazar, until all the gold melted out through the floor. Or when we had saved the universe from the devious Kizkim by hosting a dance-off, which, in turn, had inspired quite a few universe-saving dance-offs across the galaxy.

"What's the plan, Zan?"

I rolled my eyes. Blayde was back.

"Don't call me Zan. And I have the perfect way in."

CHAPTER FIVE

SWAT TEAMS MAKE TERRIBLE ALARM CLOCKS

SALLY

There might be nothing worse than being ripped from a weird dream and thrust into a nightmare. Especially if the thrusting is done with a loud, singing cellphone, and the nightmare is your reality.

I'm being dramatic, but only a little bit.

The thing about waking up in one's own bed after spending the past few days visiting countless worlds light-years away is that you're never quite sure how grounded you are. There's a feeling of anything being possible. A feeling of waking and slowly coming to terms with the fact you were now being eaten by a giant banana slug. That didn't happen, but it was one of those things that felt as if it just could happen, if you were unlucky enough.

Add to that the buzz of alcohol consumed while making awkward eye contact with your best friend's fiancée who you know is hiding something, and you're a little unsettled to say the least. After being accused by a perfect stranger of having ruined their life, no less.

The thing that woke me was my phone, ringing and buzzing on my nightstand, making the world around me shake. I had been through this dance before: It's how the worst mornings started.

Half-asleep, I reached up, fumbling for my phone as the song continued. My fingers wrapped around it, and I pulled it over to my ear as I lay under the sheets, my cocoon of warmth against the harsh cold of winter. I should have turned on the heat, but I had forgotten it was something I could control. The cold didn't bother me as much as it once had, and I couldn't tell if it was just a mild winter or if I had just grown thicker skin.

"Hello?" I said groggily, glaring around my room for any sign of the hour. It was pitch black outside. That or there was another balloon draped over my house. Couldn't rule that one out either.

I sat up. There wasn't a balloon. That was real, middle-of-the-night darkness.

"Sally." The voice said it as a statement, not a question. The monotony of it made my spine tingle, and I straightened as I sat.

Oh crap. I could tell by the tone of their voice that something awful was going down. And I was still in my TARDIS pajamas.

"Who is this?" My hand extended to switch on the light, though in the dark and the cold, it was an almost impossible feat.

"Whatever you do, don't make any sign you're awake," the voice ordered hastily, and I yanked my hand back like it had been struck by lightning. "Don't get up. Don't turn on the light."

I pulled my hand under the sheets in a flash, the tone of the stranger's voice told me that they were serious. She was serious—a woman, with a voice deepened by whispers and worry. Dead serious. I pressed my body against the wall, away from my window.

"Why? Who's calling?" I asked, terrified, my voice a low whisper.

"No time." In the background I heard people moving, rushing. "Get out of there. They are coming. Good luck."

The stranger hung up, leaving me confused in the dark of the early, early morning. I checked the time on my phone: 2:53. Barely an hour of sleep since I had come home from Marcy's. Not early enough to be considered early; still late enough to be called late.

I wanted to believe the voice. I really did. But I was tired, groggy, and not quite sure which way was up. At least I was in my own bed, on my own planet.

And then I heard it. The almost imperceptible crunch of tires on an icy driveway, the sound of a large vehicle coming to a stop. Braking right in front of my building, right below my window.

So much for the universe not throwing me shit anymore.

Something inside of me clicked into motion. Without thinking, I rolled out of bed, staying below the window, landing in a crouch on the floor and hustling out of my room. As if I had formed habits in the few days I had been in adventure mode, as if my body knew what to do before I did.

It was dark, oh so dark. I kept my hand on the wall, my fingers trailing on the cold plaster. My ambling led me to the bathroom. The small window above the commode had a nice view on the street below, so I edged myself up on the toilet lid to look out, crouching low so just my eyes were visible. If it was dark enough in my apartment, no one outside could see me.

I hoped.

There was a van on the street in front of my house. A black van, blocking the driveway. No markings, no license plate. Shifty, very shifty. It looked like something out of a spy movie.

To make matters even more double-oh-seven, the back doors flew open and out came men in full black tactical gear, holding large guns. Because of course they were. These were not just run-of-the-mill men with guns. These men were serious.

Well, who with a gun wasn't serious and terrifying? But this was like watching an action movie come to life.

On my driveway.

My heart pounded, pumping adrenaline in my veins. Seven men had flown out the back of their van. They were coming for me; why else would the stranger have called? My fear rose as I saw them talk amongst themselves, my time to escape slipping away with every second.

What would Zander do?

"Don't do what I would do!" his voice seemed to scold in my head, though I knew it was the chemicals in my brain speaking. *"You're not immortal. You're not trained in hand-to-hand combat. You don't even own a gun!"*

Then what do I do? I shouted at my subconscious, my head spinning, eyes darting this way and that, trying to find a way out like an animal in a cage.

"Sally, you have to run*!"*

I flew out of the bathroom, my heart racing. I had to get out of my apartment, somehow, but they were blocking the exits and probably had me surrounded by now. There was no escape. I couldn't jump out a window, too dangerous. I couldn't take a stand, I wasn't prepared. Focus, Sally, focus. There's always a way out. Always, right? Sure, I wasn't able to transport myself halfway across the universe in the blink of an eye, but I could do something. I had to.

Every passing second I wasted thinking of a way out, these creepy assault guys were getting closer. I was going to have to do something stupid.

Like the balcony.

I grabbed the blanket off the couch and tied it around my neck like superman. It was below freezing outside and I could take a run for it, but I would probably die of frostbite before getting far. The blanket would have to do.

The balcony of this level of my apartment was connected to the one next door by a single wall. In theory, it was simple: All I had to do was climb up on the rail and work my way around the separator. But in the cold and the snow, without being seen? Slightly more difficult.

I rushed to the sliding door in the living room, turning on the spot as I realized what they must be after: my alien artifacts. It felt strange calling them artifacts, having just acquired them mere days before, but governments would still be clambering over them if they ever learned about their existence.

Probably.

There wasn't anything else about me that would remotely interest them. I was just a boring little human in their eyes.

Maybe someone had spotted the robot sentry in my apartment. Or that stripper had gone to the FBI for something I hadn't even done. Betrayed by complete strangers for being in the wrong place in the wrong time. Isn't that always the case?

I rushed back to my room, grabbing the large shoebox I had hidden everything in. I slung it under my arm as I took off to the door, sliding it shut behind me just as I heard footsteps in the stairway. I punched the doorframe a few times, forcing it to lock behind me. No trace of my escape left behind.

Even though there were lampposts in the street, the way the building stood blocked the light from me. It was impossible to see, the cold even more chilling outside, making my eyes plead to be shut. But I couldn't close them, not when I was desperate for any light they could let through. I forced them to stay open despite the chill.

I ordered my feet forward, throwing my shoebox onto my neighbor's terrace and climbing up on the rail. It was slippery, but it only took two steps to climb around the wall. I jumped down silently, wrapping the blanket tight around me as I picked up my extraterrestrial souvenirs and hugged them tight against my chest. There, I curled up in a ball, receding into the dark corner between the separator and the wall.

My door creaked open.

I was glad I wouldn't have to explain to my landlord why two of my doors has exploded this week. Still, it was unsettling as they slipped into my apartment, silent as the night. The gentle patter of heavy feet rushed into my home and invaded my life, filling my ears and breaking my heart. I squeezed my eyes shut against the cold and the fear that began to eat me from within. Which one was making me shiver?

And, more importantly, who had been the stranger on the phone? Why had they warned me? Why were there people in my house, and what were they searching for?

The balcony door slid open like a whisper, the sound of footsteps on my icy terrace. The blanket wasn't enough protection against winter's frosty bite, and it took all my willpower to not let my teeth chatter away.

A match struck; the smell of cigarettes filled the fresh air. The man breathed heavily as he stood in place. I heard another pair of feet join him, though I couldn't see a thing.

"Smoke?" a gruff voice asked.

"No, thanks." Seconds went by like hours. "Wonderful. Just wonderful. We get called up in the middle of the night, and it's a wild goose chase?"

"I know, right?" the first man responded. I could hear him exhale air heavily, the smell of nicotine heavy in the air. "And seriously, they could have gone with half the squad. A girl shouldn't put up too much fight. Why bother?"

"Red knows," the other man said confidently. "Red!" He slid the door open, yelling into the room.

"What?" Red said as he joined them on the terrace.

"No luck?" the smoker asked solemnly.

"None."

"Why'd you need us, anyway?"

"Just re-enforcement. The files said she might put up a fight," Red replied simply, and my heart stopped.

"A girl?" The men laughed.

"I know." Their leader chuckled heavily. "I didn't believe it either. But she's smart, I'll give you that. Her bed was still warm when we arrived. No idea how she fled."

"Could she still be here?"

"We're looking, but there's no sign."

"What's so important about her, anyway? By the look of her house, she's not very—"

"No idea. But she has something they want."

"MI6 or CIA?"

"MI6 *and* CIA."

"Shit."

"What's she got that's so important?"

"I dunno, but they wanted her alive," Red pro-claimed. "I'm not in the loop or anything. But I recognized her name. Sally Webber. Ring a bell?"

"Who?"

"That girl who survived that explosion at the plant those years back?" The non-smoker shuffled nervously. "Why would they want her? If they wanted to know how she survived, why not ask her two years ago?"

"You have a good memory."

"She looked hot in the photos."

"Seriously?"

"She was, though."

"She was probably warned by someone," Red said suddenly. "Have Jack pull up the phone records."

"Yessir." I heard the sliding door open and shut again, leaving two men alone outside. A sudden crackle of radio static cut the silence.

"Red, you read me?"

"Loud and clear. She's not here. What's the next move?"

"The mission's been cleared."

"Wait, what?"

"I mean it's been erased. Put on the kibosh. Canceled."

"Seriously?"

"At two-fucking-thirty in the morning?" the smoker repeated, clearly annoyed.

"You've been ordered to pull out," the voice on the walkie-talkie crackled.

"Where's the order from?"

"From up the ladder, if you know what I mean," the voice sputtered, words cracking through the device. "Report back to HQ to fill out any discharge of weapon forms if there were any, then you're free to go home."

The radio fizzled out, the only sound left being that of the cigarette man crushing his smoke with the toe of his boot.

"Three in the fucking morning," he grumbled. "For nothing."

He continued to whine as he and his superior went back inside, ranting until his voice was cut off by the sliding door.

I let out a breath of relief, but the cold was still there, trying to gnaw through my blanket. I couldn't move, not quite yet. Not with them still in my apartment. My mind raced, trying to figure out what they could want with me.

I was nobody. Nobody, freezing her ass off in the cold.

I waited until I was sure I heard the van pull away before I got back up. I needed to get out of the cold, as I was numb pretty much everywhere. It was harder to scale the separator now that the adrenaline had run its course through my veins, but with one mighty heave, I managed to get back on my side of the fence.

My apartment had been tossed. As I hit the switch, light fell on the overturned couch cushions, the fallen blankets, and fruit. Anything that hadn't been inside a cabinet was now on the floor. I guess these guys didn't care much for the homes they were hired to infiltrate. So, now on top of having to tell my landlady that my bathroom door had "inexplicably" shattered, I had this mess to clean up too.

Who where they, anyway? I folded the blankets, my hands trembling as the effects of the panic slowly wore off. Not government, but working ... for them? Side by side? What would the CIA want with me—or MI6 for that matter?

One thing was clear: They didn't care about my alien knickknacks. They wanted me. They wanted Sally Webber, and no one was going to tell me why.

Could they know? Did they know where I had been, what I had been doing, who I had been spending time with? If Taylor's mysterious friend Felling was any basis, someone was interested in monitoring my bloodwork or something. Whatever that meant. Maybe they had decided it was time to take me in because of that. Because ...

I blanched. As in, I could actually feel the blood rush away from my face. I hadn't made the connection before, not since my mind had been fogged by grief. But Nim had been saved with Zander's blood. I had been there, saw him save the boy myself.

The same way Zander had saved me, after the incident at the power plant. Only he didn't remember it.

My hands lifted in front of my face. What had I become? Why were the creepy guys in masks with their guns and their cigarettes interested in me now, after all this time?

I dropped my hands. I needed to go. I couldn't stay here tonight, not after what I had just seen happen in my own home. I needed to go somewhere safe.

I threw on the clothes from the top of the pile, grabbed my wallet, and left. I had to get someplace safe. I had cash, which was a relief, in case they were monitoring my movements through my credit card. I hastily shut off my phone, hoping that would stop them tracking that, too—whoever 'them' was.

I couldn't go to Marcy and Dany's. No way I could put them in danger too. Same with my parents, not to mention last minute flights to Miami were expensive.

I locked and left my apartment, realizing for the first time that, as terrified as I was, I was only shivering because of the cold. Somehow, I knew I was going to be okay.

I had one last place I could turn to.

CHAPTER SIX

THE WONDERS OF PYRINIAN ADMINISTRATION

ZANDER

Hours later, on the other side of the solar system, a hopper landed on a launch pad on Pyrina's northern airstrip. It slid easily into one of the docks, hissing as its landing gear touched down and the planet's gravity took over.

The door flew open, hitting the tarmac with a resonating thwack, like a dumpster hiding an entire brass band from the tuba player's ex-hubby being thrown down a hill. Being the last ship to land on the deserted strip made the noise echo across the entire lot, and the boy stepping out of the ship cringed.

He was a young man, or still a boy, you might say, at the sight of him. He wore crisp livery, though his black boots were caked in the mud of a world millions of miles away. In his arms, he carried his mistress's uellun, a small fluffy animal, which looked remarkably like a moldy bowling ball if bowling balls sprouted legs so small they could be mistaken for fur. The legs constantly kicked outward, making holding the creature quite literally a handful. Seeing the gray-green fuzz from afar, you might be wondering who let the strawberries out this long.

The woman who followed was strikingly handsome. She wore a coat that could have been made of the same tiny legs as the pet's, which clung to her body in the trending fashion of a tight-fitting jumpsuit with an oddly dropped crotch.

Her long blonde hair was pinned upwards with gravity-defying pins, which she readjusted as she stepped out of the cramped ship and onto the dock. She took in a long, deep breath of the cool night smog.

"Ah," she said, patting her curls, "wonderful weather, isn't it now, Perkins?"

Perkins would have rolled his eyes, but he restrained himself. "Yes, ma'am.".

The woman turned to look the man in the eyes, an almost cross look flittering over her calm expression.

"Come now, Perkins." She raised an eyebrow. "It's been quite a long time since we've been to Pyrina. You are allowed to take in the sights, you know."

"Which I am already doing." He readjusted the pet in his arms. All fifty thousand legs were trying to push against him at once, to wriggle free from his grasp, and he desperately wanted to put the thing down.

"Do not let Morelli's little feet get dirty," she said,

indicating her beloved pet. "This tarmac is filthy."

"Of course not, ma'am."

"Well, now." The woman glanced around the space strip, looking for the entrance to the terminal. Spotting it, she let a grin creep onto her face, showing her sharp white teeth. "Let's go catch a shuttle."

They strode across the empty dock, meeting no one else on the way. It was getting late, the evening mist rising through the city and almost touching the bottom of the dock, making it seem as if they were walking on a path through the clouds. Which, in a way, they were. The smog was the only cloud there was on Pyrina.

Lights switched on automatically as they approached. The woman fiddled idly with the straps of her purse as she walked, her long, silk gloves wrinkling as she fussed. She seemed to have trouble walking in her jumpsuit, the fabric too constraining for her, as if she never wore anything tight in her day-to-day life.

The boy, Perkins—because he was much too young and bright-faced to be a man, however tall he still might be—followed his mistress into the terminal, all the while admiring the city that rose on either side of the landing pad with a strange fascination. He seemed genuinely amazed by the everyday hustle and bustle of people in their everyday lives, coming and going through the buildings that caressed the sky.

The inside of the station was full of commuters, trying to get out into Pyrina's incredibly confusing transport system. It was easier to travel thirty light-years than thirty blocks in this city, as the computer programs in charge of managing city planning had grown sentient and despised each other, refusing to communicate for any reason. Many programmers had been brought in to fix the problem, but each time they were rebuffed. Currently, all fifty-seven city planning AIs were in couples counseling, and while they were beginning to see progress, none were ready to open up and talk about sharing bus lines.

Even when one of the programmers tried to change CM43's mind by seducing it, it was to no avail. Though today they are quite happily married.

Luckily, neither Perkins nor the woman in red would be riding city transit. Free of the dirty tarmac, Perkins put down Morelli and took the creature's leash. It was only then he noticed how much they stuck out, even among a terminal filled with dozens of races from the entire Alliance.

No one was as elegantly dressed as her, and though the strange way she wore her hair clashed with the rest of the ensemble, she was, by far, wearing the most sumptuous clothes in the room. But even with this excessive amount of oddity, no one batted an eyelid; they were used to strange and exotic people walking through those doors. It was even normal compared to some beings that entered through the glass doorway from the strange planets, some more beast than man and others more gelatin that beast. After strange sights like those, seeing such a fabulous woman in expensive clothes was nothing new, certainly nothing to lift one's head (however many one had) to watch.

"Oh, *veesh*. Morelli! Stop that this instant!" screamed the woman, rushing to her pet and ripping it off the other ball of fluff it had merged with. The owner of the other creature dashed over to try and help, and with loud grunts, they managed to pull the two apart, much to the annoyance of Morelli and its new friend.

"Bad uellun, bad!" she scolded the fluff ball, but if Morelli seemed bothered by this, it gave no outward sign. Not that it gave any signs of feeling anything, anyway.

The woman glared at Perkins. "Well, this is going to be a mess."

Perkins nodded, tightening his fist on Morelli's leash.

Still fuming, the woman stormed off toward a kiosk, pulling out a hairy wallet from her purse, an accessory from a border planet, where the more exotic creatures were found right outside the doorsteps of even the most Alliance-friendly homes. Perkins followed, though only barely paying any attention to her. He dragged the uellun behind him as he stared up through the glass ceiling at the purples and oranges of twilight, the first stars of the evening peeking out through the veil of sunset and smog. He smiled.

"Look, we need two tickets to the Suspended Islands, as in now," the woman said to the attendant, who looked to have as much personality as Morelli, even shared between all three heads. "Make it snappy. I'm in a hurry."

"Do you have a permit for that?" the drone's middle face asked from behind the desk, their voice monotonous. They sighed audibly as they stroked the computer keys, filling out the dull forms of authorization to the Blue Valley.

The woman held up a bright blue piece of paper, which glowed with an otherworldly haze.

"I'm Ms. Harolds. I have to fill in the last of the

papers to turn over my Alliance-granted child hire to the UPA's use. Boring, I know. But then we got held up on one of the outer planets, and we couldn't make our connection because they had to reroute it around a comet. You understand, I hope."

Perkins rolled his eyes behind her back. Why was she always this dramatic?

"Um-hum." The attendant's three heads nodded sheepishly. Well, two did while the third stared at the floor. "We have one shuttle left tonight. There won't be another one 'till tomorrow morning, but I doubt you'll make it. It's on the other side of the terminal, and it leaves in half an hour."

"Ma'am," the third head droned, "your uellun is making a mess on the floor. You do understand we have restrictions on uellun breeding inside the terminal."

"My uellun—oh, frash a supernova! Morelli! Bad Morelli!"

Perkins stared at the purple chalk on the floor. Where Morelli had once been, now sat two identical uellun, each about half the size of the original Morelli, though a shade of gray darker. Quickly, they were growing back to full size, making Perkins's job now twice as hard.

"Ma'am, we do not allow asexual reproduction in the lobby," said the formerly staring head, now glaring. "We're going to have to ask you to escort your pets outside."

"Look here," Harolds snapped. "We have an appointment. Perkins has been working for me for over ten years now. I can't bear to think about finding someone to replace him, but it has to be done. People are waiting on me, higher-up people who could have you fired from your position quicker than your heads can come to an agreement about where to eat tonight. So, you get me on that shuttle, or you'll never find any work on this planet—or anywhere else in the Alliance. Is that clear?"

The attendant looked bored at this, possibly because the argument wasn't exactly new. With a large roll of her eyes, Harolds slapped a crisp bill on the counter, which promptly disappeared under a glitzy, bedazzled claw. The three-headed lizard typed something on their keyboard, and, an instant later, two small, white hexagons came shooting onto the desk.

With the tickets paid for, the woman removed both her shoes, and with a wave to Perkins, she took off toward gate Delta Fish *52 Scrmjor*. Perkins balked, but he grabbed both the uellun and took off after her.

Two became four, and Perkins stumbled.

They reached the gate with time to spare, though Perkins was struggling to wrangle all the uellun together, as there were now sixteen small, furry balls and only one leash between them.

"Tickets?" The woman at the gate seemed chirpy, uneasy. She grinned at Perkins as his mistress let herself into the shuttle, looking back at the steward with a sour expression. The young woman backed off.

They were alone in the shuttle, except for the female attendant and the thirty-odd balls of fluff. Running low on food and energy, they would either stop multiplying or keep on at this rate, only growing smaller and smaller each time.

The attendent closed the doors with a loud slam, to

which she bit her lip in obvious embarrassment. She went to the cockpit, squeezing her way past the herd of fluff, not saying a word about them. The emptiness of the shuttle was now more looming than before, broken only by the sound of the almost-silent hum of the engines and occasional squeaks from the pets, who should not have been making noises at all considering they didn't have mouths.

Perkins hung his head over the seat, the weight of the things to come so unbearable he found it hard to keep it together.

"Perkins, it's going to be all right," his mistress said, halfheartedly trying to sound soothing.

"I seriously doubt it, Ms. Harolds." He grinned slightly, though, to show there were no hard feelings. They both missed the simpler days. "Though this is exciting, right now. Going to the Suspended Islands and everything—"

"Anything I can get you?" The attendant asked in a sweet, chirpy voice as the shuttle started on its course.

"Some achilan for me, water for the boy," she answered promptly. The attendant returned with the drinks, though she was extremely cautious as she carried them from one end of the shuttle to the other. She almost tripped over one of the larger uellun, who hadn't split yet. Perkins had lost track of how many there were now, and most were too small to see. That would be the end of Morelli, though some of its offspring would live on in the stale, canned air of the shuttle.

"Bad day?" Perkins sputtered. His mistress glared at him, but what did he care? She was no longer the boss of him, really. The stewardess handed them the drinks.

94

"Yeah. First day on the job. Child hire turned shuttle attendant. It's not as easy as it seems, closing doors and making drinks." She sighed, then hid her mouth with her tray out of embarrassment. Perkins watched her turn and walk away. Ms. Harolds put a hand on his shoulder.

"I can't stop you from talking to her," she murmured. "Not anymore."

He smiled, and she smiled back, though both were awkward and slightly flakey. She hadn't said anything about the infinite iterations of her once favorite pet, which he took as a good sign. Perkins got up, following the cute attendant to the back of the small ship. She looked up from putting away the tray, startled at him being there.

"Your hair is really nice," he said, pointing awkwardly.

"Thank you, sir." The attendant smiled, blushing a bright shade of red.

"Don't call me 'sir.'" He grinned. "I'm still just a hire. Well, for the next hour I am, then I get reassigned."

"That's nice." She grinned back. "I got my new orders yesterday. Shuttle wasn't what I expected, but there's a lot more freedom than in any other assignment."

"Do you know what else they're giving out?"

"They've got tons of job openings, but they pick you on what your master or mistress either trained you in or in what they suggest in their recommendation. I worked as a waitress for a line of cruise ships, so they put me here. But small shuttles are a little more complicated to work on; here, the suspension is terrible. Before, it was just handing out drinks here and there. Now, I've gotta do everything on this shuttle, 'cept pilot it."

Proving her point, the shuttle suddenly lurched over a patch of turbulence, making the drink cart jump. The woman caught one of the bottles with lightning fast reflexes as it fell, putting it back on top where it belonged with a sideways smile, as if to say, *You see what I mean?*

"I was more like a stable hand back at my mistress's ranch," the boy said quietly, eyes wide in admiration of her trick. "They don't have any jobs with animals, do they?"

The stewardess could only shrug. "They might, but nothing big. All we get are the service jobs no one else wants. You know, so the populace can take on more intellectual roles. They might put you in food processing, though. Not too bad of a gig. It pays well."

He seemed to ignore her, his eyes exploring the small kitchenette. "My mistress hates coming down to the capital. That's why she seems all jumpy. Hey, have you ever heard about the monks of Berbabsywell?"

The woman's eyes went wide, her eyebrows then climbing back down her face to knot into a frown.

"Are you crazy?" The woman sputtered, then hid her mouth again. She dropped her voice to a whisper. "No one knows what goes on there. Why would you want a job there?"

He shrugged. "The knowledge, I guess."

She glared at him, as if he had said something horribly offensive. "I doubt they'll hire a stable hand, if it's even real. What's the use?"

"Fine." He dropped his shoulders, defeated. This seemed to reassure her.

"Now please. It's my first day on the job; I don't

want to get caught dawdling."

"Sure."

"Plus, I have to clean a few billion uellun off the carpet," she said. "Didn't anyone tell you never to bring ring planet pets onto a public shuttle? This is what happens!"

Perkins left, sitting back down next to his mistress, who barely noticed his presence as she stared straight ahead, her eyes darting back and forth in the small enclosed space. The boy leaned his head against the window dreamily.

They landed shortly after, the darkness making it impossible to see the beauty of the Suspended Islands. All that could be made out was the light straight ahead and the sound of water hitting the sides of the path to the building. The shuttle remained tethered to the dock, turned boat for the evening.

Ms. Harolds exited first, Perkins close on her heels, as she nervously made her way to the main building, stumbling slightly in her stilettos. He tossed the leash into the bay; they wouldn't be needing it now. He turned back to look at the pretty stewardess, who was in deep conversation with the pilot, arguing about something and not caring one bit about their passengers now that they were off their shuttle.

The glass door slid away to let them in. They entered the small building then rode the elevator up from the dock to the island above, a large metal block that hung in the air, silent as a whisper.

They stepped off the elevator in unison, following the distinctly marked arrows that led to the Ministry of Abductees. But the instant they stepped into the office they were grabbed by guards, bags stuffed on their heads, and marched to another location, Ms. Harolds screaming and kicking, unable to fight back with her stilettos.

The bags were ripped off, and they were now in an office identical to the one they had just entered. Maybe it was even the same one. Perkins was shocked to see a uellun on this man's desk, rolling around like it owned the place. But what was perhaps more shocking were the twenty or so heavily armed guards who surrounded him and his mistress, clutching weapons a little higher grade than the stunners most security carried.

"Three minutes ago, our Office of Abductee Processing was broken into," a strange, heavy-set orka'ha droned in the characteristic monotonous voice as they watched Perkins from across the desk. "The coordinates for the Berbabsywellian Abbey were stolen. And you two are the only newcomers on this side of the island."

"We only just arrived! What are you talking about?" the woman sputtered. She lashed out and kicked again, the heels of her shoes shattering on the concrete floor as she threw them wildly against her restraints to no avail.

"You know what I think?" The man grinned. "I think we just caught the Blade and the Sand."

"What?" The woman froze, suddenly petrified. "But they're a child's tale. A mere myth, if anything."

"Ms. Blayde, You're under arrest for ... what's the latest charge?"

"Bank fraud, identity theft, blowing up the central island."

"This has got to be a mistake!" Harolds crumbled

under the weight of the pressure. Surrounded by guns on all sides, she couldn't keep her composure any longer. "I'm from a ranch on the rim planets. We raise cattle for Pyrina—"

"You expect us to believe that?"

"It's true!" She lifted her hands, since no one had tied them, slowly and careful, her hand going for her purse.

"The laser! Stop her now!" A guard grabbed her hands, ripping the purse from her grasp, throwing the contents on the floor for all to see.

"No laser here," said the guard with a cocky grin. "If you need us to pat her down—"

She screamed like an animal, thrashing on the chair as her hands were cuffed behind her back. The boy jumped up, punching the guard out cold. Other security officers rushed in, sitting him back on the chair and cuffing him as well.

"Ah, the ransom. The sum we'll receive!" The man chuckled. "You think we're idiots—you two just marching in here and stealing our property?"

"Sir?" A guard pointed at the computer on the desk. "You have a new message."

"The computer can tell me that much," he snapped. "Don't interrupt while I'm dealing with terrorists."

"It's marked urgent."

"Not now!"

"It's from Zander and Blayde, sir."

"I said not—wait, what?"

His hands trembled as he pulled up his inbox on the laptop he was handed. Yes, it was from them; yet, how they had known his address was anybody's guess. He pulled up the message, the looming voice reading out a solemn message.

Stop calling me Sand. Give me a catchier nickname, then we'll talk. Bye!

As the man screamed in anger, a lone shuttle rose above the island. The cute stewardess was changing out of her uniform into her familiar leggings, pulling on her favorite red leather jacket to cut the chill. She smiled at her brother, who rolled his eyes, and pushed the shuttle toward their new destination.

"He was mildly handsome," said Blayde, as she threw her uniform into the trash. "Way too young, though."

"You're millions of years old. Everyone is too young for you."

" Don't you know it's rude to discuss a lady's age?"

She climbed into the cockpit beside me, stretching in the copilot's seat. She was back in her usual clothes, the silvery leggings making her legs look like cyborg upgrades. She kicked them up on the dashboard, leaning back into her plush seat.

"I really don't get how they mistook him for me," I said, pretending not to pay any attention to her. "And come on—Sand? How come you're the *Blade,* and I'm the *Sand?* My name literally means protector, but they refer to me as silicon. Really, really lame." I punched in the coordinates for the library abbey—or should I call it librabbey?—into the autopilot, then returned to my sister. She beamed, happy to have my focus.

"Don't take it hard on yourself," she replied. "If they always underestimate you, you keep the element of surprise."

"I guess." I shrugged. They had known about us for millennia, not much of a surprise there. Then, again, we made it through an excellent heist with nothing getting in our way, so I guess it didn't matter either way. They never learned from their mistakes.

"And I was outright *giving* him the eyes, and he didn't even *try* to flirt with me! Have I lost my touch?" Blayde pouted, but the grin on her face told me she was just joking.

"As if you ever had it," I muttered, then jumped away as she tried to swat me. I didn't want any broken bones right now.

"Brain chip, remember?" I pointed out. "He'd probably get a zap if he did."

"Ah, right. We should really do something about that. Their program is getting out of control."

"Agreed. Pencil it in for Tuesday?"

"What's a Tuesday?"

"So, you have a plan for when we get there?" I asked, trying to change the subject. Tuesdays came from Earth, and Earth would just make us angry again.

"Can't you come up with something this time?" she asked, crossing her arms and leaning back into the seat. She had gone cold far, far too fast.

It would always be hanging over me, wouldn't it? My time of Earth was a knife, and every mention of it cut to her eternal mind. We would have to get past it, get over it; only time could heal those kinds of wounds.

But I wondered how long it would take for her to forgive me this time. And how many times had we been through this song and dance before; I could no longer remember.

An eternity of love, anger, and blame. But she was the only family I had, and that counted for something in this infinite universe. One of us would have to cave in and forgive—like every time before.

CHAPTER SEVEN

DRUNKENLY STUMBLING ON
EARTH-SHATTERING SECRETS

SALLY

Sneaking out of one's house in the middle of the night was cakewalk compared to, I don't know, sneaking into a royal palace on an alien planet, so I had that going for me. Easy peasy, lemon squeezy.

I took the rarely used back exit of the building, slipping through the shared parking lot with our neighbors and onto the street opposite, hoping that anyone watching the house would be none the wiser. Who knew if my car was being tracked? If my phone was being bugged? Who and what these people wanted from me?

I had shut off my phone entirely, not wanting to go so far as to kill it. I mean, these things are expensive, and I'm not sure insurance would cover acts of military vandalism. I flagged down a taxi, surprised there were any running at this time of night. When I told him where I was going, he said nothing, but the look in the rearview mirror was that of disgust and confusion.

I mean, going to a pub at three in the morning wasn't really the behavior of a proper young lady.

The Peacemaker was nearly empty, save for the people I wanted to see. Huddled in a booth, the little club of off-worlders were digging into some good old middle-of-the-night jalapeno poppers, excitedly trading stories and laughs without fear of being discovered by the pub's dwindling clientele. Friends—no, not friends, acquaintances—I had met through Taylor when they were living in my apartment and trying, like Marcy, to get me to go out more. They thought seeing aliens would make me feel better about losing mine. It didn't work out that way, but, hey, they were cool people.

"No way!" Shanshan, a petite Regulian in a trim college student's skin, flapped her heavily ringed hands excitedly. "And you survived?"

"I'm here, aren't I?" I wasn't quite sure what planet Tevin was from. Every time he opened his mouth to say it, a bird would fall to the ground in front of him, then get back up and peck at his feet. He was humanoid by birth: his bulky, *Wreck-It Ralph* physique wasn't part of a skin wrap, even if he was the one man in the group who looked like a fake.

Taylor's expat group was a fun bunch. They were all on Earth for their own reasons, which most of the time they didn't find worth sharing. The one thing they did share was a love of Earth beer, so every week they came to the Peacemaker Pub, a fake-Irish joint that shared an alley with Scintillance.

And I was allowed to tag along, perks of befriending-slash-dating the odd alien.

Fighting a leechin had won me brownie points, and they had taken me under their wing. But all I could remember from that night was the dead homeless man, the one who had been just as unlucky as me to be stuck in this alleyway at that exact time, who was just slightly too early to be saved by the mysterious James Felling.

"Room for one more?" I asked. I hadn't expected to be this nervous, but by the time I had reached their table my knees had begun to wobble, worse than when I had faced the beast in the great Undercity of Da-Duhui. All eyes were fixed on me as I stood before their booth, hands awkwardly stuffed in pockets.

"Well, well, well," said Tevin. "Look what the car dragged in."

"Cat, Tevin," said Rochelle. Kind, warm Rochelle was actually glaring at me. Rochelle! The woman had so many eyes the skin suit couldn't cover them all, allowing for some very odd pimples on her soft brown face, so many that Taylor said she could see right into your soul. I had nothing to hide but hurt and betrayal. "The cat dragged in some week-old trash."

"Wow, okay, I'm definitely not wanted here," I stammered. Definitely not the welcome I had been expecting. By no means did I think they would immediately pull up a chair and order me a drink just at the sight of me, but this was a whole new layer of cold I had never seen in the group before. Even Shanshan averted her gaze.

"Let her speak," said Finn. The man had apparently come from a planet where everyone looked like a Swedish lumberjack, so he had no trouble at all blending in with us humans. Although he sometimes got asked to pose with paper towels. "Sally, what the hell are you doing here?"

"They came for Taylor," I muttered. "The Ordran. One of their robot-cop-thingies broke out of my bathroom and tried to kill me. Insanely slowly, I might add."

They pulled their eyes away from me, only to tangle their gazes into unholy knots with each other. Rochelle's many pimples blinked and then closed. I tried to not cringe at the sight.

"They said they were leaving because they needed space," Shanshan piped up, staring at my shoes. My well-worn chucks covered in pieces of the galaxy cleverly disguised as common mud. "Because of you."

"They told me that too. And then the robot showed up. Lectured me about running and stuff—Taylor did, not the robot—when they were the one running away. And now people are after me, and ..."

The floodgates opened. Tears streamed freely down my face, even as I tried to reel them in, but I was tired, so damn tired. Tired of being chased. Tired of always being in the middle of someone else's mess. Tired of people looking for me for no goddamn reason.

I had almost lost my life ten feet away from here while Dany was proposing to Marce. I thought things would calm down now that I wasn't some major alien attractor, but it seemed like it would never, ever end.

Zander had claimed the universe wanted me for

something. He blamed it on the hot-air balloon that had set everything in motion almost two-and-a-half years ago, for running into signs everywhere we went. But then I fulfilled my role as Selena. That part was over, and the universe chewed me up and spat me back out. I thought this had meant no more aliens attacking me in dark alleys, though I still wished I knew who the mysterious monk was, who gave the prophecy to the elders of Aquetzalli and Atlan. No, the only drama I needed was wedding planning panic as my best friend prepared to walk down the aisle.

Didn't I deserve that?

Tevin didn't even ask. He wrapped an arm around me and hoisted me into the booth along with them until we were all squeezed together, joined at the hip in the tiny, cushy booth at the back of the dark bar. He slid his drink toward me.

"It's been hard for you too, huh?" he asked.

I nodded. "You wouldn't believe the half of it."

I took the beer and drank it thirstily. After everything that had happened tonight, I needed something strong to wash away the terror I felt.

People were after me. People were after me.

"You owe me the new round," said Tevin, and I put down the now-empty glass with a jolt. Dang. First the champagne, now beer. I was developing a drinking problem all over again.

"When Taylor had left, they said it was because I was stuck on this whole ... Zander thing. Living in the past. Not moving beyond the explosion at the plant, imagining he could still be alive so I wouldn't have to come to terms with the fact that both he and Matt were dead. But now, it turns out, they were just as much running from their past as I was."

They all nodded. Nestor took the opportunity to grab the dish of peanuts on the table, placing them on his lap where his real mouth could start devouring them. If anyone else noticed, they didn't say a thing.

"Fine, I'll get the next round, then," said Tevin. "When you put it so nicely."

"I probably shouldn't be drinking," I muttered.

"And I shouldn't be operating heavy machinery," he said, winking. "And, yet, here I am, walking and talking. We need drinks."

Finn returned from the bar a few minutes later with a full platter, which he slipped onto the table before returning to his booth. Margaritas. Mojitos. Beer. Wine. The man didn't discriminate.

"Dude, come on," hissed Rochelle. "We're supposed to be blending in with the humans!"

"We are blending in," said Nestor, the wine glass gone from the table, but by the sound of splashing, it was currently being enjoyed by the Voth. The meek burp confirmed this theory.

Rochelle's many pimples blinked. "If you say so."

"It's three in the morning," added Finn. "Humans at a bar so late?"

"We should go to Denny's," Shanshan agreed. "People don't seem to mind us so much there."

I reached for another beer. My head was already spinning with the whole "almost got kidnapped by a SWAT team" thing, and now I was sitting with aliens in a darkened pub in the middle of the night, which didn't make things much better, but they sure made it more bearable.

I chugged.

"Woah there. Steady," Tevin exclaimed.

"I almost died tonight. I deserve a little pick-me-up."

"That's fair, I guess."

"To Taylor!" roared Finn. "For leaving us losers and moving on with their life!"

"Taylor!" the table cheered, me included. To you, Taylor, for making things worse than they were supposed to be. Thanks for paying half the rent, though.

Two beers down, and the only thing that seemed to happen to me was the slight buzzing in the back of my ear. What, did I finally develop that tinnitus I had been so terrified of getting? Probably not.

But what scared me most was that this had, at one point, been my limit. Sally the lightweight, three shots and she's down. Now two pints in, and she wasn't even tipsy.

Add a third. Nothing.

And a fourth, okay, maybe things were starting to get a little fuzzy around the edges. Maybe I had just reached the point where I was drunk enough to not think I was drunk. But by the looks of the faces around me, I was faring rather well.

"I know what we should do!" roared Tevin, glass held high. "When's the last time we went for a middle-of-the-night joyride?"

Shanshan laughed. "We haven't gone in ages! But I still have the tools in the car."

"I've got mine!" added Rochelle, positively beaming. Fifteen shots of vodka would do that to a person, no matter how tolerant one's species is.

"That settles it!" Tevin grabbed his napkin, pulled a pen from his pocket, and started drawing elaborate, interlocking circles on it. The off-worlders leaned in, trying to get a closer look.

"Oh yeah, we can totally do that," agreed Finn. "With the six of us, two hours, tops."

"What do you say, Sally?" asked Tevin, rolling up the napkin and slipping it into one of his endless pockets. "Are you with us?"

"With you?" I hiccupped. The world was bright and glistening, every second worth savoring. "I don't even know what you're planning."

"Call it some good, old-fashioned alien pranking," he said. "Come on. Get your coat."

I picked mine up from where I had tossed it on the floor—when had that happened?—and staggered out of the booth. Shanshan rushed to take my hands, giddy with glee, pinching my cheeks like I were an adorable five-year-old.

"It's so good to see you!" she said, again, positively bouncing up and down.

"You too, Shan," I replied, and she squealed with joy.

Rochelle took my other arm, and together they whisked me out of the pub into the cool breeze of a February night. And by cool, I meant "oh Derzan, I am an ice block." The cold was so intense I thought I had plunged head-first into a frigid mountain lake.

We all piled into Shanshan's truck, Rochelle having thrown what looked like planks and rope into the back, while Finn and Nestor hunted through their cars for flashlights. I sat in the front, crammed between

Rochelle and Shanshan wondering where the hell we were going at an hour like this.

Were we going to murder someone?

Oh god, was I going to be on the other end of an alien abduction?

Luckily, we drove right out of the city. Far out, in fact. Far enough for me to stop wondering who we were out to murder and begin to count down all the different ways my friends could kill me. Shanshan didn't even touch the wheel, letting the coolest autopilot drive the way, but still refusing to tell me where the hell we were going.

Until we stopped in the middle of the road, in the middle of the night, in the middle of nowhere.

"Everybody out," she insisted, though no one else seemed to need instruction. I shuddered. This was happening; this was really happening. I was going to be murdered, and I was too tipsy to find my way out of the stupid car.

Rochelle led me out of the truck and helped me get my bearings overlooking a field of weeds. Nestor handed me one of the planks and an old headlamp.

"Please don't kill me here," I said, not addressing any of them in particular, but staring out into the field where I was surely going to die. "I know it's not messy here, but ... I'd like to—"

"Hell no, kid." Tevin slapped me hard on the back. "No one is going to die tonight! Are you kidding me?"

"What's the one thing astronomers would not expect?" asked Shanshan, reaching for my hand. I took hers and stepped into the field behind her.

"I don't know, to find a little blue box on the moon?"

"Yeah that," she said, chuckling a little. "Tell me, have you ever seen a crop circle?"

"A crop circle?" I glanced around me, then up. Oh my gosh, I was going to watch a ship create an actual crop circle!

Suddenly, memories I thought bore no importance flooded back to me in a wave. The hours I had spent chasing rabbit holes on the internet. The arguments I had gotten into with friends or on random forums. The questions I had tried to ask Zander, only for him to either have no answer to or one so weird I had to dismiss it entirely.

Zander. Missing him. Betrayed. I shook my head, trying to free myself of him.

"You see, people of Earth have two leading theories whenever a crop circle is found," Shanshan continued, dragging me deeper into the dark field. Frozen stalks snapped under our feet, the ground hard and ice cold, even through my chucks. "Either an alien entity made it with their superior technology, or some local pranksters made it with wood and rope."

"There's a whole science into figuring out if aliens made the circle or not," added Finn, from a few feet away, his lamp blinding me as he glanced my way. "A checklist to follow. Human traces to look for. So far, no crop circle has stood up to that close scrutiny."

"So, we're going to change that?" I looked up at the sky: still no ship in sight. "Make our own?"

"Yup," said Tevin, tossing me a length of rope and dropping his board to his feet. "Now, don't you move an inch, all right?"

Don't move? The world was already moving so fast,

spinning above my head and beneath my feet. I wanted to sit, to lie down, to roll over on my back and stare at the empty night. Breathe in the crisp air. Take a nap.

"You see, the big question always boils down to: If the aliens didn't use superior technology, why did they bother at all?" Tevin continued, pulling our rope taut and using it to guide him as he pressed a circle into the icy stems with the board at his feet. "Why would aliens travel millions of light-years with their super fancy ships and tech, only to resort to boards and rope to make such an elaborate shape in a field?"

"The answer is because we *can*," said Finn. "Because why the hell not?"

The world spun around me, or maybe it was just Tevin. Like a kid around the maypole, he looped around my post, crushing plants expertly under foot. Their icy stems snapped under his board. The field was filled with the soft crunch of four other aliens doing the same thing.

"Here, now you fill out the circle," he said as he returned the rope to me "It's easy. Watch."

I watched as my foot got into the motion of it, stepping, squashing, stepping, squashing, pressing the weeds into the earth. It was easy, mechanical. My entire mind focused on this one thing as the rest of the world dimmed and faded around me. I felt like my great-grandmother, spinning wool, only colder and surrounded by aliens.

"Circle complete! Everybody drink!"

"Drink!"

The cries rose through the field, and even through the foggy murk of an already buzzed brain, I worried that someone out here could hear us, even though there was no one here for miles. We were closer to the old GrishamCorp plant than anyone ever liked to linger.

"Come on, Sally. Squash them like you mean it," said Shanshan, handing me a bottle. I took a swig, brain on autopilot. "I like to imagine they're the heads of the mob. The ones who chased me off Da-Duhui and want me dead. I always see that stupid slug squealing—"

"Maakuna?"

I looked up from my squashing foot, my mind suddenly clear. Shanshan's eyes were wide with fright.

"You've heard of him?" she asked.

I nodded. Slowly. Any faster, and I would have thrown up all over her.

"I thought Da-Duhui was under new management?" I asked, suddenly feeling the cold in my fingers all over again. "After the ICP uprising?"

Her eyebrows knitted together. "Girl, what'chu talking about? Da-Duhui has been in the Travoshella family for centuries. Nothing has happened. The ICP uprising?"

"But I ..." I shuddered. None of this made any sense. "Do you still get news from there? Updates?"

"Yeah, I watch the news. I have to. You realize I would give everything to get back there, right? It's my *farshing* home."

She stood there in the middle of the field, bare hand clutching the freezing bottle, staring up at the stars. The same way I had stared at the stars on every world I had visited with the siblings, desperately hoping to catch a glimpse of the sun.

I let myself gaze at the stars and think about what I

had lost. A friend. No, friends. Plural. Friends and worlds and possibilities. Blayde and Nim and all the people along the way. I made myself look away.

"Sally, I know you're drunk," she muttered, "but I really don't appreciate you messing with me about these things."

"I'm sorry. I must have gotten some faulty info."

Shanshan nodded demurely. "I need to get back to Nestor. We have some weeds to squash."

So that was that: relationship with Shanshan now forever ruined as well. If destroying friendships was a video game, I would be leveling up left and right here.

"You guys think if I pee here, ufologists will interpret it as being vortex plasma?"

"What the hell is vortex plasma, Finn?" asked Rochelle. She was at the far end of the old field, a good two hundred feet away. Holy cow, our crop circle was going to be huge.

"I don't know, but it sounds catchy," he shouted through chattering teeth. "And exactly like something they'd come up with."

"Do it!" said Tevin. "I've got some toy rocks I got at the Franklin Institute gift shop last week. I could spread them around!"

"Too obvious, Tevin!" Rochelle cried.

I finished filling out my circle, all the while trying to keep the terrible thoughts from swirling in my head. Nothing had happened to the ICP. Had the whole thing been in my head? No, not possible. The mere fact I knew who Maakuna and the ICP were meant I had been there. I had visited Da-Duhui. I had the cheesy souvenir photo to prove it.

So, why hadn't Shanshan heard about it?

Maybe I was just too drunk to make sense of these things, but even my spinning mind had enough sense to realize that something wasn't adding up.

CHAPTER EIGHT

A SHIP IS BORN

ZANDER

Here's a few words of advice for the budding space explorer.

For starters, make sure to have packed a light snack. The void of space can be large and terribly cold, so having a snack bar on hand can help you deal with the crippling anxiety of an infinite and eternal plane of which your mind cannot possibly comprehend. Keep that blood sugar up!

It's also always a wise idea to have a clue of where you're going. It's all well and fine to chart a course into the unknown, but when you remember that matter only makes up a tiny percentage of the universe out there, you could find yourself wandering for centuries, even if you're going in a straight line. At least pick a direction with interesting landmarks. I, myself, recommend the Kasser route through the Alliance rim systems where you'll get to see a beautiful failed Dyson sphere, which is the perfect place for a suntan.

And finally, make sure you don't enter enemy space. Some people think they own portions of the universe, and, while they're completely wrong, they also tend to have large guns, and I for one don't like being on the wrong end of a large gun.

"Shit," said Blayde, as she bit into a stick of moola jerky. "I thought this sector was unoccupied."

"Apparently not, now will you please sit down?"

It's not an easy thing, piloting a tiny shuttle across vast distances of space when it probably wasn't intended to make it out of the solar system. We had bought a proper interstellar drive back on the outer planets of the core system on our way out into interstellar space. It was larger than our shuttle, so we looked like a fish clinging to the belly of a shark, but it wasn't about aesthetics. This baby had power. There was no point in getting a massive ship for just the two of us.

But a drive this big was sure to draw attention, and unwanted attention at that. A shuttle like ours didn't have a weapons system, which made us easy targets.

"Turn off your engines and prepare to be boarded," said the voice through the com. *"If you do not comply, we will—"*

I slammed my hand down, cutting the voice mid-hail. I could see their ship, all firepower and shields, scavengers and bandits who preyed on the weak travelers who marched through their space like idiots without checking who claimed that area first. Their ship was a monster, easily dwarfing our ship by a factor of a hundred.

Thousand.

"Buckle up," I hissed through gritted teeth, punching the ship into manual. As soon as the enemy ship realized we had hung up in their face, they kicked into attack mode. I slammed my fist down on the thrusters, shooting us a good twenty meters off from the first flurry of plasma shots.

As well as I knew the risks, there was something oddly thrilling in the chase. It wasn't often that I felt I had my own life in my hands, but when I did, I could almost imagine something inside of me racing. The place where my heart should be, pulsing in terror.

I wasn't afraid. I was elated. Unbeatable odds were fun to beat.

The controls felt right in my hand—even as a blast hit our tail and sent the entire ship rattling. I could only grip the wheel tighter and ride it out. Somewhere, an alarm was blaring, but I reached up to swat it off. Thanks, but no thanks.

Blayde finally clicked her seatbelt in place.

"I don't need this," she stammered. "I'm not a child."

"You're also an immortal, which would be a more compelling argument," I pointed out. I was too focused on the controls to pay any more attention to her, my mouth on autopilot while my ship was on manual. "I just need you to stay put when I do this."

"Do what?"

Something insanely dumb, but wicked cool. I snapped off the inertial dampeners for a split second, long enough for me to execute a complete one-eighty. The force of it pushed Blayde and me back into our seats, crushing our ribs in the process. I shot the ship forward, threading the needle, belly-to-belly with the other ship. The oversized warp coil overhead threatened to rip off, taking the ceiling with it, but I threw the dampeners back in place before it could.

Blayde hissed.

"What?" I said. "Don't you want me to get us out of this mess?"

"I hate it when you crush my lungs."

"Ah. I'd apologize, but it's way more fun than the whole being-blown-into-smithereens thing, forcing us to wait out being rebuilt atom by atom and then the whole freezing hellscape of space until some other idiot ship flew out here to stumble upon us."

"True. Though, I'm pretty sure this was the polar opposite of shutting off the engines. Let's just talk our way out of this. Or we could bash in some heads! You know how much I love bashing in heads. Oh, look, they've managed to turn on us."

She was right. Somehow, the lumbering enemy ship—I should really stop calling them enemies; they were nothing but a bunch of jerks—had managed to turn on its axis almost as fast as we had. Veesh.

I sputtered off in the diagonal, riding our tiny ship along the axis of the ship of jerks. Spin. Spin. Spin. Like a roller coaster that could only go down.

"And what's this supposed to accomplish?" Blayde groaned.

"Annoy them? Wear them out?"

"They have all day, and we have a fancy warp coil. You sure I can't go in there and smash some heads?"

The ship set off another volley, this one blowing the

bathroom out entirely. A blue cloud filled my rear-view mirror as the disinfectant sublimated and turned to gas in the cold vacuum of space.

"That'll be us if you don't hit the gas," chided Blayde.

"You think I don't know that?"

We couldn't hide. We couldn't outrun them. We were sitting ducks, no matter how fancy my flying. Plasma shot past us as the ship gained on us, and there was only so much evasive maneuvers we could do at this point.

I powered up the engines as high as they could go, feeling the vibrations in the ship rise. The window of opportunity here was small, and every second counted. That is, if it would even work at all. We could be blown to smithereens, which would be fine, seeing as how we'd survived worse. But, then, being stuck in the void of space for a few years until a passing ship came along and scooped us up would be an unpleasant experience.

This is also coming from experience.

"Oh no," said Blayde, as the floor beneath our feet began to heat. "This is insane!"

"I've seen it done before!"

"By the *Traveler*?" she stammered. "You were with me last week, weren't you? Remember, the whole thing about it just being a TV set?"

"Hold on tight!"

I released the engine the instant it burst, flipping on the shuttle's impulse engines instead. The core exploded, sending waves of energy in every direction, and I, quintessential surfer dude of the beta sector, rode that wave right over the enemy ship and straight into warp.

"Shit, it's working," said Blayde, incredulous. I found myself grinning; it took a lot to impress my sis.

The shuttle shuddered under the pressure of our speed. Our warp tunnel was small, and the hull groaned as we forced our way through, riding the wave as far as it could take us. I gripped the controls, keeping us steady, feeling the rush of elation that came from insane flying antics.

I felt alive.

But, apparently, so did the ship, because the second we dropped out of the warp conduit, it let out a cheer.

"What was that?" Blayde unclasped her seatbelt, flying to her feet and throwing her face against the windshield.

The ship was laughing now. Already, I could feel the controls edging away from me, the thousands of buttons flicking on and off, seemingly at random. I threw my hands up in the air away from the panel, trying not to panic as the ship ran amok.

Behind us, the coffee maker turned on then off, dropping hot milk onto the carpeted floor. The drink cart rumbled forward then back, despite being empty of any drinks, which we had sold off in exchange for the engine. A disco ball dropped from the ceiling in the cockpit, fell on the floor, and rolled to the back of the shuttle through the open door.

"I ... I ... I can move!" said a voice through the com, despite there being no other ships in sight. I let out a breath of annoyance. This was not how I imagined our trip would go.

"And now you gave the shuttle sentience," she snapped. "Smooth move, Zander."

"Hey, I got us out of having to negotiate with mercs, didn't I?"

"I could have bashed in their heads, Zander!"

"All this negative talk is making my coils rust," said the suddenly sentient shuttle. "Here, let me lighten the mood!" It opened a hatch in the ceiling of the cockpit, but the only thing to fall out was a dead fly. "Strange, there should have been a flashy light in there."

"You already dropped the disco ball," I pointed out.

"I did? When?"

"When you were playing around with yourself."

"Ah, well, imagine it's there," said the shuttle, somehow sounding gleeful. "It's the thought that counts. And I can say that, now that I have thoughts."

"It has thoughts, Zander!" Blayde snapped. "Shit! What did you do?"

"I didn't do anything," I replied. "It's not like I go around elevating the state of consciousness of minor electronics every day!"

"Hey!" said the shuttle. "Watch who you call minor!"

"You're a minute old," I replied. "You're *exactly* what I would call minor."

"Oh, for *Derzan's* sake!" said Blayde. "Will you two calm down? Thank you. Now, Zander, how in holy hell did the ship become self-aware?"

"My bio-nuclear framework is based on the working of a human mind, to imitate astrogation on a smaller scale," said the shuttle, smugly. It had far too much attitude for a consciousness that was only three minutes from having been a hunk of metal.

"And I brought a mimetic mind through a warp conduit." I smacked myself on the head. Idiot! I had no idea the Alliance was using that kind of tech yet.

"So, you woke it up?"

"Tada, I'm alive!" said the shuttle. "So, where are we going next, gang? The three moons of Kendra? The graviton falls of the Bibi system?"

I traded glances with Blayde. This was not going well at all. Way to change everything up, universe. She shifted her gaze quasi-urgently to the control panel. I responded with an almost unnoticeable incline of my head. I wasn't quite sure how or even if the shuttle could see its passengers, but I didn't want it to get startled. I tapped a button gently, carefully—and absolutely nothing happened.

"Ha, that's weird," said the shuttle. "I'm not quite sure I like that. Why don't you leave the busy work to me, friend?"

Blayde's glance quickly became a glare. I had royally screwed things up, even if it wasn't entirely my fault.

"Look, I didn't know that riding this shuttle through warp would give it consciousness, okay?" I said to her and smiled, a feeble effort to cheer her up. Needless to say, she was not swayed by my dazzling smile. "The point was to save our hides, and that's been done. We cool?"

"Yeah, we cool!" The dashboard flooded with lights. "Thanks, dude!"

"The shuttle just called you dude," Blayde muttered. "Which means you're responsible. Wake me up when you reach the library, okay?"

She scooted deeper into her chair, rolling her eyes before making a big show of pressing them shut. So much for rekindling the family relationship. So much for a road trip through the stars. Blayde was leaving me alone at the helm of a ship I had just brought to life.

Shit. This was not how I saw this trip going.

"Aw, damn, we're going to a library?" said the ship. "You guys know I can't read, right?"

"We literally know nothing about you," I said, taking my hands off the controls. It felt oddly disturbing touching them now that they were part of a nervous system. "We just met. You realize that. Right?"

"Does that make you my ... father?"

Oh.

No.

"Let's stick with the whole buddy thing, all right? Keep calling me dude. And I'll call you ..."

"Stormbringer! Bringer of storms!"

"Really?"

"Starchaser!"

"You don't want a more ... I don't know, unique name? Every starship and their sister wants to be called Starchaser."

"What else would you have me call myself? Dave?"

"Truthfully, I haven't met many ships called Dave."

"Fine then. Dave it is. Dave from Accounting. It's in my database as the most boring name ever."

"Hey! I was an accountant for two months, and those Daves bring an important service to—"

"Boys!" Blayde's eyes snapped open, and she surveyed us with this look that usually precipitated murder. "Will you calm down, please? And maybe grow up while you're at it? We have a library to find and monks to interrogate. I need my sleep. Understood?"

"Do we have to?" Dave from Accounting whined.

"Look, I just found this absolutely fab little planet; it's right here, not even a light-year away, and it we land there right now I can get some fuel and the two of you can get cotton candy and—"

"Dave, I don't need cotton candy. I need to solve the mystery of my past."

"Wow, entitled much?" The lights in the ship dimmed for a split second, the disco ball rolling lazily into the cockpit from the galley and tapping my feet as he spoke. "Not everything needs to be about you."

"Look, usually ships don't get much say in the places they go, okay?" said Blayde, one hundred percent awake now. No more faking sleep—or trying to.

"Well, I want to go to Tiga's World and get fancy fuel. Who's driving?"

"Pretty sure Zander is."

"Even if I do ... this?"

The shuttle got distinctly colder in an instant. Blayde, roller of eyes extraordinaire, shared one of her ocular loop-de-loops as the air became thinner.

"Gnnnnn!" Dave from Accounting gritted his teeth, even though he had no teeth to grit. It was incredible how his programming had created that eventuality, despite never predicting, you know, how sentient the ship would become.

"Dave," said Blayde, unfazed by the lack of oxygen, "please don't tell me you've turned to murder in the five minutes you've been alive."

"How are you ...?" the shuttle stammered. "I thought humans were ... you know. It's called life support for a reason!"

"We're not humans, Dave," she said, "but if you take

us to the library, we might be able to tell you what we are."

The space warmed. The lights returned to the cockpit. The air thickened, tasty oxygen rolling over my tongue.

"You guys never told me we were solving a mystery," he said, giddy with excitement. "Okay, where are we going exactly?"

"Literally to the coordinates still on your dashboard," I said, still trying to wrap my head around the sudden company. Accidentally creating life was far too easy in this universe.

"The Library Place? No waaaaay."

"Dave," I said, trying to make my voice sound calm and assertive. It was hard to craft a dad voice despite never having a father. Maybe the library would change that.

Holy crap. What if I had a family, outside of Blayde? I hadn't dared to hope. Not in a few centuries, at least. But right now, I was too busy with this ... life I had created, this ship that was no longer ours but something different, more.

"Look, the library is just a short stop," I insisted. "Trust me. Once we get out of there with the stuff we need, you can go wherever you want. Heck, you won't even need us anymore."

"But I like you guys," said Dave. "I'd be happy if you never left me. Now, who wants some cake?"

Something pinged in the room behind us, and a hatch opened, revealing a burnt phonebook.

"Don't worry about us, Dave. Just get us to the library. If you can."

"What, you think I can't?"

Blayde sunk deeper into her chair, which basically meant sitting on the floor at this point. She shot a glance at me, a glance that told me it was all my fault, as per usual. Just my luck that the coolest piloting of my life had been suppressed under the responsibility of having created a new consciousness.

At least Dave wasn't too bad. He trudged on toward the library. I hoped it was the library; it was hard to tell, what with all control reverting to him, our futures in his hands.

Not that he had hands.

It gets really hard to travel space with all these little details. Space explorer tip number four, is it? Don't do anything stupid while you're out here. Everything you do has massive repercussions across the universe, no matter how small. Trust me.

It never gets any easier.

CHAPTER NINE

BOOK FIVE, IT'S TIME FOR A WEDDING!

SALLY

It's not every night you make crop circles and it's not every morning you wake up hungover, but when both happen the day of your best friend's wedding, you realize you might have screwed up.

Big time.

I let out a small groan as I twisted my neck, every joint and muscle aching. I stretched and realized this wasn't my bed. This wasn't a bed at all. Was this my sofa? How did I get here? And why was my neck so sore? I got up, my head throbbing with every move. Not again—hung over. What had happened the night before?

I dragged myself to the bathroom, through the shattered, splintered door, and caught my reflection in the mirror. In an instant, it all became clear. The SWAT team. The pub. The field.

Oh crap.

My hair was a mess. Hell, my face was a mess, my life was a mess, my apartment was a mess—courtesy of certain lovely soldier-types who had come to visit. My breath—gross—smelled of rotten eggs and way too much vodka. Way past deviled eggs now; more like thirty thousand demons of hell and Lucifer eggs.

One thing I had learned from traveling the universe was that speeding was not the scariest thing you could do. It was painfully slow compared with flying a shuttle.

My heart didn't agree with my mind about that. It pulsed a million times a minute, terrified.

But screw the heart! I had a wedding to get to!

I reached the old observatory in mere minutes instead of the recommended half an hour my GPS had planned. I flew out the car as if it were about to explode. I threw the keys toward a valet and rushed to the bridal suite, where Marcy would hopefully already be in her dress.

"Marce!" I screamed, sprinting through the door. "I'm sorry!"

"For what?" she asked, clutching her towel tighter around her chest. "Bursting in here without knocking? If you wanted to see me nude, Sal, you just had to ask. Legally, my booty belongs to no one but me for the next five hours. Then you'd have to ask Dany first."

I was panting, my heart practically bursting through my chest, so hard I had to clutch it to help my rib cage keep everything contained. Marcy, however, was calm, dressed only in the towel, her black hair dripping onto her shoulders.

"I'm not late?"

"Not unless you wanted to help me shampoo?"

"Oh, thank god," I said, crumpling into the chair by her bed. My body felt as if it had been pummeled by sacks of potatoes.

"No offense, Sal, but you're a right mess," she said, stomping back into the bathroom. "You look like you've crawled out of a coffin."

"I might as well have, my—"

I stopped myself. It was Marcy's wedding day: I wasn't going to freak her out with stories of SWAT teams in the middle of the night, even if I toned it down to a banal home invasion.

"What?" she asked, through the cracked open door.

"Just a really, really weird dream. It was nothing."

My phone buzzed as a news alert rolled in. I held back a laugh; someone had spotted our crop circle. The thing was massive, with spiraling, intricate designs I had been too buzzed to take in the night before.

"Nothing from this Earth could have made something so complex," a specialist was quoted having said. "Remarkable. The circle boasts perfect understanding of the golden ratio, of Fibonacci, and perhaps more we haven't interpreted yet. The being who created it must have a mind like no other."

Drunk aliens and an equally drunk human buddy. It seemed like the answer to most of Earth's UFO problems had something to do with a combination of the two.

Marcy's mother arrived half an hour later with the dresses—thank god mine hadn't been in my apartment last night—along with the hair and makeup artist, who got straight to work on me as Marce got finished in the bathroom. Soon I was all dolled up, and my hands were free to help with the last-minute wedding preparations, so I made myself useful in the reception hall.

The restaurant looked so different from when I came here on my weird date with Matt. The one that ended with Zander crashing through the glass ceiling and dragging me up to a UFO. Fun times. No bathroom breaks for me today, lest I get abducted by Killian ambassadors again.

I took a deep breath, trying to not dwell on the memories. They would either make me angrier or sadder, and neither were emotions fit for today.

"Hallo," said a voice, and I turned to see a man who was easily over seven feet tall, pushing eight. I jumped.

"Are you here for the bride or bride?" I asked, then realized the error of my ways. "Marcy or Dany?"

"Flurm." He cleared his throat. "Danirsh'ni'ah?" The man cocked his head slightly, much like a puppy. It was oddly endearing. I wondered idly why my translator hadn't given me anything to go on.

Dany flew into the room, looking absolutely stunning. It was as if someone has poured melted gold over her and let it solidify into a dress. Her many earrings had been replaced with what looked like engagement rings, each with a different stone.

"Frank Flurm! So glad you could make it," she said, taking the giant by the hand and ushering him away. "Please excuse my cousin. He's foreign."

"Oh, that's fine," I stammered. "This isn't the first of your cousins I've met. You look gorgeous, Dany."

"Thank you." She beamed. "I can't believe this day is finally here! How's Marcy? Is she okay? I haven't heard from her at all this morning. It's enough to make me go on a Liam Neeson-style rampage."

"Her mother has her busy getting dressed, so I doubt she's been allowed to touch her phone."

"The photographer's poised and ready, the caterers say all is a-ok, and the florist has finished setting up. Everything is going great. Can you tell Marcy? I know it's bad luck for the groom to see the bride before the wedding, but when there are two brides, it could probably be a disaster and implode the universe."

"I'll let her know."

Dany nodded, but I was already rushing back to the hotel wing of the old observatory, letting myself back into the bridal suite just in time to see the stylist pin the last strand of hair around Marcy's tiara.

She looked beautiful. The white lace climbed up her neck and down her shoulders like it was a part of her skin. The rearranged bustle of the dress enhanced her curves, giving her the silhouette of a Hollywood starlet. As she turned, her smile grew with delight.

"Holy heaven on a hot plate, Marce," I stammered. "Any room for a third bride?"

She laughed, staring down at herself and stealing glimpses of the dress in the mirror.

"Don't mess up your dress!" Marcy's grandmother rushed forward. "It looks perfect!"

"You're going to step on her train!" I sputtered. To my amazement, the woman not only stopped, but both she and Marcy stared at me like I had turned into the *Thing*.

133

"Sally!" Marcy's eyes filled with tears. "You speak Mandarin?"

I panicked. Freaking translator. "I learned it so I could speak with your family on your special day! Surprise!"

"You're the best maid of honor any bride could wish for." She reached forward to hug me, then looked down at her dress in worry. We air hugged instead.

"Girls, it's time!" Marcy's mom fluttered in, admiring her elegant daughter, fighting back tears. I slipped out of the room, finding my place next to the other bridesmaids and posing quickly for the photographer.

Outside in the garden, I was surprised to see how packed Marcy's side of the church was compared to the barebones of Dany's. Other than cousin Frank, along with the two other cousins I had met the night before, about five people had bothered showing up. Most of Marcy's family had flown in from China, though mostly because Dany had spared no expense on their flights. Marce had been insanely excited when they had RSVP'd yes. Dany hadn't said anything when none of her invites came back.

I cried happy tears as I watched my best friend say her I do's and as she kissed her gorgeous wife, a picture-perfect moment under a trellis of fresh flowers. She glowed beside Dany, the two of them now bonded for life. I could not have been happier for her.

Marcy had wanted all the clichés: the slideshow of photos of them as a couple, the eating of the cake, the throwing of the garter, every wedding tradition in human history. Although I was asked to dance a few times, I didn't really do much for the rest of the evening.

I was exhausted from, well, everything, still a little off from the night before, details of which were still missing.

"What, no plus one?"

I wasn't in the mood for anyone else's relations flirting with me, or conversation in general, really. The adrenaline that had kept me sane from the night before and functional through the wedding was dwindling now, leaving me with a sense of emptiness that would quickly show as annoyance. The apathy before the depressive episode; I had learned to recognize the pattern.

"Do I know you?" I said, coldly. I didn't even need to look up to confirm I wasn't interested.

"Oh, come on, Sally, don't be like that."

That voice. I froze, turning to look at the woman as she sat down beside me, finally recognizing her. A woman I hadn't seen in person in over a year, dressed in the same blue pantsuit she had worn when I had met her. Probably packing heat, too.

"Felling? What are you doing here?" I blinked a few times, refusing to believe this was real. Yup, not a figment of my imagination. The stranger, the friend of Taylor's I had met on New Year's after killing the leechin was here. In the flesh. "You shouldn't be here."

"It's a party!"

"It's my friend's wedding."

"I was in the neighborhood," she said calmly, staring out at the crowd. "Wanted to make sure that you were all right. Are you?"

"I'm fine."

"No, you're not." She turned her chair so she was

facing me, her head close, her voice hushed. "I'm going to tell you a secret, so please return the favor."

"We're back in grade school now?" I scoffed. "Are you going to tell me who has a crush on me?"

"I need you to be serious here."

"It depends," I said, trying to hold that air of mystery Blayde always managed to emit. I didn't want James Felling to know I needed her more than she needed me. Why was it that every time I had conversations now, I had to think like a diplomat? "Secrets? Come on, agent whatever, this is plain odd."

"Here's the deal," she said, ignoring my question, "remember that blood work I told you was being monitored?"

"How could I not?"

"After your recovery, they found nothing strange in your bloodstream," she said, as if we were not in the middle of a wedding reception. "But yesterday when you came in for your regular checkup"—she handed me a sheet of paper with confusing medical terms on it—"the doctors think they found some new antibodies they never dreamed of. And some other weird ... things. Things that only exist in theory."

"Oh wow, my blood has weird antibodies?" I scoffed. "They didn't screw up at all on their end. This isn't science-fiction; this is real life. Can you please just leave me alone? There's nothing in there to monitor."

"They could be dangerous," she muttered.

"Are they dangerous? The chemicals and the anti-bodies, I mean?" I asked. "And while I'm at it—*what the absolute hell?*"

I started to tremble. The SWAT team. The weird

blood work. This was all too much.

"They're not dangerous to you," she replied, somehow still composed. "But they want to do more work on you. I took the liberty to deleting their files. I also had to pull some strings and have your sample destroyed. Well, I say 'destroyed,' but everything's in my hands now, so you're safe."

"Thanks," I said, silently wondering if she was doing this out of friendship, or if she was considering blackmail. She probably was. I made a mental checklist of all my belongings and holdings. It was a short list. "You were the one who called last night, weren't you? The one who warned me."

She nodded. "They were going to bring you in. I didn't know what they were planning until the men were already sent out. It took a lot to bring them back in, let me tell you. I had to call in a lot of favors."

Relief flooded over me, mixed with more confusion. I was a target, and there wasn't much I could do to hide. I was literally sitting out in the open right now. For all I knew, this mysterious friend of Taylor's had me completely surrounded by whatever team she led.

"What do you want?" I said, trying to hide the flood of emotions. "I assume you didn't just do this because you like my face."

Felling smirked, but the expression never touched her eyes.

"I took care of you without wanting anything in return," she insisted.

"Then why don't I believe you?"

"Because you don't trust anyone," she said. "Or that's what you want me to think. That you're not feeling something under all those layers. And because I'm a woman with answers you desperately want. And you're a woman with answers I desperately need."

"You trying to seduce me? Fair warning, I'm not some kind of bond girl."

"And I'm not James Bond," she replied, stoic. "I'm an entirely different kind of James. But I'll tell you how I know all this if"—here came the 'if'—"if you tell me what happened to you in the past month that changed your blood work so much. Oh, and why you can suddenly speak so many languages."

" What are you talking about? What languages?"

"You don't have to whisper. No one's going to understand you."

"Wait, what?"

"We've been speaking Latin for the past few minutes." She grinned. "How can you not have realized that?"

"Maybe I got carried away on Duolingo."

"I started with French and German. I just had to know."

I glared at her then grabbed her hand and pulled her outside to the balcony, closing the doors behind us as quietly, even though I wanted to slam them. The sun was setting, an eerie twilight, but we were alone out here, no chance of eavesdroppers listening in, Latin or no Latin.

"Fine, I'll tell you. But this is just between us, okay?" I breathed deeply, having the sudden urge to tell someone. Just this once. And I trusted this woman. She had, after all, saved my life.

"I can keep a secret," she said calmly, but I could tell

she was more than eager to hear what she needed to hear. She probably would have said anything to get me to speak.

Maybe I should have let her seduce me after all.

"Zander and Blayde came back." She didn't seem the least startled, as if he had been expecting this all along. "Just over week ago. They invited me on a trip, but we got lost. Somehow, we got back in under five hours Earth time, but it was still well over a week out there. That's it, nothing more."

"Where are they now?"

"They took off the second they dropped me home."

"And will they come back?" Was it me, or was there disappointment in her voice? The look on her face showed that she was sorry for something, but was she sorry for me or sorry her hero had left before giving them a chance to meet?

You and me both, buddy.

"I doubt it. They have no reason to." It was hard to keep my composure at this point, my annoyance at the siblings rushing back in a torrent. I felt my nails digging into the palm of my hands as they made fists. There. That was much better than crying again.

"Sorry about that," said Felling. She raised and dropped her hand, finally lifting it to put on my shoulder, an awkward sign of reassurance, though I could tell she wasn't used to having to comfort people.

"So, you keep your end of the deal?"

"What? Oh, yeah. Everyone's gathering inside. Should we join them?"

"Yes, later, but explain. Please. A deal's a deal."

"FBI," Felling muttered, pulling out her badge in a

flash. My heart fell. Okay, so not a joke.

"The FBI knows about aliens?"

"*I* know about aliens," she said, smugly, putting her badge back away. Once again, I saw the holster of her gun and a shiver went through me. "I just happen to work for the FBI. They give me their weird cases, and I get them results. They don't really care what I'm up to in between."

"Oh my gosh" My heart leapt in my chest. "You *are* Agent Mulder!"

Felling laughed. "Mulder and Scully mixed together with one tight bow," she said, with a conspiratorial wink. "Only I'm hotter and get paid better."

"And your name really is ... James?"

"I'm a black woman working alien cases for the FBI," she scoffed, handing me her card. And, yes, the name James Felling was printed on it, along with the FBI shield. "The name helps a bit. On paper, I'm just the creepy dude who takes on the supernatural cases."

"So, the government *does* know about aliens then?"

"Well, they won't take me seriously, even with the stack of evidence I've formulated over the years. But the day will come ... and meanwhile, I still solve *normal* cases, so I have enough credibility to pull a few strings and put a few missions on hold. I know the right people."

We walked back inside the reception hall, and I could tell by the way her lips moved that she had switched languages again. The translator really did work anywhere. Awesome. Even if the buzz behind my ear was returning, my head ringing only slightly as I kept up with the conversation. I hoped it wouldn't short out; I had no idea where to find replacement parts this end of the universe.

"So, which branch of the FBI, exactly?" I asked. "I mean—"

Thwack.

The bouquet hit me straight in the face, like a cannon ball. I stumbled, grabbing anyone for support, but Felling wasn't there anymore. I fell to the ground, the other guests rushing around me, most of them laughing at the absurdity of the situation.

"You okay, Sally?" Marcy asked, worried.

"Destiny's giving her a sign!" One of the guests giggled, and suddenly there was a hoard of well-dressed laughing people all around me, eyes wide, staring. I laughed to show there were no hard feelings as I clutched my stinging eye.

But as I got up and dusted myself off, James was nowhere to be found, leaving me alone on the dance floor.

Story of my life right about now.

CHAPTER TEN

CRISIS-PROOFING YOUR TEENAGE SPACESHIP

ZANDER

I was pretty sure libraries were supposed to be filled with books, not, you know, rows upon rows of horned slugs.

"Blayde," I said under my breath, as we stepped into the marbled lobby of this mysterious lost planet, my face bogged down with the thickest fake beard I had ever worn, "I don't think this is where we're going to find the monks."

"Why? Because slugs can't pick up the cloth?"

"No, because the slugs seem to be eating each other. I'm pretty sure they can't be trusted with books."

"You think too small, brother of mine," she replied, taking every step with delicate poise as she struggled to avoid the trails of green slime crisscrossing the path before us. "Just don't squash any of them, okay?"

The man who appeared behind the counter was no slug, and he seemed as annoyed by their presence as we were. He gritted his teeth and forced a smile.

"Are you two here for the convention?" he asked, as a trail of green slime squirted across his face. One of the slugs had devoured the other so quickly, it had simply exploded.

"We're trying to get to the library," I said. Beside me, Blayde was pretending to be interested in a flyer on Space Madness, while using it to shield her face from the same fate.

"You're on the wrong side of the planet for that, friend." The concierge smiled apologetically, green goop dripping from his bushy eyebrows. "I am sorry for the state of our lobby. Ever since the fall of the Da-Duhuian ICP, gut slugs have been out of a job and have been struggling to maintain population, what with all the cannibalism. The conference was supposed to be a meeting of their top thinkers trying to find new options, but their keynote speaker has just been disemboweled. Either way, I have a feeling they won't be dealing with unemployment for too long."

My head snapped up: the ICP. The gut slugs. What had happened to the people of the Undercity and the people who had survived the uprising? This was news I should know, having been on the front lines saving these people. But rarely was I around long enough to see what came next.

"Lovely," said Blayde, nodding. Either she didn't care or was more pressed for time than I thought. "So, tell me, how do I get to this top-secret library?"

"Secret? Oh, you mean the monks' library! I thought you were talking about the public library. Berbabsywell, yeah? You truth-seekers?"

"I guess you could call us that. Any indication on how to get there from here?"

"You just waltz into a hotel lobby and expect me to know where the best-kept secret in the universe is kept?"

"You're a concierge. Isn't that your job?

"Good point, but no. I don't know where it is. They say only the penitent will find it, if it even exists. Now, if you'll excuse me ..."

The man removed himself from the conversation just in time to duck from an explosion of slime from the dying Minister of Foreign Affairs, according to the tiny name tag that landed on the counter before us.

"Great, so that was no help at all."

Blayde was stoic as we left the hotel, careful not to track slime with our shoes. She didn't glance back at the dying species in the lobby, eating themselves to extinction.

"Should we be doing something about that?" I asked, pointing my thumb over my shoulder.

"Not my circus, not my monkeys." She pulled her journal from her pocket and flipped through the pages, despite the fact she knew them all by heart. "Sally's not here anymore. You don't have anyone to impress by saving a few slugs from unemployment. Not to mention, I remember them giving her a terrible welcome on Da-Duhui."

So, she did remember. She just didn't care.

"What do you expect to find in there that you don't

already know?" I asked, reaching a hand to pull the book away. Manic Blayde scared me, one step away from a cataclysmic fit of rage. I wasn't going to set her off by asking questions that scared even me.

"I don't know, anything," she muttered, ripping the book back. "A clue. A way in. A way out. Something. Berbabsywell might be the hardest place to find in the universe, but we've done crazier things, haven't we?"

"We're not exactly in a rush, you know. We have all of eternity to find it."

"So long as it continues to exist, and you've seen how fragile mortal constructs are. They crumble to dust in the blink of an eye."

I stuffed my hands deep into my pockets, staring up at the purple pastel sky, the sunset of a star I had only just met. Somewhere out there, Sally was looking up at the stars too. How long had it been since we had left her? A month, a week, a decade? Was she even alive anymore?

My breath caught in my throat, and I allowed myself to choke, kept the air from my brain long enough for the dizziness to wrap around my mind. I couldn't help but think about her, imagine her life without us, without me. Her happy life, her successes, her family, comfortable, happy, *living*.

I hadn't given living much thought until I had been with her. She had shown me what it was to take all of one's mortality and put it on the line just to be ... more. How much more wondrous the universe could be if you lived between the heartbeats, the glory of the stars and the worlds, all different, all maddening, beautiful and ugly and raw. I had never been dizzy before I had seen the universe through her eyes.

And I would never see it again.

I turned back to Blayde, who was nose-deep into her own journal, eyes so close to the page I wasn't sure if she was reading or breathing the words.

"Where to next, sister of mine?"

"Back to the ship, I guess."

"Right. The ship. Dave from Accounting. Look, wouldn't it be better if we got another ship? One that wasn't sentient?"

"I don't see why we need to. I know we have all the time in the universe, but it still feels like a waste of it."

I said nothing, instead leading her through the empty streets of Oohoma City, her arm wrapped around mine so that she could keep reading even as she walked, enraptured by the words of a Blayde who had lived centuries ago.

"Blayde, are we the same people we were when you wrote that?"

"What do you mean?" she asked, not removing her face from the pages.

"We die and regenerate, over and over again ... how much of us is the same, how much of us was even there? I mean, neither of us can even remember that far back, so—"

"So what? We have trouble remembering; it doesn't mean it hasn't happened."

"But then who's there to say it did happen at all?"

"Oh, come on," she snapped. "We're not going down this existential rabbit hole right now. Let's find the library, find the Berbabsywell monks, and all the answers will be there."

"What if the answers aren't there?"

"We won't even consider that option," she muttered.

We turned into the shuttle dock, neat rows of little planet hoppers sitting on the asphalt, ready to take to the stars. And then, there was our little ship, sticking out like a sore thumb: the ugly, massive engine sitting precariously on top of the tiny UPAF shuttle.

A shuttle that bleeped and lit up at the sight of us.

"So, did you two have fun?" it asked, surprisingly gruffly. "Or was the experience pointless in the grand scheme of things?"

"Fun?" I exchanged glances with Blayde, who only gave me the usual roll of the eyes. "No. And no luck either. Are you sure these are the right coordinates.?"

A pause. "Yes."

"You hesitated, Dave," said Blayde, as she pressed the door release button. Needless to say, the door did not release.

"I did not."

"You did."

"So, what if I did?"

"Just open the door, Dave," I said, but it was hard to sound intimidating to a spaceship. I had once convinced the emperor of Detronas to give up his crown just by storming into his chambers, but I couldn't get a newly conscious space shuttle to tell me the damn truth.

I reached up to where I had so carefully welded the engine's core matrix into that of the shuttle, wrapping my hand around the cord. One, two, three loops. Steady and slow.

"What are you doing there, Zan?" The ship's voice

was more monotonous than it had been before we left, as if the rest had zapped it of all emotion.

"The name is Zander, and I'm going to find a ship that'll take me to where I want to be," I said, voice even, hand steady. "And I'll be bringing my warp core with me."

"But Abryria is an awful place; you don't want to go there," the ship stammered. "Not to mention it's restricted. Why does anyone want to do anything? It's all meaningless."

"The coordinates lead to Abryria?" I turned to Blayde, and her expression fell. We both knew the planet, though we had never been. We had helped refugees escape the slaughter there.

About a century ago, the Alliance council decided they had a surefire way to bring an end to all wars: a peace museum. Which, admittedly, was one of their more well thought-out plans. However, they decided the best way to instill peace was to clone key figures from their history and fill their minds with the memories they could piece together from historical archives. Needless to say, the exhibits were accurate as hell, down to the butt-hurt generals of lost wars, and the bloodlust was perfectly replicated. Leave the most intelligent and evil thinkers alone in a museum overnight, and it all comes down to *Jurassic Park*-style cataclysmic failure.

The planet had been off-limits ever since, leaving the clones to their own devices, protecting the outside universe from the most dangerous minds brought back to life.

Not to brag, but Blayde and I had been the ones to bring an end to a lot of Alliance screw-ups in the past, however long we had been alive. Which meant that half those exhibits were born hating us for their defeat. So, it was rather logical that the next step in finding the Berbabsywell monks would be hiding on a planet pretty much built as a middle finger to my sister and me.

"Dave," I said, biting my lip to keep myself from screaming, "We gave you coordinates for a reason. If you refuse to take us there, we have no choice but to take another ship, any other ship."

"And we're taking our engine with us."

I could feel the coils in my hand run cold.

"No, you can't," said the little shuttle, but there was a hesitation in its voice, a knowledge that we were not bluffing. Not that I wanted to threaten a ship that was barely a day old with being dismantled, but I was breaking new ground here. Parenting—for lack of a better word—a spaceship didn't exactly come with its own handbook.

"You can take us to Abryria and leave us there if you wish," said Blayde, "but we're getting to that planet with or without you. But if you take us to Abryria and help us find the library, we'll make it worth your while."

"You can't give me anything of value," it pouted. "The universe will end, and we'll all end with it, a blip in the universe, not leaving our marks."

The door slid open without any further argument, and I did a double take. The interior had changed dramatically since we left Dave: the plush luxury seats now entirely black, the window blinds pressed shut, only the red emergency lighting to liven up the place. In place of the little disco ball up front, there was now a little pile of ash.

"Blayde," I hissed, "I think our ship is depressed."

"It's not," she said, shaking her head. "It's entered its goth phase. It's completely natural and will pass soon."

"It's not a phase!" Dave snapped, more emotion in its voice than I had expected possible. "It's who I *am.*"

"Yesterday, our ship was a newborn," she said as she led me into the cockpit, throwing herself haphazardly on a seat. "It must have hit puberty around the time we landed. The gothic thing just came out of that."

"Stop calling it a thing, mom."

"I'm not your mom, Dave, but I am an authority figure you can try to rebel against if the urge overcomes you," she said, inspecting her nails. "Emphasis on the try."

"Dave, will you take us to Abryria or not?" I asked, trying to ignore my rising frustration, pushing it down, deep down, along with the other things I would only deal with when this adventure was over.

Such as a sister who thought she knew what was best for me.

"Fine," said Dave, and the door shut behind us, hissing slightly as the hull pressurized. "But you don't touch any of my knobs. Got it?"

"No knobs. Understood."

We took off into the purple sky, diving into the inky blackness of the interstellar void, throwing ourselves gracefully into full warp speeds, into the stream of faster-than-light travel.

Immortality breeds patience, so no words were said, not even by Dave, who was embracing his goth phase so entirely he refused to speak. It was hard getting used to the long periods of nothingness once more. A few weeks ago, I wouldn't have blinked twice at the prospect of spending days with my body on hold. But ever since Sally, where lingering spaces were filled with voice and sound, I found that letting existence pass me by was more tedious than finding things to say.

"What is that sound?" asked Blayde, after we had been sitting in relative silence for a few hours.

"I don't hear anything."

"You do. Listen."

I shut my mouth again, tuning my ears to the slow *womp, womp* of Dave's warp core running. The regular thrumming was broken every few seconds by an extra beat, out of rhythm with the rest.

"It's just the engines," I said.

"Dave, are you trying to get under our skin?" Blayde ignored me, speaking directly to the ship. "Turn that racket off."

"It's not a racket," said Dave. "It's who I *am.*"

"He seems to have progressed into a phase which I believe is called *emo*," she explained to me, her voice low.

"*He* can hear you, you know."

"It seems Dave is deliberately running a beat through his warp core, Zander. Do you have anything to say to that?"

"Keep me out of this! We have much more important things to deal with."

"Oh, so *now* you're willing to talk about the library?"

"What are you talking about? I was always willing to talk about the mission."

"Oh yeah? I haven't heard any speculation as to the

nature of their information on us, and I—"

"Will you two stop fighting?" sputtered Dave. "Stars! Some days I wish I was never born!"

"You were literally born today, Dave."

"I wish I wasn't!"

"Dave's right about one thing, though," said Blayde, her eyes fixated on the empty dash. "We should stop fighting; get on the same page."

Not this again. She couldn't expect me to just forget about all she had done to get us here. She couldn't expect me to forget about Sally and how we had left things. I was allowed to hold a grudge. I'm sure I held lesser grudges for worse things in the eternity we had spent together, and I'd forgotten all about them in a lifetime or two. We would forgive each other eventually; we had to. But right now, I wanted to fume.

"We are on the same page," I replied. "We both want to go to the Library and find the monks. I just don't understand what on earth it all has to do with Abryria."

"Excuse me?" Blayde looked up at me, her eyes wide. "What does Earth have to do with any of this?"

If my heart was beating, it would have skipped a beat right then and there.

"Nothing, it's just an expression."

"A dumb one. I mean, it's like saying 'what on Pyrina' when we're light-years from that gods forsaken place."

"Relax, will you? I just picked up an expression. it's no big deal. I thought you said you wanted us to stop fighting."

"I want us to stay focused. You don't sound focused."

What Blayde wanted was none of my concern. She

had already gotten what she wanted, while warping past anything I might have asked for. Like, I don't know, a proper goodbye?

She was right about one thing, though: I was distracted. And while I had a right to be, this was neither the time nor the place.

"Abryria," I said, bringing us back to the subject on hand, "I wonder what it's like now. A hundred years after the clone uprising. Do the clones live forever, or have they interbred? Are they even capable of that? If so, there could be a whole generation of children, born of the worst criminals in the galaxy, with their own planet to rule. I wonder what that civilization is like now."

"I can't imagine they want us anywhere near them," said Blayde, "so we'll have to find a creative way to infiltrate the place. Who knows? Maybe they haven't heard of us."

"I hate to break it to you, but what year do you think this is, exactly?"

Dave's voice was surprisingly un-angsty when he spoke. Even the sad, awkward beat of the engine had stopped.

"Not sure," said Blayde, "but there's been at least a hundred years between us and the Abryria catastrophe, right?"

"According to my charts, that happened five years ago."

"Five years?" Blayde and I exchanged looks, her brows knotting and furrowing as she tried to work out the math on this one. No, it was impossible. We had done so much, gone so far since the day we had shoved survivors into escape pods on the surface of Abryria.

The timeline didn't add up.

"Doesn't matter," Blayde said quickly. "It just means we have to plan for a different entrance."

"And you think the library will be there? Greatest library in the universe, containing all information, in the heart of a planet overrun with the universe's most dangerous criminals?"

"No, it's not going to be there, of course not," she said, shaking her head. "The coordinates, though, will be."

One step closer to answers. One step closer to finding who we are.

But things were just not adding up.

"It doesn't bother you?" I asked, staring at the ceiling. Dave had dimmed the lights to make the whole thing look an odd shade of red, making me wonder if he had slipped through his emo phase and into the vampire one.

She stared up at the ceiling as well. "We could ask him to set the light back."

"Not that. The whole… century not having been a century. This time burp, for lack of a better term."

"Oh? I mean, our math was off. It happens."

"But both of us thinking the same time has passed when it hasn't?"

She shrugged, her shoulders making a scrunching noise as leather rubbed against leather.

"Hey, I spent twenty years looking for you, only for you to have taken a two-month vacay. Time distortion happens."

"Yeah, but… in that direction?" I forced my eyes to

look into hers, and she held the gaze for only a second before pulling away. Her Earth-green eyes didn't let anybody in, not even me.

"You're trying not to talk about Sally for my sake," she said. "Thanks. But I know what you mean. Five hours passing on her planet when we were gone much longer than a week. Time squeezed into a long dinner. I'll admit that's odd."

"And now, this one-hundred-years-only-being-five thing. The math doesn't add up."

"Maybe history repeats itself? This could be Abryria 2.0, the Alliance starting over."

"And screwing up all over again? They're dumb, Blayde, but they're not that stupid."

"Put that on the list of things to ask the monks," she said, closing her eyes and settling back for a nap. "You see? You do have interesting things to ask them when we get there."

CHAPTER ELEVEN

I GET MYSELF AN ISLAND

SALLY

One thing they never warn you about when you return to Earth is just how dull your life becomes in comparison to everything you've been through.

A month ago, I had been a goddess and imploded a bomb as I fell out of a spaceship. Granted, that adventure had ended poorly, but my heart hadn't raced anywhere near as fast since. Nothing on TV could even compare.

So, right now? Now, I was bored.

Very, very bored.

I flicked absentmindedly through the channels, nothing there grabbing my attention for long enough to make sense. Okay, maybe Alejandro Vasquez's abs. Those were sharp, beautiful, and definitely the right number.

Maybe I was just a pessimist. But it was better than anything else at this point.

But those abs; man, those abs. Maybe I could find some optimism in those perfectly sculpted ...

Shake it off, Sally. I got up to get a cup of water, trying to stay hydrated. It was impossible to do anything fun with Marcy being on her honeymoon and Zander and Blayde still gone. The most interesting it got over here was when I spilled stuff on the floor and spent a few minutes cleaning up my mess. Which, incidentally, was what happened next.

Only this time the water landed on the kitchen island where my journal was sprawled open at its latest page. The water hit the paper with an almost slow-motion splash, the ink smearing, the words fading to a blur. I swore under my breath.

I got a paper towel and set to work cleaning up my mess, disappointed that yesterday's work was ruined. I had desperately been trying to recall all the details from my off-Earth adventures, putting pen to paper to record the truth, the whole truth, and nothing but the unbelievable truth.

Seeing as how I had some money, work was no longer on the forefront of my mind. Perks of being named in the will of a very rich, murdering alien boss before he realizes you're onto him. Though why he thought I was worthy of his money, I would never know.

When all was clean again, I had nothing to distract myself anymore. I went back to the couch, hoping the television would have more to offer than the biggest grossing film of the year.

"The solar system is a—"

"Oh no! The aliens are coming! And they want our corn—"

"The unnamed lost city recently discovered in the middle of the Atlantic has had a lot to offer to archeologists, though not many of them have grasped the meaning of the many glyphs that cover its temple walls.
"

Now, that wasn't at all uninteresting. I put down the remote, lifting my feet onto the coffee table and grabbing a pillow, clutching it to my chest like a cozy shield. The camera panned over the ocean floor, showing large stone blocks from a long-lost civilization. A column jutted out of the sand, fish swimming around the ornate marble, narrowly avoiding the film crew.

The camera cut to bright sunlight, a woman standing on the deck of a ship, her curly hair waving in the sea breeze. She was in her late sixties, early seventies perhaps, a bandana tied around her neck, sun-kissed fingers wrapped around a water bottle, which swung with every gesture as she spoke.

"There is so much for us to sift through," she said, waving her hands excitedly. "This might be one of the, if not *the,* most important archeological finds of our time. An entire civilization is down there, five thousand years old, kept frozen in time by the ocean. What can we learn from them, about these people? So much!"

The narrator took over, panning across the ship. It looked like there was almost fifty people on board, some gently lifting artifacts from the ocean floor, others cleaning those that had already been brought up. Golden jewelry seemed to be the catch of the day.

"The settlement has been found to be quite large, with two cities and small towns dotted around what would have once been a coastline," the voice said. "The most astonishing thing is how the land mass it belonged to sank quite suddenly and all at once. Many researchers are hailing this as the discovery of the lost city of Atlantis."

I scoffed at the television. But then I saw them on the deck, their pixie cut glowing in the sunlight.

Taylor.

They had done it. They had taken the job; they were off hunting lost civilizations with people who didn't know their face. Exactly as they had said they would do.

I guess I hadn't thought they were being honest. That they just wanted a way out, a way away from me. But here they were, on a ship in the middle of the ocean, ducking their head to avoid appearing on camera. They were taking a brush to what looked like a gilded breastplate, the kind a soldier would wear to match their cyborg cyclops friend.

I froze, but only for a second. I shook my head as the video continued, trying to put the image out of my head. The image of a man in that same breastplate, coming at me with a spear.

No. I was home now. Safe now.

But I was still shaking.

Good for Taylor. I watched as the camera panned to another part of the ship, and the narrator began speaking of the many things they uncovered on the ocean floor. *They deserve to be happy. To be free.*

"The city must have sank thousands of years ago,

although the cause has not been determined. It must have been a sudden and devastating disaster that caused the town to be so perfectly preserved. From what archeologists have already found, the town itself was devoted to the goddess of the moon."

Shouts of excitement rose from the ship. People rushed to the railing, looking out into the sea. Something was being pulled up and out of the water, and apparently it was causing quite the fuss.

"The team has just found an important artifact," the narrator said, "which might open an entirely new field of study in this expedition. A statue of one of the city's gods has been discovered in the ruins, and they are currently bringing the deity's head to the surface. This is the first time this god will see the air in over five thousand years."

The crowd parted, and my heart stopped.

My own face looked back at me.

The ancient carving of my features was lowered onto the deck. My eyes, my nose, my mouth. A little green, sure, but still me. My face.

My heart let out a feeble beat, a whimper of fear. It was as if my entire life had suddenly been thrown upside down and shaken until it threw up on the floor of my world. This couldn't be happening; this couldn't be real.

And yet, here it was, making perfect sense.

They had found Aquetzalli.

The city had been real, and I had been right. It *had* been my moon I had looked up at, my air I had been breathing.

Zander had found Earth; we'd just gotten here too early. Five thousand years too early.

Zander could travel through time.

I don't know how long I sat in front of the TV, clutching the cushion so tight to my chest it was starting to hurt. The realization was so much of a shock that my body couldn't process it. No wonder they couldn't recognize a planet, even if they were there before; no wonder Blayde felt no trace of their visit to Meegra, even though Ter back on the *Traveler* knew their legend; no wonder everything that had gone down with the ICP on Da-Duhui hadn't happened yet. It wasn't the theory of relativity that made them arrive weeks after, even though they spent just a day away—it was jumping through time.

Which meant the weirdness Zander and I had encountered—in the hospital, in the park—those had all been temporal flukes. The stripper who claimed I ruined her life *did* know me; I just didn't know her yet. None of those things had happened yet, even if it had happened before.

I was shaking. We had travelled through time. *I* had travelled through time. I had come to Earth and lived as a goddess on Atlantis before allowing it to be devoured by the sea. I had failed my own people, my own species.

Oh god. I was a disaster.

In that moment, there was only one person I wanted to talk to. Someone who could tell me it was going to be all right and actually mean it. One person who would make me feel better: Zander.

But he wasn't here. He could be anywhere in both time and space, never to be seen by me again.

So, I had to call the second-best thing. I stood up,

dropping the cushion, grunting in determination like a caveman who had just spotted some mighty fine berries. I still shook from the shock, my lip quivering, but I forced it still. I saw them on the TV, trying to stay out of frame as the camera panned over my stone head. Yes.

As much as it hurt, it was time. I had to do this.

I picked my phone off my table, hitting their number gently, hoping, praying it would get through to Taylor on the ship. At the same time, I hoped to high heaven they weren't going to pick up. I wasn't ready. Thanks, anxiety.

No. I had to be ready.

The phone rang over and over. It was obvious Taylor wasn't answering, so I took it as a sign and hung up. It wasn't meant to be. And seeing how I had left things the last time we had spoken, I wasn't sure they wanted to hear from me.

But this was about more than me: this was about time travel. It was about a lost civilization I had had the privilege of meeting. It was about something bigger than I ever was. It was about Angee and Ancha and Bismuth, who would live on beyond death.

I had to see them. I had let them die, after all. Me and my empty promises. Me and the goddess I was not. They had all died because I had been too slow to act.

I had to see them. I just had to.

I grabbed my laptop and searched for the contact info for the expedition. They had a number you could call, which I did. But they knew of no-one named Taylor and wouldn't patch me through to "the gorgeous non-binary person with the cute pixie cut." They hung up on me quite quickly, and that line of communication was down.

I glared at the documentary, which was still running on my screen. I felt myself scowling as Taylor appeared on screen, only to try and sneak out again. So, they didn't want to talk to me. Fine. If they were going to play hard-to-get, I was going to play hard-to-miss.

I pulled open my computer, opened an email to someone I had never wanted to email, but whose card now sat awkwardly on my coffee table: Felling.

James, I wrote, *I need to get in contact with Taylor. Please. It's urgent.*

Sent.

On the TV, they sidled up next to the face and froze. I watched Taylor shake their head a few times, possibly in confusion, the same confusion I had felt when I first set eyes on the statue, two weeks ago or five thousand years ago. I wondered if they recognized me. I wondered if, when they did, why they didn't call me.

I knew why. But it still hurt.

My computer pinged. A response.

Sally, I read, *I don't think they want to talk to you right now.*

I let out a loud groan. Had Taylor told her not to let out their info?

It's life or death here, I wrote, exaggerating only slightly. *I need to talk to Taylor. Now.*

Sent. Reply.

Fine—and then a number.

I punched the number into my phone, before even taking the time to thank Felling for hooking me up. I just had to speak to Taylor. I had to.

This time, they answered.

"Hello?" Taylor sounded confused. I guessed not many people had their new number. I was relieved to hear their voice, their musical notes, the voice that had rocked me to sleep on my worst nights.

"Taylor," I said. Instantly, I sensed them tense up.

"How the hell did you get this number?"

"Our mutual friend." Well, this was going fantastic. "Don't hang up! Please, please, don't hang up. It's urgent."

"Give me one reason why." They grunted.

"The statue," I said.

There was a heavy pause on the other end of the line, Taylor holding their breath. I waited.

"How do you know about her?" they asked, slowly.

"Because I am her," I said, my mouth running a mile a minute, "or at least, I was. Taylor, Zander and Blayde came back. And they can travel through time. I think? It's the only thing that explains it. Taylor, last week I was the great goddess Selena."

"Sally"—Taylor let out a massive sigh—"you're crazy."

"Not about this!" I stammered. "I've taken my meds. I'm more level than I ever was. But I'm the reason Aquetzalli is under water. I know you don't want to talk to me or see me, I get that. But I need to see Aquetzalli. I killed them all."

"Aquetzalli?" Taylor stammered. "How ... how did—"

"I was there, Taylor," I said, insistently, my voice rising as I stood up from the couch. "I was there when it was submerged. I met the Atlans, too."

"We never made that name public," they said, trying to stay calm, but there was a tremor in that beautiful voice that was pushing to be heard. "No one knows about Aquetzalli but us."

"Well, I do," I said. "Is that enough proof for you? Or should I tell you about the Temple of Selena?"

I realized my words were coming out sharper than I wanted them to. I was getting angry; not at Taylor, but at myself. For not having seen it earlier. For being behind this all.

Holy shit, I had submerged Atlantis. Plato, get a load of me!

"Taylor," I said again, slowly, forcing myself to be calm.. "I need you to help me. I need to go there. I need to be absolutely sure. I need to see the damage I've done."

Taylor took a breath.

"You're asking me to believe a lot," they said. "I mean, time travel? Come on, that's just not possible."

"And finding cyborg cyclops on the bottom of the ocean is?"

"Fair point," said Taylor, "but this is insane, really. Even for everything I know about the universe. Time travel shouldn't be possible."

"There are higher dimensional beings that exist beyond time," I said, wanting to laugh at my words. "Trust me. I've met them. Zander and Blayde, they just never knew. How could they? Every planet looks different to them. They never stay long enough. They never ..."

Stay. I choked on the word. Not again. I swallowed, waiting for Taylor to reply.

"Oh hell, Sally," they said. "I didn't realize."

"It's okay."

"No, no, it isn't," Taylor spat, though thankfully not at me. "I take it he's gone again."

"Yes," was all I could make out.

"I know you're panicking, but you're going to be okay, all right?" they insisted. "Call doctor Schumann. She'll help you. You're—"

"You think I'm making this up?" I snapped. "That I just imagined all this because, woah, I'm unstable! That's it, isn't it?"

"I mean, Sally ... come on," they said, sweetly.

"Zander came back, Taylor," I said. "He came back, and we left for Da-Duhui. You know the name, right? I'm not making this up. Then we were on the *Traveler*. I met Captain Kork! And then I was the goddess Selena for a while before coming home. And then Zander left. And I have piles of alien junk to deal with, but it's enough proof for anyone to see I'm not making this up."

"Deep breaths, Sally," said Taylor, slowly, gently. "It's all right. I believe you."

"You do?"

"I do."

"Then you'll let me come?" I asked. "I need to see the city. I need to see the damage I've caused."

"If that's what'll help you." They let out yet another sigh, like they were deflating. "I'll figure out how to get you on the ship. Do you still have your translator?"

"I do." My fingers absentmindedly went up to the back of my head where the small, washer-shaped metal ring sat, making ridges in the skin behind my ear. "I ran into our mutual friend again. Well, she crashed my friend's wedding. Reminded me I can speak any language now."

"Perfect," Taylor said. "Right. Now, you're a linguist. I'll have Felling make you a good backstory. I'm going to hire you as a contractor, okay?"

A smile blossomed on my face. "Sure. Anything you can do to get me on that ship."

I could hear typing somewhere down the line. Finally, Taylor spoke again.

"I'm not Taylor here," they said. "I go by Robin."

"I like it," I said. "Robin. It ... it suits you."

"You think?" Taylor, now Robin, chuckled. "Felling set it up for me. I'm not sure why she chose it, it's a little too cutesy for my taste. Anyway, you'll need to get to Baltimore. You'll have someone to pick you up there at the train station. And Sally?"

"Yeah?"

"I missed you," they said, breathing into the telephone. "I'm sorry for how things ended. I hope we can still be friends."

"Friends," I agreed. "I'm sorry too. And Robin?"
"Yeah?"
"I miss you too."

CHAPTER TWELVE

COMING FACE-TO-FACE WITH THE CLONES OF OUR PAST

ZANDER

By the time we had reached Abryria, Dave had moved out of his emo phase and begun his college years, which meant that our ship was the next great Alliance author.

"I've written another poem," he said as we entered orbit around the restricted planet. "This one is about my dysfunctional childhood. Do you want to hear it?"

"Maybe later, buddy," I said. "We have a heist to plan."

"It's short-form," he continued smugly. "I've become fixated on the structure of quara'ha verse from Meegra. Eight verses of eight syllables. Let me begin."

He cleared his throat, though he had no throat to clear. The coffee pot in the back of the galley gurgled.

"*I was born without a mother; and a father who didn't care,*"

"Dave, you're a spaceship. You're not supposed to have parents," Blayde interjected, unplugging the machine from the wall before the pot could overflow.

"You made me lose my flow!"

"Did you at least manage to bypass the restriction on the planet?" she shouted over the angry hum of the sullen ship.

"I had to put in an official request with the Alliance, and they were rude as hell," scoffed the ship. Of course, shuttles can't scoff, so really he just blew a wave of cool air out of the recyclers, as loudly as physically possible. "They were all, 'what, an A-type shuttle? In interstellar space? Is that engine legally modded?' How rude! I'd like to ask him if he's legally modded, that piece of—"

"Dave," I interjected. "Calm down. You are illegally modded."

"What? How could you do this to me? This explains so much about my early childhood and the persistent effect this has had on my upbringing and current mental instability."

He snorted again, making the shuttle go cold, but he put himself in orbit around the planet, nonetheless.

"Right, access refused," he said. "You're going to have to switch to plan B. Damn, five and nine syllables. You've really pulled me out of my groove. But then again, aren't we all just beings with a vast, empty page before us, waiting to be filled with our experiences?"

Blayde stormed into the main cabin, tapping the floor panels with the heavy heel of her foot. "Zander, what are we looking for?"

I watched as my sister ripped up one of the shuttle's

tiles, extracting the emergency exit gear. She tossed me a pair of goggles, which I slipped over my eyes reflexively.

"We're aiming for the old visitor's center," I explained. "From the blueprints on Dave's database, that's the most likely place where Alliance information would be held."

"Too bad we don't have time for recon," said Blayde. "I'd like to know what we're getting into before, you know, hopping into a world full of our literal worst enemies."

"They're just clones, Blayde."

"I'm not sure they know that, brother of mine."

She shrugged, zipping up her red leather coat. Dave was now orbiting close enough to the planet that we could see the beginnings of continents: large brown-and-green landmasses over bright blue water, so close to Earth's colors it hurt. I focused on the pressure inside my chest, forcing it to loosen. I didn't need anything holding me back right now.

"Ready for a bit of fun?" she asked.

"Only if you are."

"I'll see you two soon," said Dave, sounding, somehow, impossibly bored. "I need to work on my free-form prose. The silence will do me good. You two are always holding me back."

Whatever he said next was drowned out by the rapid depressurization of our cabin. The door flew open, and the air was sucked right out, pulling us along with it. Though I couldn't hear it, I could see Blayde laugh, her grin spread wide on her windswept face.

There was simply nothing like falling through the

atmosphere of a planet. Feeling the wind rush against your skin, ionized particles coming along for the ride. The heat building up on your chest as the friction threatened to ignite you. A quick jump to shake off that momentum and start anew. Falling, falling, falling, stop. Hands out, legs spread, nothing but you and a quickly approaching planet.

Terminal velocity isn't terminal for everyone.

I couldn't help but throw my head back and scream, letting the air pull the sound from my mouth. Tucking my neck to my chest and flipping upside down, twisting my body to get a good spin going, dancing through the frigid air. The closest thing there was to flying without wings.

Too quickly, it was over, and I was standing in an empty field with Blayde by my side, readjusting wind-swept hair and stuffing the goggles into my pocket. I glanced up to where I had been standing just a few minutes ago on the edge of space.

"See? You wouldn't have been able to make that kind of entrance with Sally around."

I knew better than to murder Blayde. The last time I had, she had sulked for a month. It probably wasn't worth it to strangle her here. No, I'd reserve that for when she truly crossed a line.

"This way," I muttered, extrapolating from the old blueprints and the position of the sun. Blayde said nothing more, following me out of the field onto a surprisingly well-kept road.

The visitor's center hadn't changed in the supposed five years since we had helped pull everyone out. Even from this distance, it was easy to tell that it was well maintained. The building sat like a delicate crown in the valley before us, concentric rings hiding dangerous traps to keep the convicts in and the surrounding nature out. The only thing that had changed or simply not been fixed was the obliterated second outermost ring, the guest terminal.

We jumped closer, cutting a good day out of our walking time. Now we were just beyond the first and outermost ring, the barrier against the encroaching nature. In an act of supreme idiocy or sheer brilliance, it had been built out of a strongly reflective material, curving and bulging the image of the forest beyond. Every few minutes, the wall was programmed to throw out a handful of hurtful slurs about the trees' physical appearance, apparently shaming the trees into keeping their distance.

The odd thing was it seemed to be working; nothing grew within twenty meters of the wall, making us the only idiots to walk the no-go zone.

"Don't you think you've had enough sunlight?" asked the wall, as Blayde and I approached. "Maybe you need to go on an all-rain diet."

"Does it know we're here?" I asked under my breath. The wall was at least sixty feet high, which was easy enough for us to jump but nonetheless unsettling.

"I doubt it," Blayde said. "I think it's just a solar-powered insult launcher. It'll be screaming at the forest long after the forest dies. Come on."

We jumped to the top of the wall, hopping easily down into the sentry walk. From this vantage point, the entire complex looked deserted. The ruins of the terminal ring were hauntingly empty, the museum's third ring too dark to tell.

"Do you think we're alone?" she asked.

"Please. With those roots? It's like you don't even care about finding water."

"Except for the insult launcher, of course," she said with a grimace.

"I can't imagine they all left in just five years," I said. "The universe wouldn't be so ... quiet if they had all escaped."

"Always the optimist." Blayde shrugged. "I'm working under the assumption they all murdered each other."

We jumped to the third ring.

Blayde clutched her laser pointer as she drew a circle through one of the upper windows, letting us into the old museum complex. The smell hit me first: not a smell of rotting corpses, not the smell of abandoned buildings, but the heavenly scent of roasting meat on an open flame.

"You see what I mean?" said Blayde through gritted teeth. "Cannibals. Better avoid."

I nodded. I'd been eaten by a cannibal once. Apparently, capturing a man with a leg that kept growing back made me his golden goose. If it wasn't for the fact that they grew tired of picking their way through leg hair, I would probably still be being consumed by the chief of Nazar.

I wonder how he was doing now. He made a mean margarita.

The halls of the old museum were clean and empty. Not a sign of a body anywhere in sight: no death, decay, destruction, or anything we had expected. Just empty halls that seemed to go on forever.

"I guess they did all get out." She indicated the empty cells. We had just entered what was meant to be a temporary exhibit on the last stand of the Gramoccin empire, the walls lined with scenes that were supposed to represent the conflict. Pedestals sat empty where the clones were meant to stand.

"This place gives me the creeps," I said. "Let's get the information and get out of here."

"You've got the creeps? You?" Blayde laughed, her voice bouncing off the empty walls. She pushed open the door at the end of the exhibit, leading us into the main lobby of the museum. "Zander, please. If anyone was left here, it would be you that would scare them, not the other way around."

"Oh wow! It's Zander and Blayde! Does anybody have that good bottle of Jujaka? Quick! Set another place!"

Blayde and I froze, her hand still on the door handle. Before us was a massive table, long as the lobby, with fifty or so people crowded around it, plates full of meat. The smell was unbearably good, impossible to ignore. Where the information desk used to sit was now a gleaming fire, massive animals roasting on spits.

And there, around the table, were our worst enemies—smiling at us.

There was Jesmina, the butcher of Jaspon, scorpion queen of the three sister stars; Ravit, the emperor of the Golar, last of his kind; Tresmine, scholar of Nevith; Bob. Freaking Bob.

All of them looking as us like we'd just joined them for lunch, not, you know, once brutally ended their reigns of terror.

"Hey, Zander, Blayde, grab a chair!" said Kizkim, the mad scientist who had once eradicated an entire solar system by teaching them a form of tango which, once started, one could not help but dance until their lungs gave out. "We have fresh meat! All synthetic, in case you've gone vegan. Seeing as you're here, anything could happen!"

Neither I nor Blayde could get a word out edgewise as we were ushered into seats, squished between Kizkim and Jesmina, who was devouring a juicy cut of something blue and smelling oddly of bubblegum. Before we could ask what was happening, Bob, freaking *Bob*, had handed us heaping plates of food.

Having had nothing to eat since Earth—no, before; I never did have a chance to drink that tea—I was grateful for the meal. Blayde shot me a quick look. We didn't know their intentions; we couldn't be sure the food wasn't poisoned. I didn't quite care either way: I'd been poisoned before, and it wasn't worse than, I don't know, having your liver eaten every day, over and over again.

Had that happened to me, or was that someone else? I couldn't remember if it was a memory of something real or from a story someone had told me. I vividly remembered the time my leg was eaten, that much was clear, but the liver, now that was foggy and ...

"What brings you to Abryria, folks?" asked Kizkim, delicately slicing his fruit before bringing the flesh to his mouth. What a madman. "I take it you're not here for all the smiling faces."

"Can you speak louder? Some of us can't hear!"

shouted a voice from the end of the table.

"We're trying to have a normal conversation, RrRr!" he said, the name a crash of two boulders. "We'll tell you later!"

"What about the saltshaker?"

But Kizkim didn't pull a phaser out of his pocket and disintegrate him on the spot, no. He smiled and returned his attention to us, an eager, completely average host.

"You look surprised," he pointed out. "I suspect you were not expecting such a warm welcome."

"To be honest, we weren't expecting anyone left alive down here," said Blayde, politely pushing her food around on the plate as if she were actually eating it. I had already finished two steaks at this point, and I hadn't tasted any poison on the way down.

"What? Because we're the worst the universe has to offer?"

Kizkim didn't look like the evil type from the outside. His race, the Huggalottans, were furry and large-eyed, meaning they were always thought to be more cute than deadly. Part of what make Kizkim such a popular exhibit had been the fact that he was pure evil in such a sweet shell, meaning people had constantly been trying to break him out of the museum because he couldn't possibly-wassibly be a baddy-waddy.

Then again, the rest of his race died out centuries ago because they had all fallen asleep one day and been invaded, then woke up and thought it completely normal that they were now under alien occupation. That, and their mating rituals were so violent that none of the Huggalottans thought it was worth the trouble to reproduce.

"The Alliance expected us to kill each other off the second we had chased them off the planet, but what was the point?" said Tresmine. "None of our memories were real. We're products of the Alliance's propaganda machine."

"Hear, hear!" said some guy halfway down the table. Couldn't remember who he was. Had I killed him once? Maybe we didn't know each other.

"We've been living in peace and harmony ever since," said Kizkim. "And happily so. Here, no one sees each other as murderers and cosmic butchers. We're just bunches of cells grown from the worst slime of the universe."

"Just the galaxy," said Jesmina, curling her x's.

"And the Alliance leaves you alone?" asked Blayde.

"Apparently it's more expensive to bomb us than it is to clothe and feed us," explained Kizkim. "It's not like the population will grow. None of us are genetically compatible."

Relief flooded over me, and I breathed easy, devouring a fourth flank steak in less time than the other three. It was odd to look into the face of Kizkim and not feel an immediate sense of deep hatred. The last time I had come toe to toe with him, I had been so violently tangoing that I had already lost three dance partners. I tried not to remember the look on his face as I swung my head at him, the betrayal in his eyes when he realized my flirtation had been a ploy.

Blayde hadn't been there for that one. Where the hell had she been?

"Is it weird that I have kissed at least half the people

at this table?" she muttered, low enough only I could hear. "Ugh, do you think the Alliance knew I dated some of them? Did they implant those memories too?"

"I sure hope not," I shuddered. "Or we'll both be in a lot of trouble. What's more worrying is that we both seem to have a type."

"Do our romantic partners try to take over the universe before or after our breakups?"

"You still haven't told us what brought you here," said Kizkim, his voice rising over the din and shutting us up.

"Oh right." I put down my food prongs and forced myself to look at him. This was not the man I had danced to death with. No, this was a copy, a copy *aware* his memories were fake. It was not his fault he was alive. "We're looking for the library. The coordinates we ... Acquired ... from the Alliance brought us here. We assume you know where we need to go next?"

"Oh, yes, you're in the right place!" Kizkim clapped with glee, his blue, fluffy ears twitching excitedly. "We're an indexing node of the library. We can definitely get you to where you need to be."

"You're a what now?"

"How versed are you with quantum information?" asked Kizkim.

"Information being physical and all that?" said Blayde.

"The library contains all information in the universe," said Tresmine. "But it cannot contain any information about itself. That would break the laws of quantum mechanics, creating a rupture in space-time. Imagine a black hole, though rather having an excess of mass, it would contain an excess of information."

"So, we contain all the information about the library that the library cannot contain itself," added Jesmina. "Which makes us intrinsically linked to the library. We tether it to the universe. Without us and the other nodes spread across the cosmic web, the library would exist but would be inaccessible to anyone who wasn't prepared for a one-way trip."

"Talk about a paradox," said Tresmine. "The library is either the most stable or the most unstable place in the universe—or both at the same time."

"The Library can only be accessed through a node like this museum," said Kizkim. "It's one of the reasons the Alliance didn't blow this planet when we revolted. The abbot paid them handsomely to buy this planet, just so they could use it as a node."

The library was sounding more and more fascinating by the second. A place containing all the information in the universe; now that sounded like a promising place to discover one's own past.

"You can show us how to get there?" I asked.

"Show you? We can take you! The abbot established the transit tunnel in the old museum core. Finish your meal, and we'll go right there."

It was as if entire weights lifted off my chest. Not only was Abryria calm and welcoming, but they almost literally were holding the door open for us to find the Library.

Maybe things were finally coming up.

CHAPTER THIRTEEN

RETURNING TO THE LAND OF THE LOST

SALLY

I was accosted before I even got on the train.

Well, when I say accosted, it might be worth mentioning that this was cooler than any spy movie. I stood at the station, waiting for the train to pull up, when a man in a black suit tripped over my suitcase.

"Terribly sorry," he said, rushing away.

"Sir, you forgot your ..." He had dropped an envelope, and by the time I reached for it, he was already gone.

I was never here, said the note inside, along with a passport, Florida driver's license, and a wad of cash.

And it was my photo in the passport—my face, a picture taken from the DMV's records. I had never had a passport before, and I guess I had been dumb in thinking I wouldn't be needing one now. The name, however, was Sandra Weaver.

Well, I guess I'm Sandra now. Neat.

Sandra got on the train and read a book on the short trip to Baltimore. When was the last time I had taken the train? I had learned a new way of travel, seen the stars up close. Trains just didn't compare. But at least I was here in one piece, the only discomfort of my trip caused by the gross nose picker who sat beside me.

There, at the station, a man was waiting, holding a sign with my new name on it, scrawled in nice, round letters. It took me a second or two to realize that Weaver was supposed to be me. I pulled my suitcase along behind me, my trusty duffel hanging off my shoulder.

"Sandra Weaver?" the man asked, meeting my gaze. He was dressed in an easy button-down shirt and loose khaki pants. Not a driver, not that I would recognize one from experience.

"Yeah, yeah, that's me." I extended my hand to shake his. I wondered if Sandra Weaver needed a new personality. Should I give her a strange accent or a fancy gait? Realizing it was too much work, I just smiled and took his hand.

"Oh, it's so nice to meet you! Call me Kyle."

"Likewise!" I said. "Not the Kyle bit, but it's nice to meet you too."

Shit. There goes Sandra's sense of cool. Five minutes into existence, and she's already an awkward duck.

"Robin has told me so much about you," he said, ushering me through the crowd, out to a car that was waiting for him in the parking lot. "They say you have a real knack with languages."

"Yup," I agreed. "I hear I have my work cut out for me."

"Lost civilization means lost language." The man laughed. He took my bag and put it in the back of his rental as I climbed in the passenger side.

And then the words just spilled out of him. We didn't drive long, but by the time we reached the harbor, I knew his entire life's story. Apparently, Kyle was an archeologist with a focus on ancient Greece, more specifically Sparta, and had been the grad student of the woman who located the lost city, the woman from the documentary. He was already in Baltimore on a resupply trip, so the timing was perfect for picking me up.

I guess the universe was starting to pay me back for the shit it put me through. Nice feeling.

We arrived at the ship, and Kyle showed me to my tiny cabin, where I dropped off my bag. I had never been on a ship—an ocean ship—before, but this was just a small one, Kyle kept telling me. Still, there was something unique about being on the deck and seeing the waves crash around the prow. The smell of salt was warm and reassuring; I felt at ease on the water.

Until a few hours later when I started throwing up over the prow. Apparently, I didn't have what one would call sea legs. Space legs, sure, but go figure.

Kyle was obviously excited for the company because he was still talking this entire time. I wondered how he had time to breathe. He spoke as we walked; he spoke as we ate; he spoke well into the night when all I wanted to do was sleep. I never even got to speak with the rest of the crew.

Here he was, telling me about the different eras of ancient civilization and how they tied to the civilization they had found. The architecture of the columns, for example, which showed they had a remarkable influence from Greece, though how they traveled to the main continent nobody knew, seeing as how no ships had been found.

"Maybe they swam," I suggested. Kyle found that hilarious.

He went on about the giant coral reef that sat in the middle of what had once been the island, a reef that unsettled the researchers if they went too close. He told me of the huge statues they had found of the great goddess, of the temple they were trying to enter. He spoke of a sunken pyramid, beautiful cities and what appeared to be a prison, carved into the cliffs.

And all the while, I was forming the connections, my heart sinking as the evidence around me grew. I had travelled through time. I had been here before, thousands of years ago.

"But the technology!" he said, letting out a slow whistle as he stood next to me by the rail I had just puked over. "You have no idea. They had mechanical men, actual robots! And we think their spears could be used to conduct beams of electricity. Sounds like science-fiction, but I've seen it with my own two eyes!"

He was like that for the next two days. Which I suppose was fine, but the knots in my stomach made our nautical knots look like play dough. All I wanted was to get there, to see Aquetzalli with my own eyes, to be sure it was all true. That I wasn't crazy. That I had been there. That I was a time traveler.

I hadn't seen any paradoxes yet, but there were bound to be some. If I had learned anything from television, it was that time travel always brought on a mess of trouble.

"You say you're an expert on dead languages?" This had been the first time in two days when he had asked for my input. "You're pretty young, aren't you?"

"Yeah, but I learn languages quickly. I recently discovered I can pick up on anything anyone says to me."

"How many languages do you speak?"

"No idea. I keep learning."

"Can you understand what I'm saying?"

"Yes."

"And now?"

"Still yes."

"What about now?"

"I hear you loud and clear. Why?"

"I just spoke to you in Spanish, Portuguese, and Latin."

"Huh."

"And you answered me in each of the languages. When did you learn them?

"I don't know. I just like words."

"That's amazing."

"I guess so, but it makes it confusing. My brain translates so fast I can't tell if you're speaking another language than English. Or if I am."

"And some of us are stuck spending years to learn a single language, and you can do it in, like, seconds. You psychic or something?"

"Don't think so… "

"It's okay if you are. My mom was." He paused, waiting for me to object or ask something more. When I didn't, he continued, "She could feel the emotions passed into an inanimate object. If she were alive today, she could touch a stone in the buried city and tell you what happened there. It was amazing. It drove her mad in the end."

"I'm sorry." I was bad enough in knowing how to deal with my own grief, let alone someone else's. I tried to change the subject, allow him to take over once more. "It's amazing you found the city so intact."

"It really is! Now, if we could only understand what the cataclysm was that sent it under water. An apocalyptic flood is very Old Testament. But an entire continent being swept under the waves? There has to be a reason."

A giant spaceship's shockwave as it entered Earth's atmosphere? Maybe?

And then, after days of nothing on the horizon, the research ship came into view. Compared to our little skiff, this thing was a monster. I stared at it as Kyle rambled on, my heart pounding a mile a minute. Below us, right now, was all that remained of Aquetzalli. And before me was the ex who had broken my heart.

This was going to be fun.

We climbed into an inflatable raft and were driven over to the ship, which waited for us with a rope ladder. I slung my duffel bag on my back and began to climb, each one of my steps wobbling as my nerves grew.

And there they were, waiting for me.

Taylor. Robin now, but they had been Taylor when we met, when we kissed, when I whispered their name under my breath in the dark. And here they were, staring bashfully at the deck of the ship they had left me for.

"Welcome back, Kyle, you jackass!" A man sprung forward and grabbed my guide in a tight bear hug. For the first time in two days, Kyle was speechless.

"Ah, you must be the linguist," said a voice. I tore my eyes off Kyle in time to spot a woman pushing her way out of the crowd. Her hair was wispy white and billowed around her face like dandelion fluff. Instantly, I recognized her from the documentary that had brought me here.

"Dr. Finbar, but you can call me Isla," she said, shaking my hand. "A pleasure. I'm looking forward to having you work with us."

"Sandra," I said. "Me too."

"Talking to your references, I didn't realize Dr. Barcasian even took research assistants. I'm amazed you managed to solve the language's codex before he could himself."

"He pointed me in the right direction." I blushed, having, of course, no idea who that was. Probably someone who owed Felling a favor. "But it's going to be so different in the field. I can't wait to get down there and get to work."

"Want to start right now?" Isla laughed. "We've got a sub ready to dive, and we're—"

"Heck yes!"

"I was joking." She crossed her arms as the breeze picked up and chilled us both. The ringing at the back of my ear got stronger. "But I'm glad to see you're this eager."

"I just ..." I took a deep breath, centering myself. "I

really can't wait to see this place. I've been dreaming of this city since I was a child."

"We are making history here," said Isla, "by finding it. And you're right, there's no point in putting it off! Kyle will show you to your cabin so you can put down your things. We'll dive in thirty."

When I came back on the deck, the tiny sub had been lifted into position. The crew was helping the pilot get settled in, Isla watching from below, checking off items on a clipboard. I made my way to her side.

"Have you ever been in a submarine before? It's too claustrophobic for me; I never go down anymore. I hope you don't have a problem with small spaces."

"I'm all right, thank you," I said. I was too antsy to see the city that my anxiety didn't have cracks to poke through. As it reminded me of all the ways I could die, I beat it back with the hammer of *shut up*.

"Since you're so eager to begin, we're putting you on an exploratory mission," she explained. "You are going to photograph any instances of text you can see and start finding ways of translating it as soon as possible. It'll help us understand the city a lot more."

"Perfect." I nodded. "I won't let you down."

And there they were, slipping into the submarine without a glance my way. The only person on this ship I wasn't ready to talk to, and I was going to be stuck in a ship with them one-on-one, under the sea. Robin turned, saw me, and their gaze fell. I gave a feeble wave.

"You," They started.

"Hey, Robin," I replied. "It's good to see you."

They hadn't changed a bit, not that it was long since I had last seen them, even if it had felt like an eternity.

The pixie cut was cute and fit their face well. Now, it was short and almost military instead of the swooping shape I had suggested. They had told me it was too much like a mullet. We had laughed about it together, back when things were warm between us.

There were probably things much more awkward in the universe than being trapped in a tiny submarine with the roommate who broke your heart, but I didn't know of many. And right now, my genius plan to see the truth about this place was looking like the dumbest idea in the universe.

The submersible was a small craft, with enough room for two people to sit and not much else. Notice I didn't say we'd fit comfortably. We were surrounded on all sides by notation equipment, pressure gauges, and who knew what. So, while my initial plan of visiting Aquetzalli sounded like a work of genius and a fair bit of spy work, now that I was here, I wanted nothing more than to go home.

We dropped into the water, the swirling bubbles enveloping the sub as we dove into the deep end. At first, the water was bright blue and tranquil, but the world around us quickly darkened as we dove deeper into the void.

I say "we," but Robin was the one doing all the work. I just sat there, wondering if maybe I was afraid of closed spaces on top of extreme heights, then realizing it was probably tight space with Robin was what I was afraid of. Or maybe the whole "seeing the ancient ruins of a civilization you had visited a month ago" thing.

But I needed proof. Proof that I could see, proof that I could touch. I needed to know if time travel was possible—and if I had experienced it for myself.

I imagined the pressure inside the submarine felt the same in here as it did outside the hull: crushing, squeezing, a cold and dark void. Not pleasant. Robin was as silent as the deep ocean and seemingly twice as cold.

"So, um, how are you doing?" I asked, trying to break the tension.

"Are we really going to do this?"

"Do what?"

"Come on, Sally." Even their reflection in the large bubbled window didn't want to make eye contact. "You can't possibly be this naive."

Maybe I was naive. Maybe I wasn't a hundred-year-old gas cloud living in a human facsimile. But I was also the other half of that relationship, dammit, and that didn't count for nothing.

"Let's just get this over with," said Robin. "I missed you, but it doesn't mean I'm ready to spend more time with you just yet. Let's get down there, translate some carvings, and get you back off my ship. "

"Your ship?" I stammered. "Look, Robin, I'm not here for you. I just want to find my answers and get out."

"So, we're agreed?"

"I guess we are."

"Then why are we fighting?"

"I don't know. Maybe because it's all we ever do? Maybe because fighting is all we know?"

"That's so… stupid," said Robin. "I mean, come on, Sally. I've been around the block a few times, and it's never that easy. You can't boil down a relationship to a few words over why it worked or it didn't."

"We never worked."

"Exactly my point," they continued. We were still lowering deeper, the blue ocean around us becoming darker as we sank. I kept my eyes riveted on the empty sea before us. Even if I wanted to run, there was nowhere I could go at this point. "We did work. Sometimes. And other times, we didn't. We just chose to discontinue the experiment."

"Hold on, what? *We* chose to discontinue it?" I sputtered. "You're the one who walked out on me, Taylor. I mean, Robin. Jeez. And for your information, I didn't want to have this argument. I meant what I said—I just want to get to the bottom of this, literally. If I did want to draw this out, I would tell you about the robot who assaulted me looking for you."

The was a chill in the air. "A robot?"

"From the Ordan."

"Shit. What did you tell it?"

"Nothing. I offered him tea. Well, I threw it at him, so he had no choice but to accept it. I still haven't been compensated for the broken door."

Robin snorted, but they were as tense as ever. Relieved they were safe. Scared by how close it had come. All that on top of their own relationship anger.

The ruins were coming into focus now. The columns of a long-forgotten temple loomed out of the deep, and Robin switched on the headlights of the small sub. From a distance, it looked like the ruins of Pompeii, except, you know, at the bottom of the ocean.

"I didn't know it was so close to finding me," they said. "I'm sorry. I never meant to put you in harm's way."

"Yet, you walked out on me."

"Tell me, Sally. If Zander had come back at any point during our relationship, would you have hesitated before going with him? Would you have thought about me?"

I couldn't answer. I knew exactly what I would have done; it was what I had done to Marcy, a week before her wedding day. Not a second thought in following Zander to the stars.

"That's what I mean," they said. "Everything about our relationship revolved around Zander. We had an expiration date: the day he would return. And even if that day never came, you would still be waiting. You refused to invest yourself into making us work, so I left. But you can't blame me. You had one foot out the door from day one."

"That's not true."

"Yes, it is." With a chugging noise, the sub stopped its descent. Robin toggled controls above their head, and, with a slow rumble, we moved forward through the deep blue water. "You were waiting for him. Refusing to move forward until *he* came back. We could never be until you let him go. I was a rebound. Stop me when this looks familiar."

"Well, he came back, broke my heart, and I'm over it." I shrugged. "Can we focus on the fact that a place I visited just last month is now dead and under water and has been for five thousand years?"

"Veesh, if you got over him so quickly last time, maybe we would have had a chance," they muttered, pushing the sub forward even more. "Did you tell him about us?"

I sat on my hands to keep them from fidgeting as I watched my world go by. There was the temple where the wise women of Aquetzalli had washed and bathed us, where Angee learned the truth about who we were. There was the beach where we had the bonfire party, where the Atlans had attacked just to get their hands on the fake-as-hell goddess. The city that had been vibrant and alive moments ago, reduced to a shell of what it once was.

"You keep answering my questions with silence," said Robin. "You're just proving my point. You edit out your past. Life kept moving forward while you were waiting for Zander to get back. You can't edit chapters out of your life because they hurt. The only way to move past something is by moving through it. Are you... crying?" They glanced over at me as I furiously wiped the tears from my cheeks. "I'm sorry, okay? You see why I didn't want to have this conversation. Here, of all places."

"I had friends here," I said, avoiding their gaze. "I screwed up. They're all dead because of me."

Robin scoffed. "All this? Because of you? You give yourself too much credit."

I told them the story as we moved silently through the ruins. I told them of the people I met: of Bismuth, Ancha, and Angee; of the cyborg cyclops and the mysterious temple in the now dormant volcano. Robin listened, saying nothing, controlling the sub as they silently contemplated the world outside our window.

"I took pictures, if you don't believe me," I said. "You're probably the only person I can show them to.

I'm not sure I can ever share them with Marcy; I wouldn't know what to say. One day, maybe, when I'm ready. Why are we turning around?"

"Oh, sorry," they replied. Was I imagining things, or were their eyes welling up too? "It's just... there's this reef we avoid. It creeps us all out. So much."

"The whispering forest survived?" I strained my eyes against the blue, seeing nothing but dark forms in the distance. "Score!"

"The what now?"

"A ... Kimmy cluster."

"Krimoge?"

"Yes, that!"

"Right, now I have to find a good reason to keep the team from exploring *that* madhouse."

Robin turned the sub back toward the city of Aquetzalli, and I tried to place the vistas I remembered over the world I was seeing now, but it was impossible to see the rolling green hills, the lush forests, the vibrant cities.

And I sobbed for the downfall of Aquetzalli.

I was still crying when the sub was pulled out of the water, though I had wiped my tears on my sleeve by the time Robin had opened our door to the outside world.

"So, how was it down there?" asked Isla, reaching out a hand to help me down. "Make any breakthroughs yet?"

"You laugh, but this girl has already got her bearings," said Robin, speaking up for me as I struggled to recapture my voice. The ringing in my ears was louder now, the little chip behind my ear on the fritz. I would need to find a way of getting it out as inconspicuously as possible, but now was not the time. I snapped my eyes shut until the sound of feedback died down, the sudden pain distorting my senses.

"Did anyone hear that?" asked Kyle, glancing up from his phone and looking around wildly. Had they all heard the sound as well? It wasn't just me? No, they all shook their heads. "It sounded like a foghorn. We're not meant to meet with other ships right now, are we?"

"There it was again!"

"I heard it too!"

"Yeah, what is that?"

"I didn't hear anything."

HOOOOOOOOOOONNK.

A deep sound echoed through the sky.

"I heard it."

"Definitely."-

"Oh no." I gasped, praying it wasn't true. One by one, we all looked up, lifting our heads to the stars. I felt the trembling deep within me—the knowledge of what was to come.

"Isla? There's something weird on the radio," said a young woman, appearing from the galley, holding a slip of paper. "All the channels are saturated. The same message over and over again. It says ..."

"Show yourself!"

The voice came from the sky, like God above sticking his head out of the clouds. The voice echoed through the air as the sea rippled and waves crashed hard against the ship, making the deck shiver and shake.

"What is that sound?" Robin's hands flew up to their ears. I stood paralyzed in place, unable to move, pinned down by the words in the sky.

"How long has this town has been underwater?" I shuddered.

"By our estimates, five thousand years. Give or take." They took her hands off their ears, staring at me awkwardly. "Why?"

"The Sky People are back." I wanted to scream, to run, but there was nowhere to go to escape the solitary, well-armed prisoner transport ship. Not while I was standing on top of a research vessel in the middle of the Atlantic. And this time, no Zander, no Blayde. Nim, dead and buried. Selena nowhere to be found. And the last picture of the Zoesh they have on record is mine.

CHAPTER FOURTEEN

HAVING FUN ISN'T HARD WHEN YOU'VE GOT A LIBRARY CARD

Zander

"I feel bad for abandoning Dave."

We stood in the dark core of the museum, surrounded by copies of our worst enemies, all smiling and kind. A little cathartic, if you ask me, though *farshing* creepy. Blayde kept her lips in a tight, straight line, revealing nothing.

"Dave needs to grow up," she said. "It's time for him to leave the nest. Go and see the universe for himself. Get out of his parents' basement."

"He's a ship. He doesn't have parents, and there's no basement involved."

"Exactly, so he has no reason to feel guilty."

Kizkim sat at a terminal, communicating with the

196

library to prepare for our arrival. All our work preparing Alliance aliases fell apart the moment we had walked in on a banquet of the worst the universe had to offer, but he assured us the abbot accepted anyone who requested entrance to the library, no matter their position with the Alliance. They were above such petty squabbles.

"Don't you think this is a little too easy?" I asked Blayde. She clutched her laser lazily, rolling it between her fingers like a cigar. "I mean, this is a restricted planet and all. Yet they open their doors, share their food, and go out of their way to get us to their library."

"The Alliance Coordinates sent us here, and we stole them right off the Pyrinian database. It's not like they knew we were coming."

"But these monks have a way of knowing what's going to happen, don't they? Remember the whole Sally-Selena debacle?"

"You say it as if that didn't just happen last week," Blayde scoffed.

"Well, the monks were involved thousands of years before that, planning everything. What makes you think they didn't set us up? Put this whole thing in motion?"

"Do you want to go to the library or not?" Outside the glass doors, the former museum exhibits were watching us with eyes wide and smiles even wider. Were they happy to see us go or planning something far more nefarious?

"If the monks had set this all up, don't you think they would have asked the Alliance to give us access to this planet?" I insisted.

"Maybe they wanted us to think it was all our doing, make us work for it."

"Then why would these guys, literally carbon copies of the people who hate us most in history, be so chill with us using their magic bridge?"

I must have been staring too hard at Kizkim because he looked up, waving at me with that adorable teddy bear smile of his. Big, white eyes and blue fluff just made to hug, cute as a button, exactly the opposite of the violent killing machine I had known him to be.

"We're connecting," he said, smiling wide. "The bridge is forming. Take a big step back."

The room erupted in cheer as the center of the floor lit up in brilliant yellow light, a beam rising to the ceiling to meet the growing pool of light. The clones whooped in excitement as the beam held stable.

"All you have to do is walk through there," said Kizkim, leaving his panel to meet with us again. "And on the other side are all the answers you could ever want."

"It goes without saying," I said to Blayde, gently taking her hand, "that we shouldn't keep our hopes up. They might not know anything about us. This is just a lead. Nothing more."

"The first lead we've had in centuries."

"Still. We need to prepare ourselves for the possibility that none of this will pay off. We need to be ready to jump and start over again."

She nodded, though the words weren't hitting home. She was too focused on the beam, the thrill written on her face.

"Always running," I muttered.

"What was that?" she asked, though I knew she had heard me quite clearly.

"I'm not saying anything."

"Why do you always have to go and ruin good things? Veesh. We'll talk about your issues when this is over."

"What do we do if we find our life story in there?" My free hand trembled, and I forced it into a fist. "Should we try to make it back to what we used to call home? It probably doesn't exist—or at least, not anymore. What then, Blayde?"

"We'll figure it all out after."

"I don't want to know who I was before, not anymore," I snapped. "It's more trouble than it's worth. Whoever it was, it's hasn't been me for millennia."

"You would prefer"—her lips curled over her teeth, a reminder that she was a predator by nature—"to find a nice, cozy planet and just stop, even though you have no idea who you were, are, and what you are?"

"I might not know who I was, but I know who I am," I said with as much confidence as I could muster. "That's enough for me."

"Well, not for me. You can stop yourself from seeing the truth, but don't stand in my way."

A minute went by, an eternity in which we stared at the glaring yellow beam, our eyes burning from the intensity, both too stubborn to turn away. I held her hand in mine, and she clutched my fingers tight, tying my heart into knots.

I couldn't remember the first time I had held her hand. I couldn't remember anything about us. All I knew is that every morning I woke with her name etched in my mind: my sister, my partner, my friend. Through thick and thin, through everything. She had been there for me, and I for her, our strength in the other one's heart.

"Maybe you don't need to know," she said calmly, squeezing my hand tighter, "but aren't you dying to?"

She was right, of course. She knew me too well. Curiosity overcame me; it had been filling me up without me realizing, but now I was full to bursting.

"That's my bro," said Blayde. "Now, let's go find the truth, Sand—"

"One more word, and we're going back. Dave's probably wondering where we're at."

I didn't notice the pipe in my ribs until Blayde ripped it out, kicking Tresmine square in the chest and sending him flying toward the light, only to be caught by someone I'm pretty sure I remember once shooting through the head. Except now Blayde was the one with the bullet through the eyes, falling backwards on the carpet with a limp *thump*.

"Assholes!" I screamed. "You realize brain matter is really hard to get out of fibers, right? Don't expect me to clean up after you!"

The room had transformed into a war zone, with my sister and me in the middle. I was sure I had a nightmare like this before, only it ended with Captain Kork calling me "cadet," which at that point had been the coolest possible thing I could think of. I wondered what Kork was up to now. Hope he hadn't been fired after that whole Consortium fiasco.

Wrong time for that train of thought. I ripped the laser pointer from Blayde's cold, dead hand, twisting the dial to a nice strong burn setting that wouldn't lightsaber off somebody's hand. My body moved mechanically, muscle memory taking over, my sister's hand in mine as I jumped us out of the circle, my heel catching Bob—*farshing* Bob!—in the neck, winding him and sending him straight into the light beam, where he promptly fizzled out of existence. Swinging the laser, holding off the hoard of angry clones from my sister's still-recovering body, raising long lines of burns along the exposed flesh of their skin.

"Kizkim, what the hell?" I spat, punching a man-spider right between the mandibles before flinging him into the chest of an advancing spider-man.

"You can't blame Tresmine." The fuzzy blue man had climbed atop his computer terminal, bearing his fangs at me across the distance. "He did what we've all wanted to do."

"I thought you were better than your false memories!" I ducked and rolled as Jesmina swung a Rolandian meat cleaver at me, the blade sinking five inches into the post behind me.

"They might be false memories, but they are still *our* memories," he hissed. "The only ones we have. The worst moments of the wars, none of the good of the rest of our lives lived. None of the heartwarming childhood dreams and games. No first love, first kiss, only the murder and massacre our genetic identicals left behind. And all of us with one thing in common: our mutual hatred of the siblings. The Iron and the Sand."

"Oh, will you shut up with that nickname?"

"I tell you all this, and you're just mad about what I called *you*?" I didn't think a bear could look so forlorn, but here I was being proved wrong. "No wonder we all hate you."

"I don't." A bright cloud flickered nauseating shades of impossible colors in the middle of the mangle, fighting clones passing right through him. "If anything, I'm rather indifferent. I don't know him."

"My man!" I called.

"He has absorbed two trillion lives," said Kizkim.

"Ah. Wait, him or the cloud he's cloned from? I thought you were trying to make a point about not being them."

"Will you shut up and get to the bridge before it closes?" said Blayde, rising from the dead and ripping the laser pointer out of my hand.

"I still don't know why they're all trying to kill us," I stammered, "and each other, apparently?"

"The abbot created this outpost specifically to prepare for your arrival," said Kizkim. Jesmina had managed to pull her cleaver from the post and swung it at me once more, but this time I hopped over it, bringing my heels down hard on the blade itself. She lost her balance for a split second, and I twisted the blade with a swing of my hips, toppling her to the ground.

"Oh, great, see what Zander was telling you about these monks being on top of things?" said Blayde, halfway to the bridge already.

"Most of us just wanted to see you go, let the library do with you what it wished. But the other half wanted to see you suffer for what you did to us."

"It's not like we can't each take a turn, you know?" said Tresmine, squirming under the grasp of some other guy I didn't know. "You heal. We can all stab you until we get the stabbies out, and then you can go to the library, everything on schedule. It's not like the library is worried about the passage of time."

"I really don't have time to discuss the passage of time in an informational anomaly," Blayde shouted. "Zander, come on, we have to go."

"Thanks for dinner, man," I shouted over the din. "Sorry about the mess."

I jumped to Blayde, and, together, we threw ourselves into the beam of light, only to be swept into atoms along the cosmic web through no control of our own. Which was unsettling to say the least, seeing as how usually one of us was driving. An instant later, we were flung onto the cold floor of what I sincerely hoped was the library, the beam of light flashing out of existence before we could thank it for the ride.

"Blayde?" I called, pushing myself up onto my feet and sweeping my gaze over the empty room. The walls were stark white and barren, giving no indication of where we had landed.

"We're not alone," she hissed, tossing a body at my feet. Kizkim groaned as he rolled over, staring up at us both with wide-eyed terror.

"Oh shit," he stammered.

"Shit is right," I said, placing my boot upon his chest. He didn't resist, didn't squirm. He simply lay there looking up at me, patient, as if knowing I wasn't going to squash him. "What are you doing here, Kizkim? I thought this was a trap?"

"If it were, you'd probably be too smart to fall into it."

"Idle flattery isn't going to get you anywhere," said Blayde sternly.

"Fair enough. Truth be told, I always wanted to come to the library, and they don't open the bridge for just anyone. I'm part of the faction that doesn't give a crap about what you did or did not do, so if we can just go our separate ways, we're fine, okay?"

I removed my foot. He had a point, and in any case, neither of us truly had any say over who visited the library or not. This wasn't the Kizkim I had ended to save the galaxy, just some copy with fake memories and matted blue fur. He gingerly got back up to his feet, inching away from us.

"So, what now?" asked Blayde, crossing her arms and leaning back as she surveyed the room. "So much for a welcome party."

The air hissed as the doors to our small cell slid open. Outside was a dull, gray docking bay, not unlike all the other docking bays in the rest of the universe, except maybe for the ones on Pansus, where their shuttle bays are made entirely out of the dried-out bones of mammals that had once inhabited their planet, always making you crave some kind of jerky.

A man was waiting for us there, dressed entirely in dull gray. His head was completely hairless, eyebrows included; his strange blank eyes stared at us, piercing through us completely He stepped into the room without a sound, even as he tapped on his clipboard.

"Nimien?" I sputtered. The sight of him made my blood run cold, the failure still fresh in my mind, the loss palpable. But the boy was all wrong: his eyes were not the right color, and I knew that gaze well, having seen the life drain out of it not once but twice. He furrowed his invisible brows in confusion.

"I do not bear such a name," he said. "Welcome to the library, Zander, Blayde."

"Thank you," I replied, clearing my throat awkwardly. I couldn't get the resemblance out of my head. "We're here for—"

"Yes, we know why you're here."

I glanced over at Blayde, who only shrugged.

"You must be Kizkim," said the boy. "You should not be here."

"I'm Kizkim's clone. I've come seeking the library's sanctuary."

"Wait here then. We'll have someone process you shortly." He nodded slowly and made a note on his clipboard, which erased in a matter of seconds. "As for you two, follow me."

Damn, I was craving jerky now. Nervous hunger, I assumed, though it was a relatively new feeling.

He led us out of the room, shutting the door behind us. A flash soon followed, though I didn't have time to work out if that meant Kizkim was dead or simply returned to his warring home world. Either way, pretty unfair.

Also, not my problem.

"You said you knew we were coming?" asked Blayde, trotting beside him, hands clasped behind her back to keep them from fidgeting. She obviously didn't care about what had just happened to our fuzzy blue frenemy.

Why did I? Months ago, you couldn't have made me care, even if you had promised me ice cream. But now, the possible death of even my worst enemy was suddenly twisting my non-existent heart into odd knots.

I was even feeling bad for Dave, sitting in orbit around Abryria, never knowing if we'd return for him or not.

Maybe Blayde was right: All that time spent on Earth, lowering guards that had been raised for a reason, replacing survival habits with luxury, had made me weak. Over-thinking everything.

"It is our duty to know everything in the universe," the boy said, eyes fixed straight ahead. He waved an arm at the large door that led out of the hangar bay, indicating for us to follow.

Blayde looked up at me, eyebrows crossed. I nodded. The experience was odd to say the least. But I wasn't the only one to see Nim in those features.

"So, what do we call you?" she asked the boy. "Do you have a name?"

"Of course," he said. "You may call me Monk Randall. Or simply Monk. I am the librarian assigned to your case and will help you to find your reference materials. You will probably not encounter anyone else during your time here, so there will be no confusion."

"Oh, are you the only person working today?" she asked.

"In a way. The library exists out of time, so we're simultaneously working all at once and not at all. Try not to think too hard about it."

"Working hard or hardly working?" I suggested.

"Ah, the ancient Earth proverb. Accurate, in a way. In many more ways, though, not."

"That's my brother. Stuck on Earth for two months, and he comes back sprouting ancient wisdom. Join any cults I don't know about?"

"Shut up."

We followed a polite distance behind him, alert, absorbing everything around us in case we had to make a daring escape. The monk paused at the next door, flipping open a compartment in the wall, entering a code quickly, and the entryway slid open for us to pass through. I committed the code to memory.

"Are all the doors here coded?" Blayde asked casually, glancing around the hangar as if she had never seen one before.

"No one can enter or leave the library without a monk to lead the way. And all of the documents are protected, so they cannot leave this place either. Only copies, if ever allowed. You see, we take security very seriously here. As we know everything that has occurred and is yet to come, we cannot have anyone trying to change the established timeline."

"Uh-huh," Blayde nodded earnestly. We knew full well that we wouldn't need a monk to help us back outside.

"Wait, does that mean we really do live in a deterministic universe?" I asked. "Everything truly is set in stone?"

"No, quite the opposite." Randall shook his head. "Everything that can happen is happening. It is only through observation that the outcome becomes determined. Thus, until the information is seen, all possible outcomes exist at once. Do you understand?"

"Not really. What's the point in having all the information in the universe when reading it renders it useless?"

"Not useless. But you can see why we don't let just anyone in here."

The inside of the library was not as I expected. It was clean and white, with thin hallways crisscrossing this way and that, making it almost impossible for me to get my bearings. Blayde would have the place memorized within minutes, though, which was a relief. The monk led us though what felt like miles of corridors until he finally stopped in front of a door like every other, entering his code on the keypad of the lock, which unlatched to let us in.

It seemed like a small office, though when I say small, I do really mean small. There was only enough space for a desk that held a large monitor on it and a few nondescript chairs. There was a tiny porthole in the back wall, in which was a picture of a small, fluffy animal and the caption "Case of the Gazorpnas."

I guess they didn't have Mondays in a place outside of time.

Randall took a seat, gesturing for to us to do the same. We waited as he booted up the computer, typed in password after password, until he finally looked at us again, fingers poised on his keyboard to enter our every request.

"It's your turn, now. Where would you like to start?"

"I don't know, why don't you tell us?" said Blayde. "Seeing as how you knew we were coming and all."

"This is one of those times where I need you to state your request," said Randall. "Just because we expected you to come doesn't mean we know what you wanted to see within our walls."

I glanced over at Blayde. Once again, this was so simple, the universe finally parting to allow us to reach our goal. It was like with Sally, when all the dominos fell so that she would eventually save a world. The monks had probably engineered that, too. It had surely been one of their kin who brought the prophecy to the people of Aquetzalli and Atlan.

The universe had wanted her there, just as it wanted us here, now. We just had to take our chance and not throw away our only shot.

"We take it you know who we are, then," said Blayde.

"Zander and Blayde. The siblings. The Iron and the Sand. Though you've gone through many different names over the course of history. Yes, I know who you are."

"And you're not going to turn us in to the Alliance at the end of this."

A smile crept up Randall's dull face. "The library takes no sides. We have no intention of releasing you into anyone's custody but your own."

"Then we'd like to see the oldest reference to us there is," she said, readjusting herself nervously on her seat. "The first time we appear in history. We need to know our truth."

"You've come to the right place then." The man continued his relentless typing, his brow furrowing in concentration.

"Wait a minute," I sputtered. "If this library contains all information in the universe except about itself, then how are you meant to find any books?"

The monk sighed heavily. "Very, very carefully."

"That doesn't answer my question. You're either breaking the laws of physics or playing with fire. Not literal fire, but—"

"Zander," Blayde growled, "it's what the nodes are

for."

"In any case, the file you are looking for is so old that to read it thoroughly, you have to see the manuscript itself. The language was impossible to decipher, even by the abbot himself, so it has not been digitized as of yet."

"Is it possible for us to see it in person, right now?" I urged. To my surprise, he nodded.

"I don't see why not." The monk kept his face expressionless, though his voice changed to an excited pitch, like he was going on a field trip. And without even waiting for a response, he rose and left the room, a difficult feat as he had to scoot around us and manage to open the door, all while we scooted so close to his desk we almost collapsed on it.

The truth, so close at hand. For so long, it had been held from us, hidden, believed non-existent, or at least to have faded into nothing over time. And after all this time, all we had needed was the right place to look. Everything was here. Everything was offered to us on a silver platter, without question. The universe finally wanted us to *know*.

"Or is it all too easy?"

"I know," Blayde replied, though I hadn't realized I was speaking out loud. "But we're this close, Zander; this close! You're not going to throw this chance away on a whim, are you?"

"My instincts aren't always wrong."

"They aren't always right either."

I was hurt. Blayde was always the level-headed one. Maybe sometimes she went overboard, but it was always within reason. Although, recently, she had been acting a little more eccentric than usual. I was so focused in having her accept me once again that I had failed to notice that maybe she needed to make an effort too. I couldn't have made her this paranoid.

Or was Blayde right? Was it me, my perception, my opinions that had changed?

But change or no change, it didn't stop me from feeling like something was definitely off. I prepared myself to fight, if I had to.

We followed the monk in a silent procession through the hallways, marching deeper and deeper into the core of the library itself. Finally, our guide stopped in front of a lone door. He reached into a bucket and handed us head-to-toe clean room suits.

"These are our physical manuscripts," he explained, as we pulled the plastic suits on over our clothes. "The rest we keep in virtual format. But these cannot leave the library, whatever the reason. They're being held together with nothing but a prayer. These were hand-written, and most of them have been illuminated. They are more art than record. Some others are too old to decrypt, and yet some the abbot orders us to keep in a hardback copy. He says that the written word is more powerful than any computer's database. So, we keep them here, to be cared for and admired."

"Shouldn't they be kept in a museum?"

"They're safer here. We appreciate them more than the average public would."

The sudden change in architecture wasn't anything we had been expecting. Tall, wooden arches loomed above us, with shelf upon shelf of books of every shape and size to please even the most indifferent reader.

Randall led us through the forest of shelves, into the very heart of the hall itself, where one short half-shelf stood alone, holding only a handful of books. He reached out and pulled out one small sliver of a volume, bound together with primitive techniques in red leather.

"It looks brand new!" Blayde exclaimed in a small, almost reverent whisper.

"Take your time." He checked his wrist watch, though what it could tell him in a library outside of time was a mystery. "I'll let you read in peace. Do not touch the other books in this room. You have no authorization to do so, and I will know."

He left us alone, alone at the carved wooden desk with a simple lamp and alone with our book—the book that would tell us the truth, the entire story of everything, the story of us.

I folded open the first page gently. It was blank, except for a sprig of an unrecognizable plant, drying between the covers. Blayde lifted it to her nose, inhaling deeply before handing it to me.

"Does it smell like home?" she asked, almost pleadingly.

"I can't tell." I tried not to feel disappointed at this. "You ready?" I asked as she caught her breath.

"Ready as I'll ever be." She reached up her hand, and I grasped it, and I turned the first page.

A diary.

In Blayde's handwriting.

Her grip tightened, as together we read.

CHAPTER FIFTEEN

WORST CONTACT

SALLY

They had come back. The Sky People had come back.

Why did I keep calling them that? They had another name, the Youpaf. But saying that the prisoner ship had come back just wasn't as real as realizing that they were the same ones who had once instilled fear upon countless generations of old Earth.

"What the hell is that?" Kyle screamed. The motors of the ship had calmed down to a whine, a low hum, but he still raised his voice as if the sound was a shriek. "Is that a fucking spaceship? Are we going to be abducted? Oh fuck!"

"No tidal waves this time," I muttered, finding myself surprisingly calm. Then again, this had all happened to me before.

"What?" Robin yelled.

All around us, people were screaming, running in circles helplessly, hiding, praying. Which was an amazing feat when you took into account how small this ship was. Robin and I were the only ones who hadn't moved, our eyes riveted on the sky. They clenched their hands into fists.

"Holy fucking hell," they growled. "This is them, isn't it?"

"In the rusty metal flesh," I said. "It's the prisoner ship. I guess some prophecies do come true. It's like 2012, but a few years too late."

"And what do they want from us?" Robin tried to stay calm, yet their breathing was harsh and rapid. This did not bode well for them.

"They're probably still looking for that prisoner they lost years back." I watched the ship hovering above us, blocking out the sun. "The World Eater, they called it, but he went by Zoesh too. Heard of him?"

"Holy shit, Sally!" Robin spat, taking a step away from me. "You knew the Zoesh was on Earth, and you didn't tell me? Veesh! He ate an entire fucking planet, Sally! He burped up a moon!"

"Aliens are about to incinerate us, and you're mad at me?"

"Yeah, I'm mad at you!" They crossed their arms in front of their chest. "When you hear a mass-murdering alien is on a planet, you tell people, okay? Bad breakup or no."

I gritted my teeth. This was the least of my problems right now, the priority being the giant spaceship currently hovering above me. Which, unfortunately, happened to think I looked just like the prisoner they were after.

"Okay, what do we do?" Taylor's breathing was finally under control, their voice was as normal as it could be in such a situation.

"I... I don't know," I said, shuddering. Crap. I really had no idea. I needed Zander here. I needed Blayde. I needed their amazing, last-minute plans. I couldn't do this on my own, not without their knowledge and skills and—

"You have to call Zander," Robin said, saying exactly what I was thinking.

"I can't. You know I can't. There's no way of getting in touch with him, and he doesn't want me around either. No. This is up to us."

"Sally and Robin, defenders of Earth?" Robin scoffed. "Yeah, that's going to work."

"Felling! We need to contact Felling. She'll know what to do. She's trained for this sort of thing."

"I'm not sure the FBI, or whatever, trains their people to deal with alien threats, Sally."

"Do you know anyone else?" I spat, maybe a little too harshly. Okay, a lot too harshly, but there was a spaceship hanging over my head as I was arguing with my ex over whether or not to call their crush. This was worse than it ever had to be.

"No."

"Right," I said. "I need your phone."

"Don't have her number," they said, a little sheepishly. I was impressed; they had indeed made a clean break, and not just from me. Even if they had got Felling to do the whole identity-creating thing.

"Do you have Wi-Fi here, at least?"

"This way."

Now, getting through a ship becomes ten times harder when the people around you think it's the end of the world. Which, of course, it might just be, but there's a bit of decorum we all need to follow in times like these, so, I don't know, maybe those who want to stop us all from dying will manage to do something. In any case, I had to elbow a dude in the face just so I could get through the bulkhead and into the ship.

Robin led me through the tight hallways into a room where the woman from the TV documentary was screaming wildly into a radio. She wasn't making much sense, not through all the sobbing, punctuating every sentence with a muddled cry that sounded like, "pizza, please!"

The computer was shoved into my hands, and I pulled my eyes away from the sobbing woman. Robin tapped the screen wildly.

"Looks like Felling's in the loop," they said, coolly.

Their Skype inbox was full of messages, all from our favorite federal agent. *Call me. Call me. Call me. When you get this, call me.*

"Needy much?" I scoffed.

"How can you be so calm in a time like this?" Robin spat. "They want to incinerate us!"

"Geez, relax, will you? I've seen them before. We can handle them."

I was surprised by how calm I was. I was never cool in situations like this; that was kinda something that defined me. I smiled, realizing that maybe my medication was finally working the way it should be, keeping the panic at bay.

Only now was a pretty rational time to panic.

Call me!

Oh, right. I put the computer down at the desk, ignoring the sobbing scientist, and hit the call button. Instantly, Felling picked up, looking the same as she always did, suave and sophisticated despite the panic in her background. Apparently, our ship was not the only place full of rushing, terrified people in hallways.

"Sally," Felling said, as if expecting me, "is Robin there?"

"Hey," said Robin awkwardly, leaning into frame.

"Good," said the agent, nodding. She was combing her hair back urgently, flattening it tight against her scalp.

"Are you seeing this?" I asked.

"You mean the spaceship?" Felling grinned, almost excitedly, for a whole second before returning to her serious exterior. "Everyone is seeing the spaceship. Every single government in the world is seeing it. The satellites picked it up the second it came into orbit, and we've been monitoring it since. Somehow decloaked in a snap. Any ideas what it is?"

"Sally says she's seen this before," said Robin. "It's some type of prisoner ship, and they're looking for an interstellar fugitive. And if we don't offer them up, then we're toast."

"They've issued threats?" asked Felling, freezing with her hands in her hair. "What kind?"

"Literal toast, Felling," said Robin. "They're going to roast us through and through."

"Ah." The agent went back to combing her hair.

"Right. And Sally's dealt with them before? How? When?"

"It's a really long story."

"Yeah, well, the world's at stake here. Let's not waste time."

I took a deep breath and stole one last glance at the woman with the microphone. She was out of breath now, staring at the radio transmitter with a distant look on her face. I had to shake myself out of it.

"Well, it turns out Zander and Blayde can travel through time as well as space, even though none of us knew it," I said, incredibly quickly, taking in Felling's look of shock in one stride. "We arrived in the ancient city of Aquetzalli about five thousand years ago, and they thought I was some goddess sent to save them from the Sky People, which turned out to be this gigantic prisoner ship looking for this thing called the World Eater or the Zoesh, a huge creature that can change its form. Though when I saw it, it was the size of a stadium, looked like a dinosaur, and lived underground so it could hide from the prison guards. You following?"

"What the ..." stammered Felling. "The extra dimension in our calculations! It was time all along?"

"Don't interrupt," I said. "Focus on the dinosaur. Now, the Zoesh can control people's minds, but after a while, they all end up looking the same, something to do with his preferred human form. He controlled every single one of the emperors on the mainland, which I think now was somewhere in South America. The Sky People or the prisoner ship or whatever you want to call them would burn the planet in search of this creature, so they started to do it where I was—again, just assuming here—somewhere in South America until, somehow, the minute I pointed the ship in the right direction, he just ... disappeared."

"Because that's just what giant mind-controlling, world-eating dinosaurs are known to do." Felling rolled her eyes.

"I pretended to be the Zoesh in human form, so they would arrest me, but then I got possessed by the actual goddess Selena, who's not an actual goddess but the Zoesh's ex who lives in the sixth dimension or something and hangs out on the moon. Only that was after setting their ship to a new course, and they continued on their way, searching the solar system for the Zoesh."

"But it must take thousands of years to circle the system," said Felling, eyes wide. She finished with her hair, all of it pulled back into a professional bun. She tugged the wig on over the top. "They must be pretty malformed from all the, well, incest."

"I tell you a true story about time travel, alien criminals, and giant robots, and all you get out of it is ship incest?"

"Sorry, sorry." She snapped herself out of it. "Too much to take in."

"And if you were wondering," I added, "they used to take the kids from Earth to replenish their gene pool, but I don't know from where. I just know that the people I spoke to were forced to give up theirs. I managed to get them back. They might have stolen from other continents as well."

"Like the story of the labyrinth, the tributes? Maybe

there's a connection?" asked Felling.

"I still can't believe you went to ancient Atlantis." Robin let out a low whistle. "With Zander and Blayde. You have to tell me more."

"Not right now, Robin!" snapped Felling. "We have more pressing matters at hand. Sally, if they still think you're the Zoe or whatever, we can work out a plan. I'm coming to get you. Hang tight."

"I'm the middle of the ocean, Felling."

"Get on a dinghy and get as far away from the ship as possible," she ordered. "Straight west. I will see you in an hour."

"In an—"

But Felling was already gone. I looked up at Robin, who nodded thoughtfully.

"Well, it looks like we're going on a boat trip," they said, a grin drawing up on their face.

"You know how to steer one of those?"

"I can figure it out." They shrugged. "Come on. We have no time to lose."

We ran back up to the deck, leaving the archeologist to cry in the corner. I knew I should have helped her, have said something, but things were heated already as they were. Up on deck, a riot had seemed to have broken loose. Some of the team were fighting over the miniature sub, throwing punches over who would get to ride out the end of the world safely underwater. Robin and I exchanged tense glances.

We avoided the crowd, crouching and making our way around the prow of the ship as quietly as possible. The little boat for the diving team was toward the back of the ship, and the riot was between us and it, which was not ideal. And to make matters worse, the spaceship was still shouting angry slurs at us.

"Give up now, you fat cow!" shouted one person on the loudspeaker.

"Yeah! Your mother was a space whale, and your father was a methane moon!" said another.

"We will burn them all!" said the first one. "I mean it, I really do! We have fire! And lots of it!"

I rolled my eyes before realizing I was the only one here who understood a word they said. Robin gave me a confused look.

"Hurry," they said, taking my hand in theirs. "We don't have much time!"

Why the prisoner ship wasn't acting, I didn't know. Were they actually waiting for the Zoesh—and by extension, me—to give myself up? Or could they simply not see us? Either way, they hadn't attacked yet, and I for one didn't want to wait to test their patience.

Robin and I made a mad dash for the back of the ship, using the rusted artifacts to hide our escape. It seemed to be working. Once we reached the back of the ship, no one was following us, which was a definite win. And there before us was the inflated ship, in all its vibrant orange glory. I climbed right in.

And stepped on Kyle's face.

"What did you do that for?" he snapped, grabbing my leg and giving it a twist. I fell backwards onto the ship, hard.

"Sally!" cried Robin. "Kyle?"

"Where do you think you're going?" he asked. "You do realize there's nowhere to go, right? Horta is 950 km north of here. You don't stand a chance."

"So, what are you doing here, then?" Robin grabbed an oar with both hands, digging their nails into the wood.

"Avoiding the crowd, of course," he said. I pulled myself back up to my feet, wary of what he might do next. "If it's the end of the world, I'm going down quietly."

"With a bottle of Scotch, it seems," said Robin. "You smell like Suds Mckenzie's ass. We need this need this raft and you don't, so move, asshole."

"No can do," he said, and Robin slapped him in the face with the oar. The man toppled backwards, teetering lightly, then fell right over the rail.

"Robin, what the hell?" I stammered, reaching for Kyle, but it was too late. His unconscious body had fallen into the deep, dark ocean below.

"He was in our way!"

"You could have just killed the guy!" I said, leaning as far over the rail as I could go. Nothing. Kyle was sinking like a stone. "We have to save him."

"How the hell do you want us to do that, Sally?" Robin scoffed. "The submarine is currently the source of a minor disagreement, if you didn't already know."

"We can't leave him to drown!"

"Sally, if you want to save the omelet, you're going to have to break a few eggs, or so I think the expression goes. Now come on."

"It's the end of the world. Not everyone is going to be cool with that!"

"He was in our way," they said, climbing into the raft. "Now, are you coming or not?"

I clambered in after them, and Robin winched us

down to the water. All the while, my eyes were fixed squarely on the spot where Kyle had disappeared under the waves. His death had been senseless, meaningless. I looked back at Robin and saw them under a completely new light, and it wasn't a light I liked.

"What's gotten into you?" I asked, my mouth dry. "Who does that?"

They said nothing. Instead, they pulled the cord on the motor and set our little raft in motion. I clutched the sides as we flew across the ocean, our ship growing smaller and smaller in the distance as we did.

The spaceship above us, however, did not. It was so large it barely seemed to move in the sky, as if it was following us as effortlessly as it hovered there. I pulled my eyes away, looking forward. Felling had better have a damn good plan.

I felt it before I heard it: water droplets rising and spraying my skin. The sound, then, mechanical and cold, chilling me to my core. I threw my hands over my ears to block out the growing roar.

"They're here!" I cried, dropping my head between my knees. "They've found me!"

"But they won't get you," insisted Robin, increasing the motor's speed.

We flew across the water, made choppy by the shuttle overhead. The water splashed up from the ocean, and I was drenched within minutes. I didn't care. I wasn't looking. I had stuffed my head down low between my legs and was holding myself together with my hands.

"It's not going to help!" I stammered. "They found me once already! They'll find me again!"

"No, I won't let them," they said.

"They can vaporize entire buildings," I stammered. "They destroyed a pyramid made entirely of gold, Robin."

"What do you suggest we do?" they shouted over the roar of the motor.

"I have to surrender."

"No, you don't."

"It's the only way!"

"Fine! Well then, I'm sorry, Sally. We've come a long way, you and I, but I won't give up so easily."

"What are you ..." I began to ask, but the question was going nowhere. I glanced up from my knees to see Robin stand and strip off their clothes and toss them into the sea. "Robin, I—"

"Goodbye, Sally." They smiled weakly. "I'm sorry it has to end like this. I really did like you, but I need to get away. And, apparently, this planet isn't big enough for that. Please try and survive."

There was a glow of blinding white light, and I closed my eyes to block out the pain. There was no sound except that of a pile of skin hitting the deck of the ship, rubber against rubber. What had been Robin's human body collapsed on the plastic like a limp noodle.

They were gone.

They had abandoned me.

I stood on shaky knees in the plastic boat. Robin had cut the motor, but I hadn't even noticed over the sound of rotors above us. Me now, I guess, since Robin had left their material flesh behind and gone off as a happy-go-lucky patch of sentient haze.

Figures my ex would turn into a literal fart.

I closed my eyes against the salt, raising my hands high above my head. This would be the end, but I was doing what had to be done.

"I surrender!" I yelled over the turmoil, spitting out the salt that stuck in my mouth. "Don't shoot, I surrender!"

Something hit me on the head, hard. I desperately tried to open my eyes, but the onslaught of water on my face made it almost impossible to do so. I stood there, trembling, unable to move. This was going to be the end. I knew it.

"If only everyone would do that when the authorities arrived, the world would be a way safer place." The voice wasn't who I had expected. Then again, the ship's captain had probably been replaced a few hundred times since I last saw him.

"Just arrest me already!" I sputtered. "Get it over with!"

"Why would I do that?"

I opened my eyes, but it wasn't a prison guard who met me; it was *her*. James Felling was hanging out of a helicopter, grinning at me as if I had just told the most hilarious joke she was not allowed to laugh at. "I got here as soon as I could. Hop on."

James was leaning oh-so-casually out of what seemed to be a silvery cross between a helicopter and a jet, which I'm pretty sure the military would deny all claims of existing. Her lips curled into a smile, a twinge of pride for the large entrance she had just made and the effect it had had on me.

"How did you get here so fast?" I stammered as I started to climb the ladder out of my small raft.

"This baby's engineered for speed," she said, and I took her extended hand as she hoisted me into the helicopter thing. "It's not a very pleasant way to travel, but it's as fast or even faster than the Concord. Where's Robin?"

"They ascended to another plane of existence without us," I said. "Or turned into a fart. Either way, they're not joining us."

"What the hell?"

"Right," I cleared my throat, "they were an alien. I forgot they never told you."

"They never ..." James looked completely taken aback at this. "Shit. An alien? They were secretly an alien?"

"You get used to it," I said, as she pointed to my seat then took a second to adjust her hair. "I know I did."

CHAPTER SIXTEEN

CAUGHT READING MY SISTER'S DIARY

ZANDER

Day 7

Red. Everything is so red.

I don't think I've ever seen so much red in my life: red dust, red trees, red sky above us. Red has always been the color of violence and no-goes. Halting and pain. Now it's the color of my liberation. I claim this color as my favorite. No one else can have it.

We've been here for a week, give or take. The days are longer in this place, and the nights even worse. We fall asleep at the wrong time, wake up when no one in the world is stirring. But we're adjusting, slowly. I still get hungry when there's no food to be had, but when there is food, there is so much of it. Fruits and vegetables, and meats from animals I have never heard of before. None of that mush I've been eating until now: protein, curds, and whey.

No one here can explain what happened to us. One minute we were in that room, that terrible room, a silent execution, and then, then we were here. Here in this place with a red sky and red dirt.

I seriously believed the outside world would have a blue sky, a sky like we had seen in pictures and Wednesday-night movies. I guess it's safe to say: I do not know where we are. I don't think anyone does.

The locals say we just appeared in the wilds. One of them saw us flicker into existence, and now they all think we're some harvest omens or something of the sort. We told them—in as many words and hand signs as we could muster—that we were not. I don't think they believe us. At least they treat us really well as a result.

They're nothing like the people at the institute. They dress in animal hides or woven wools, which they dye in many colors, mostly more shades of red. I haven't seen the color white in days, and it don't think I ever want to again.

The people here eat what they hunt or find. It's good, hearty meals. Our stomachs could not handle them the first days, but now we've adapted. We try to help with the cooking; I really like it, honestly. I've never made food before or even seen how it's done. We put a lot of things in big pots over fires.

Fire! More glorious red! I love fire. I want to curl up in it and wear it like a coat. I want to hang embers as jewelry and rival the stars with my own personal flame.

Stars! How could I not mention the stars? The books never do them justice. As soon as the sun goes down, the heavens above turn into the most gorgeous sight in the universe. Hundreds of thousands of candles stretching farther than the eye could ever see. I could stare at them for hours. I want to go there, up there, be among them, shine bright like them, and watch time go by.

The people here have rudimentary paper and ink, and they were kind enough to let me take some for myself. Binding this journal took me days, but at least now I can document everything. Putting it in writing makes me feel like this is real and not a fever dream I'm having as I lay dying on a table under adult supervision.

Still, I must write sparingly. I don't have an abundance of paper, and the point is to chronicle our new lives here, not to dive deep into my psyche and undo the harm that's been done there. That'll be for another day. Once we're settled.

I am so glad I'm not alone. If I had arrived without him, I would never have survived here. We now go by the self-appointed names Blayde and Caesar: I picked mine because I think it defines me, though Caesar (feels odd calling him that) got his from an old book back home. He always did like ancient civilizations. Not that he's really settled on the name.

It's nice to use our play names instead of using them to hide. The pain is over. We are free.

I told him we should be lucky to live in a civilization like that, but he just laughed and said that we predated ancient. I'm scared. What if he's right? Did we travel in time?

Day 63.
(The natives say it's the 5th day of the month of the dog, whatever that means?)

We're fully integrated into the society now. It's amazing how fast we learned the language; it's almost impossible. But obviously now, I know it was only just improbable. The impossible is impossible, apparently. Take it from the girl who popped into existence in the middle of the forest.

Hold on, I just realized we'd never play paradoxes with Tyche again. I wonder where he thinks we are. Sometimes I wonder if we died in that room, and this is what the afterlife is like. I doubt it, though. Not enough angels. I totally want to see angels.

I have to write down their names: Tyche. Sandino. Moira. Apple. The people I'll never see again, people who probably think me dead. Remembering them keeps them—and me—alive.

I'm getting more used to the food here. My stomach never complains about the mystery meat and strange berries anymore, and I'm finally gaining strength. I'm stronger than I ever was, even back when I first had training. I run faster than anyone here, can climb trees in split seconds if I have to. I love it. The freedom of a world without walls. I can't stay still, so every second of my life is devoted to movement.

My arms and legs are thick with muscle. I'm losing the baby fat that coats my belly and thighs. My face is leaner, more angular. I actually like my reflection now.

I convinced some of the men here to teach me their ways of the warrior. At first, they complained of my gender, telling me that my time would be better spent either gathering fruit or washing my hair. So, I chopped my hair off. Right below the ear, in one cut with a blade. The next man who commented on it, I dropped to the ground in seconds. Minutes later, I had a spear in hand, and they were showing me the proper way of handling it. I've never had so much fun!

I feel at home here, more so than back at the institute. Sure, I share a hut with fifteen other women, who apparently really like to spoon, and my only true possession is this book, but I still feel like this is permanent. I want to be here, and I can leave whenever I want—not that there's anyplace else to go. I explored the hills sometime last month but didn't find another camp for miles and miles.

So, this is home.

Zander's fitting in even better than I am—yes, he's Zander now—and he seems to be the center of a whole lot of attention. Men and women love him, especially since he's decided to stop wearing shirts. My brother, ladies and gentlemen. "Brother" sounds like the best word for it.

20th day of the month of the dog
Day 78.

The son of the chief proposed to me today.

I didn't know him. He's not one of the small group of hunters I train with. Probably a good twenty years my elder. He had never spoken to me before, but today he spoke of how an alliance would benefit the tribe. He was strong, and, in his own words, the best hunter. I would make a good wife.

Would I? I never thought of it, back when we lived in the institute. I'd always assumed I would live out my life in those rooms, Zander by my side for however long I would last. I didn't know anyone over twenty back there—except for the Coats—so I planned to die off like the rest of them.

I had never seen myself as a wife, in any way, shape, or form. Never even considered it, seeing as how it was never an option. Wives were for the men in coats who joked about having someone mad at them for missing dinner when a test ran late. Wives were the women in coats with high ponytails and bright rings on their fingers who glared at them when they said that.

I gracefully told the man I would think about it. I said that I wasn't sure how long I would stay with the tribe and how I didn't want to get tied down.

But it's what he answered me that made me fill with rage.

"I assumed that Zander and Zella were an item," he told me. "And that they would stay together here. If he were to stay, you'd need a husband."

Zander and Zella. An item.

The thought was so foreign to me, I zoned out for long enough that the stranger just walked away. What did that even mean? This was all very confusing. I knew they were friends, and she frequently and very openly spoke of how nice his stubble was. What did an item even mean?

After asking around, I learned it meant they were courting. Which means the pre-wife stage. Does that make Zander the pre-wife? It seems a little nicer than just walking up to a stranger and asking for marriage, here's looking at you, chief-boy.

I'm happy for him; he's been smiling so much lately. Though, admittedly, it's weird he didn't tell me any of this.

Maybe I'm just blind.

13th day of the month of the sea-beast
Day 95.

Zander was murdered today.

I woke up to go hunting before dawn and practically tripped over him on the way out of the village. His head was bashed in with a rock. I saw his brain spilled out on the dirt, red mixing with red in the light of the sunrise. The rock that had been used to kill him was sitting just a foot away, covered in my brother's blood.

I couldn't help it. I screamed.

I probably screamed for over an hour and would still be screaming now if I still had my voice. My mind spewed out a hasty drawn-up list of suspects. Zella's father, for one. He hated seeing her with my brother. Or Yana, the wise woman, who kept flip-flopping over whether or not we were divine or demonic. Either way, it didn't matter—Zander was dead.

My cries had woken the entire village, and they came to stare at me and my definitely-not-holy and apparent-ly-entirely-mortal brother. They wanted to move the body out of the road. I wouldn't let them dare. I cradled his broken head, staring at his eyes, eyes that wouldn't close. Their silver green looked so dull without his life to light them up.

He couldn't be dead. Not now. Not when we had finally made it out, when we had made it through. We had escaped; we had a new home. He has a freaking pre-wife. He hadn't died in the institute, and he wouldn't die now. Not here, not ever.

It took the entire village to pull us apart. I keep getting nasty looks, as if this was my fault. They won't let me back into the hut. I don't even know what state Zella's in.

All I know is that whoever did this is going to pay. And I'm going to make them.

7th day of the month of the sea-beast
Day 79.

Well, the revenge plan is over before it really began: Zander's a zombie.

I had found shelter at the edge of the village, near the well. Built a quick and easy lean-to, but the night was pleasant, and I wouldn't be needing it. No, what I needed was a plan of action; I needed to track Zander's killer and kill them the same way they had ended him.

Painfully.

What I didn't expect was for Zander to crawl out of his grave and come and find me.

His head was the same as it ever was, as if the rock never gave him such an enthusiastic greeting. He was covered in his own grave dirt, so red he looked like one of the pots we used to store food. I almost killed him again from fright, but he stopped me. Yes, zombie Zander could speak. I had heard of the undead before, but he assured me he wasn't one of the brain-dead sort;

he was just as scared as I was.

It got worse when we realized he didn't have a heartbeat or a pulse. He showed me how a cut down his arm would sew itself shut before he was even done slicing it; his blood was red and warm, like any living being.

On a hunch, I did the same, taking my hunting knife and etching a line from elbow to wrist. Under the line of blood, my skin was unblemished. I looked up at my brother in shock.

"What are we?"

He didn't know. I didn't even dare to think about what this meant.

So, we took our things, and we left. We couldn't stay in the village anymore, not after what they had done to Zander. Despite me wanting to shove a spike up the ass of his murderer, Zander just wanted to get away quickly, make it better for everyone.

We're on the run now, both of us: zombie, vampire, whatever he is, he's still my brother. And I will figure out what happened to him. What happened to us.

The only way to stay sane is to remember that this is not our home. One day, we will find a place to belong. One day. But for now, we have to run.

As long as we are together, we'll never be lost.

Afterward, we stood there, in silence, Blayde clutching the last page as if it were a rope and she were a kite, hoping to be reeled in from the storm only to find that the weather had made it come loose.

"That's it?"

I couldn't tell if she was surprised or angry or hurt. The three emotions rolled into one, making the hair on the back of her neck rise. I didn't dare step away, not when the same feelings were rolling through me.

And with them, somehow, relief. Relief that I didn't get anything more about the other Zander. The easily-murdered-for-love Zander. The settle-down-with-a-stranger Zander. The lost puppy who just wanted a home.

I was not that man. In fact, I didn't recognize myself at all in those few pages. As Blayde flicked through the rest of the book, conjuring images of odd alien species and worlds we must have visited, I didn't feel any sense of recognition. That, too, was a relief. If I simply kept forgetting the places I'd been before, the universe would remain eternal.

I wondered how many of these species we'd seen go extinct. How many times *I*'d gone extinct.

She landed on a page where I had been sketched in charcoal splendor: without my coat, without my hair, but still, impossibly, me. I barely looked older than a teenager, and my gaze was off, distant. Blayde must have sketched me when I hadn't been paying attention.

I didn't even know she could draw.

"Okay, so that was a complete waste of time." She slammed the book shut, a little too harshly, dust coughing out from the pressed pages. The red leather cover looked remarkably like the one she clutched now, the one hidden inside her breast pocket.

Where had they come from? Two journals, millennia apart. That alone was a bigger clue than anything we had read in that ancient text. Our own ancient history of Blayde.

"We get one name," she growled. I put my hand on her shoulder, but she cringed away before it could land, letting the fingers slip through empty air. "A single, dotty Zella. Who's most definitely dead by now. I guess she was your first, so at least now you'll have something fun to talk about at parties."

"Veesh, Blayde." I stuffed my hands back into my pockets. "You do realize I'm not the enemy here, right? The Zander who was married? That Zander died with Zella, back when the universe was young and our sky was red and we thought we were mortal. So, don't stand here and insult me when I'm here to help. I've always been here to help. Since the very beginning."

Blayde paused, catching her breath—an ironic trait since, technically, neither of us needed to breathe— taking a step back from the book. She didn't look at me, instead scanning the aisles to our left, our right, and finally the tiny shelf beneath the journal itself.

"Hello, what's this?" she muttered, pushing me out of the way so she could kneel and get a closer look.

"Why do you think it's so empty?" I asked. A single shelf, with not even a dozen books on it, the sisters to Blayde's red journal for all these years. She ran a thumb over the titles on spines.

"You recognize them?" I asked, unable to get a good look in edgewise with her taking up the entire space.

"Well, I would recognize an important book title," she said, tapping the spines. "Monk-boy sounded serious when he told us not to. Zander, these are the first books in the universe."

"What?"

"Myths, really. Can't remember where I heard about them. The Ramnolian, Thirbiva, the Sympan ... Zander, the original version of the Karshan is here. The secret historic works at the birth of the universe. If someone were to read these—all these books on the shelf—the answers to life's questions of physics, life, religion, the universe, everything. Not just a cryptic number everyone pretends to understand; actual, palpable answers."

"Okay, now that's pretty cool," I said, glancing around the library to make sure we were alone. "Why do you think your old journal was stored here with them?"

Blayde crouched in front of the well of information she had never even dared to dream of. Not what we had come for, but perhaps even better. I could imagine the glow in her eyes, the voice deep inside her telling her to open one of the books, to learn, to know.

"Randall told us not to touch."

"What, like we can't be trusted with an old book?"

"Um, not really, no," I said, as she pulled out a massive, dark tome. "Look, Blayde, I'm totally fine with the whole book-reading thing, but don't you think some things are supposed to be left unknown?"

"Like our history, you mean."

"What?"

"I know you don't want to know anymore," she hissed, sliding the book open. The pages were old but not billions of years old, so it was a wonder they had made it to the library at all. This place must have begun along with the universe itself. "But it's my turn, Zander. I've been waiting thousands of years to know who I am, and now that I know I can't, I want to know who I can be."

"Okay...not creepy at all."

"I've been protecting you since the beginning. The proof's right here, between the pages of this very book. So, for once, for this one small instance, let me do what I want to do, instead of caring for my stupid, useless brother!"

Her words cut deeper than any knife ever could. And I should know. It had barely been an hour since I had a pipe ripped from my own chest. This hurt like no pain I had ever felt, like Blayde was ripping out a piece of my heart only to crush it between her fingertips.

First Sally, now this. Her eyes locked on forbidden knowledge, words flowing into her mind that no person should ever dare read. It was clear she no longer trusted me or needed me. That I was not an equal in this partnership. Blayde had branded herself the leader, my leader, and was done waiting for me to help.

It was as if the floor I was standing on had ripped open and dropped me in the cold, empty void of space.

And then it got a million times worse because, of course, the most sophisticated library in the universe would know when you were reading its restricted material. Duh.

The monks had us surrounded almost instantly, seeming to walk through the shelves themselves. They carried heavy silver guns—what kind of monk carried a gun?—but Blayde didn't see them, her eyes were taking in as much from the book as she could, locked on the paper, impossible to tear away.

"Well, what a nice surprise to see you here," came a voice from nowhere and everywhere, punctuated by a small chuckle. My already twisted stomach lurched. That voice, it simply could not be. The gentle tone almost musical, like he was about to burst into song. I never thought I would hear it again. It couldn't be; no, it was impossible. It was the voice of a dead man.

As if in a trance, Blayde pulled herself away from the book. She shook slightly, like someone had plugged her into the main grid. She had recognized the voice too. She knew where it was from. Slowly, her eyes rose from the page to lock on those of the speaker. Their eyes locked, and her jaw dropped.

And mine did too.

I never expected to see him again. Not after I had seen his body engulfed in flames. After I had cried over his death, drank in his memory. But here he was, all grown up, taller, his features sharper. His dark hair had grown and covered his entire head. He was lean and muscular, wearing a shirt and pants just one shade of gray darker than his people, the monks flocking around him, protecting him from us.

But neither Blayde nor I dared to move. We were too shocked to act, which hadn't happened to us since that time a certain war hero had turned out to be an actor, thanks to Alliance programing.

But it's that kind of deep-set shock you get when you see someone you watched die is now definitely not dead.

"You found your way back here," he said gleefully. "Which iteration? Where are we in the timelines?"

But we said nothing. He looked so casual about this, smiling like this was his birthday and we had brought him presents.

"I take it from your shocked faces that you know who I am." His smile widened into a sneer. "Oh, how long I've waited for this!"

And with that, Nimien raised his arms and shot us both in the face.

CHAPTER SEVENTEEN
SALLY WEBBER GOES TO WASHINGTON

SALLY

Felling slammed the door shut on the abandoned lifeboat and the pudgy pile of skin Robin, formerly Taylor, had left behind. The momentum forced her back onto her seat, a hand already reaching for the buckle before the pneumatic hiss died out. She smoothed her shirt with a steady hand.

"Sanders," she said, snapping her head in the direction of the cockpit, which was less of a cockpit and more of a curtain. "Rendezvous point omega. And make it snappy: the world might be ending."

If the pilot replied, I didn't hear them, as every sound in the universe was drowned out by the roar of the ship's engines coming to life. The aircraft rose vertically in the air, forcing me down into my seat. Outside the windows, water swirled around us, curling up as if there was no gravity at all. We were inside a typhoon, a wall of ocean pushing us into the sky.

And then we were off.

To say the craft shot forward like a bullet would be an overused analogy. Instead, we *were* the bullet, fast enough to tear through the universe itself. My teeth rattled in my head, threatening to drop out. The vibration was so strong I was sure I would shake into dust.

Then there was Felling, seemingly fine with the G force, crossing her arms and leaning back in her seat as casually as if the speed were nothing, not even an inconvenience. Not a hair out of place.

"ARRRREEE YOUUUUU GOOOIOIIING TO TELLL ME WHERRRRRRE WEEEE'RRRRREEEE GOOOOIIIIIINNNNGGG?" My teeth chattered with the force of the ship. It was nearly impossible for me to speak, let alone hear myself talk over the roar.

I needed to barf. And I needed to barf *bad*. But every time it came up, the force of our acceleration pushed it right back down my throat.

Felling put a finger up to her lips. Of course, she was the smart one. No talking was better. I leaned back into my chair and tried to make myself comfortable. The ship itself was a rustic version of the hoppers we flew on during the *Traveler* incident, so it wasn't like this was my first rodeo.

Strange, me getting used to this. I never expected this weirdness to become so ... banal.

It only took an hour for us to hit coastline, though

it felt like much longer than that. I could tell we were flying over solid ground when the sound of the motor changed. I understood now why people called them choppers, even if this craft wasn't like anything else out there.

We landed in a place with sun; that was all I could tell by looking out the window. The water droplets were still there, coating the plexiglass and refracting sunlight into my eyes. I closed them, lifting my hands to brush my hair back into place. My entire body still shook as if the craft hadn't stopped moving at all.

Felling stood up and slid the door open with ease, revealing a bright green lawn, so vibrant the color almost hurt my eyes. She jumped out, and I realized she was wearing heels.

"Are you going to stand at all?" she asked, turning back to look at me. "It's going to be terribly difficult to get you to the situation room if you don't. Don't worry, the initial shock will wear off as soon as you take a few steps. It only pulverized bones in the prototype."

Dazed as I was, I somehow managed to unbuckle my seatbelt. That alone felt like a gigantic effort, like my hands were encased in lead. I did, however, manage to stand, grateful for my comfortable sneakers in a time like this.

I love you, chucks.

I grasped the edge of the chair for support, still wobbly. Felling made a face.

"What?" I snapped. "Not standing fast enough?"

"That and your outfit," she said, coolly. My dusty cargo pants and T-shirt were nothing compared to her immaculate suit.

"So, I'm slow to recover and have poor fashion sense," I said. "You can add that to my file."

"Oh, trust me, we already knew." She laughed. "No, no, no. We're going to the White House. You need a suit. Cute skirt, heels. And a hairbrush."

It was only then that I recognized the lawn. The perfectly manicured lawn. The roses I had seen so many times on TV.

I looked up from the ground and found myself staring at the White House, way closer than I had ever seen it before. There wasn't a fence between it and me this time.

I did the only logical thing: I fell right back down on my seat.

"The White House?" I said, the shock not yet reaching my vocal cords. "Why?"

"Because of the aliens, I would suspect."

"But why bring *me* here? I mean, I'm not supposed to be anywhere near these people. I'm not a government official. I'm just a nobody girl from—"

"A nobody girl who apparently can tell what the aliens want from us," Felling insisted. "Lewis, get over here!" She hollered to a soldier I hadn't noticed before. "Get me safe box 334."

The soldier saluted and jogged away, leaving me sitting alone in the craft while Felling paced outside. I stared at her in awe, the wheels in my head turning.

"So, the White House," I stammered. "Apparently, alien invasion movies have it right? The US are the ones with a plan of action?"

"It's complicated," said Felling. "On paper, the UN has a course of action, a protocol we all need to follow.

But faced with an actual invasion, what we're seeing is a lot more of each country for themselves. We're going to video conference with the UN in a bit, but first we need to be sure to put America's interests, well, first."

"And you, in all this?"

Felling shrugged gently. "I don't always get a lot of respect. But when the aliens do come, each government finally has need of me. But now, they need you more."

"So, what do I call you?" I asked, as politely as I could. My voice still shook slightly. "We're in Washington; I can't keep calling you Felling."

"You can," she said, smiling politely at my childish questions. "But I don't mind James between friends."

"Friends," I repeated, a question as well as an assertion. I guess, after all we'd been through, we were technically friends. I mean, on this planet, my friends could be counted on one hand: Marcy, Dany, and Arthur, greatest mailman in the world. Even Robin had left the station. I hadn't seen the off-worlders since our night in the field.

So, what did that make James? And why on earth would she want me as a friend?

Maybe she just needed someone to talk to about this, about space and aliens. Someone to connect her with Zander and Blayde, to tell her that her research was a valid, tangible thing. She didn't seem the type of woman who needed friends, but then again, who doesn't? And I guess she really was a friend, as I was to her, just so she could share her alien findings with someone since her line of work didn't give her many allies.

But now with the ship hovering above the Atlantic, all this was about to change. She would finally be taken seriously. She would be called on for her expertise around the world. And it was in times like these that she needed to keep her friends as close as she could.

"The safe box, Agent Felling." The guard returned, holding a large black briefcase, the kind with metal sides and clasps.

"Thank you." James took it off him and handed it to me. I staggered under the weight, while James had barely flinched. "Get changed. We've got a meeting to go to."

"Changed? I thought this was an emergency. Do we have the time?"

"You know as well as I do how much appearance matters in these things. But be quick about it." She shoved the box into my hands, urging me to the back of the aircraft as she shut the door. A light turned on automatically overhead. The soft orange reminded me of the hopper on Nim's planet, when we had met Two and Crandle was…

I pulled my focus back on the box. Hurry, Sally, hurry. Inside was everything I could possibly need. The suit fit me almost perfectly, and I slipped on the simple black shoes and pulled my hair back into a bun. The elastic was even included in the box; they had thought of everything.

"Do I look okay?" I asked as I exited the craft.

"You look fine. Now come on. We're going to be behind in the briefing." She extended an arm to point the way, and we strode across the White House lawn with a fully armed escort.

The White House lawn. My feet brushed against the blades of grass, grass on a lawn the presidents strode every day. All the history here, just beneath my feet. I trembled as I walked. All that history could be reduced to ash if I didn't play my part right.

"First time in DC?" asked Felling, noting my trembling hands.

"No, but last time was a school trip," I said. "Though we never got to see the White House. Post 9-11 and all that."

"Remind me to get you a visitor's pass when this is all over," she said, "so you can take your time to see the place. It's gorgeous. Did you know they have a bowling alley?"

"Seriously?"

"Well, a bowling lane. And a home cinema."

I felt as if I were dreaming. This afternoon was so absurd. I watched the president's puppy rolling around in the tulips in the garden as the First Lady scowled at it, her eyes focused on the animal and ignoring the soldiers completely, as if she were used to all the commotion or just didn't want to see us. I wondered if she was in the loop about the alien spacecraft.

"So," I started, awkwardly, leaning in as close as I could, "what exactly are you?"

Felling shook her head, a small smile forming at the corner of her lips. "Are you asking me if I'm pulling a Robin on you?"

"Oh gosh, please tell me you're human. I'm tired of everyone just up and changing species on me."

"Yeah, me too."

"I mean… you're not really FBI, are you?"

"You catch on fast."

Felling looked up at me, her eyes sparkly with wild

excitement. She grinned, showing all her teeth in a way that said more than her words ever could. I didn't know which branch of government she worked for or if I should be scared right now, but the power that radiated off her was enough to say I shouldn't ask questions I didn't want the answers to.

"It might have something to do with the helicopter thingy." I pointed back at our ride. "It's not every day you see something so ... not from Earth."

"Reverse engineered," Felling scoffed. "But still American-made, thank you very much."

The white steps led us up to elegant hallways, gorgeous paintings on every wall. This was the White House, the actual White House, and I was five minutes away from meeting the president.

I didn't know what made me so nervous. I had met so many important people in the past month, I lost track: mayor of Da-Duhui, Captain Kork, emperor of ancient Earth, all that. I ran this all through my mind, trying to calm my rising nerves as we rode the elevator far down into the Earth. I hadn't been down this deep since I had climbed into the Cave of Ordeals, only this time I wasn't a goddess; I was the unknown friend of a government agent who was never taken seriously—not a big foothold to get things done.

"Clip this to your lapel," James ordered as she handed me a badge with my name and photo on it. The subheading *Expert on Extraterrestrial Activity* was printed boldly in red, making my heart flutter. I guess having a few alien friends suddenly made you an expert in these things.

"Now, in there, only speak when you're spoken to

and no jokes. Nothing. We're in crisis mode here, okay?"

"No problem. I've been through this before. Only then, I could say things like 'I will strike you down with a lightning bolt!' and I was taken seriously."

"We're going to have a lot to talk about once this is over," she said, clipping on her own badge. "Remember, you're an expert, and they're counting on you. *I'm* counting on you. Heck, it seems the whole world is counting on you."

Talk about no pressure.

She pushed open the door to an empty room.

"Are we early?" I glanced down the elegant wooden table, dappled in the evening sunlight. All the chairs were in place, not a speck of dust on the table. If there was an alien summit here, it was over hours ago.

"Shit," said Felling, dropping her hands to her hips.

"Agent Felling! Hullo!"

An out-of-breath staffer ran down the hallway toward us, waving his arms wide. By the time he reached us, Felling's expression had soured.

"So?" she asked. "Spit it out, man."

"You are invited," he said, panting heavily, "to lunch."

Felling's eyes went wide.

"Lunch? But it's… four." she said, incredulously, as if the mere invitation wasn't the most absurd part of his sentence.

"You are invited for *sushi*," the man insisted, making the most obvious wink in the history of winking. I would have assumed it was some off-putting remark of some kind, if Felling didn't audibly gasp at that moment.

"You mean——" Her eyes flashed up and down the

hallway. "You mean, someone forgot to order online?" She reached back and ripped my ID tag from my lapel, shoving it into the staffer's hands.

"Sally," she said, as we followed him away from the fancy situation room, "I really hope you like raw fish."

The good news from all this was that I finally got my lunch. The bad news was I had to get back in the cargo pants.

The first time I met the president in person, he was stuffing his face with California rolls.

My experience with alien invasions was limited to being a goddess that one time and everything I had seen in movies. I imagined being surrounded by uniformed generals, nervous politicians, and the president himself, chewing on the tip of a pencil to calm his nerves. They would all seem to be in a big debate until the door behind us would slam shut, silence falling on the room, all eyes turning toward us in hope of good news.

Instead, we sat around a conveyor belt in a futuristic-looking sushi shop, men and women in ill-fitting tourist shirts getting the better rolls before they even reached me. If I stared hard enough, I could make out the shape of holstered weapons under the loose-fitting shirts of those along the perimeter of the room, looking everything like American tourists on Capitol Hill.

But instead of discussing which Smithsonian

museum to visit next, they were trying to stop the end of the world.

If I didn't know who they really were, I would never have guessed they were the top military figures in the nation. Let alone the world. As Felling explained it—translating the snippets we got from the exhausted staffer—the president didn't want the UN knowing he was convening his cabinet before meeting with them about the alien ship. It had shown up on NASA sensors before anyone else—something to do with frequencies and cloaking devices, which would probably have made a lot more sense if it wasn't third-hand information—and we were supposed to report those findings immediately.

Which, of course, doesn't happen in real life because politics and whatever.

Therefore, this wasn't a cabinet meeting. It was an "extended lunch break." The president taking his favorite officials to lunch, mid-afternoon. But it was dangerous having these highest-ranking men and women all in one place, so we had to look as inconspicuous as possible. Half an hour had also been wasted in deciding which place everyone wanted for lunch, as Marge, who usually took White House lunch orders, was home with the flu.

There was a lull in the conversation when we had slipped into the restaurant, but we apparently checked out because we were seated at the very end of the conveyor belt. The debate resumed, the generals and admirals around us pretending we didn't exist.

"We need to think about removing any *spice* from the *wasabi* before we even think about talking to them."

"How do we know if they're really from *Japan*? It could be a hoax from another *island nation* trying to make us loose our holding."

"No, wouldn't the *wasabi* be in the United States if that was the case? It seems to be stuck over the ... Atlantic site? Is that what we're calling it now? Is that politically correct?"

The two men closest to us pointed at maps of the city, putting on a grand show for the people outside. Felling, looking much less at ease now that she was out of the suit and wearing a Faded Glory shirt she had grabbed from one of the tourist vendors outside, tried to join the conversation, to no avail.

"My god, does this roll have a banana in it?" The president stifled a cry from the other side of the restaurant. "Who does that?"

"Is that code for something?" hissed the man beside me. "I'm sorry, I'm not up to date with restaurant protocol."

"No, but if he calls for oysters, we have to start singing *happy birthday* and give him enough time to escape out the back," said the general.

"Roger."

"Asking for Roger indicated you think someone at the table is an imposter."

"Who comes up with this stuff?"

The general rolled his eyes, taking some salmon sashimi from the conveyor belt. "The big cheese."

The man in question—the president, I think—was getting more flustered by the second. Even from this side of the room, the red of his face was evident.

"It's better than anal probing!" he cried, dropping

all pretense of speaking in code. Unless this was also code, yet somehow ten times worse. "They've been here before, to abduct, experiment, and to probe! Forced mating like we're lab rats!" The restaurant went silent. "It's just like the movie *Signs*. First, we get the crop circle, then the aliens arrive! They're coming here next, mark my words. They're coming to Virginia!"

You know when something is so absurd, and you do a spit take? Just blast the air before you with a wave of whatever you were last drinking? Unfortunately, I hadn't been drinking anything, so what I spat out must have been a combination of mucus and my own lungs. Which, of course, led to a massive coughing fit, which, of course, led me to drinking huge gulps of the water in front of me before realizing it wasn't my glass. The man knowledgeable in restaurant code etiquette extracted it from my hands.

"Is she *with the tour*?" asked the president. I didn't need a code translator for that one. And then, of course, the president was talking to me as I was still trying to dab gobs of water off my face, the teacher catching their student in deep conversation at the most important moment of the class.

James, somewhere between frustrated and terrified, rose to her feet. I followed suit.

"Sally, meet Robert," said James, leading me to the end of one of the plastic tables. "Robert, this is Sally, the friend I told you about."

The man dabbed his face before turning to greet me, and my heart jumped into my throat. There he was: the president of the entire nation, and he had a spot of soy sauce on his Smithsonian T-shirt.

"A pleasure, sir." I held out my hand to take his. It was already shaking before he made contact, and there I was, shaking hands with the president of the United States, and no one was there to take a picture. Shame.

"Ah, so you're the young lady with, what did you call it, James? Insider information?" He didn't seem all that happy to see me, though my outburst was probably to blame for that.

"That she is, sir," James replied firmly. "She knows everything there is to know about our guests."

"I wouldn't put it that way," I muttered, heat going to my cheeks. "But I met them once. It's a long story."

"Then, please, don't waste our time. Explain."

I wondered if maybe I should sit, if there was some way to get rid of this awful feeling that anything I had to say would screw everything up. All eyes in the sushi shop war room were on me, my own planet in jeopardy. And I could not let them down the way I had let down the people of Aquetzalli and Atlan.

"These aliens aren't here for probing, science experiments, or anything like that. They're looking for an escaped convict. A creature called the Zoesh," I explained, clutching my hands and speaking from my gut. "A shapeshifter. But they won't stop at anything to catch him. Last I saw them, they scorched half the planet."

"Did no one tell her the code?" a man in a Washington Nationals jersey hissed.

"I'm pretty sure everyone is still buying it, Stephen."

"Wait, can you go back?" asked another. "Last time? When were they here before?"

"About five thousand years ago, the same time the

lost city they are now above was submerged under the waves."

"Five thousand?" Murmurs were exchanged through the room, and it was obvious I was making no sense to them. The sushi continued to roll down the tables, the ramble of the treadmill filling the room. I stopped waiting for permission and grabbed a chair, pulling it up to the president.

"Well, this is a complete and utter waste of time," the president muttered, reaching for his glass. I'm pretty sure it wasn't iced tea in there, though he gulped it as effortlessly as if it were. He pulled his other hand out of his pocket, revealing a stress ball in the shape of a happy orange turtle. "Remind me, who exactly is this woman?"

"You think I'm wasting *your* time?"

I reached into my pocket, at the same time as I reached deep inside of myself. Reached into the moments where I had felt so helpless. The moments I had faced creatures bigger and more terrible than a mere president, creatures that could have killed me but I escaped. I reached into the part of me that clung to the painter's suits in the airlock, never letting go. That part of me had been hiding for so long, but now it was going to come out and come out strong.

I pulled out the phone, moving my thumb through the pictures to pull out the one I took of the ship as I walked back to the golden temple after the incident in the cave. I placed it on the table next to his wasabi, leaning in close.

"I am Sally Webber," I exclaimed, "and a few weeks ago, I left Earth. I have seen the universe up close and personal, seen cultures and races that would make your hair curl. I traveled through time, and I protected the Earth of old. An ancient evil is back, and I know how we can stop it. Believe me or don't believe me, I don't care, but I won't fail this planet. My home needs defending, and I'm going to be there for it, with you behind me or not."

He scrolled through with a ginger thumb. The pictures of the Youpaf ship sitting atop the glorious golden pyramid, the face of the Zoesh as I used my flash against him, even the drunken selfies on the beach during the bonfire. Everything, my past laid bare.

There was no going back now.

"This could have been photoshopped." The man in the jersey beside him stared over his shoulder, scowling.

"Carl, it's been three hours," snapped a guy from across the room. "The media doesn't even know the ship is here yet."

"But this gold pyramid in the background ... Where is it now? Why haven't we found it yet?"

"Because they destroyed it," I explained. "In one second, the pyramid was reduced to dust."

"We have to nuke them *now*. We don't stand a chance next to those kinds of weapons!"

"I doubt they can be nuked."

"Remind me how you somehow traveled in time?" the president demanded, intent. "Which country are you from, exactly, and how long have they had this technology?"

"I—" I sputtered, but James jumped in right in time.

"She got a lift from an extraterrestrial we've been tracking for some time now," she interjected. "A

257

humanoid who goes by the name of Zander."

I cringed. I didn't want his name in the hands of the men in power, but, then again, he wasn't coming back anyway. Wave the name around like a flag all you want, Jamsey.

"And where is this extraterrestrial now? We could use his insight."

"He's not on Earth at this moment. And we don't have him on radar either."

"Fine. But I want tabs on him as soon as he's Earthbound again." The president turned back to me. "So how did you stop them last time?"

"I told them I was the Zoesh in a human form. With the help of a friend, we beat them up from the inside and sent them on their way."

"Can we do it again?"

"I doubt it. They'll probably take more precautions this time."

That, and there was still no sign of Selena coming to help, and I wasn't going up there without reinforcements. Not unless I wanted it to be a very short trip.

"So, what do you suggest?"

I had absolutely no idea. These were some of the most powerful men and women on the planet, yet every eye was on me. I wasn't a leader. Or a soldier. I was just someone who had hit an alien with her car.

"I think we need to find the real Zoesh and give it up to them," I sputtered. A basic plan, an obvious one. But an essential one.

"But what tells us it hasn't died since last time?" a stranger warned. "I mean, it's been thousands of years."

"Couldn't we just ask them to leave our planet?

We're not doing anything wrong. They can't scorch us just because they can't find their convict."

"It's a generational ship." I rolled my eyes. "They've been raised for one thing and only this one thing: to search every planet in this system for this creature and kill it. I sincerely doubt they'll back down, even if we ask them politely."

"We have to work under the assumption that the Zoesh is still alive," the vice-president assured, nodding furiously. I hadn't recognized him until now, probably due to the fact I'd never seen a picture of him out of a suit, and here he was in an "I heart DC" tee that was much too small for him.

"What does he look like?" I was asked.

"Again, he's a shapeshifter. He takes over any form, controls it like a puppet," I explained. "His true form is gigantic, but he escaped last time by shrinking down, which would have severely weakened him. When I last met him, he said he needed a protector and a voice. The protector stays near the form, and the voice wants to gain as much power as he can. So, he could be anyone. But he's probably someone famous or at least well known. From what I could tell, the beast was a little addicted to the limelight."

The cabinet exchanged worried, accusing looks. For all intents and purposes, they looked like a big all-American family who couldn't agree on who was going to foot the bill. They were taking my story incredibly well, though, for people who didn't know aliens existed until a few hours ago.

"Don't worry," I said in my most reassuring voice, though it wobbled as uneasily as I did in heels. "The host tends to look like he's taken from the same mold as all the older hosts. I'll be able to recognize him."

"So, what now? We look at every celebrity's photo to find the voice? How is that supposed to work?"

A hand clapped on the president's shoulder, and the president turned away, shielded by one of his Secret Service men with his hand on his holster. It was only then that we noticed the RipCurl security all standing and the commotion outside as people took to the streets. No one was looking at the shop, not hardly. They were all focused on something in the opposite direction, something that had them all with their phones out, either texting or taking photos.

No one stopped me as I walked to the window. No one got in my way as I pressed my hand to the glass, staring up at the pink-and-purple sky to see the clouds parting in the wake of a massive bow.

I knew deep in my gut what was happening. I hadn't wanted to believe it, but here it was, following me all the way from Aquetzalli to Atlantis to America.

"I know what needs to be done," I said, my mind resolved, yet dumbstruck by the truth of it.

Silence. Could they see the ship from their seats at the table? Did they know? Did they want to pretend it wasn't happening?

"They tracked me here. I don't know how, but they followed me from Atlantis to Washington. They still have on file that I was the face the Zoesh adopted last; even if that was a lie, they've had thousands of years to sit on it. The only thing that can be done is for me to go to them and give myself up."

CHAPTER EIGHTEEN

THE ABSOLUTELY UNEXPECTED TERRIBLE DAY

ZANDER

There are worse things in the universe than being tied to a chair; being tied to a chair by a person you thought was a friend is one of them. Being tied to a chair by a friend you also thought was dead is quite near the top of the list.

I regained consciousness just as my body finished healing, the bullet cold against my face as my re-sealing muscles pushed it out. It toppled off my lap and onto the floor, making a sharp tinkling sound as it rolled away. That was followed by a second metallic sound as Blayde's face finished healing itself too.

"You're slow," said Nimien, putting down his watch. "Your return from the dead is two-point-five percent reduced compared to the norm. What have you eaten in the past two days?"

Neither of us wanted to answer. Neither of us *could* answer; few things took us by surprise. Calling this encounter surprising was an understatement.

"Nimien?" Blayde was the first to speak, surprise layered so thick in her voice that you could spread it on bread. "How are you ...? I watched you die, Nimien."

But it was Nimien standing in front of us: older, more sure of himself, but Nimien all the same. Not to mention he had hair now. The expression he wore was of a child who had found an ant he was preparing to burn with a magnifying glass. This was Nimien—but not the Nimien we had known.

"I saw it happen," I said, as if saying it would make sense of the memory. "I watched the arrow pierce your heart. I watched your body go up in flames. We had a memorial. We mourned you, we—"

My voice was becoming shrill now, too harsh for my liking. I snapped my mouth shut, waiting for Blayde's reproach, but it would never come. There were far more pressing matters.

I had to remove myself from the situation, to remove myself from the memory, the pain. We were seeing Nim alive, but we were still tied to chairs. The fact he had defied death didn't mean we could ignore the situation we were in. I was bound to the chair by my hands and legs. It wouldn't be easy to wiggle out of, but I could break a thumb if need be. I glanced to my right, trying to gauge where Blayde was. She was bound, as I was, to an ornate metal chair.

The room was small, all white walls like the rest of

the station, the floor tiled white to top it off. We could have spotted a speck of dust from a mile away, if there had been any.

Not only was there no dust, but there weren't any doors either. Now this was fun.

Nimien's gray clothes struck a sharp contrast with the stark white room. His guards at the back blended in only slightly better with their lighter-shaded clothing. Oh, and they held guns, which wasn't too reassuring.

Nimien placed his hands on the table before him, making the impression of criminal interrogation even more realistic. Until now, he still hadn't said a word. No, "how are you guys," no, "long time no see," no, "ta-daa, I'm alive." Nothing.

To make matters worse, Nimien was starting to remind me of someone else. Why did someone so familiar feel so unfamiliar? I shook the thought out of my head. I had to stay focused.

"How are you alive, Nimien?" Blayde finally asked, her voice devoid of emotion. "Not that I'm not happy you are. I am, but—"

Nim snapped his fingers, the sound like the snap of a whip echoing off the walls. His monks turned and left in complete silence, fading through the walls as if they were nothing. When the room was finally empty, Nim walked to the front of the table, sitting down on its edge. He refused to make eye contact.

"I'm surprised that you're surprised." His voice was airy and calm, like the monks of this place. How he kept his composure, I would never know. "Seeing as how you never had the decency to come back and check on my body. As you decided to save your own immortal skins, without a care for those who actually needed saving. You left me for dead. You should have known this day of reckoning was coming."

I would have laughed if I could. Not a laugh of joy, but of complete confusion and exhaustion. This was more than one mind could handle.

"How could you possibly think we'd abandon you like that?" I asked, trying to remain calm, but it was a struggle. "I watched you die. I watched you burn with an arrow through your heart. There is no coming back from that, I assumed—"

"You assumed, did you?" he spat, bringing his hand down hard on the table. Only then did he finally lock eyes with mine. For the first time in my eternity, I was faced with a stare that made me want to shrivel up and hide. "You weren't even sure!"

"You were dead and Sally was dying!" I had felt fear, actual fear, as the warriors closed in on us, as the spears started to fly. Sally could have died, and it had put me on edge. Made me irrational. Made me miss something as obvious as Nim still being alive. "I made the call. You understand that, right?"

He broke away, turning to place both hands on the table, leaving his exposed back to us. If we had been loose, now would have been the time to strike. But strike at what? Our friend?

"This isn't about Sally," he snarled. "It was never about Sally with the two of you. She was interesting while she lasted, wasn't she? And you"—he spun around, pointing his lean, perfectly manicured finger at Blayde—"you wouldn't have given a flying fuck if she had died that day. So long as nothing gets in between you and your mighty brother, you'd let the universe go down in flames."

"That's not true!" She would have bitten his finger clear off if he hadn't pulled it right back.

"Oh, but it is," he said, showing his teeth. "I own the largest repository of information anywhere in space or time. I know it; I've been *everywhere*. And I have everything ever written about the two of you. Want to hear your best hits? How many planets you've destroyed, lives you've taken?"

"Nimien," Blayde said coolly. "What exactly are you accusing us of?"

"You do know none of that is true," I added. "And what makes you think you would have done anything differently? That you are any different?"

"I was the only one of us who truly cared about her!" He was almost screaming now, as though he had this on his chest for years, building up pressure so it needed to be released. "I would have done anything for her, unlike *you*!"

"Stop that!"

"She cared for me too!" He crossed around the table placing himself in front of me and glaring down, his eyes burning holes in my face. "You had to drag her away from me kicking and screaming!"

"You know better than I that if I had left her there, she would have died!"

"You didn't even give her a chance to see for herself if I was truly dead or not! And obviously, I'm not."

"We didn't know that then!"

"You just wanted an excuse to drag her around the universe with you so you wouldn't get ... lonely."

"That's a lie!"

"And why's that?"

"Because I love her!"

When I say silence fell on the room, I mean it fell like a whale dipping out of the sky. The resonating crash left my ears ringing, burning. I could feel Blayde glaring at me, staring daggers into my chest. I knew in that moment I had betrayed her, so completely and totally. I was lost to her.

Expressions flickered on Nimien's face like the changing of channels. First, shock, his brows raising high; then, amusement, a lip curling upward. And finally, anger, as he brought his fist to collide with my face.

And that's when I felt a sensation I hadn't known in who knows how long: pain.

I let out a scream as his fist pushed teeth out of my face. I never feel pain. It's a signal sent to the brain to alert you that you are in danger, so being me means there is never any danger to signal. I stared in awe at Nimien, feeling the blood dribble from my jaw, my mouth throbbing. So, this was what it felt like to hurt.

I had felt worse before.

I snarled back at the man Nimien had become, the selfish man consumed with rage, consumed by simmering feelings turned bitter and burned. He wiped the blood from his knuckles onto his pants, leaving long red streaks down his thigh.

"Sally would have loved to hear that, wouldn't she?" He leaned against the table. "Yet where is she? Dead on Irving? On Anthea? Jana-3?" He paused for a second, waiting for an answer that didn't come. "You brought her home, didn't you? After all the lies and life-threatening situations, you actually managed to bring her home. I guess there is *one* good thing you did for her. How relieved she must be that you stopped dragging her through danger." Again, no answer. I could feel my teeth beginning to grow back, a familiar feeling, but this time, it was accompanied by a wave of what must be nausea as they pushed through the tender gums. "Won't she be happy to find out I'm still alive? And won't she just love a nice, friendly shoulder to cry on when she learns about your untimely death?"

"You can't kill us," Blayde finally said, though without the vigor she had minutes before, only a sad, resigned voice of a child being told off.

"Well, she doesn't know that."

"What the hell have you become, Nimien?" I couldn't take it anymore. This odd, twisted version of the brilliant boy I knew put me on edge. It was like looking into a mirror world—trust me, I had been to quite a few, one of which the void of space was deep pink, which was surprisingly cool—and finding the alternate version of your friend there. A monster in the place of an innocent child.

"Haven't you figured it out by now, Zander?" Nimien grinned, beaming. He held out his hands almost peacefully. "I am you."

"Come again?" Blayde snorted. "Cut the cinematic bull crap, and just tell us what's going on. Can't you tell we haven't been following any of it?"

"Well, let's start at the very beginning," he said. "Do you remember when you gave me blood back on Earth?"

"We never went to Earth with you," Blayde

answered, confused.

"Oh, I'll get to that part soon."

"If you're asking," I interjected, "yes, I do remember saving your life during the Sky People incident." I was regretting that spur-of-the-moment decision to save what I thought was a decent human being. But you can't take back actions. You can't unravel the spool of time.

"Well, a funny thing about your blood." He seemed excited, no, happy to tell us a fact that made him smarter than us. "It's restorative when it's mingled with our own. The blood won't leave the system; it becomes part of who we are."

"But what does that mean? You got cut back there. You weren't regenerative."

"Until you give the regenerative cells a nice jump-start."

If the room had felt cold before, it felt arctic now. Blayde looked at me, and I looked at her as the pieces began to fall into place in our minds. As we began to understand what we had done.

"Actually jumping them, idiot," he said. "Gods, I didn't think I was being that cryptic."

"So, you're saying ..." A shiver ran through my soul. I will never have a grave, but it felt like someone had buried me just so they could walk over it now.

"When you jumped me off the ship to save the children, you inadvertently turned me on."

"Rethink your words, Nimien," said Blayde. "You're not saying what you think you're saying."

"I'll rephrase that, then. You switched on the regenerative cells." Nimien shot her a glare. "I'd appreciate if you didn't interrupt. It's very rude. Anyway, since

I had such a concentrated dose in the few days before, well, a little spear through the heart was nothing."

"But you can see why we assumed you were dead, right?"

"Back to that later. Anyway, I wake up from the dead and the tribe finds me, and what's the respectful thing to do in that situation? Oh yeah, they assume I'm the new moon god and light me on fire to free me from my mortal body. And when my ashes rebuild me, well, they crown me emperor."

Blayde let out a laugh. The absurdity levels were beginning to rise, and I was having trouble following. Everything about this day felt like a bad dream.

"Wait, hold on, you were emperor?" she asked, tears running down her face.

"Oh yes. Emperor of a broken land. And one day when everything was set right, a usurper assassinated me. Not pretty, but as I was regenerating, I thought this place didn't need me forever. I had already made things right."

"Hard to see that coming from you," I pointed out.

"Oh, shut up. As my cells stitched themselves back together, I thought to myself, well, if Zander and Blayde can jump, why can't I?"

"Because it's complicated to do, even with experience. That's why." Blayde sighed, bored with the arrogant small talk. "Just get to the point already."

"So, I jumped. Not very well, though. I ended up in the beginning of the universe. Don't interrupt. I saw for myself the glory of the Big Bang. Hell of a performance; it was incredible. A little odd, what with the boot and the goldfish, but no matter. After that, I kept a low profile for a little while, jumping from planet to planet, *learning* to control my little ability, unlike you two. And finally, I decided I should document this world, aided by my new order, and live here, to watch the universe grow and evolve, so I could trace your footsteps and crush you."

"Wow. No ego there at all," Blayde said with a sigh.

"Finally, I found Earth, recognizing it for what it was: the planet I had died on the first time. I might be going through time backwards, but a place like that had an imprint that reached across time and space if you know how to recognize it. So, I broke the Zoesh out of his prison cell, found him a cozy cavern on Earth, gave a really classy prophecy some time later to a tribe, and watched everything unfurl. All the while, I've been living in this time bubble, safe with the history of the world and the universe. And not just the known universe, but the whole thing. I have been waiting for you to come by, keeping an eye on the only true relic of your past as bait. It was child's play."

"Then why not kill us when we started out?" I asked. If anything he was saying was true, it changed everything about ... everything. "Why not find Sally before we got to her?"

"Oh, trust me, I did." He laughed. "But I don't mess with time. I only push it in the right direction. You three had to meet, so you could meet me, and thus, I could meet her. And I had to be there, behind the scenes, to make it happen. Though I'm surprised you don't recognize my earthly alias, Zander."

So, I had met him before. He was giving me the clues, but there wasn't any sense to them. Not that I had the mind to unravel them right now, with my face still in pain—pain, of all things!—and the fact that Nimien had become an immortal like us hanging over my head.

"But we travel through time as well as space?" Blayde was the one to ask, leaving me to my spinning mind.

"Correct."

"How come we never noticed?"

"I can't answer that. I'm not you." He made a childish gagging sound. "Being you is the last thing I ever want to be."

"But you just ..." Blayde sighed, and I could hear the bones of her neck crack quietly as she rolled her head in circles. "But *how* can we travel through time?"

"Well, let me explain like this." He took out a sheet of paper and a pen seemingly from thin air and drew a long, squiggly line across it. He then proceeded to drag one finger along the line, from point A to point B. "How could I have done the trip faster?"

"If you lifted your finger off the paper?" I answered, confused.

"Exactly. To avoid the slowness of the second dimension, you simply take the third dimension to travel through it."

"Your point being?"

"To travel faster in the third dimension, since you can't travel faster than the speed of light, is to step out of the third and into the fourth: time. So, to move faster from point A to point B, you simply use time to get there quicker. Right?"

"I guess."

"So, to travel through time—"

"You move up a dimension?"

"Exactly!" He grinned. "Not as dumb as I expected."

It was an oversimplification, to be sure. Dimensions are not supposed to work like that. But the visual was both compelling and beginning to make sense. If we could travel through time, instead of just space ...

Oh, holy Derzan.

"How did you learn all this?" I asked, masking my fear.

"I've had unlimited time to research at my disposal, the mysteries of life spread out for me to read over whatever amount of time I chose to do so. It's been rather ... interesting."

"What happens to us now?" Blayde interjected.

"We have a nice cell set up for you two until I come up with something ... creative."

"You haven't changed, you know that?" He didn't answer, so I continued. "You're still the scared and angry boy we saved from Aera. Now, you just have more power, but you're still the same."

"You have no idea what you're talking about." He sneered. "I'm more powerful than anything in this universe has ever been. I know more, can do more. You and your brother have no idea what you're dealing with. This time, I'm going to make your punishment stick."

CHAPTER NINETEEN

THIS ISN'T AN ACTION MOVIE, IT'S THE END OF THE WORLD

Sally

They say the world would end in ice or fire, but I was there, and the world ended through a flurry of selfies.

I watched from inside my hotel window as dozens of people stopped to frame the alien ship well above the Washington monument before taking the shot. The street was crowded with people vying for the prime location, the best picture to commemorate the coolest thing to ever happen to planet Earth.

Too bad we'd all be dead by morning.

Isn't it amazing how in one second, you're in one day, then suddenly that day is gone forever? I turned my eyes to the clock as the second hand made its turn past the twelve, and suddenly tomorrow was today and today was yesterday. Just like that.

What would Zander do, what would Zander do? The question rolled through my mind like a train off the rails, chugging along and crashing all at once. I could feel the panic sitting in my chest, taunting me, daring me to break. It had never given me an option before. Something about me was stronger this time.

Still not strong enough to take down the alien invaders, but you know, baby steps.

"Last night alive, huh?" I said to James, as she lounged in her hotel chair. I held the clock, watching every move of its small dancing hands. "Any advice on how I should spend it? Rob a bank? Get a tattoo? I've got a lot of savings to spend in seven hours."

"A lot can change in seven hours. They'll catch the Zoesh."

"I doubt it. It doesn't want to be found." I let myself fall backward on the bed. "It's still better me than humanity. The needs of the many outweigh the needs of the few and whatnot."

"The world would never live with itself after losing a geek like you," she said reassuringly. "I promise they'll do everything in their power to keep you from going on that ship."

"Come on, James." I sat up, trying to be serious. "A quick, simple fix like getting rid of a willing volunteer is way better than losing manpower on hunting down a dangerous extraterrestrial."

"Yes, it would be, but what would the press say? That we gave up so easily? Handing in an extraterrestrial criminal will ensure international conflict resolution, thanks to the unity that sort of thing brings."

"Whatever they choose, either they will be a hero or I'll be a martyr. Both would unite the planet."

"But only one leads to worldwide celebration."

"I've picked."

"Picked what?"

"I'm going to get the tattoo."

"What?" James got up, walking to my side. "Are you drunk or something?"

"No, I just want a tattoo. Just, you know ... a tattoo. Something big and bold, like 'Don't trust aliens.' A good reminder for me to think on for the next six hours and fifty minutes of my life."

"What on earth has gotten into you?"

"I don't exactly know."

I sat up on the bed, placing the clock down gently beside me. I could break it, throw it against the wall so hard it would shatter into a million pieces, taking the wall along with it. It would be easy.

"They don't even want me in the room with them," I muttered, staring at the blank TV screen. "When we finally managed to reach the Youpaf ship, the president refused to let me talk to them. Me, the willing volunteer and all."

Of everything, that probably hurt the most. Going from being a useful part of the team to being relegated to the sidelines. I might not have political experience, but I knew what was going on, and I had a right to be in the room when they decided my fate, dammit. I was the only one who had seen with my own eyes just what the Youpaf were capable of, could name them and speak their language, but they thought me better suited to waiting in a hotel room.

I wasn't going to pretend I didn't know what was going on.

"He was probably worried about having a diplomatic emergency on his hands."

"The one I'm supposed to die for, yup."

"Seriously, stop saying that."

"Well, then why are we here?" I threw my arms wide, indicating the hotel room. "Don't pretend this isn't a cell. You're here to make sure I don't run before my time to shine. I'm well aware of this being the last hotel room I'll ever see. They could have at least splurged for a suite or something. I don't want my last meal to be lackluster room service."

James said nothing, and I fell back on the bed again. I just wanted to feel like myself for once, especially in my last moments. But what did feeling like myself even mean anymore? The me I met in my brief moments of lucidity as I drifted through my depression or the me who gathered her wits and yelled at aliens to get them to leave me alone?

The drunk girl in the middle of a freezing field, staring up at the stars as aliens made crop circles around her, wondering why the only person I truly wanted to see was light-years away.

"I wish Zander were here."

"Me too," said James "If I had one wish in the world, it would be to meet him."

I hadn't realized I had said the words aloud. I could picture him, hold him in my mind, that face, that smile. The hair that reached for the heavens. The grin of polished teeth, deadly and kind. A tongue for saying the sweetest words or bringing civilizations to their knees.

Just some weird dude from space I had hit with my car and went on a few adventures with. That guy. The guy I couldn't get out of my head, no matter how much pain he had caused me.

"Why are you so obsessed with him?" I asked, still not moving from the bed. "Who is Zander to you?"

"It's a long story."

"It might be the last one I'll ever hear, you know."

"Then it really isn't worth me telling it."

We said nothing for a while. We knew what was happening here. She saw her role as jailer and I saw mine as sacrifice, the same way Angee had prepared for her part in the prophecy all those years ago. It didn't stop her from screaming on the way down.

"Next time Zander comes to Earth, will you introduce me?"

I rolled over, taking her in. She glanced up from the hotel brochure she was reading, lifting the corner of her lip slightly, somehow apologizing for words still left unsaid.

"If I'm alive at that point, sure."

"Sally, do I have to keep telling you you'll be fine for it to actually stick?"

"I might die of old age before he decides to come back."

"Funny."

"No, I'm serious. He's not coming back. At least, not to me."

Maybe I had been too cruel in the way I said those words, but James didn't press the matter. She returned to scanning the hotel brochure, though there was nothing interesting there. Not like the spaceship hovering over the city just outside the window. Maybe she, like me, just didn't want to look at it.

The absurd drained out of my life, replaced by very real ships in very real Earth cities, with the entirety of my world on the line.

I wanted to find something to laugh at, but there was nothing there.

"So, you know aliens," James piped up, once again looking up from the brochure. "What can you tell me about the crop circle near your place from two weeks ago? Was there an alien landing? Did they come to Earth to—"

"We were out drinking. It's a thing they do when tipsy, apparently. Helps them cope with the fact they'll be in hiding forever. Though I guess that's about to change."

"Hey, just so you know, I've been doing an amazing job keeping this situation maintained," she said, tossing me her phone. "Check the headlines."

I pulled down the menu and scrolled past the weirdest collection of news reports I had ever seen. Coca Cola claiming the ship was a publicity blimp. Buzzfeed rating which of the underbelly rust spots looked most like celebrities. A religious group already claiming it as the next coming of Jesus, though Jesus had a cool new car.

Not a mention of invasion anywhere.

"How did you pull this off?" I sputtered. "Oh my gosh, *you're* the government coverup? When conspiracy theories inevitably arise, they'll all revolve around you!"

"I still had some favors left over, even after saving

you. A lot of people owe me a lot of things."

"This whole air of mystery thing is seriously giving me the creeps. Will you ever give me a straight answer?"

"Probably not until you're willing to be straight with *me*, Sally Webber."

"How can I be more honest than I already am? You know more about me than I probably do at this point."

James didn't say anything. Instead, she got herself a glass from the mini-bar in my room and drank its contents in one quick gulp. She then proceeded to hand me a glass of water, which I downed in a single swig before laying back down on the bed again, my head hanging over the side so that the world was upside down all over again. I stared out at the ship hanging limply in the sky outside my window.

Hey, the left-most rust spot did bear a striking resemblance to Scarlett Johansson. Fancy that.

And there, beyond the ship, a big, bright moon. It hit me in that instant that if the Sky People were here, the Zoesh still here, hell, Aquetzalli being on Earth, Selena must be alive. Right here, right now. She lived outside of time, after all. But the mere fact she wasn't *here* told me that the version that gave a damn about us wasn't around.

"If you're going to continue moping all night—"

"Dying girl. I have a right."

"Well, if you refuse to believe that we're going to get you out of this and still keep moping, can we at least turn on the TV? You're allowed to watch on-demand movies and everything. And we'll order room service."

"Wow, fancy movie, fancy food, private hotel room—what, is this a date? The night before I die?"

I rolled over so the world was the right way around again. I tried to understand the look on her face, but her agent training kept it devoid of any incriminating emotion.

"Do you want it to be a date?"

"Not if I'm about to die, no."

"Well, you're not. And I'm just trying to make this more bearable. For the both of us."

"Fine then, put on a movie. Something that will numb the brain cells a little. I don't want to have to think."

"I have just the thing."

She cycled through the movies in a surprisingly long list. All movies I would never get the chance to watch when the morning came.

"So, this just came out two, three weeks ago," she said, landing on a title, giving my heart a little leap. *Squeal and You're Dead.* It's a terrible, terrible action movie masquerading as science-fiction. If anything, it'll serve as an example of how things could be far worse for us right now."

"I just saw this with Marcy," I said, sliding to the back of my bed and getting cozy on my pillows. "But I wouldn't mind watching it again. It was truly awful. I think it requires multiple viewings to capture the complete awfulness."

"Alejandro Vasquez has this way of always picking the more eye-rolling movies. And yet he's won how many awards?"

She ordered us a pizza and shut up, leaving us to enjoy the awfulness of a script with so many producers involved it was more likely written by a computer that had been fed ten thousand action films and asked to come up with its own. The only editors it had ever seen were a few hundred monkeys on typewriters who got really excited when they discovered the word "fart."

Sprawling vistas over a decaying Earth were not a great way to get into the movie-watching mood. More death and destruction were probably not the best morale boosters.

"Five hundred years in our future, there was a war. A great war," the narrator intoned.

"Bet you five dollars I can predict what happens next."

I almost tossed a pillow at James. "You've already seen it, and so have I."

"Even so, it's terribly predictable."

"Need I remind you, you picked it?" I glanced back at the screen. Too bad, we had missed the part where they told us how human greed blew up the planet. A nice, friendly reminder of how screwed we are.

The lead baboon rose from the rubble, waving a banner high. The baboons were having a grand old time rebuilding civilization, complete with factory bylaws and human suffering. Just, you know, now entirely in baboon form.

The camera panned deep into the bowels of the Earth, where Vasquez and his fellow human survivors and descendants were living in the quite literal shadows. Vasquez was an everyday working shmuck in New Chicago, an underground version of New York, who used to be a neurosurgeon before his wife died in a cave-in. Johnathan Joe got fired five minutes in for refusing to keep working when another cave-in kills his partner. Still unsure of what job he did, because future babble, but now without a job, he couldn't get the medi-grains for his very sick gran, so everyone is sad.

Then a government man shows up and convinces him they need his neurosurgeon prowess to create cybernetic implants for pigs, to send the pigs to go fight the baboons and reclaim the surface once and for all.

So, this all becomes a weird mash-up of *Babe* and *Space Jam* as the pigs become a team, rallied by Johnathan Joe, and have to fight the baboons in an elaborate game to avoid an all-out war.

Pass me the popcorn. You couldn't make this crap up. The baby cybernetic pigs get read bedtime stories by Papa John while discovering the thrill of farts, supplying the casual viewer with an endless supply of stale fart jokes and terrible visuals they would have to scrub out of their eyes.

And then, every time that stupid face of Johnathan Joe appeared on screen, I once again had to remember the face of the emperor, who had banished me to the Cave of Ordeals, who had abandoned his people, who had been a puppet of the Zoesh for so long he was beginning to look like him.

It took me a few more terrible fart-filled puns for it to actually hit me. That smile. That swoop of black hair. The way his brow furrowed when he tried to look pensive.

The last time I had seen this movie, I was convinced Zander and Blayde were simple space travelers. Well, way more than that, but time hadn't been anywhere near the equation. But now, now I knew the truth. I had seen the ruins of Aquetzalli with my own eyes. I had witnessed the return of the Sky People.

And now, I looked upon the face of the Evil One, and I saw it for what it really was: a mask, a fraud, a puppet just like the emperors of old.

"What happened?"

James was suddenly sitting before me, blocking my view of the now-paused movie. I didn't remember blacking out, but my brain must have actually snapped. The pieces had finally come together, and they were terrible to behold.

"I have some good news, and I have some bad news." I retrieved my shaking hand from hers. "The good news is I found the Zoesh's current puppet. The bad news is that he's the most beloved action movie hero the world has ever seen. Any idea where we can buy some pitchforks?"

CHAPTER TWENTY

THE SIBLING TRAP

ZANDER

"Push-ups? Really?"

I shoved my body away from the floor, hoping for, begging for my muscles to burn, for them to feel anything. There was nothing to fight in this dark place, so fighting myself would have to do. The boredom wasn't even the half of it; being alone with my thoughts, and awful thoughts at that, made my situation infinitely worse.

"You're going to have to talk to me eventually," she said, coolly. Not the tone of a woman who cared. Not the tone of someone who wanted to make amends. Just pure, unadulterated boredom. "You always do."

Of course, I always did. I could go a human lifetime without speaking to her, and still, she would be there, waiting. Sometimes the thought was reassuring: When the universe would reach its end and all life around us had fizzled out, she would be there, beside me, with me, every step of the way.

But other times, times like this, a lifetime of ignoring her didn't seem like enough.

"Cut it out," she ordered. "You're acting like a Julkan crab."

I breathed heavier. Not because I needed to, mind you. Hell, I was pretty sure breathing wasn't necessary at all. I needed the sound to overwhelm me, to block her out. There was nothing around for miles that could do the trick. Just me, my thoughts, and the air from my own lungs.

"You know, you're really immature for your age. You can't give me the cold shoulder forever."

Not a drop of sweat on my brow. Not a spark of fire in my muscles. But at least I wasn't sitting on my ass doing nothing. That would truly make me a madman. Or a Julkan crab, even. Rocks until the ocean told them otherwise.

"Just stop it!"

I kept pushing myself harder. Pushing her out of my head. Pushing away from the world around me. From our prison cell, from the end of the road.

From Nim. From Sally. Please, gods, let her be safe.

I couldn't remember how I'd gotten here. From sitting in those cold metal chairs to this dark place where nothing existed save my sister, the darkness, and me.

And a floor. I was grateful for the floor.

But how Nim had gotten us here—and for that matter, what and where *here* even was—I was stuck.

Nothing I could remember even compared to this. I had tried jumping—in fact, that had been the first thing I had tried—but all that left me with was a resounding headache, which wasn't pleasant. For once, I had no point of reference, no idea what to do, and simply no options.

"Please, Zander."

The tone of her voice had shifted. I knew how easily Blayde could slip into a role, how little effort it took for her to fake an emotion. I doubted she had any real emotions at this point, save for jealousy, perhaps, but that was neither here nor there.

I stopped my push-ups, though. She was right; I couldn't keep ignoring her forever. Immortal patience be dammed, a lot of shit had just been thrown on my plate—our plate—and we needed to work through it.

Like adults.

Like equals.

I stopped, dropping myself to the ground, turning to take in my sister, half-expecting to find a child in her place. Her eyes locked with mine, and she was either an extremely good actor or I saw something real for once behind those bright brown irises. Her voice was frail, weak, terrified. Easy to fake, difficult to believe. It was as fragile as porcelain and as cold as the void of space we hung in.

The voice somehow reminded me of Sally as she gripped that ladder, ready to climb down into the dark depths of the unknown. The fear that was so evident there, so poorly masked anyone could see right through it.

But Sally was human. Fighting that fear made her

brave, exceptional. My sister was... well, the jury is still out on what we are, seeing as how the library didn't give us a chance to solve the riddle of our existence.

But Blayde was scared. Somehow, I knew this was not an act.

And I had no idea what to do with that.

I couldn't remember a moment when Blayde was scared before. Worried, maybe, but terrified? I didn't have any experience with this. But if you were immortal, fearless, a warrior for as long as you could remember, and not even scared of death, what would terrify you?

Loss.

The fear of loss was the only thing that could ruin her like this.

And the loss of hope was even more devastating.

I stood and made my way across the stone tiles toward her, trying to avoid looking at the sheer drop just inches to my right. Blayde sat on the marble bunk our jailers had allotted us, and I joined her, putting my arm around her shoulders. She ripped her arm away.

"What the hell do you think you're doing?" she asked, sputtering spittle on my face.

"I'm trying to reassure you."

"Why is your arm there?"

"I'm giving you a side hug."

"It feels weird. How is this supposed to reassure me?"

"I don't know, but I can go right back to push-ups."

"Ugh, no. Leave the arm if you have to, so long as you're not over there acting like macho supervillain."

"How do push-ups make me look like a supervillain?"

"Remember Chandrakar?"

"He was an ass."

"And he was a supervillain," she grunted. "The only other man I knew who did push-ups in the middle of the day to help him think about the biochemical weapons he could create. He used to shout out his count and ask me if I was still watching. Gave me ample time to sift through his research and bring his ass to the ground."

"I don't remember seeing him at Abryria."

"True. Maybe they all got tired of him and offed him before we got there."

"Is that what we're going to do?" I asked. "Run through our greatest hits to pass the time? Change the subject every time it gets uncomfortable?"

"I can't see you coming up with any better ideas, and it does take the mind off our situation."

"What situation?" I waved my arm around the massive expanse before me. "You mean, us being trapped in a prison with no end? With no doors to break out of, with no walls to climb, with no window to tell the time of day?"

She shrugged my arm off for good this time, finally rising to her feet. There was barely any room to move on the platform, only about five meters in each direction. Tiled in cold stone, it was the only place with any kind of substance in our prison. Beyond it was the void: darkness stretching out, eternal, everlasting, in every possible direction. Above us, darkness. Below us, a pit so deep you couldn't see the bottom and so wide you couldn't see the sides.

"How long have we been here?" she asked. "Do you even remember how we got here? Because I sure don't."

I remembered being furious at Nimien, terrified imagining what he would do to Sally—and then, nothing. Just the platform. Just the push-ups.

Questions ran through my mind with no answers in sight and no one to ask for clarity. How Nimien had managed to cause me so much pain, for example. Or who was hiding behind those familiar eyes. He was Nimien, but he was someone else too.

"We'll get out of this," I said, with as much assertion as I could muster. "We always do, don't we?"

Blayde reached her hand out into the darkness, but it did not go far. Her lips were a thin line, her brows knotted together like the rigging of a sea ship.

"Where's the light coming from?" she muttered, ignoring me. Five seconds ago, she was panicked and hopeless. Now, she was back to investigating. I'll give that to the power of side hugs.

"No idea. It's like it's from the platform itself, but it won't cut the darkness."

"If we find the power cable, we can grind around it with our nails or something until it's big enough to crawl out of ..."

"How long would it take?"

"Twenty? Thirty years? Doesn't really matter. I mean, it turns out we travel in time now."

She stifled a little laugh. "How come we didn't notice?"

I shuffled uncomfortably on the stone cot. I had slept on worse, but still, they could have given us some bedding in here.

"Maybe we did notice and then we forgot."

She sat on the edge of the platform, dangling her

legs into the void. Our clothes had been changed while we were unconscious, leaving us dressed in the same gray uniform as the library's monks.

"I guess we're not like Nimien," I continued. "He had that time full of hatred. His anger made him discover his abilities faster than we ever did."

"And us?"

"We had each other." I gave her a squeeze. "We had more fun running around discovering the universe and putting out fires to actually care about our destination. Plus, whenever we would arrive, the planet would have changed so much that we thought it was someplace new."

"He said he could feel a trace, though."

"Didn't you say you could, when we got separated? Somehow you could, I don't know, feel where I had been? Maybe we just can't tell when we're together because we're joined at the hip."

"If we could control where we went, we could just have brought Sally home and we never would have met Nimien. He would never have become what he is now."

"And I would never have known Sally."

She paused, as if she was reluctant to ask her next question. Maybe she was scared of the answer. I didn't know what to think of Blayde being scared. It was a completely natural emotion to have, but she'd never had it before.

"So, are you ... really"—she paused—"you know. Are you in love with Sally?"

I shrugged. She rolled her eyes, crossing her arms before staring me down once more, all hint of fear replaced by that judgy look she liked to sport. The one with the thin-yet-pouty lips. Yup, that's the one.

"Be honest. Come on."

Now I was the one who was afraid. Why, though, I couldn't put my finger on it. It was stupid of me to be afraid, of my own emotions, no less. Or was I more afraid of what Blayde would say when she heard them? She wasn't the best at feelings.

And I was going off on a tangent again. I didn't know how I felt about Sally because I simply refused to think about it. Inconvenient thoughts needed to be shoved down, deep down, until they were forgotten and gone for good.

Except, I liked what I felt for her. I liked being around her. I liked the way she lit up when she discovered something new. I liked how she was completely terrified of everything, yet, she made herself do what she thought was right. Even when she tried to be a more selfish person, she sucked at it—and that's probably what I loved the most about her.

Loved. Love. Bright and new and electric.

"You're staring into space, Zan," said Blayde. "Should I be worried?"

"Hush. You asked me a tough question. It's not like I don't have the time to answer it."

"Okay, fine, think about this dumb yes-or-no question for hours while you're at it." She threw her hands up in the air. "It's not that complicated. Do you love her? Yes? No? A little bit with coffee and cream?"

"I don't know."

"That's not what I heard you tell Nimien."

"I was trying to piss him off, you know." It had been the first thing that came to my mind that I knew would rile him up. His creepy obsession with her was unsettling, and I knew I had to step in, instinctively, even though these were instincts I never knew I had.

"Still, very confident. Very smooth."

"Okay, fine," I snapped, and the barrage broke. In an instant my heart clenched—actually clenched!—and I found myself taken by a current when an instant earlier I had been standing on solid ground. "I love her, okay? And I'm not used to saying that because I haven't felt this way about anyone for as long as I can remember. I love you too, but it's not the same. You're like a part of me, like my very own arm or leg. Sally? Since the day I met her, I felt like I had an entirely new set of organs. Like she's another arm or second heart or even my brain. Maybe she took over my mind because I can't stop thinking about her. She's gorgeous and she's smart and she's funny, and I can't help the fact that being away from her is like missing a part of my soul. And I know I'm rambling now, and I can't understand why I'm yelling, but I am scared, Blayde! Scared for what Nimien has planned for her! Scared to remember who he was on Earth to me! I'm terrified for her, and I need to protect her, and I—"

"There's a whole lot to unpack right there, Zan," she said. Not mad nor happy, but a corner of her thin-lipped frown turned upward. "For starters, I'm so not your leg or your arm. That's frashing weird."

"Sorry. I got a little carried away with the analogy."

"And you suck at analogies," she added. "Any other day, I'd probably laugh at you, you know? This is everything I warned you about. Getting attached to a mortal. Putting down roots. Getting too wrapped up in the little details of the universe when we should be trying our best to keep our distance. But even if she's the reason we're in this mess, I still understand you."

"She's not the reason we're here," I said, trying to unravel the confusing response and the weird mess of feelings that had just exploded inside me. "I was the one who decided to save Nimien. I didn't know the extent of what our blood could do at the time, but that doesn't change the fact that I'm the one who created him."

"Because Sally made us bring him along."

"I could have let him die there."

"No. Once you get attached to mortals, it hurts to see them die. I know. I grieved Nimien with you. I could have stopped you from saving him in that temple, but I didn't. I'm as responsible as you. But we still wouldn't be in this mess if it weren't for Sally."

"Saying that isn't going to change my feelings for her," I snapped. "It's too late for that."

"Which I should have realized when I tried to save you from her." She shook her head. "I thought cutting you off, a clean break, would heal the both of you, but the roots were already holding."

"So what if they were?" I let out a sigh, falling back on the cool metal slab to stare at the massive expanse of nothing. "Would it hurt for us to enjoy a genuine connection from time to time?"

"Have you not been listening to what I've been telling you?"

"Blayde, I love you, but I need space to make mistakes like this. And I'm only calling it a mistake because you see it that way, but in my eyes, I need to be allowed to feel something. Just a little bit. I wouldn't mind having my heart broken from time to time if it meant being with a woman like Sally Webber."

Blayde got up, reached the other edge of the small platform, and swung her feet over the edge, much like Sally had when we sat on the top of the pyramid. I remembered the night, the breeze that blew us closer together, dancing on the beach to let off the pressure of being a savior to an entire human race. The way she had looked at me. The words I so wanted to tell her but reason told me I couldn't.

I moved next to Blayde again, putting my hand on her shoulder, and once again tried to jump out to no avail. It was like insomnia, the thought that you would never fall asleep again, rooted so deep down that it stopped you from getting a peaceful slumber. Like I had forgotten how to jump, how to split my cells and send them into the cosmic wind. I had forgotten the key to getting out of this nowhere place, forgotten if there even was one. Already the memory of my being able to do so was slipping my mind, wiping my memory clean as a slate.

"You can't either?" Blayde whispered.

"No."

"How are we going to get out?" she asked, her voice hushed and frightened once again.

"By trying. And when we fail, by trying again."

"And when we fail again?"

"We try again. And we don't lose hope."

She put her head on my shoulder.

"I hate this place," she said, so low I wouldn't have heard, except for the fact it was so empty and silent here. "We have to get out of here. I'm losing time. I'm losing myself. I'm losing you."

I hugged her close, shielding us from the dark. "I am too, sis. I am too. But we'll get out. I know we will. And you'll always have me."

In the darkest times, hope is something you give yourself; that is the meaning of inner strength. So, I willed myself to find hope. To be stronger than my physical strength and turn inward, where things were dark, cold, and musty. A memory grew there. Planted like a seed. Slowly, the more I nurtured it, the memory grew into something much bigger. A tree of hope grown from the seed of a memory, the memory of an event not yet happened.

I started to laugh at the impossible situation I found myself in and the impossible resolution it could have, my mind linking together some random phrases in the past weeks.

"What's so funny?" Blayde whispered.

"Not funny, amazing."

"Fine, what's so amazing then?"

"Hope. Hope is an amazing thing."

CHAPTER TWENTY-ONE

SAVING THE WORLD IN ALL THE WRONG PLACES

SALLY

It was hard to believe the dark, empty vastness under the highway, in some little town I had never heard of before, would be the last place I'd see before I would die.

You're probably getting tired of me reminding you how many other times I had almost bit the dust. It was too easy to remember, too complicated to forget, and I'm discovering I have a bit of a blabbermouth on me, so let's get straight to it.

I had almost died way, way too many times for a girl my age. They had never been pleasant, and most had involved me facing my greatest fear: heights. While you might call that confrontation therapy or something, it just made things more traumatic. Don't let me drive on a bridge anymore or you'll have a screamer in your car.

Tonight, I was on firm land. Practically underground, which ironically made me think of New Chicago far beneath old New York, in the world where pigs and baboons had a reason to war. Which I guess was what most of our wars looked like to people like the Alliance.

Some puddles lay on my path, dark as crude oil, reflecting the stars that shone through the openings between the streets above. Off in the distance, some bundles lay, probably the cold homeless bundled against the harsh winter chill. I pulled the thin jacket tighter around me. The stilettos and nylons were a very bad idea in this early March weather.

What made the situation colder, though, was the fact I was totally and completely alone.

Which I guess was good for one thing only: No one would have to see me in this godawful dress. Marcy, herself, would never be able to look me in the face again if she had seen me now. The cheap red fabric was irritating, leaving my skin tender in long swathes underneath. James and I had taken what we could get on such short notice, the only way for me to look so wholly unremarkable that I could walk through the underpass like an invisible woman. She had a box for everything, and box 356 had last minute party attire. Just not very nice quality stuff.

I felt the ruby red makeup sticking like glue to my dry lips. The discomfort of too much coverall layered on my face. The weight of my hair as it was pulled back in a strange knot behind my head.

It was humiliating.

Even more so, when I caught his eye, I knew that the man standing in the moonlight just a few feet away was the one responsible for the murder of Angee and subsequently Nim.

He turned away from the other moonlit stranger, slipping a thin envelope into his leather jacket. If you had asked me five hours ago how I would feel meeting the incredibly famous Alejandro Vasquez, I probably would have been fangirling so hard you wouldn't get an answer from me.

You probably wouldn't have expected a cool, collected, "I'm going to murder him."

Because that's what this was: an execution. For the millennia the Zoesh had ruled Earth, for keeping the entire planet at the mercy of the whims of the Sky People. I had never wanted to kill someone this intensely for—no, I had simply never wanted to kill someone the way I wanted to end the Zoesh. Rather, I wanted him dead, and since neither Zander nor Blayde could make that happen, it was up to me, Sally Webber, the weirdo from Earth, to bring the Planet Eater to its knees.

"Fancy meeting you here," I said, impressed with my calm. "You know, it's been forever since we last talked."

The bait had caught. He stepped forward, toward me, toward the skimpy red dress, toward the cheap perfume and the even cheaper lipstick.

"Do I know you?" he answered. He lifted his lips into a smile, baring his white teeth. If I had been a rational girl, I would have sped off right now.

But I didn't run. The wire in the top loop of fabric connected me with James, hidden in the shadows, ready to get me out the second I was in trouble.

But I wouldn't need her. I could handle the Zoesh myself.

"We met in Mexico, a long while back. Before you were an actor."

"Oh yeah?" He moved closer, putting an unwelcome hand on my shoulder. The smell of whiskey wafted over my nose as he spoke, and it took all my restraint not to puke. "What was I back then?"

I could feel him pushing at the edges of my mind, trying to find an in, to gain control. But it was weaker than I remembered, a poke rather than a prod.

He had not recovered, not from losing so much mass so quickly. He had shapeshifted into something smaller to escape us the first time, but a period of five thousand years was only a blip in his lifespan, not enough time to grow any larger.

Which meant the true Zoesh was somewhere nearby, hidden, small. Destructible.

"I think you were an emperor. Or a dinosaur. But that was a long time ago, wasn't it, Zoesh?"

He took a step back, even as his mind pushed harder. I swatted him away like one would push a toddler from taking seconds. I stood my ground, mentally, physically.

In an instant, the man changed. He was taller, taller than a human *should* be, every muscle stretching, pushing the bones to their limit. He towered over me like an ant before an aphid.

I take it all back. Here comes the terror. Hello, fear!

I begged myself not to scream, biting my tongue to

keep my mouth shut. So much for this new, brave Sally. I was just as tiny and messed up as I was pre-Zander days.

"Hey, I know you!" A grin spread wide on the Zoesh's face. " Selena, right? Goddess of the moon?"

"The one and the same."

"You caused me pain." His hand was around my wrist before I had a chance to do anything about it. He squeezed until the skin turned white. "It took me millennia to get that song out of my head. You planted it so deep I needed to pry it out with an ice pick."

"Well, you killed thousands of my people, so, you know, you win some, you lose some. I'd say we're even, but we're far from it."

"Get lost, human." He thrust my hand aside, and I almost fell over with the shock of it. "Go home. I don't do that anymore. I'm an actor. It's a much more fulfilling career. I don't talk to riffraff."

"Riffraff that was alive five thousand years ago?" I asked, but he was already making his way away from me. Shit, already losing him. "Or who, I don't know, the wardens think is you?"

He stopped. With slow, precise movements, he turned to face me again from over five meters away. His figure was dark under the overpass, his face impossible to interpret.

"What was that?"

"They think I'm you. The Youpaf, I mean, and in case you didn't notice, that is their ship in the sky over DC, and they're looking for the World Eater."

"Then why are you here? To ask me to turn myself in? To go up there and tell them you're not who they think you are?" He let out a snort, so loud it shook the ground I stood on. "Not likely."

"That's not why I'm here."

"Then why?"

"I guess because I can. You're not a hard—what's the word? Man?—to find, you know."

"So, you're here to taunt? To gloat? Then why not let me gloat a bit. I can snap your neck in a second, so if you're done gloating, I'm hungry."

"Would you?"

"Without batting an eyelid."

"I don't think you would."

He snarled, an inhuman, retching sound coming from his mouth. I tried to stay strong, not to show my growing feeling of dread in the pit of my stomach. He looked less and less human by the minute.

"You underestimate me."

"No, I don't. You can't kill me, or you won't have a scapegoat anymore. I'm as safe as I ever could be. Well, goodbye, nice seeing you again." This time, I was the one who turned to leave, taking careful measures not to trip in the heels. "Oh, and lest I forget, if I don't turn myself in, they're going to roast the entire planet, and either you burn or you lose your entire fandom. It's going to look a whole lot like your weird pig flick in here pretty soon."

"Stop!" The Zoesh was practically screaming now, to the point where I imagined feeling the droplets of his spit on my exposed back as I walked away. I didn't: stop that is. I kept on, letting his anxiety rise a little. I knew how overwhelming that felt. "Stop, I tell you!"

Like lightning, he stood in front of me, so suddenly

that I almost walked into him. Quite the opposite of what I wanted to do.

"You want to talk? Fine. I want answers."

"You want answers? You? The space dino they all want dead wants answers from a lousy human? This is one for the history books."

"I'll trade you." His voice was a low whisper, a hiss. The desperate voice of a desperate man. Well, man-dinosaur thing.

"A bargain?" I tried to channel my inner Blayde, exaggerating the arch of my eyebrow, drawing all my focus on him and solely him. "What could I possibly want to trade with you? I already know you are not going to give up your life. And that's the only thing I need right now or I'm dead the second they find me."

"How about answers for you." He ran his tongue over his parched lips like a lizard. "Three for three. Answers for answers. Huh? What do you say?"

"I say fat chance, buddy."

I had him right where I wanted him, which was him wanting me. The second I became more valuable to him than he thought he was to me. After all, wasn't that the reason I was here? To get answers?

"And if you don't come quietly—" I felt the barrel of a gun nudge the small of my belly, cold metal sharp and nasty against the already harsh night—"then none of us are getting what we want."

I was expecting this, but that didn't stop a shiver crawling up my spine. Lovely. Great night all around.

"A question for a question," he insisted, nudging me harder. "Deal?"

"Deal," I cracked. "Can you take away the gun?"

"Not a chance in the universe."

I took deep breaths, slowly and quietly, trying to calm my racing heart. Fear pulsed through me, my body a live wire. I thought this would all be over now that I was home on Earth. Instead, I was making nefarious deals with gross dinosaur men in the middle of the night.

"So, first off. How did you find me?" he asked.

"The government is tracking your phone. We knew you were doing your evening shopping down here."

In a flash, he took his phone out of his pocket and slammed it on the ground, crushing it with his foot. A thousand-dollar phone gone in a split second. Felt like an Ai Weiwei piece.

"Your turn," he grumbled.

"How did you survive?" I asked. "From the incident all those years ago?"

"You mean after you—that was you, right?—blew me up?" I nodded. Maybe this would count as one of his three questions but probably not, seeing as he was the one holding the gun. "Following that, life wasn't that good. My new protector died, though not from me. I spent the next years forming myself into a vapor of consciousness that I could more easily impose on others. I simply possess a human for his full lifetime, leave when he dies. Wards off suspicion, though confining."

What was with me and all these gaseous beings? First Taylor, now Alejandro Vasquez, a.k.a. the Zoesh, favorite actor and least favorite dinosaur person.

"My turn," he growled. "You're a pure human, though somehow you survived for five thousand years.

How?"

"Time travel. But don't ask me how that works because I don't know. It was an accident."

"What sort of accident?"

"I don't know if the right word is kidnapping or eloping. With an alien."

"Where is he now?"

"Sorry, it's my turn for questions."

"Then proceed," he said with a sharp-toothed grin.

"How did you escape from the prison all those years ago?"

His grin turned from a sneer to pride. "It was simple. A friend gave my cell door a little push. I possessed the guard. He got me a ship and flew me here. I messed with the natives, hence the dinosaur guise, and have been living on this planet ever since."

"For sixty-five million years, they haven't been able to catch you?"

"I know, it's pretty rad," he said, flaunting his acquired Earth slang. "They still have no idea that it's me." He stopped suddenly, his gaze flying to the sky. "Why did the stars just go out?"

"Is that your question?" I asked. "Are you blaming me?"

"No, my question is, if they think you're me and you're on the surface and everything, why aren't you already on their ship?"

It was my turn to grin now.

A bright column of light fell from the overpass above, exactly on the spot where the Zoesh stood, wide-eyed and fearful, his eyes squinting at the sudden blindness of everything.

"How?" His face turned to one of full terror. "It's her you want! She's the Zoesh! She admitted it herself!"

I stood my ground, laughing slightly.

"What's so funny?"

"You. You flaunt your so-called amazing intellect, but all you've ever been relying on is others. You should have stayed underground."

"What the hell are you talking about?"

"Simple. I realized the ship was tracking me the second it broke atmo' above the patch of sea formerly known as Aquetzalli. Which was confirmed a few hours later when it followed me to DC. I knew they had their eye on me, but I couldn't figure out why they didn't just abduct me."

"Get to the point, lady," said the Zoesh. He could have run, but something kept him frozen there in the beam of light, almost as if he was glued to the spot, a certain monolith technology, perhaps.

"It turns out the prison wardens were eager to have our full cooperation on their case since they've been working alone for so many years. They've been listening to this conversation the whole time. So basically, yeah, they know who you are, what you are, and pretty much everything else. Did you get all that, Youpaf?"

The Zoesh threw back his head, farther than any human should be able to, and let out a roar so vile, so alien, that the blood drained from my face in an instant. Light poured down on him like water from a bucket, collapsing him with a beam so bright I needed to avert my eyes. My heart pounded, the panic welling up in my chest, but I was ready to scream along with him if that came to it.

But the attack wasn't going to come. Not now, maybe not ever. Okay, no, that was too optimistic. But I felt good in that moment, powerful, strong, and able like never before. I had taken down Earth's most ancient enemy with nothing but well-placed words. No help from an ancient goddess, no help from immortal aliens, no powers or strengths beyond what I was born with.

Sally Webber had just saved the world.

"I think it's my turn for a question," I added, feeling the power course through me. "How long do you think will be added on your prison sentence now that you've evaded them for over sixty-five million years?"

One too far.

I had been riding so high on that horse of mine I hadn't glanced down to see that he had never put the gun away. Why would he? You couldn't shoot at the Sky People, but you could shoot the girl right in front of you, the one who had willingly given you up to them. The reason you were trapped in the first place.

I didn't feel the bullet go through my body. I didn't feel it come out the other side. All I saw was the Zoesh rising, up and away. He was trapped. At long last, I was free.

And meanwhile, my hand felt like I had stuck it in a vat of ketchup.

I felt a warm stickiness on my fingers, as my hand tried to keep the spilling blood within my belly. Then, the cold as it came for me, my name on its wintery lips as it called and coaxed me toward it. The ground rushed up to greet me like an old friend whom I hadn't seen in so long.

Hello, ground.

Did you miss me?

The asphalt and my head collided, making my ears ring more than they had been already. I wanted to cry out, scream into the cold darkness of this place. I could see the blinding light, the one people warned you of when death was near. It looked so far away, yet it was still within reach, as if it hung in the air before me, waiting for me to grab it.

Which is when the whole 80s flashback sequence occurred, but you already know all that; you were there for it. Kinda fun in my last moments, but still a pretty terrible way of viewing my life as it passed me by.

I sobbed. I couldn't tell which was the part that hurt the most: the wound in my stomach, slowly killing me as my skin both burned and froze; or the thought of never making things right between us, of never seeing their faces again, of never telling them everything I had intended to.

I wanted to get out, get away. Away from the cold, from the dark, from the death. I would go—but not here, not now. I didn't want to stay in this place. I wanted to leave it all.

I thought dying was supposed to be a calm process, of numbness and transition.

I was dead wrong.

Finally, the shriek escaped my lips. Finally, I felt air rushing through my lungs. But the blood was still spilling, quicker and quicker, through the red dress and onto the dirty ground. I didn't want my blood on the ground.

Fading, fading, fading. I tried to stop the thought

process, to keep myself calm. It would go easier this way.

Sorry, Felling. The Zoesh was taken away. Sorry that I'll never be able to introduce you to Zander. Sorry I couldn't tell you more about him. Sorry I couldn't tell him how I felt.

Why didn't I say all that while I was still alive? It sounds so ... sincere. I'm sorry, Zander, I couldn't tell you how I truly felt. Maybe I couldn't even let myself know.

And, Blayde, I'm sorry nothing worked out between us either. You won't mind now, will you? Did you really want me dead? If you did, here's your wish come true. I won't be bothering you any longer.

But I couldn't die yet. I hadn't offended that stripper!

Which is when I felt the nudge. More than a nudge. My skin bulged under my hand, my stomach reeling from the pain.

Why did it bulge?

Every cell in my body was alive with fire, the searing flame chasing out the impurities. I could feel myself burning from a heat I could never have imagined. Was I going to hell? Oh, please no. It's too hot. So hot. So hot.

I could feel myself fading away.

So hot, too hot.

I'm dissolving.

But it's still too hot; stop the heat.

I'm only atoms in the wind.

CHAPTER TWENTY-TWO

PRETTY BADASS RESCUE, IF I DO SAY SO MYSELF

ZANDER

A cry of pain rose out of the nothingness that bordered my world.

I spun around, but Blayde was just as perplexed as I was. She sat up straight on the concrete slab, her palm pressing into the stone like she was trying to crush it into the ground. She looked up at the sky, if you could call it that, and scowled at the darkness.

Were there other cells out there? Our eyes met, if just for a second, and I could tell she was wondering the same thing.

And then the cry came again.

It echoed somehow in the infinity, resonating against

nothing, sending a shudder through my core. Because I knew that scream. That scream had given me nightmares since the very first time I had heard it.

"Is that ...?" Blayde was suddenly at my side, her touch gentle as she took my hand. I gave it a tight squeeze, trying to keep in my rage.

"It is," I said, feeling myself tremble, something I hadn't experienced in a long while. "They're trying to torture me. This is how Nimien tortures us."

Sally was in pain.

Somehow, her voice echoed through our cell, inside this weird emptiness that Nimien had created.

And as terrifying as her scream was, I couldn't help but be scared of my own reaction as well. How the cry of this woman from Earth was ripping me apart from the inside out.

Blayde let me crush her hand in my grip as I tried to deal with this rush of emotion. She was not unaffected by the cries; her fierce exterior always snapped when someone she cared for was in pain.

Even if no one else saw it.

"Why her?" I asked, hissing between my teeth as I listened to Sally sob. It was as if she were right beside me, though her voice was louder than thunder. Like she was crying in my ear.

"It's not really her," Blayde said, maybe a bit too harshly. "She's not *actually* being hurt. We know torture techniques, seen them before. Hell, we've used some. They would be showing you a video to get you to react if it were *real*."

"You're just trying to make me feel better," I croaked. "You know as well as I do, they got the voice from somewhere."

I thought of Nimien, on Earth, stirring among Sally's friends and family, scooping her up in the dead of night just to capture the screams that would punish me for the crimes I had committed. What had he done with her? Had he left her alive?

Sally was crying now, low, quiet sobs, the kind of crying you did when you thought no one else was around to see you. My fists were shaking, unable to remain still.

"If they hurt her—"

"Zander ..."

"I mean it, Blayde."

"Zander, look."

There, in the sky, on the ceiling, whatever, just hanging in the darkness, it was her.

Floating?

I guess they did have a video to show me, after all.

She was floating in the sky wearing a tight red dress, her feet clamped in stilettos, which dug into her skin and toes. And that horrible makeup on her face, it was like it had been applied by a child.

Then I saw the dress again. Then I saw the blood.

The blood was bright and vibrant, fresh and flowing. Her hands were covering the wound, pressing down as she cried in the air. Her eyes were squeezed in pain, and she let out the soft sobs I never wanted to hear leave her lips.

Oh, Derzan have mercy. She had been shot.

Sally was dying.

"It's fake," said Blayde, coolly. "It has to be."

And then, the cries stopped. Sally took in one last

breath, and there, before my eyes, she died, floating in the nothingness that made up the prison of my mind.

Blayde was looking at me, but I couldn't meet her eyes. This couldn't be it. This could not be the end. Sally was supposed to have a life, to grow old, to have a family, a career, all the things I would never have. She was supposed to be free from the tragic shit that made up my life.

And she had died from a gunshot wound to her stomach.

I finally met Blayde's eyes, and she reached up, wiping a tear from my cheek, shaking her head. No. This wasn't real. And if she believed it, I should too.

So why didn't I believe it?

And then, Sally *breathed*.

She flew upright, gasping for air, her hands clutching at her throat, as if that was going to help. She was shivering, gasping for breath, her body trembling so hard she looked almost blurred. She was panicking, terrified. Her hands went to her stomach, where the wound had been.

With trembling legs, she got to her feet. No platform, just standing, right in the middle of the darkness.

And she screamed again.

It lasted for what felt like an eternity. Yet it wasn't pain. It was a scream of shock, of confusion. Relief swam over me. She was alive. Somehow, Sally was alive.

Blayde and I watched as she gathered her wits about her and calmed down. I felt uncomfortable, seeing her without her knowing I was here. Then again, I wasn't sure exactly how she fit into all this, how and why she was floating in nothingness.

Why she was here in my cell with me and my sister. She could have been a hologram; that would make more sense than her physically being here in the dark. A hologram or an illusion, or maybe a shared hallucination.

Sally was growing pale now, but it wasn't from blood loss. In fact, she wasn't bleeding anymore. Her face contorted into a mask of fear as she lifted her fingers to her neck. She stood still for ages, shivering.

I feared I knew what she had found there.

I didn't know what any normal human being would have done at this point. But Sally wasn't normal—not before and, obviously, not now. Instead, she got herself under control, breathing deeply, looking around in the darkness. She touched something in front of her; she wasn't in the same darkness as we were.

"Zander!" she screamed, making me almost leap out of my skin. And her body grew and stretched, taking up more and more of the sky. Blayde did not react; she was fizzing in and out of existence, as if Sally's presence was pushing her away just by being there.

"Zander? Zander, please wake up. Zander? Please. Wake up." Yet her face was too big, taking up my whole field of vision.

My cheeks felt hot, and I didn't know why. It tingled, like it had been plugged into a live circuit. All the while, my mind raced, trying to make sense of her words, but they meant no sense; there was none to be had. I was awake, and she was a hallucination. I was awake.

Or was I?

And then, I couldn't breathe.

There was a short moment of panic when I realized air was no longer reaching my lungs. Oh well, that tended to happen sometimes. Hadn't caused any lasting damage to date. But the rest of my body felt weird, like there was a pounding in my chest, like the steady beat of a drum, two, three, four.

I sputtered as my eyes flew open, the dark cell replaced by blinding white. An oxygen mask was thrust on my face and I inhaled deeply, trying to ease the discomfort of my tingling lungs. I breathed in and out, blinking out the brightness around me.

I was sitting in what appeared to be a reclining chair, fluffy and covered in velvet. Electrodes covered me from head to toe, except for two, which now dangled, useless, as if my arms had grown vines. Frenzied hands flew over me, ripping the wires off my skin.

I spotted Blayde in a chair like mine over to my left, same electrodes, yet she was still asleep. The prison had never been real. It had been in my mind.

And to my right was the most beautiful face I had ever seen in my entire life.

Sally's face.

She was frantic as she ripped the wires from my body, like my life depended on it. Her hair was a mess, most of it spilling out of the bun she was wearing, the makeup I had seen covering her slim face mostly gone by this point, as if wiped away by an invisible hand. The red dress, still stained with blood, seemed uncomfortable on her, not even her right size.

She turned to face me, and her eyes lit up. Her mouth stumbled around my name, like it couldn't decide whether or not breathing was its job too. In an instant, she flew at me, her arms wrapping around my neck, and she breathed a heavy sigh of relief into my hair.

314

I could have cried if I wasn't so exhausted. But inside, my heart was doing somersaults, relief washing over me so powerfully I was glad I was sitting down or I would have been knocked over.

I wrapped my arms around her and clutched her tight, never wanting to see her gone again. The feeling of her warm body against mine made my every cell quiver with joy, both a feeling of relief and the pure amazement of truly being alive.

She had survived. She had lived through death itself. She had somehow made it from Earth to this random place, the library at the heart of the universe, a random jump bringing her right to me. And she was somehow still hugging me, despite the fact I had abandoned her on Earth.

Not what I had wanted to do, quite the opposite, but she didn't know that.

Somehow, we were together again, even though there was a one-in-a-billion-trillion chance of that happening in the universe. She was here.

I guess, some days, the universe lets one slide.

"If it wasn't for the fact that it's an awful thing to do"—she licked her lips in that awkwardly endearing Sally way—"I would slap your face right now."

"You should."

"I'm mad at you."

"I know."

"You left me."

"I'm sorry."

"You were there, then you just were gone! Not even a warning!"

She shouted in frustration, turning her back on me

and mumbling incoherently. Ah, that was more like her. Good to see she really was here, and not just an illusion. I ripped the remaining wires from my arms and legs as she continued spewing truths.

I knew she would have been hurt. It felt just as terrible hearing the words as she spat them out at me as it had been hearing them from myself. I had abandoned her. I had deceived her. I had betrayed her.

And I nodded. I agreed. I had left. There was no point making excuses because from her end, it would have been the same whether it had come from Blayde or from me.

"Not that you'd believe me, but would it help if I pinned the blame on Blayde?"

"A little."

Finally, she was done and out of breath. She leaned forward, panting, winded. Her hands were still a sticky red, the same shade as the lipstick she wore. She reached up to undo the bun, letting her dark blonde hair fall lightly on her shoulders. She wiped the rest of the heavy makeup off her face with her wrist,, letting the coverall flake and flutter to the ground.

"I did miss you," she muttered, lifting her eyes to meet mine. The warm brown was as beautiful as a sunrise over a new world.

Without knowing what made me do it, I took a step forward and kissed her. And she kissed me right back, grabbing my hair and pulling me down close to her.

It was unlike any kiss I could remember and would be one I could never forget. Because it was Sally who was pulling me in, begging me to stay, and there was me trying to respond, simultaneously shocked and over the moon with her response. Knowing she wanted this kiss as much as I wanted to kiss her.

I folded into her arms, and she melted into mine. I drew her in, my hands wrapping along her back as hers dug at the nape of my neck, fingers locking through my hair. There was the gentle skin of her shoulders, soft against my hands, the warmth of her body stoking a fire in my chest.

All the panic I had been feeling melted away into nothing in her embrace. We drew into each other like two flames becoming one, all the rest of the universe melting away.

Then, of course, she pulled away, and, poof, the magic moment was over. Gone.

She stepped back, a strange look on her face, her eyes wet, my arms cold from the lack of her. Was she sad? Happy? Confused? I couldn't tell. She looked at me as if she'd never seen me before, her eyes wide, her lips quivering. She was waiting for me to speak, just as I waited for her to.

"Blayde!" she shouted suddenly, breaking the silence, rushing to her side in seconds.

Ah, I probably should have expected the sister component.

Sally carefully removed both the electrodes attached to my sister's temples, keeping the oxygen mask firmly in place this time. Blayde bolted upright in an instant, breathing heavily.

"What the hell was all of that?" she panted as she quickly surveyed the room and assessed her situation. "Brilliant. Prison of the mind. No wonder we couldn't jump away."

Then she noticed Sally and gave a quick, high-pitched, squawk.

"Where'd you come from?" She glanced from Sally to me, trying to make sense of it all. "Whose blood is that?"

"It *was* mine," she answered, giving my sister the most awkward smile the universe had ever seen. The most beautiful smile.

"Well, thanks for getting me out." Blayde ran her hands down her arms, popping the wires from her skin.

"Even if you ran off on me last time?"

"Especially since I ran off on you that time. Now this can go one of two ways: either I say I made the right decision because, hey, you came and saved us! Or I apologize profusely because it was a totally jerk move."

She looked up at Sally and held her wrist gently in hers. Sally couldn't help but stare right back down at her, awestruck, angry, and confused.

"You have every right to be mad at me."

"I don't need your permission for that, you know."

"I do know."

"I haven't heard an apology yet."

"I'm very, extremely, irrevocably sorry," she said. "There's no excuse. I saw you as Zander's weak spot, and maybe you're just his soft spot, but really you're stronger than I'll ever be."

Sally turned a bright red. "Really?"

"I'm totally the best at apologies. Also, how did you get here?"

"I don't exactly know." She kept her eyes on the ground, as if she knew the answer but didn't want to say it.

"She jumped," I said quietly. "Somehow, she jumped."

"You jumped, and you're not dead?" Blayde eyed Sally from head to toe, taking in every detail. "Oh, *great*. Just great. Another me on my hands."

Sally looked even more confused than she already was. Trying to move out of Blayde's intense stare, she sat down on the end of one of the chairs and removed her stilettos, throwing them over her shoulder carelessly. The skin beneath them was rubbed raw, but all signs of the straps were gone within seconds. Sally's eyes went wide.

"How long's it been?" she asked, awkwardly, looking back up at Blayde. "On your end?"

"About a week? Give or take." Blayde shrugged. "Maybe even less. Five days?"

"Oh."

"And you?"

"Over a month."

"Sorry about that." Blayde, amazingly, apologized *again*.

"Why did you go? Why did you two run out on me?"

"You're not going to like this," my sister said, sternly. "You were home, and I was free of you. So, I jumped him. Twice."

"You could have told me our partnership was over—"

"I could have, but Zander would never have gone along with it."

"Of course he would have. You're his sister. He lost you once; I don't think he could handle it again."

"You think so?"

"I know so."

"I was just so ... hasty. I can't take back what I put you through."

"Put me through? I learned more about myself in the past month than in my entire life. You didn't put me through anything I didn't need to be put through." She closed her eyes and took a breath. "It was still terrible and awful and doesn't make what you did right."

"I will do whatever it takes to make it right." Blayde sounded relieved. "So, what did you do back on Earth?"

"For starters, I realized you guys can travel in time, too. Did you know that?"

"Not until very recently," I said. "As in, a few hours ago. How did you find out?"

"Remember I said the ancient civilization we visited looked a lot like Earth?" she said, a twinkle growing in her eye. That's the Sally I knew. "Turned out it *was* Earth. And the Sky People came back. A lot happened."

"What?"

"The Zoesh was on Earth all along," she explained, lighting up. "We tricked him, me and this really nice government agent I met through Taylor after I stabbed a leechin a few years back. Super chick. Hey, she doesn't know where I am right now." She was rambling now, in shock, switching from one subject to the next as if she was changing the channels. "Oh crap, I've been shot! Why am I still alive? Why don't I have a pulse? I'm dead, aren't I? Oh, sweet Derzan in a pickle jar, what's happening to me?"

She breathed deeply, trying to calm her panic. Blayde turned her gaze to me, nodding in Sally's direction. My turn to say something. Something important, something relevant and…

"Let's get out of this place before anyone notices we're not trapped anymore."

Presto. Good thinking, Zander. Your brain does not compute well when it's riding the high of having actually kissed Sally Webber.

"Hold on." Blayde got to her feet, her voice rising to the commanding tone she used when she was confident or when she was completely out of ideas. "We can't leave without the book."

"What book?" asked Sally, equally buzzing with excitement and anticipation as she came to terms with what was to come.

"A field journal, from when we first ... how to put this?" Blayde turned to me for help.

"Basically, a record of everything that happened after our first jump. Blayde's first journal."

"And I need my current one back too, thank you very much. And I'd like my jacket back while we're at it."

"Good. Sally and I will try to find a way out of here," I said confidently. "We'll meet back in the room that connects to the Abryria node of the library."

With a curt nod, Blayde ran to the door of the secondary cell, putting her hand in her pocket and removing it empty with a curse. She took a step back, and, with a spur of energy, ran to the door, kicking up at the last second to break it down.

"And while you're looking for a way out, do you think you could find me my laser pointer?" she demanded. And without waiting for an answer, she was off.

CHAPTER TWENTY-THREE

TOTALLY NOT A ZOMBIE ROMANCE

SALLY

I was dead, then I was alive. I was on Earth, then I was in space. In front of Zander.

These were the few things I was absolutely certain of, even if none of it made sense. I mean, it made sense if you considered I had actually died and this was my afterlife, being reunited with Zander and sort of appreciated by Blayde, who was suddenly, what, emotionally available?

It made more sense than anything else I'd seen so far.

Only the flush I felt at holding Zander's hand was anything but the emotions of a dead girl.

"So, this is a prison?"

It was the only thing I could think of asking. The

other questions were too bleak; questions like, "How did I get here? And why am I not dead or am I actually a ghost right now?" were a little too much for me to handle. Too much, all at once, like living through Da-Duhui, the *Traveler*, and Aquetzalli all at once.

Zander nodded as he led the way through the corridors like he knew the place. He paused at every intersection, checking if the coast was clear before ushering me to follow him. Not for a second did he let go of my hand.

We paused inside a small room, where racks and racks of gray clothes were hanging on the walls. He nodded to himself, grabbing a hanger and handing it to me.

"We're in a library," he said, searching through the racks for something he himself could wear.

"Oh. I don't see many books." Usually I would be happy to, you know, be in an alien space library, but without books, it didn't really fit the criteria for me.

"It's not just a library, it's *the* library. The greatest repository of information in the entire universe. So large, in fact, that it bends space-time around it. You see, information is physical and can be seen as being related to entropy, and by that I mean chaos, by—"

"Why are you in library brain jail? Did you forget to return your books past their due date?"

He didn't laugh. His face was more solemn than ever, avoiding my gaze.

"Zander," I stammered, "what's going on? Why am I here?"

I was afraid I knew the answer. At least to the question of how I had survived death itself and found myself, suddenly and quite spontaneously, in the middle of a giant intergalactic library with my best friend, the alien man and his sister, the laser-wielding ninja.

And now, of course, things had just gotten much weirder. Because Zander was removing his jeans and shirt, replacing them with light gray pants and a light gray hoody. And within seconds, he had become the man from the hospital and the same mysterious Zander I had thought I would never lay eyes on again.

One revelation at a time, Sally Webber. Your brain can only take so much.

But actually, I felt saner than I had in months. Maybe even years. It was as if blinders had been lifted, and I could see everything all at once: the colors, the motion, the world around me. I could hear the quiet movements of the library; I could sense it was a ship from the tiny rumble under my feet. I could smell the detergent someone had used on the floor two days ago.

I felt aware, of everything. Aware, and totally calm.

There would be a time for panic later. My mind agreed and promised to wait, for the first time in my entire life.

"So," I started, but my sentence went nowhere.

"So," Zander replied, looking as unsure about anything as I was right now.

What I actually wanted to say was "let's make out some more in this empty closet so I don't have to think about the fact that I somehow crossed the universe to find you, and I'm dead but not really." That would have been much nicer right about now. Knowing that he and I had found our way back to each other again. That his hands were waiting to wrap around me, that his lips were waiting to taste mine again. But I couldn't run

S. E. ANDERSON

from the truth forever.

Especially now that forever was going to last a long time.

"What did Blayde mean when she said that I was another her?" I asked, embarrassed the second the words left my mouth.

"I think you already know."

I think I did know, deep down inside. Not even all that deep, seeing as how the nagging voice that usually lived inside my head was refreshingly silent. Feeling stronger than I had ever felt before, in control of my every move and thought. Like a Bene Gesserit in my prime.

I was no longer Sally Webber.

I was more me than I ever was before.

I was both, and I was neither. A walking paradox.

"I'm like you," I said, the awareness of it pulsing through my veins. Slowly, because the heartbeat was enjoying the slower change of pace.

"Yes." He nodded. "And you jumped, across all of space and time, through the fabric of the universe itself, to find me. It should not be possible."

"And, yet, here I am. Hi!"

He didn't smile. He watched me the same way a man would assess an alligator that had just appeared before him.

"How did I become like you? I mean, I was definitely not born this way. I've been injured so many times I've lost count." Yet, my broken nose when I had been taken by the Atlan had been forgotten about. The many, many times I had fallen from great heights and simply brushed it off. I had hurt, yes, but not for long.

325

"A few hours ago, we met another like us," he explained, slowly, as if somehow trying to diffuse me. "They explained that one needed two things: a blood transfusion and a jump. Combined in the right order, and you get ... us. Now I know we've jumped you many times before, but never once have either of us given you blood. We never had a reason to."

"Only you did." The memory of that day was clear in my mind, brighter than the sun. "The day I was dying in the hospital. You came, and you healed me, putting your blood in the IV. I didn't know it was blood at the time; I thought it was alien medicine."

"But that never happened."

"It hasn't happened *yet*," I realized. "Don't you see? When I told you about this on the *Traveler,* you were adamant it never happened. But we didn't know about your time travel back then! You travelled back in time from somewhere in the future, to save me."

"I did this?"

For the first time since I had known him, Zander was dumbstruck. He fell backwards against the clothing rack, not even trying to hold up his own weight. His mouth was open in complete confusion, the knowledge so overwhelming in that instant that he couldn't even speak.

I crouched beside him, putting a hand on his chest, no longer afraid of such a personal touch. He reached up and wrapped his hand against mine, pressing it there, above his heart, as he met my gaze and didn't let go.

"I did this to you," he said, lip quivering. "I cursed you."

"This isn't a curse, Zander."

"Isn't it?" I could see his eyes going wet, redness in his cheeks I had never seen before. "I've turned you into me. I was selfish, or I will be selfish, and I took you away from the only life you've ever known. For what? For me? To turn you into one of only three people in the universe who I wouldn't have to see die?"

"Zander, it's all right."

"No, no, it isn't," he said, freely crying now on the floor of the closet, clutching my hand in his. "I had no right to do this to you. I had no right to take from you the only thing that links everything in the universe—an ending. I love you, Sally, and that love has—"

I didn't know what else to do. I pressed my finger to his lips, turning his tears to confusion.

"Whjaja?" he asked, through pressed lips.

"Shhh."

"Are you shushing me?" He reached his free hand up to push my finger away.

"I dunno. It's how they do it in movies," I said. "Though, come to think of it, it's weird when a girl does it, isn't it? Actually, I take that back: It's pretty creepy when anyone does it."

And then I was kissing him, again, trying to pull all the sadness out of him in one go, as if I could make him feel better just by being so close. He held me there, muscles softening under my touch, tension easing as I pressed myself against his chest.

I had wanted to do this for so long, I hadn't even thought it was possible. But now I was kissing my best friend, and everything was going to be okay.

"I don't blame you," I said, as I finally pulled away. "You saved my life. I saved the world. Twice! I think we're pretty even."

His face went grim once more. "Sally, this is eternity we're talking about here. I can tell you right now I want to be with you forever, but I can't even remember who I was a millennium ago."

"You want to be with me forever?"

Screw emotion, I was kissing him again. He loved me. Zander loved me. Zander *loves* me, and now I'm kissing him again, the greatest privilege in my life, the most exciting thing to happen to me ever, even counting the fact that I was an immortal space jumper now.

"I love you, too," I said, and he melted into my arms. At this point he'd slid so far down the wall that his neck was at an odd angle, but even with a double chin, he was the most beautiful man I had ever seen.

"We still need to talk about this," he said, between kisses, "and we still have to get out of this place."

"Right, right."

I pulled away, giddy and excited in ways I'd never been before. I hopped up to my feet in one swift move, holding out a hand to pull him up. Now standing, he reached down to kiss me once again, hands on either side of my head, wrapping me in a box of warm, happy Zander smooches.

"I've always wanted to do that," he said, breathing warm breath over my nose.

"Me, too."

"I guess we're star-crossed lovers, you and I."

"That would mean the stars don't want us to date, though, wouldn't it?"

"But you literally crossed the stars to get to me, you realize that, right?"

"Oh, jeez, I hope I didn't make them too cross. I would hate to offend the stars."

We stepped out of the closet, both on track, both determined. Blayde's laser pointer needed to be found, and next, the exit. Though I could only bring moral support at this point, seeing as how I had no idea where we were.

That, and my entire body was filled with butterflies. Super unhelpful, but unbelievably fantastic.

"So, what is this place?" I asked. "You say it's a library, but it feels like a hospital and looks like a prison."

"It's actually an abbey for the Berbabsywell monks."

I almost stopped in my tracks, but excitement urged me forward.

"Berbabsywell monks? The men who know everything there is to know about the universe?"

"Are you one of them? How did you know that?"

I shrugged. "I heard about them a lot. I thought they might be a big deal."

"They are. Remember the monk who gave the prophecy to Aquetzalli and Atlan? He's one of their order."

More pieces falling into place. I thought the universe was done with me, but it evidently wasn't. From the hot air balloon to the monk librarians, it seemed everything wanted me to be here, now.

My story hadn't ended as Selena. It had been another stop along the way, leading me to this place.

But for what? To save Zander and Blayde? To become like them? Is that what the infinite universe truly wanted of me?

"We wanted to find answers, and we felt like this

was the place to find them," he continued as we walked. He didn't seem to take notice of any of the signs, though they were printed with gray lettering on white and impossibly hard to read anyway. "Blayde and I travelled here. But it was a trap. The abbot lured us here with the promise of answers."

"Wow, quite the adventure you went on."

"It was a mess. It involved breaking into the emperor's offices to steal coordinates that our ship didn't want to go to because it was experiencing puberty. Showing up here to know it was all for nothing? Now that sucked."

I wasn't going to pick up the bait. That was a story for another time. "Not nothing, if Blayde is going back for her, what did you call it, field journal?"

He nodded. "The first one she ever had. Tells us nothing, but maybe if we explore it deeper, it will reveal some clue as to where we came from."

After running around the plain white corridors for what seemed like forever, we realized the monastery was set up in the form of a circle. After that, navigating the corridors became easier. Luckily for us, we didn't encounter anyone in our wild search.

After who knew how long of running down the corridors and climbing random stairs, we stumbled upon a more extravagant hallway than the others. It was like setting foot on a completely different ship. The walls were made of wood and tapestry, the floor of Lithorn panels—I was proud to recognize, though with a sense of unease, as the wood of my alien boss Grisham's desk was made of the same alien material— with fancy rugs from all over the galaxy spaced out across the floor, leading the way to an enormous, ornate room. The domed ceiling was made of glass, the light shining in from glowing, moving shapes and motifs on the walls. Like clouds, they moved and reshaped themselves, making completely different designs. It was hypnotic.

"Right, if this isn't the place, then I'll pop back to Earth right now," I said, quietly wishing that this was my own office. Not that I needed one, but a girl could dream. "Here, laser-laser-laser."

Zander rushed to the desk, pulling open drawers and riffling through documents, somehow still keeping an eye on the door behind us. I made my way to the massive window, excited to once again be up close and personal with the stars. I didn't know how far removed we were from the universe or whatever, but the stars felt closer than ever, sparkling brightly with their beautiful light.

The universe would never cease to amaze me.

Would I still think that in a hundred years, a thousand years? Would this feeling of wonder wear off? I glanced back over my shoulder at Zander, thinking of all the places we'd been together, the joy on his face as we explored and adventured together. No, I don't think it would. If there were two things I wanted to stay immortal for, it would be to explore the universe as deep and as wide as it went and to love Zander for as long as was eternally possible.

But then I saw past Zander, and my heart, or what was left of it, fell.

The wall nearest the door, hidden to us as we entered, was nothing but a floor-to-ceiling flat screen TV. A TV with a screensaver, images drifting upward as if reaching for the stars themselves, photographs that chilled me to the bone.

Because every single one of them was of me.

There I was, sitting in the ice cream place next to karate class, sneakily sharing an ice cream with my mom as some stranger snapped my photo through the store window. There I was going to prom, John leaning in the photo, barely a month before his terrible accident. My heart caught in my throat. There I was fighting the leechin outside Scintillance, which meant this person had seen me but hadn't tried to help. Always in the distance, always taking pictures from the shadows.

The pictures drifted upward on the stream of pixels, each one both familiar and distant, my life held at arm's length. I stared at them for longer than I'd like to admit without making a sound, overwhelmed by the terrifying sensation growing inside me with every passing breath.

Someone had been following me. Stalking, since birth. Someone—or something—had collected these private moments from my life and compiled them on a computer outside of the universe. This person ran the largest, more absolute depository of knowledge in or outside the universe, yet, all the pictures here seemed to be of me.

For an instant, I thought this might have been part of this mysterious abbot's plan to trap the siblings. Use me as a lure, somehow, even though I was supposed to be light-years away and my immortality hadn't awakened yet; it felt odd to think about it like that, but it was growing on me.

It all got a thousand times worse when Matt Daniels, my ex-boyfriend, who was supposed to have died years ago and light-years away, strode into the office with a beaming smile on his face.

CHAPTER TWENTY-FOUR
HERE'S TO THE NICEST GUY I KNOW

SALLY

"Matt!"

I couldn't help myself. I flew over the desk and wrapped my arms around his neck, practically crying into his shirt. Matt Daniels was alive, alive! He hadn't died for me in the hellfire of a self-destructing ship.

Nope, he was somehow alive and well in the magical mystery library, dressed like a monk, no less.

"How did you survive?" I asked, absentmindedly moving a tuft of his hair out of the way. All fear and panic at the sight of the weird images had washed through me alarmingly fast, allowing me to focus on him, on Matt, the man who had sacrificed himself for me, the man who ...

Should have been dead. Why wasn't I focusing on

that?

"What happened to your hair?" I asked instead, unable to pull my questions out without ripping a tooth as well.

"You like it?" he asked, his voice the same as it had been two years ago, beautiful like the setting sun.

Hold on. I had never thought that. His voice had been rather nasal, like—

"It's so cool!" I said instead. The all-too-familiar panic began to rise in my gut again, alarm bells ringing. I was not in control.

"And how are you doing?" he asked me, holding me out at arm's length to examine me. "I like the new outfit!"

"Get away from him, Sally," said Zander, somehow distant now. "That's not Matt Daniels."

As if his voice was an arm reaching down to pull me out of the water, I broke the surface and breathed. But something was pushing me back under, into the bubbly, happy feeling that everything was right with the world and it was totally normal that Matt was here.

"I ... Saw ... You ... die," I managed to spit out, before my eyes got fuzzy and everything but Matt blurred.

"You haven't changed a bit," he said, as if I hadn't said a thing. "How long has it been for you?"

"Over two years, now," I said, wondering why I found his question odd. "And you?"

"Oh! About the same."

He brushed a strand of my hair behind my ear, and I caught another glimpse of the creepy slideshow. Once again, the illusion shattered, the need to run suddenly overwhelming. Matt couldn't be here; Matt was dead. Matt was lying somewhere under the rubble of the

GrishamCorp power plant.

Matt *couldn't* be here.

He couldn't be.

"Zander," I said, still fighting the spell I was under. "Did you know Matt was here?"

"That's not Matt," he said, sounding more distant by the second. "That's Nimien."

Realization hit me like an out-of-control *Traveler* falling through the atmosphere of a hostile world. The eyes; it has always been the eyes, the ones I had caught in the kitchen of a lost colony, that I had both seen and failed to recognize because they belonged to an alien boy and not a human man.

But Matt Daniels wasn't a human man, was he? Because Nimien hadn't died during the Sky People's raid. He was the other immortal Zander had mentioned but refused to call by name. Nimien was immortal, and he was also Matt-freaking-Daniels, my dead ex from Earth.

Neither dead nor from Earth, I might add.

The spell broke the second I recognized those eyes of his. In that moment, the baby fat that had coated his once-adorable face and the beginnings of a belly I had found so endearing faded away. In their stead stood Nimien, now fully grown, bold and beautiful in the way a king python was. He did, in fact, have hair now, a field of magnificent hair, grown in thick and full, enough to rival Zander's. His body was toned and muscular, strong and sturdy like a block of marble. There was a sharpness to his face that hadn't been there before, neither in Matt or Nim, making the only true link between the two those dramatic, deep brown eyes.

"I meant what I said." He grinned, holding on to my shoulders. "It *is* so very good to see you, Sally Webber. We have so much to discuss."

Zander roared as he flew over my shoulder, leg extended to kick Nim straight in the face, but Nim stepped to the right, avoiding the foot entirely. When Zander crumpled on the floor, he let out a yelp of pain, a cry so intense you'd have thought he had landed in a bed of red-hot coals.

Only it couldn't have been. Even if the floor had been literal lava, Zander wouldn't have cared, wouldn't have screamed. Yet now, he was writhing on the floor in evident agony.

"What have you done to him?"

I rushed to Zander's side, reaching out to touch him, but when my hand brushed his skin, he screamed harder. I watched helplessly as he suffered alone.

"A little invention of mine," Nim replied, somehow cheerful about all this. How I could possibly have seen him as Matt baffled me. This new hybrid of a man had nothing of the softness of those two men. He was nothing but pride and rage. "Have you ever heard about those stories where mothers lift cars to save their own children? It's all caused by adrenaline, making your muscles use their full capacity, a superpower that's kept from you by your own body, to keep yourself from muscle degradation, among other things. So, I thought to myself, 'Immortal? Why couldn't my muscles work like that all the time? My body tissues will never degrade.' I spent a few years on the project, finally coming up with a serum that forced your body to go into a rush. With one annoying side effect—pain."

"You drugged him," I stammered. "You're the leader here, aren't you? Matt, Nimien, I don't even know what to call you anymore. You created this trap for him, and now you torturing him? Why? What happened to you?"

"Do you want to tell her, Zander, or should I?" he asked. Zander could only scream. His every nerve must have been on fire. A cut on his face belligerently refused to close. Nimien must have nicked him as he soared past.

"Tell me what?" It took everything in my power not to call him an asshole or shit face or any kind of awful name I could think of. None felt like they were strong enough. Now that I was a few feet away, the sickly-sweet scent that surrounded Nim couldn't alter my brain either; he had been trying to drug me as well.

Stalk me. Drug me. Trap me.

Like I was prey.

"He's been lying to you," the hunter said. "Tell her or I'll do the honors."

Zander slowly regained his composure, fighting with all his might not to scream. He fixed Nimien with determined eyes and spat at him, though it didn't go very far. Spittle ran down his cheek onto the gray carpet. Still, he choked out his words.

"Tell her about you?" he hissed, before dropping his head back against the carpet, eyes pressed closed against the pain.

"Tell me what?" I just wanted Zander's agony to end, to be able to do something, anything, that would stop him from writhing on the floor like that.

"So, so many things."

Nimien took a seat behind his desk, closing the

drawers with a swift kick of his heel. He pulled Blayde's laser pointer out of his top pocket, placing it on the table before him. I didn't leave Zander's side.

"Did he tell you, for example, that he was scared of me?" he asked, crossing his legs on his desk. Behind me, the wall still scrolled with images of my childhood, stolen moments on display. "Did he tell you that he knew what I was, what I could be, from the moment I took control during the Battle of Bonfire Beach? How he distanced himself because of that and left me to die on that pyramid because he was intimidated by me?"

"That's just not possible," I sputtered, but I remembered the look on Zander's face as he carried me away from the spears of fire, so determined that Nim was already lost without bothering to look back.

I remembered what Blayde had said at Nim's funeral. How she had realized how truly genius this boy was, only for him to be taken from them so early on. Was it possible that they were, in fact, scared of Nim?

I couldn't blame them. Not now, not when I looked into the eyes of the boy I had cared for and the man I thought had cared for me. The fact they were one and the same filled me with so much disgust it turned my stomach. I would not throw up on Zander today, no, sir. Even if I had a damn good reason to.

"Did you know Zander and Blayde were toying with you?" he continued. "They could have taken you home any time they wanted. The universe is big, but it's not that big. Not for us. That's how I always find you, Sally."

I shuddered. The tone of his voice, the words might have sounded sweet, but they were terrifying. But they also ... fit. As I laid dying, the last thought in my head was how I wanted to make things right between Zander and me. And then, I had woken up, literally at his side. That was no coincidence.

"I could keep going," said Nimien, practically smirking, "but you're smart, Sally. I know you can already sense the truth. You have seen how dangerous Zander and Blayde can be. You've seen them be judges, juries, and even executioners of the universe. Their version of good isn't universal; it just *is*. And they have wasted their power on the petty squabbles of the universe. Killing a president here, an emperor there. Did they tell you that to reach my library, they had to go through a planet inhabited by their worst enemies?"

They hadn't told me anything of the sort, but there hadn't been time for that, had there?

I didn't know if his words made sense or if he was drugging me again. I decided that any man who wanted to drug me for me to see his way didn't have any valid arguments to begin with.

"What happened to you, Nim?" I asked, pushing myself to my feet. Zander had grown silent on the floor, the pain so overwhelming he couldn't even scream. "The last time I saw you, you were saving children from alien invaders. And now you're here, what? Making a collage of my life?"

I pointed at the creepy wall of pictures, and he flicked a switch, making it go blank. Instead, a single picture appeared: Matt and me, at Grisham's Thanksgiving party. The two of us dressed to the nines, standing so happily together.

But Matt Daniels was a lie.

"Why are you telling this to me?" I whispered.

"Because you deserve to know. Something Zander or Blayde don't understand."

"They do."

"Then why not tell you?"

"I dunno. Maybe because they themselves don't know?"

"I can remember every second of my existence. They're no different."

Zander's silence worried me. He didn't whimper, plead, cry; he didn't utter a sound. He just lay on the floor, watching.

"No, they're different."

"How would you know?"

"Because I trust them."

"How can you? After he abandoned you ... twice? After he almost killed you, got you lost in space, turned you immortal against your will?"

"I forgave him for that."

A low chuckle escaped Zander's lips. He still wasn't moving, but he was alive, listening. I stood taller and stronger.

"I saw the way he left you when he disappeared. You were tortured. In pain. And you forgave him, just like that?"

"Like you saw a lot of things," I snapped, motioning the wall again. "You stalked me, Nimien. Since I was a baby? That is so insanely creepy! You tricked Zander and Blayde to come here, tortured them, tricked me to come here, and insulted my intelligence by thinking any of this"—I flailed my hands to encompass the room— "would turn me against them. Instead, it has done nothing but smear the memory of two men I cared for dearly."

Nimien looked colder now, the shadows on his face deeper. He took his feet off the desk, all pleasantries over.

"How can you be so naive after everything you saw?" he asked, keeping his eyes fixed firmly on mine. Those eyes! How had I missed them when I had seen Nim? How could I not have known who else they belonged to? "Do you see them? The thousands, millions of worlds around their own personal sun. Some of them think they're alone in the universe; others have siblings scattered across galaxies. Stunning perfection." He turned back to me. "Zander and Blayde? They destroy that perfection. Like a cancer that destroys the cells of an organism, they go from one place to another, leaving a trail of destruction. And, somehow, you get pulled into it." He was suddenly close, too close for comfort, his breathing heavy on my neck. "There's still time to escape it. You don't need to be a part of it."

"They're not destroying anything."

"How can you be so sure? You can't trust Blayde. She's a killing machine, a bomb ready to go off. A psychopath. And yet you trust her?"

"I do. And she's no psychopath. She chooses what emotions she lets control her life. I don't always think she's right, but she's trying harder than anyone else I've ever met."

"She left you. Abandoned you. Always hated you. Are you forgetting that?"

"She betrayed me, and I forgave her. She acted irrationally, out of fear, out of jealousy, but I love her. Even now, after everything, I trust her more than you.

She was always honest with me. You, well, you ..."

I didn't even know where to begin with him.

"And Zander, what, you think you have a chance with him? He's not even your own species. Who knows his history? I do. It's not pretty. Impressive, the thousands that have been in his bed. And you think you're any different."

"Wow, Nimien, jealousy is not a good look for you. "

"Jealous? Me?" he spat. "No, no. Though I do not understand for the life of me how you still trust him so firmly, after everything you've seen."

"You want to know why? Because even when times were tough, he treated me as a normal person. Even if I was more hassle then help, he never showed it, and always treated me like an equal. Because even though his sister wanted me gone, he stood up for me. Is that not enough? You know he never spoke ill of you, ever? He was torn and messed up after you died in his care. I will always stand by their side. Because whatever happens, whatever is said, whatever is done, they showed me love. And because he could have left a long time ago, but he's still here, right here, in this very room—even though he could jump away whenever he wants. "

Nimien shook his head. "He's weak, Sally. What you see in him aren't signs of strength. Hell, he probably would have left if he wasn't in too much pain to function."

"And whose fault would that be?"

"Understand I cannot be jealous of him. Unlike Zander, I always knew you would find your way to me. I made it so. Everything is by design."

Somehow, those words chilled me deeper than anything else he had said. I forced myself to stand tall, refusing to shiver, instead fixing him with the delicate stare of the girl I always wanted to be.

"What design, Nimien?" I asked, terrified of the answer. "What are you talking about?"

"Haven't you asked yourself why the universe seems to revolve around you?" he asked, smiling that charming smile of his. For a second, I could see the boy that he had been, the one who had danced so happily with me on the beach in Aquetzalli.

"Actually, I have."

"You noticed." He nodded. "Good. You've been at the center of it for longer than you think. As Zander already knows, at this point, everything I've done since I discovered my abilities has been for you. To find you, to see you again, to bring out the real you."

Now, that caught me by surprise. I didn't think anything else could at this point.

"The real me?"

"The Sally Webber who was always meant to be." He smiled, walking from behind his desk until he was in front of me, leaning back like the most casual man in the universe. "I have been playing the timeline since the beginning.

"I was the one who told Grisham where to build his new power plant. Who took Matt Daniels's identity and wooed you back on Earth. I orchestrated everything, from Marcy's party where you met me—why do you think I was there that night?—to you getting hired by my business partner. Grisham was never in charge of anything; I was, though the idiot never pieced together my two identities. And I killed him in the end, leaving my alias with him, to prepare you for your trip to the stars.

"I orchestrated absolutely everything. On Da-Duhui, I helped the ICP plan its heists, putting all the pieces into play. I was the one who made certain you would meet Sekai at that party, to remind you of the people you had already saved, to prove to you that you mattered in the fabric of time. I made sure you knew how special you are. Everything I did was because of this.

"I was the one who got the other Matt Daniels, the real Matt Daniels, booked on a spaceship on its way off Earth and later saved him when his ship exploded, making him captain for his efforts. I'm a kind man. I knew what he would become, that he would thrive in the universe, and I knew that I would have to meet him in order to save him from that dreary life he was never meant to live. I'm the one who triggered a virus in the colony's AI, making it ready to release me—the real me—when the time came. That same virus that activated in the ICP, forcing Zander and Blayde to lose focus and, as a result, to lose Earth.

"I was the one to release the World Eater, and find him refuge on Earth. I was the one to tell Selena she needed to find herself. I was the one who brought the people of ancient Earth the prophecy of your arrival."

"You were the monk," I hissed. The revelations were too numerous, too overwhelming, and I struggled to cling to a single one before another shattered my view of the world or my life. "You played both sides. All the sides."

"I have come so far from the boy who toggled his point-reader back on Aria," he said, proudly, "just for extra food after lunch hours. Or who poisoned the director to force him to find a kidney donor, leading him to believing I was his son. I always knew I was meant for more than that place, a life of servitude and control. I built the library to bring in my greatest foes, setting the perfect trap so they would come here and you, when you were finally ready, would follow them. I orchestrated your life before you were even born, Sally Webber, just for this moment, right here, right now."

I was visibly shaking now, unable to control it anymore. Nimien, Matt, whoever he was, he was a sociopath. Manipulating everything to get his own way.

"Don't you see?" he said, reaching for me, but I stepped backward, still reeling from his words. "You believed in me the first moment you met me. And I believed in you. I did all this to save you, to make you the person you always wanted to be. If you hadn't followed the path I laid out, you would still be on Earth, fighting the hopelessness of a glitching mind and the loss of those you hold dear. I freed you from that. I fixed your brain and elevated you to the most powerful being in existence."

I shook. The man was sprouting gibberish. It was the universe that had wanted me to save the people of ancient Earth, wasn't it? Wasn't that why it put the pieces of time together to bring me there, so I could fulfill my role and save my world not once, but twice, both past and present?

Only it wasn't the universe pulling the strings. It was a boy. A confused, angry little boy who wanted something so desperately he had moved time and space to bring it into his hands.

I was not a thing to be had. I was not a broken puzzle to be fixed. I was, and am, Sally Webber, and I didn't need anyone to tell me what I can and cannot be.

"What happens now?"

I clenched my fists as I stared at the entitled man who had once been my friend, my lover, the trigger to my pain. He smiled and did not reply. At least, not with words. Instead, he grabbed my hand, and we jumped.

CHAPTER TWENTY-FIVE

SALLY'S CHOICE

SALLY

Wind whistled over the stalks of wheat, and I felt the cold on my skin. I felt it the way one might feel a stranger's stare: the odd feeling that it was there, but there was nothing tangible to confirm it.

Strange. It was cold outside, but I wasn't cold.

The smell of wet grass saturated my nostrils. It was a cold evening, the sun setting over the field we found ourselves in, casting long shadows as it went. We were the only ones there, Nim and me, standing in the middle of this empty place like we were the only ones in this entire world.

"Where are we?" I asked, coolly.

Nimien smiled. "You don't recognize it?" he said, waving his arms wide. "You don't feel the tug of your

348

own home world?"

I shuddered. "We're on Earth?"

"Hey, presto. Gold star for Sally Webber!"

I glared at him. The man was flaunting now, his arms towering to the sky like he was going to summon lightning on me. I folded my arms across my chest to cut back on the cold, a cold I both felt and couldn't feel at the same time. But I would worry about that later.

"Okay, Nimien, I'm lost," I said. "Why on earth did you bring me, well, to Earth? Take me back right now!"

"You can leave whenever you want," he said with a shrug. "You're able to do that, you know."

"No, I'm not."

"Yes, you are," he insisted. "Look at you. You travelled across the universe and through time itself to find me, like I always knew you would. The only reason you're not leaving now is because you don't want to."

I frowned. The man no longer looked like Nim; he didn't look like anyone at all. I understood now how I had never seen the resemblance between him and Matt earlier because right now it was as if it had never been.

In an instant, Matt was a man who had never existed, a fiction conjured by Nimien in a convoluted way to see me again. To date me. To seduce me. I shuddered as my memories of Matt gave me an acrid taste in my mouth.

He had not only created Matt but also killed him. And now, he was taking my good memories of him. Every nice thing Matt had said had been a ploy, a manipulation from this boy, a boy under the delusion that I was madly in love with him. Everything I remembered of the man was tarnished by that knowledge.

Our good days were now bad days. Our bad days, well ...

"No, it's because I don't know how," I said, edging away. "And I'm not like you, Nim. I'm human, just human."

"You're more than that." He reached forward, trying to take my hand from where they were folded over my chest. I flinched from his grasp. "Haven't I always told you, I can see the potential in you?"

"Fuck my potential," I snapped. "Stop beating around the bush and tell me why you brought me here."

"I thought you'd recognize the thing that changed your life, Sally." He jerked his chin to the right. I followed his gaze, my jaw dropping.

It was a balloon.

A hot-air balloon, to be precise. Red and yellow stripes crossed upward, as if running away from the flames below. A hot air balloon that had been seared into my mind for years, ever since I saw it collapsed on my roof that fateful day.

The day my life was thrown overboard. The day the hot-air balloon had cost me my job and set the dominoes in motion so I would be at the right place to hit Zander with my car.

"No," I said, my voice barely a whisper. "It can't be."

"Oh yes, it most definitely *can* be," Nimien said, punctuating his sentence with a chuckle. "And, as a matter of fact, it is. Now, do you understand?"

"Still no." I turned to him, and he held my gaze, assessing me from the outside in.

"Immortals are special, Sally." He took a step closer

to me. Two steps too many. "We're not born this way; we chose this life. We chose this burden. For better or for worse, we all make the decision that makes us who we were."

"Um, no," I said. "I know two immortals, and neither of them wanted this life. I still remember you dying at the foot of that pyramid. What are you talking about?"

"We're time travelers," he insisted. "Our decisions affect our past as well as our future. Everything is connected."

I nodded, understanding nothing. He kept saying *"we"* like I was just like them, but I wasn't. I couldn't be. I was still human; I knew that. What had happened back in the library was Selena or some other higher dimensional being coming to rescue me. Maybe it was Robin. I doubted it, though. I wouldn't count on that traitorous cloud of gas to actually have a heart.

"Then why are you still here?" I asked. "If immortality is such a burden, why keep it?"

"A burden?" he said, holding back a laugh. "Whoever said it was a burden? I'm immortal, Sally! I can do anything I want! I thought I would never have the time to see the universe, but guess what, ha! I'm cataloguing the entire thing. I am the most powerful being in existence. Why would I want to change that? No, in fact, I ensured it happened."

"Hold on, what?" I stammered, confused. Well, I was already a whole lotta confused here, but everything he was saying made it worse, not better. "How?"

"Oh, you know," he said playfully, "you just have to talk to the right people. I made sure those two idiots wanted to hijack the *Traveler*. I left the coordinates for my home world hidden in deep lines of code, so the ship would immediately go there if there was trouble. Oh! And I made sure to put a virus in the computer interface in Aria, creating the AI I hated so much. All so you'd come under the exact conditions I remembered, the conditions that made me who I am today. The computer virus had the unintended side effect of spreading too far, seeing as how I made it during the great pilgrimage of humanity, but you took care of Da-Duhui with no trouble at all."

"Wait, you're behind the AIs?" I asked. "All the AIs going off at once?"

"Face it, Sally"—the grin on his face spread so far, too far, more than humans should possibly be able to do with their skin—"I'm behind *everything*. Anything that happens in this universe happened because I willed it so."

I couldn't help but snort. I mean, you would have too. This guy, who had been nothing but a teen just weeks ago, was now so full of it that vanity was just pouring out of his ears. He didn't like this reaction, though. The grin turned quickly to a glare, and I was the source and focus of it.

"Don't laugh, Sally, I'm being serious."

"I'm laughing *because* you're being serious. I mean come on, you can't possibly be behind everything."

He shrugged. "Suit yourself. There's one thing I'm not behind, and that's you. This is my gift to you, Sally."

"What?" I asked. "The hot-air balloon that derailed my life? Should I stab it or something? Is this supposed to make me feel better, get closure?"

"Not closure," said Nim. "Quite the opposite. A beginning. This is the morning before, Sally. This is the morning before your life changed. Before the hot-air balloon that changed everything."

At this, I blanched. I could feel the color drain from my face, as if the wind had blown it clear off. Whoosh.

What the hell? I mean, what the absolute hell? Things were starting to become clearer now, to weave themselves together, forming an image that shocked and revolted me. I would have thrown up if there was anything left in my stomach. I just stood there, staring at Nim, my mouth opening and closing like a fish. My hands went limp at my side; I couldn't keep them crossed anymore.

"What?" I stammered, staring at the balloon. "Nim. Why am I here? Why am I really here?"

"Because," he said, taking my dead arm. He covered my hand in both of his, like he was about to propose without getting on one knee. I was frozen, petrified even. I couldn't have moved even if my life depended on it. "My life is so entirely intertwined with yours, Sally. You're the reason behind me being the way I am, for everything I did to put things in motion. I would never have been able to pull off my transformation without you. You freed me, Sally Webber. And in exchange, I free you."

"You're not serious."

"Entirely," he replied. He looked slightly offended, but it was getting harder and harder to tell as the light of day dimmed. "I'm giving you a choice. Right here, right now, to take control of your life. You can get in that hot air balloon and ride it, take it to your house, and set your entire life in motion. Or you can stay out of it. Wait until the sun rises and see where time will take you. Because if you chose that path, Sally, the past two years of your life will never have happened. You'll go to work that day and keep your job. You'll go to Marcy's party and have a fun time. You won't meet Matt Daniels; he'll never have existed. You won't meet Zander. His sister will follow his unbroken jump, and the two of them will leave Earth without having met you. You'll never meet anyone not of this Earth. You'll never go to space."

"And you?" I said, shivering. It wasn't from the cold. "You said it yourself. Without Zander, Blayde, and I, you'd still be on that planet, living under a dome under the thumb of an AI."

"That's the power of the choice I'm giving you, Sally," he said. "My life hinges on yours. Change your past and change our futures, or make our lives happen. Either way, my fate depends entirely on yours. You see the power I give you?"

I took a step back, my legs shaking. I hadn't felt this level of fear for a long time, if ever. It was more than being threatened with death; I was being threatened with life.

"You can't make me decide," I said. "How cruel are you? This is not my decision to make!"

"That's where you're wrong, Sally," said Nim, almost angrily now. "This is entirely your decision! Your responsibility! It's your life; take control of it!"

"Screw you!" I spat, turning to walk away from him. I stormed off, knowing he'd try to follow me, but I didn't care. "You can't throw this on me!"

I was wrong—he didn't storm off. He simply jumped in front of me, appearing in the air like he had been there all along. If my eyes hadn't already adjusted to the dark, I would have run into him head-first.

"Sally," he chided. "Sooner or later, you're going to have to stop letting things just happen to you. You're going to have to make things happen.'"

"What, you have a problem with how I live my life?" I asked, angrily, turning to my right and heading off in that direction instead, cutting a zigzag through the wheat field. The grass was tall and itchy, but I was too mad to care.

"Yes, I do!" he said, once again appearing in front of me, forcing me to stop dead in my tracks. "Seeing as how I'd like to be a part of it!"

"Well, screw you!" I had run out of insults to fling at him. "Did you ever consider that I might not want to spend my life with you?"

"Yes."

"And you'd be okay with that?"

"I'm an immortal. I would never stop trying. Sooner or later, you'd see that you feel the same way about me."

"No means no, Nimien!" I spat, furious.

"No's don't last long, in the grand scheme of things. Your life lasts an eternity. Decisions can be changed."

"You're not making a great case for that right now."

"You might think differently in about a thousand years or so." He pulled a flower out of who knew where and handed it to me. "We have all the time in the universe and then the multiverse, too, if we find that too short."

I slapped the flower out of his hand. "Even if I were

immortal, I wouldn't spend even a fraction of that time with you."

At this, he frowned. It was evident, now. The boy from Aria I had known was gone for good. Had he been real at all? Or was he the cunning creation of a master manipulator? Nim no longer existed. Nimien was here in his place.

And he wanted me.

I cringed. Nimien was giving me a way out, though. A way to clear him out of my life, for good. But the consequences of that action would ripple through time and space. If I purged myself from Nimien, took up his offer to stop the hot-air balloon from ever reaching its target, I would be responsible for the Zoesh never being found on Earth, letting the monstrous ship continue incinerating the planet every few thousand years.

Unless—unless me avoiding conflict meant Nim was never Nimien, and he had never set the Zoesh loose in the first place.

I glared at Nimien. How much of what he told me was true? Was it possible he was responsible for those issues in the first place, giving me a reason to doubt giving up my past? But if he had created them, wouldn't they go away if he was destroyed?

"I love you, Sally Webber," he said, taking my hand. "Heart and soul, I love you. All my life, my thousands of years of existence, I've had one thing in mind: to make you the happiest woman in all the universe. And if it takes thousands of years more to make you love me the way I love you, well, then, you're worth the wait."

Contrary to what he was intending, his words chilled me to the core. They scared me in the primal part of my brain, the part that was shouting *run, Sally, run!* These were not the words of a lover; they were the words of a stalker.

"You don't love me," I said, coolly. "You love the idea of me. You hardly even know me."

"I know your own life more than you know it yourself."

"That's not love!" I tore my hand from his, making him scowl. "That is an obsession!"

"Love is obsession!"

"No!" I snapped, wanting to run more than ever now, but feeling trapped and small. "No! All those things you told me, when you were Matt. About how you saw how great I was and shit. I thought it was romantic, but it was just your ... Your ... it was your charm! It wasn't substantial! You wanted me, and you would say anything to have me, even if you didn't believe them to be true." I glared at him. "I don't know why you want me, Nimien, and I don't care. I am not yours, nor am I anyone else's. Now leave me alone."

He reached out to grab my wrist before I could move. But his face wasn't angry; it was calm. He squeezed, tightening the pressure. I didn't know whether to stare at him or at the arm he was slowly breaking.

"This is because of Zander, isn't it?" he snapped. "He clouded your mind. You're in love with him, aren't you?"

"It's none of your business whether I love him or not. I understand, now, why you pushed him away when you were Matt. God, I should have seen the red flag when it was hoisted in front of me! It wasn't charming;

it was possessive! And I am not a possession. I can befriend anyone I want. You do not control me."

With that, he twisted my arm, snapping my wrist in half. I felt the snap—I heard it, too—yet the searing pain I expected never came. I saw my arm dangling before me, but I felt nothing, not even nausea. Instead, I picked my hand up, my body filling with shock as the bone knitted itself back together.

Oh Derzan. I really was like them.

I didn't have time to dwell on the realization. Nimien stood so close to me I could smell his breath, heavy with the scents of mint and sea. The smells, which I had once loved, now turned my stomach.

"The choice is yours, Sally Webber," he said, breathing on my face. "Get in that hot-air balloon and make yourself into the woman you were always meant to be, give yourself the gift of immortality, take the keys to the universe for yourself—or stand here all night and stop it all from happening. We will never meet. At least I can be content with the fact you won't remember Zander."

And then, Nimien was gone, leaving me alone in the field, in front of the balloon that had changed my life. Leaving me with a choice I never wanted.

And a decision that had to be made.

CHAPTER TWENTY-SIX
A GOOD OLD-FASHIONED FIGHT SCENE

BLAYDE

Some days, *"I told you so"* just doesn't cover it.

Dealing with my brother's frayed decision-making skills had always been what kept me going. Well, it gave me a purpose, other than just a wild existence, a bundle of chaotic atoms that refused to just lay down and die. Cleaning up after Zander had driven me forward, so of course, the one day I want something for me, I end up in a mess of my own.

Which turned out to be one of Zander's messes. Again. I should probably say I'm not surprised by any of this, but that would be a lie: It was an understatement, seeing as how I practically expected it.

I didn't bother changing into the monk robes. I

wouldn't give Nimien or his acolytes the satisfaction of seeing me stoop to their level. I was already sticking out like a supernova, so why bother trying to play by their rules?

I had a simple goal in mind: getting my hands on my journal. The first one, the disappointing one, yes, but also the one that held our beginnings.

That, and I needed my current journal, which I suspected was kept in the same place. He could take my book, take my pointer, but he couldn't take my dignity.

My vision swam with blurred whites and grays as I flew down the corridor, my feet barely touching the floor. I pushed myself faster and faster, letting instinct take over. I wasn't running; I wasn't jumping—this was something new. Or old. Hard to tell. Always hard to tell.

Good brain, running so fast. Smart brain, finding the way. I would have crashed into the wall by now if I hadn't put it on autopilot, millennia of reflexes leading the way.

This library was one big ball. Rolling, spinning like a planet. Gravity pulled me down.

By that line of logic, the best way to find this center, was by going down.

Down is fun.

I reached the end of one of the many corridors to be faced with a difficult decision: elevator or stairs?

Stairs. Definitely.

I slammed the door open, even though I guess I could have opened it normally, but where's the fun in that? In three quick steps, I jumped over the rail into the empty shaft that led to the center of it all.

Falling was fun. Falling was fast. Falling reminded me of what it's like to fly. I remembered flying once, though the memory is vague, fleeting. Landings flashed by my face, faster and faster and faster, until they, too, were nothing but a blur. The silence was deafening; the silence was free.

Ground in sight; heart take flight. Muscles clenched, relaxed. I stood at the bottom of the shaft, all gathered momentum gone and not a sound of my arrival.

Unceremoniously, I brushed off imagined dust from my shirt. Habit. Always gave me time to check my surroundings while giving the appearance of not truly being there. The coast was clear.

Nimien had obviously not expected Sally to come to the rescue. Hell, *I* hadn't expected Sally to come to the rescue. We had gone from two immortals taking on the universe together to two mortals, a romantic entanglement, and a nemesis factor.

It had been ever so long since I had a nemesis. I had never truly expected it to be Nim, though. I pushed open the door and stepped out into yet another white corridor, unsurprised yet again that it was empty. Perks of superimposing moments of time was that you simultaneously were all there at once and completely, utterly alone in your world.

Nim's world. Nim's stupid world. Nim's stupid trap.

Was the journal even real? Instincts pointed to yes, the feeling deep in my gut that I had written those words. Even if the logic wasn't all that sound. Although I had no memory of the book itself, it felt familiar, the cool touch of the leather on my hands stirring old feelings.

Another hall, same as the others. But recognizable. I strode through the corridor, muscles tense, ready. No weapons except for my own hands and feet. Perfect.

The monk didn't have time to see me before I jumped behind him, arms around his neck before he could utter a word. Squeeze, slip, safe. Then he was unconscious on the floor without making a fuss, good boy. I found his key pass and opened the door he had been protecting, ignoring the usual protection policy. No time for a bunny suit now.

I couldn't blame the monks for doing their job. It was a cushy gig, after all: going from being the errand boys of the Alliance to suddenly running the most powerful collection of information in the universe was quite a step up. He'd be fine once he slept it off.

In another life, I would probably like it here. Though I was not one for reading, I was all for knowing. Reading was so time-consuming, but the information received was worth it. If I wasn't in such a hurry to get out of this place, I would have snuck a peek in any one of those old tomes.

The oldest books in the universe. I was older still. It's always hard to see yourself as old, especially when you kept the complexion of a mid-twenty-year-old human for as long as I had and the memory of a computer crossed with a rather small sieve, a photo-graphic memory unless said memory had been cleared for more space.

The details it chose to keep were confusing and comforting all at once. I could remember all the lyrics to the Julkan funeral dirge, a twenty-seven-hour rant about how cooking one's eggs to the proper temperature saved lives. I could remember how to defeat the last boss in the popular Avarethian VR immersion—throwing the other members of your party at his many eyeballs until his allergies acted up. I could remember promising this one girl I would be back with her groceries in a few hours, but I hadn't been back in five hundred years, and at this point, it doesn't really matter anymore.

But I couldn't remember my home, my mother's face, any of the milestones people found so important in their lives.

I didn't have a life; I had an eternity.

There, in front of me, was the stand that had held my book, but it was gone now. Lovely. Further proof of the setup.

I felt a pull toward the old books as I had earlier, the pages that contained all knowledge of good and evil. I felt them call to me, their wrinkled, old pages reaching for me and trying to bring me back to them. I froze, fighting desperately to escape their grip on me, the temptation of all this knowledge, and was unable to take another step.

Maybe I deserved a little peek at the other tomes. I was older than they were, to be quite honest, and I wasn't planning on coming back anytime soon.

I glanced over my shoulders, left then right. Up, down, and a dozen other directions. Nada. Zilch. I was free to read and read I did.

Come to mama.

The first book was nothing special. Cryptic, that's what it was. Dark and weird and full of tentacled beasts.

Prophecies for the end times, which by all accounts had already passed. I did remember the oozing green planet covered in slime, but was that past or future?

Veesh. There goes my sense of linear time. My own history, the part of it I could remember, were in shambles.

The red leather was a symbol, I read to myself. Oh, hello. This sounded familiar. The woman warrior. *They had no different word for red and blood. They called her a weapon. Called her the blade, though she claimed it as her name.*

Spooky, showing up in someone else's history like that. At least, I think it was me. My ego has a habit of inflating when I get angry; I've been working on it. Even so, a shiver traveled through my spine as tiny fragments of memory danced in front of my eyes, just out of reach, daring me to catch a full glimpse.

I had only read one page, the words floating in my consciousness like the old memories. Unable to hold onto them. My brain tried to purge itself, as if the words were a virus and could not be saved.

"Find anything interesting?"

I almost jumped out of my skin—believe me, it had happened already; not very pleasant—at the sight of him there. Nimien, looking polished and altogether pleased with himself, leaned over the reading lectern as if he had just caught me cramming for an exam. Somehow, he had jumped to exactly where he had wanted to be without blinking an eye. I wrinkled my nose in disgust as I smelled his gel, a sign he mistook for a scowl.

"Good to see you again, Blayde. What? No hello?"

For the first time in recent memory, I was at a loss

for words. I couldn't understand why I wasn't moving either. I knew that if I wanted to, I could snap his neck in three places. Yet my arms refused to move.

"Don't stop reading on my account." He jammed a delicate finger on the page, crinkling the old paper. "There's so much more to learn."

"Shut up."

Blayde, who can decimate armies with a look.

Blayde, who once saved a planet with a poker chip.

Blayde, who talks about herself in the third person.

Whose comeback ability had been sorely reduced to that of a child.

I'd spoken to his lot before, yet never one this powerful. So full of themselves. I guess I probably was like that sometimes. Maybe that's why I despised them so much.

"What do you think of my collection?"

He waved his arm toward the library, and I remained transfixed by him. Stuck. Trapped in my own body. For the first time that I could remember, I felt fear. Real fear. Panic? My cells were beating in unison, the human equivalent of a heart racing. I felt my whole body pulse with the emotion I thought I had purged. I did not fear death; immortality had to end sometime. No, I feared this knowledge.

I feared the facts contained in those books.

All the while, he spoke of how he acquired them, the secrets I would learn if I read them. I wanted to yell, to run, yet with every step, their call was harder to resist. Tricks and traps and an eternity of controlling the universe. A scared, angry little boy playing at being a god.

"You're one smart woman, Blayde." Nimien patted me on the back as he pulled out another book, a smaller one, bound in silvery gray like storm clouds. "Smart enough to escape the mind cell I created. I think it's only natural I should reward this intelligence, don't you think? Not let it go to waste."

My eyes were riveted on the large purple book on the shelf, the golden words on the binding swirling, fading between every language imaginable. Symbols, letters, cryptograms.

The Sympan. First book ever written. A detailed account of the first years.

The universe in a tomme.

"I don't want to," I managed to say.

" Of course, you do."

"No, some things aren't meant to be known." I felt my resolve growing, but I still could not move. My mind was foggy around the edges.

"Blayde, it's just a book. There isn't anything wrong with books, is there?"

I shook my head, unable to think of an argument. Unable to dig deeper in my mind, as if the only thing I could think of at that moment was the book.

"Books are meant to be read. Why else would they be written?"

"Not all truths are good to tell."

"You're right. Sometimes information must be kept from those who can't handle it. It's for those who need to know the information."

"I don't need to know."

"Sometimes people must put aside their own needs for the needs of the others." His perfect white teeth were too close to my face. If I had my wits about me, I would have punched them out. "And the knowledge needs to be known. By someone."

"Not me."

"Who else?"

We stood facing each other in silence, the call of the books so prominent in my mind it was like they were shouting. My skin pulsed. I forced myself to keep my eyes on his, but it was as if the pages were clawing at my face.

"Not. Me."

"You've saved worlds many times over. The universe, on some occasions. I know the history of the universe and its future. Some of your actions stopped small events from escalating to total destruction. Some events are yet to come."

"I do not need more responsibilities." I breathed deeper, my skin crawling with the lust of the books. "The universe doesn't need me to be any more powerful than I am now."

"Yet only you have the power to know this knowledge without letting it overcome you."

"No."

Nimien grinned. "One page. If you can't handle it, stop."

"Stop yourself."

I couldn't restrain myself anymore. My gaze drifted down, seeing the words yet not interpreting them.

"It's the truth you're looking for. Don't be afraid." I felt Nimien's hand on my back. I could feel his face distort into a grin. "You will become a god, know all, both good and evil."

I felt a shiver go up my spine. Was it still fear? Or was it excitement now? And with a deep breath, a deep exhale, I began to read.

I absorbed the words faster than I could understand them, their sweetness filling me, every letter making me feel stronger, more powerful.

And I continued reading.

Without seeing or knowing how, I flipped the page, reading on.

Faster and faster, the words blurred before me; my cells pulsing to the invisible beat of the universe; my eyes reading at the speed of light. Nimien's grip on my back was harder yet more and more welcome by the second, tethering me to reality.

I felt something wet roll down my cheek. A tear? Was I crying? I escaped the book for a second, following the journey of the tear as it slipped off my cheek onto the book below, the fall feeling like an eternity.

A silent plop. A quiet splatter.

The scarlet drop staining the page.

The feeling of more rolling down the other cheek.

Tear after tear of red liquid escaped my body, shattering my concentration.

At first, I felt hate. The blood disturbed me, my reading—I must stop it so I could continue; I must keep on with the flow of words, with the truth, with the knowledge of the universe filling my brain and making me stronger.

And then a single thought shattered it all: this hate was destroying me.

I didn't want this power.

I didn't need it.

Yet my hands were still on the wrinkled, old pages, still stuck there.

The place Nimien's hand touched my back turned hot. I knew heat, lived by it. I had been burned more times than I could count, explored the deepest reaches of volcanoes and scorching dry worlds. But this heat was unbearable, bringing my focus to a pinpoint, to a single goal: get away.

I screamed, the weight of the information gone, letting me breathe freely. I spun around and shut the book. Nimien—gone. As if he were never there.

The burn on my back wasn't going away, like all my cuts and bruises I had ever had, but all I felt was relief. I was free of the spell, whatever had overcome me, free of his control.

The fact he had managed to hold me so still chilled me to the core.

There he was, standing a good ten meters away, waiting with his arms crossed over his chest. Waiting for what? For me to strike? I knew better. Everything in this place was a trap.

To break free, I would have to change.

But he could see what happens next, couldn't he?

"Well done," he said, inclining his head. "There's the Blayde I know and love."

"You call this love?" I spat. "What kind of sick game are you playing, Nimien?"

"No longer calling me 'kid,' I see."

"No, I reserve 'kid' for friends. And I seem to remember that's what you were, at some point."

"Before you left me to die."

"I said I was sorry."

"Look, I'm still willing to extend an olive branch," he said, "seeing as how you came here for answers, and I have them. Come with me."

Why did I follow him? The answer was simple: Because I wanted to. Enemies and arch-nemesis are fine and dandy, but I wanted answers more. I had walked right into a trap, but the trap was baited with something real.

"I want my journal," I said through gritted teeth.

"Oh, you'll get it. Promise."

He led me through the hall of books, down the rows and rows of hard copies, the histories of civilizations risen and gone spread out along the shelves, along with copies of those that had yet to see the light of day. I wondered how many more Zander and I were in. How many Nimien had played a key role in creating, in destroying.

No one man should have so much power.

I decided, then and there, that Nimien probably deserved to die. And I would be the one to end him.

Of course, my timing could not have been worse because it was then that he turned the corner, marched down the row of floor to ceiling bookshelves, and extracted a small, red journal.

"See? I always keep my promises," he said, as he handed it to me. I took it gingerly.

"Which one is it? The old journal or the one you stole from me?"

"Don't you understand, Blayde?" Nimien threw his arms wide. "You see so little. Look around you. Every journal is your old journal."

I almost dropped the one I held. Because I was an

idiot. A stupid, blind idiot. A stupid, blind idiot standing between two shelves, each one covered in the same, unremarkable book, one after the other after the other until the end of time.

Journals. Thousands upon thousands of red leather journals, each identical, each mine.

"You gave them to me willingly." His lip curled up in a sly, proud smile. "Every single one. Well, except for the very first. That one I found, once I knew where to look."

"No." My mind buzzed with millions of voices screaming at once, *Not possible, not possible!*

"Every few centuries, you come here, falling over and over again into my trap," he continued, shaking his head. "I would give you a journal to read. We'd drink and eat and have a good time. I had no qualms with those versions of Zander and Blayde. They were not the selves who betrayed me. They were quite fun, actually. Every time, you would leave feeling like your mission had been fulfilled. You'd give me your old journal for safekeeping and head off on a new trajectory to find your home. But, inevitably, you would come back, all memory of the encounter just ... gone."

He snapped his fingers, and I clutched the journal tighter. This was just a story, a taunt, not the truth. Nothing he said could be true.

I would know, wouldn't I? My past in his hands?

"But now you are here—the right you—and I can finally get my revenge."

The scream that came out of my mouth wasn't mine. It was the scream of Blayde across the ages, scorned over and over again by this lying asshole, this poor excuse for an immortal if I ever saw one. It was a battle cry amplified by lifetimes of lies and deceit.

I flew at him, faster than I had ever moved before, yet he was gone. Jumped away at the last second like the coward he was. Always playing puppet-master from the shadows. He knew what I would do before I would even do it.

There, at the end of the row, my leather jacket hung in a display case. Zander's beside it, looking more battle-worn than mine. My laser on a silver platter. Huh. Last place I expected to see it.

To defeat Nimien, I would have to defeat time itself. Do the one thing Blayde would never do.

I smashed the glass with my fists, freeing my coat, my pointer. There would be no going back. I slipped the jacket on and clutched my pointer in both hands. I would have to destroy the one thing that kept bringing me back.

I turned the pointer on its highest setting and took aim at the red shelf. In an instant, the flames took hold. The books I treasured more than anything in the universe, my histories. The fire grew and spread, taking with it the pages of my lifetimes.

I took one out of the fire, for good measure. Saving one, a single orphaned journal: the first. The rest would go, ending the brutal cycle that constantly brought me back.

The library burned.

The core of knowledge of the past, present, and future melting in a silent fury of flame, consuming the words no one must ever read.

CHAPTER TWENTY-SEVEN

TROUBLE IN PARADOX

SALLY

There was a lot going through my head in that moment all at once. My ideas jumbled and merged together, creating the kind of collage you tell your child you're proud of but blame the dog for destroying when you never hang it on your fridge.

First: Nimien was alive; Nimien was immortal; Nimien was Matt.

Second: I was immortal. Zander had made me immortal, the same way he had done to Nimien, by trying to save my life. Once again, he had gone above and beyond. He had saved my life, only to give me too much life to know what to do with.

Third: Nothing in my life *just* happened to me. It was orchestrated by a creepy stalker who had an unhealthy obsession with me for who knew what reason. Only now I was supposed to take control of my life and make it happen, or whatever bull crap Nimien had spouted.

And, last but not least: I had no freaking idea how to pilot a hot-air balloon.

A decision had to be made: Do nothing and change everything, or fight for the life I was living now. A life that was knitting itself together, the choices of my past culminating in this moment of truth. Did I want this? Could I have it?

I would never know Blayde. I would never know Zander, feel the love for him I felt right now, deep in my chest. I never wanted to be immortal, no. There had been so many things I had wanted in my life, and a longer one wasn't one of them. More than anything, I wanted John back, the brother who had died before he truly got to live. If I had one wish, it would have been to save him. Not to live this life, a life without end. I saw how it made Blayde, bitter and cold. But I also saw how it made Zander: constantly amazed, strong, and stronger than the metal forged at the heart of dying stars.

I wanted that strength. I wanted to be the person I was becoming, someone who couldn't let a civilization die without doing something about it. Someone who pushed the boundaries of what should be possible because the alternative was impossible for the universe to bear.

I wanted to take up that mantle. To be strong when others couldn't. To be the girl they called to help. The woman who *did* something when no one else could.

So tonight, I would do. Not because of some stalker creep who wanted me to, but because it was my choice. I had never felt like my life was in my control, not when my mind consistently turned on me. Not when panic forced my chest to tighten and my lungs to starve. Not when grief overwhelmed me so easily. Before, I couldn't trust my own mind, but now, I was seeing clearer than ever before.

My absurd life had never been absurd; it had all been staged. To change the past, I would have to stand back and do nothing. To take control of my future, I would have to do everything.

First step: create me. I would forge myself through the pain I felt now, create someone capable of dealing with whatever the universe threw at her.

Next, I would come after Nimien and stop him from imposing his will on the universe. I would make myself for myself, not for any man, no matter how much he believed he was in control of my destiny. If I had learned anything tonight, it was that fate is something that can be forged.

And finally, I would end the library. The universe did not belong to a single person. It belonged to all of us, living, breathing, fighting.

Build myself. Take control. Save the world.

I climbed into the basket of the balloon, flying over the wicker wall and grasping firmly at the ropes. Time to turn this around.

Okay, after I looked up how hot-air balloons worked first.

So, there I was, standing, seething in the middle of a field, power coursing through my veins, the knowledge that today I would become eternal, all the while cradling a tiny phone in my fingers and trying to look up YouTube videos about flying this sort of thing.

No, I didn't have a license, thank you very much, but I had this guy's permission, and if I didn't, all the future would be changed, so there's that.

But what would change if I didn't accomplish this? I lit the burner and let the flames grow, golden tongues reaching into the ever-darkening sky. Slowly the balloon filled, but in the quiet, my mind began to fill with doubt. What if I didn't do anything, let the night run its course, wake up in the morning, and go to work? Would Grisham come to Earth if Nimien never left his homeworld? Just how much of my life had this man controlled?

Would there be a Da-Duhui to save if the ICP never went rogue? Would the World-Eater Zoesh ever escape to Earth if Nimien hadn't showed him the way? How many people had I saved from something other than Nimien?

Was I being selfish, believing that I would make such a big difference in the universe? That if I went to work every day like a normal, twenty-one-year-old American girl, it would change the outcome of some alien world on the other side of the galaxy?

The balloon filled swiftly with air, slowly growing above me in the soft moonlight. I recognized its every fold, even now, seeing it with a focus I had never known before. I was so strong, steady, even-minded. I felt fear and knew that it was secondary. Would giving all this up be worth it, to keep Nimien trapped in his bubble world?

But Nimien was smart. If we hadn't let him out, the genius teenager would have done something himself. He didn't need us to free him.

The universe needed me to stop him.

And so, it was with that thought lodging itself in my mind that I threw out the last of my ropes, and rose with the balloon into the sky, confident it would take me to where I needed to be.

I rose high above the field, the ground falling away below me, and while I knew I should be scared, the distance was nothing but an afterthought. I had shed my fear of heights, apparently, or simply subdued it through determination. I could remember what it was like to feel my knees go weak at the sight of the ground striking below me, but tonight my knees were steady.

The fall no longer scared me. What scared me was knowing that after the fall, I would stand up, shake out my shattered bones, and continue on my way.

The city looked so different in the pale moonlight. Clusters of lights sat where buildings stood, diamonds on the earth, a dull echo of the starry night above. There, in the distance, a lone power plant, finishing touches placed on the site of the Killians' exploitation. I was doing this for them.

Or was I? I remembered Sekai at the party, giving me advice to make it through the madness. Sekai, who had only been there because of Nim.

Nimien would pay.

The burner above me sputtered, and the balloon sank. Shit. I hadn't been paying attention to it, not that I knew how to tend to it exactly. Case in point: Now we were sinking steadily, the balloon and me, and we were still miles from chez Sally-of-the-past.

Before I had time to do anything, except dumbly reach for the burner with my bare hands, out of nowhere the basket hit a roof. It slid along the shingles before being dropped once again into the void, dangling over empty streets before finally coming to a full stop across the road.

In a garden I recognized well.

I stepped out of the basket, waving my charred hands in the air to cool them as the blackened skin was replaced by baby-soft, new material. There had been no pain. Only a sense of heat, a sense of unease, and then the knowledge it was going to be all right. The air smelled of bacon, and it was disturbing I found the smell of my own burning flesh to be so breakfasty.

But back to the problem at hand. Because I knew the yard I was now traipsing through, knew the grass and the patio, knew the people who would be standing here in just twenty-four hours. Because this was the yard I had met Matt in, Matt who was onto me since the beginning, Matt who was never really Matt but yet another alien in my life, trying to make history play out the way he liked best.

So that was the night I grabbed Jenn's grill from her porch and stuffed it into my hot air balloon, knowing full well that this was meant to be, though I wasn't all that keen on the details.

"What are you doing?" she called dreamily from her window, wiping the sleep from her eyes as she stared down at me and my balloon.

"I just need to borrow this for a sec," I yelled back. "Don't worry, this is just a dream, okay? Go back to sleep."

I was getting really good at the dreaming lie. So good, in fact, that she slid her window shut and tomorrow morning would tell Marcy it had all been in her head.

I hooked up her propane to the burners, let the flames rise as it filled once more with hot air, and we drifted upward again. Next stop, if the wind was favorable: my apartment, and sleeping me.

It was very favorable. Maybe Nimien controlled the wind as well. Who knew how far his touch extended? I shuddered at the thought. At the memories I had shared with Matt, at the thought I had been so close to someone so disgusting. I had slept with him, loved him, trusted him. I had listened to him when he told me to keep my distance from Zander, not realizing that there was more there than just a jealous boyfriend. He had been trying to undermine my relationships, turn me against my friends, make him my sole focus.

I felt like a queen on the way to long sought-after vengeance, my hands at the prow of my ship, at the neck of my dragon, not on the edge of a wicker basket. All I had to do was set the pieces in motion to make Sally Webber have the worst day of her life and change her world forever.

Touchdown. Propane dying, flames dimming to a cool nothing. The balloon draped over the house as delicately as a doily placed on a bedside table. I leapt out of the basket and landed lightly on the pavement behind my home, enjoying the feel of the cool asphalt beneath my bare toes. I took my keys out from under the flowerpot, let myself into my own home, cold and dark in the early morning hours. I no longer needed the lights; my eyes were fine in the dark, comfortable even. It seemed as though moonlight would guide me after all.

As I closed the apartment door behind me, it struck me how much had changed in just two years. The room was warm, smelling gently of fresh laundry. Rosemary's pillows were still strewn on the couch. I walked past them, drawing my fingers over the soft fabric. The smell of the place, the smell of home years ago, like a memory caught between the pages of a favorite book. This had been my life. All I knew, the day before I had met an alien—technically two—and everything had changed.

No, it was today. The clock on the oven told me as much. Today was the day my life became something more.

I let myself into my bedroom and froze on the threshold. I had thought this part would be easy, but no. Because there was me, sleeping in my own bed, clear as daylight even with the balloon draped over the glass. Me, with my greasy, thinning hair fanning out on my pillowcase. My clothes were strewn on the floor from when I could barely find the energy to do my laundry. Me, hours before I would discover a more chaotic universe.

Last chance, Sally Webber. Last chance to save yourself.

I picked up the alarm clock off the nightstand, popped out the batteries, and jammed them under the mountain laundry pile. That would have to do.

I had done my duty and made myself, well, myself. All I had to do now was get out before anybody caught me.

Except that Rose was waiting for me in the hall.

Not for *me*, exactly. maybe she was waiting for my past—her current—Sally Webber to come out and console her. Maybe she just wanted to think somewhere other than her bedroom. But my roommate was standing before me, her face wet and red, nose sniffling with every breath. She wore her favorite pajamas, the ones with the little foxes on the pants, and clutched a ripped tissue in her fist.

"Sally," she said, as if she was simultaneously surprised and relieved to see me. She had her hand on the bathroom door, as if she were on her way there before I caught her, though I could barely believe that.

"Rose," I replied, happy, so happy to see her. I hadn't heard much from her since the day she had eloped. She'd messaged me on Facebook to apologize for how quickly she had left, and then I guess I had too much in my life keeping me from staying in touch. I saw that she had had a baby, a beautiful girl that she and Ben had named Karen, all rosy cheeks and wispy blonde locks. She was happy, in the future I knew.

But in the present, my past, she was devastated.

"Ben and I broke up," she said, and my heart was crushed. There went baby Karen in the blink of an eye. I couldn't see the future, but I had lived some of it, and I knew this was not how it was meant to be. I wrapped her in my arms and held her as she sobbed as the current Sally Webber slept a deep and restless sleep in the room next door.

"No, no, no, no," I said soothingly, a mantra and a plea. "What happened?"

"I just ... it just hit me"—she sniffled—"that he was not as serious about us as I was. That he was never going to ask me to marry him, you know?"

"Never?"

I pulled away from her grasp, kissed her on her forehead, and placed her on the couch where she could rest her tired head. I knew once more what I had to do. For the universe, for me, and for future baby Karen.

But as I took her keys and drove her car into the night, I found myself wondering what had gotten over me. It was a silent drive through the city, lights green all the way, but the hesitation and anxiety that usually writhed in my gut were silent. And while I liked the freedom, I couldn't help but feel afraid.

What was I doing? If I drove back there now and asked sleeping Sally what she wanted, would it be what I was deciding for myself right now?

I was already changed. How could I know that my decisions were truly my own?

I didn't know how Zander and Blayde could do this, all day, every day. Questioning their identities as their treasured memories withered to rot in the back of their minds. I could turn this car around now, let history play itself out differently, let Rose wake me up in the morning and save me from getting fired from the clothing store.

Every moment allowed for a different outcome. So many futures, all branching out from every single decision. Nimien, keeping all our lives in his mind, the strings crossing galaxies and history itself, going mad from the strain.

I kept driving.

Ben's light was on in his living room. I took this as a sign of things going as they should. Before the engine had cooled, I was banging at his door, mind racing with the words I was going to say.

"You go to her right now," I said, before he could even ask what I was doing. The half-nude man clutched the door in one hand and a pint of cookie dough ice cream in the other.

"Sally?" He blinked in confusion. "What are you doing here?"

"I wanted things to run their natural course, but it looks like I need to step in." I stood firm in front of him. "You and Rose are meant for each other. So much so that she's breaking down because she wants you more than her own mind can handle."

"This isn't your business, Sally." He moved to close the door, but I placed my hand on it, pushing back. My muscles didn't scream as I exerted my force, and he struggled to budge the wood even an inch.

"It damn well isn't, but the fate of the world is literally in my hands, and you two need to tie the knot today," I snapped. "You two have been in love for years, and I know for a fact that you have the ring ready and waiting. Don't ask how I do. You've been waiting so long for the perfect moment that the girl slipped by you, and I'm not going to let that happen. You go to her now, tonight, and you bring that rock, and you get down on one knee and tell her how you've felt since the moment you met her. And you marry this girl now. No sense in waiting another second. Because the universe is mad and chaotic and frantic and beautiful, and something as fickle as love shouldn't be lost over a detail. When you find your person, you don't let logic get in your way. The two of you want to be happy together, so go, be happy together. Heck, go to Vegas if you have to, but don't you dare let this moment slip away." I handed him Rose's car keys. "Go now."

I watched him drive away as I sat on his stoop eating his half-melted ice cream and wondered why I had never uttered those words before. I feared myself and envied myself, both for having the guts to say what I had never had the energy to say before.

I had done it.

Every domino was in place for my rebirth, save one. But I had to find Zander for that last piece of the puzzle, and I was stuck in 2017 eating ice cream from someone else's spoon.

This was probably part of Nimien's test, right? Maybe he was meant to pick me up at the end, but he hadn't shown. Which meant one of three things:

One, there was something I had yet to do, though I doubted that. The sun was rising now, and past-Sally was soon to be awakened by a very confusing phone call.

Two, he expected me to jump back, all on my own. And while I didn't quite understand the physics of jumping, I knew that I wasn't going to do this on my own.

And three, he was meant to be here, but he couldn't make it. And since he was a time traveler, well, something must have gone seriously wrong.

Element four paraded into view almost unremarkably. The sun was still low on the horizon, and the only people out for a walk would be graveyard shifts and girls with crazy time-travel missions. So why this woman in a long, silver gown was parading down the sidewalk with her head held high, I couldn't possibly tell you.

"Hey, Selena." I stood. "I thought I would find you here, eventually."

"Sally Webber." Selena, goddess of the moon and surfing ingenue, extended her hand for me to shake. "It's been a long time."

"How long for you?"

"Not sure how to quantify it in human terms," she replied with a gentle shrug. Her dress was like something from a red carpet, liquid moonshine draped over her dazzling frame, wearing my face but not quite. "I had a long recovery from having absorbed the energy of the bomb, but it gave me a lot to think about. I just watched you arrest my husband. Beautiful work."

"The ordeal is finally over, then?" I asked. She inclined her head dramatically, blonde curls brushing against her clavicle.

"It is. I shall be leaving Earth, soon, but I made a promise to an old friend to deliver you along the way. And clear up a certain balloon. It was a rental, after all."

She extended a graceful hand and I took it, handing her the ice cream with the other. She took it without a word.

"How well do you know him?" I asked her as the ice cream dematerialized. The edges of my vision were fading now, but I felt no fear, only the certainty that this was right.

"The abbot?" Her smile was wide, her eyes sparkling. "Not well enough. But he knows you."

"Did you know he helped free your husband?"

She shook her head. No.

"I don't trust him." I said. That was putting it mildly.

"I do. He brought me you."

When the world faded into hues of blues, she was still there, and when the office of the abbot came back into view, she was still there. But when Zander rose from the floor, she was gone, and I was left with the sinking feeling that the worst was yet to come.

CHAPTER TWENTY-EIGHT

ALL THE JOYS OF TIME TRAVEL, NONE OF THE MILES

ZANDER

I can't say I ever missed pain, but I do know I romanticized it a whole lot because when I felt the real deal for the first time in time immemorial, all I wanted was for it to stop.

When it did finally stop, I wanted a cheeseburger for some reason. Like a good, greasy cheeseburger from Earth. I laid there flat on my back, staring up at the ceiling, listening to my nerves sizzle and regrow. It was only then when the numbness returned—thank Derzan—that I rolled over and realized Sally was gone.

I retract that "thank Derzan" part. There was nothing to thank, only terror and panic and panic and terror.

The only good news about this situation was that Nimien was gone. But gone where? And Sally was surely with him, which was the exact opposite of okay.

Nimien. Nim. The boy who I'd just two weeks ago taught to hold a sword, whispered him words to woo Angee, buried his memory in an empty box beneath an alien tree. Now somehow, he was Matt, a man who had hated me, resented me.

He was an immortal, the abbot of the Berbabsywell monks, leader of the greatest library in the universe, so full it warped time and space, and all this, all *this,* because he wanted the one thing he couldn't have.

Sally.

And then she was back, the papers on his desk swirling as she appeared, looking stunning in her red dress, her feet bare and brown as they touched down on the cool metal surface. But she was alive, her eyes glowing with a light I had seen only once before.

Selena.

As she descended, the light went out, and Sally was left teetering on the tabletop. I was by her side in a heartbeat, reaching for her as she fell dizzily into my arms.

And then she was crying—we were crying—her arms wrapped around my neck, my arms around her back, holding her close, as if I could pull her into my heart and keep her safe there.

But she didn't need that. She pulled herself up, wiped away her tears, and captured my gaze in one fell swoop.

"We need to stop Nimien." The certainty in her voice was stronger than ever before.

I had so many questions. Where had he taken her? What had he done? But the look on her face, that of sheer determination, was enough to keep my mouth shut for now. We would talk later about what she had just been through, when we had time for more tears.

"What do you need me to do?" I asked, and confusion crossed her features. Huh. I guess I was used to *her* asking that of *me*.

"You're not going to like it."

"We have to stop Nimien. He's out of control. No one should have all this power. And the fact he used it to manipulate you into ... into—he can't be allowed to go on. If you have a plan, I need to hear it."

"I need to finish this," she muttered, clenching and unclenching her fists. "I need you to make me immortal."

The number of immortals in the universe had doubled since I had woken up today. Sally was now one of them, making her a light in the universe that would never expire. A wild hope I had never wanted to feed, one both astonishing and terrifying in scope.

I have been the one to do it, yet it hasn't been done. Not yet.

We stood there in silence, both of us with things we needed to say but couldn't get out. Facing monsters, a black hole, invasions—fine. But gathering the courage to say the hardest words to say? You needed more than sheer bravery for that.

"I'm not ready," I hissed, taking a step back. "I thought I was, but I'm not ready to see you like that. I'm not even sure if this is the right thing to do. I can't make you immortal just because I want to share an eternity with you. Blayde's right: I have lived thousands, maybe millions of years. We have known each other for such a short time. The fact I have never felt this way before could be—I mean ..."

"Zander."

She stood taller than I had ever seen her before. Confident in a way that I had only seen the beginnings of before. Now, she looked ready for war.

"Zander, this is not your decision to make. It's my future, and I have decided. My place in the universe is to help it. I need you to make me immortal. not because I want to see where this thing goes, but because I'm ready to see where I'm going. This was always meant to be, even if Nimien thought he was orchestrating it. The cycle was in place since before either of us. It's just, I dunno, time."

Her confidence faltered, only briefly, at the end of her speech. As if she realized the weight of her words and decided to put a bit of it down. When she looked back at me again, she was nervous, her lip quivering ever so slightly.

"Are you sure you want this?" I asked. "There's no going back."

"I know. I've played my part. Now it's time to play yours. I wouldn't give up our time together for anything. Not even my own mortality."

She reached for my hand, and I took it in mine, wrapping her slender fingers in mine. No longer fragile. No longer breakable. Sally Webber was hard as steel, inside and out. A different Sally altogether, though the same through and through.

"Just one thing," I said. "I don't quite know how time travel works?"

"Oh, that is a problem."

She let go of my hand, brushing her hair out of my face before stepping around me. The wall of Sally's still sat frozen, a memorial to a mortal life.

A hunter's wall of trophies.

"Do you think you can jump based on an image?" She waved her hand toward the wall. There was a picture Sally and her brother sharing a jumbo pizza, and she cringed.

"I've never had a reason to try," I said, watching her life scroll by. "But if Nimien can do it on thought alone, I should be able to. I think."

I hoped.

Nimien, defying all odds. Doing more with his immortality than Blayde and I ever did. Building a vast intellectual empire. Unlocking the secrets to the travel in his blood, the travel we gave him. Better than us in every way.

"You know what scares me most about this wall?" Her voice was hardly more than a whisper. "It's that I recognize every single moment."

"I don't ... I don't know why you find that troubling."

"There's nothing here I don't remember. There's a certain woman back home, one who I haven't offended yet—I don't see her here. Which means these are all things that have already happened to me. *Only* things that have happened. If this wall is Nimien collecting my past, I'm afraid of what he has planned for my future."

I swallowed, hard. I reached for Sally's hand and she held it, softly. I picked an image. A hospital, hopefully hers, the right day, the right time. When I let go of her hand, I filled my heart with determination, closed my eyes, and held the image there.

I reached for the universe, opening myself before it, allowing it to take me in. The darkness enveloped me, filling me whole.

Take me here, take me here, I begged of it, the same way I had once begged it to bring me to Earth. I thought of the shove when we had landed in Aquetzalli, the way it had felt so deliberate. Had Nimien done that too? Had he pushed us into his trap? Was anything out of his reach?

I felt Sally's hand again. With a jolt I realized I hadn't gone anywhere. I opened my eyes to the wall of photos again, feeling the warmth of her touch rising through my arm.

"No luck?" she asked, as if the result wasn't already obvious. I shook my head. "You need to let go, Zander."

"Let go? Of what?"

"You're tense. Look at you."

"Of course I'm tense. Somewhere out there, you are dying, and I can't do a damn thing about it, even if it was somehow meant to be. Nimien could, though. What if he's the one you saw? What if he saved you? What if I never ..."

The look on her face shut me up rather fast.

"Zander, you're in your own head," she insisted. "I know Nimien scares you. He scares me, too. I don't know where he is right now, if he's taunting us. I can't be sure if anything I do in my life is my own free will. But you know what? I'm going to keep fighting."

She reached up and planted a kiss on my cheek, tendrils of heat growing through my skin.

"Zander, right now, you have to jump. If this is the

only time in the universe when you have to be accurate, then let it be this."

She let go of my hand again, and I closed my eyes, feeling the kiss, that tiny kiss, consume my soul. Sally Webber. The girl had crossed time and space to find me *as she lay dying*. I would find her the day she first died.

I ripped my cells away from her, shattering my body into every unique element that made up all of me, feeling my consciousness squeeze into the dark void that held everything together. The nodes and filaments of matter that ran through the entirety of existence, dark and just out of reach.

I thought of the week I had spent on Kili, dancing wild dances with the crew I had just saved, eating food made for kings, turning down proposals of every sort. All for a single reason: to get back to her. I drew on that feeling, the feeling of not knowing if she was alive or dead, the need to see her again. I felt my way blindly through the backstage of the universe, hoping, reaching for the light that was her.

This time I knew I was in the right place. The second my cells come back together, I felt the cold prickle up my spine that came with the awful sense that the worst was yet to come.

I was in a dark hallway, facing a closed ward, the window shades closed. Yet I still felt it.

It must have been the middle of the night. The lights were off—all of them. An eerie light came from under the door, a light blue light from the electronic monitor of the ward.

This was the place. The place Sally Webber died.

Suddenly I could see again, the darkness of the hall

darker, the lights lighter. I found myself gasping. No jump had ever been so difficult, so painful, as that one. But no one had seen me arrive. I looked around; no cameras in this part of the hall. I was alone.

Except for her.

"Sally?"

I pushed the door open into the room where she lay, and for a moment, I thought I had taken a wrong turn somewhere at node 24-A. Because that wasn't a human in that bed. If it was, it shouldn't be alive, let alone breathing, even with a tube to help.

No, what was in the bed was too red and raw to be human. Skin missing, bones exposed. A nose burned clear off a once-human face. Hair seared to the roots. A body so puckered and sore it couldn't belong to a person, let alone her.

This. This is what Blayde had been warning me about since the beginning. She had known. She had seen the damage we did to people and had been protecting me, and Sally, since the very beginning. Her warnings had been so distant, so fueled by jealousy, or so I thought.

But no, they were real. This was what we did to people, the real human cost. I was so thrilled that Sally had become one of us that I hadn't stop to consider the alternative. That my actions, and mine alone, would put her at death's door.

I mean, come on! Who invites someone to watch the explosion of an underground spaceship? It's not cute; it's dangerous.

Here before me was the result: a woman without a face, barely a body to rely on.

"Sally," I said again. The words didn't come. They were caught in my throat, somewhere between my anger and grief. Here she lay dying.

All because of me. What good was I saving her if I had been the one to put her here?

"It's Zander," I said, then regretted it instantly. She had no ears to hear me, not really. I paused, in some small way hoping that this would wake her up, though I knew deep down if I did not act soon, she never would. She didn't stir. The only sounds in the room were the slow bleeps of the machines by her side and the rasping sound of air being forced into her lungs through a tube.

I wanted her to wake up. To wake up and throw something at me, to scream, to yell. I wanted her to be angry at me for what I did to her. To be angry for everything: taking over her life, dragging her into mine, destroying her job and abandoning her for two whole veeshing years, taking her to space only to get lost in the madness, dragging her through the chaos all the way back.

And behind all this, Blayde, who was always right, and Nimien, who was never wrong.

"I'm sorry I couldn't get here sooner." I forced the words out. If I didn't say something now, I never would. And she never could either.

"I'm sorry I couldn't come back sooner." I looked at her, really looked at her. This was what happened when you let yourself get too close. "But I promised I would, so here I am. I can see that this means nothing to you; you might not even remember this meeting. But I had to come. Blayde's outside, waiting. She wants you to know she's pleased with how much you helped us save the Killians. They treated us as heroes when we brought them back. You would have gotten that treatment too. Now, I'm going to come back again, and when I do ..."

What was I supposed to tell her, now? I wanted to tell her to run. Get as far away from this life as she could. Run from your home. Run from me and Blayde, never let us take her anywhere. Never let us destroy her light.

But there was a Sally waiting for me at the library. A Sally who was free and alive to choose this. A Sally who wanted all this.

"You'd better be alive, Sally." I reached for her hand, then decided against it. No more pain tonight. "So, I'm going to get a guarantee on this." I pulled open the nightstand and found a sterilized needle they had left there. I jammed it into my arm, pulling out some blood, then injected it into the blood bag dangling over her body. All so easy and painless, yet the worst thing I had ever done in all my memory.

"I'm coming back to you, Sally." I left the hospital room, hoping no one would notice me being there. How on earth had she even remembered this encounter?

I closed my eyes, letting myself fade, getting sucked back through the universe to the here and now where Sally was waiting for me, safe.

She was sitting at the desk as if it were hers, expertly navigating the computer console, a determined yet confused look on her face. She looked up as I arrived. Her face was hers, once again, the same she had worn the day I had met her. The body in the bed was nothing but a terrifying memory.

A haunting one at that. A warning, for when I got too close.

"So? Is it done?" she asked, already knowing the answer.

"Yes." My answer was short, simple. She didn't want any comforting words; it would only make things harder. She had made the ultimate decision, giving up her mortal life for—it must have been more than just for me, but I couldn't look past her sacrifice far enough to understand it.

"What now?" She picked up the laser pointer. She had somehow found it while I had been dealing with her past.

"Now," I said. "Now, we take care of our old friend Nim."

CHAPTER TWENTY-NINE
I HATE MAKING TERRIBLE DECISIONS

SALLY

The library was as impossible to traverse as it had been when I had first landed there, yet it felt like we had spent an eternity in this infinite hole. Thinking about eternity made bile rise in my throat. Eternity would be a thing I would know now, whether I liked it or not. I had made the decision; I could never go back on it.

We ran into Blayde before we even got a trace of Nimien. She burst out of a doorway, practically crashing into us, smelling of old books and fire. She tossed Zander his old black coat without breaking stride.

"This place is the worst," she proclaimed, throwing wild looks at us. "Talk about torture. Ugh. Turns out we have fallen into Nimien's trap, like, a gazillion times, and the past me is an idiot who keeps giving him my journal. Veesh. I stole the first one and hope you have my current one."

Zander held out his hand, trading her book for his coat, slipping it on. Relief spread over his ashen face.

"So, wait, you're saying we've been here before?"

"It's a long, long story, Zander-boy. One for when we get out of this place. Nimien didn't give you too much trouble, did he?"

Zander's mouth zipped shut faster than an open fly on a red carpet premiere. His eyes darted toward mine, and I was suddenly aware this was my story to tell and no one else's.

Where the heck to start with this one?

"So, basically Nimien is Matt Daniels, my ex. And everything that has happened in my life has been him manipulating me into manipulating events to make myself me and bring me here. Does that make sense?"

"Oh! That explains everything!"

"It does?"

"No, but I suppose you'll explain all this to me later?"

"You got it, girl."

"Don't call me 'girl.'"

"Can we get on with it, um, fair associates?"

Zander was practically twitching where he stood, his leather coat slick and dark over his gray monk's attire, making the sound of shifting paper every time he moved, voluntary or otherwise. He clenched and unclenched his fists over and over, glancing up and down the hallway as if he were prey being stalked.

"Yes, let's get out of this place," said Blayde. "It gives me the creeps. And plus, we have what we came for."

She patted her breast where both journals now sat comfortably protected.

"We need to find Nimien first, though," I said.

"Why?" She cocked her head. "That idiot is dangerous. Plus, he'll be too busy dealing with the fact that I set his books on fire."

"You what?"

Zander and I didn't realize we spoke in unison until Blayde rolled her eyes. "Look, he kept stealing the journals of our past selves, who, don't ask me how, kept forgetting they came here. That's a dick move, so I burned all the journals. Past us would approve if they knew what was happening. But I think a few other classics might have gone up in flames too. Oops. "

That was it. An eternity of books, gone. In one instant. Moments like these I questioned Blayde's right of authority, controlling what books we read, destroying those containing information that could make us wiser.

"Why did you destroy them? Do you know how much we could have learned?"

She didn't answer, looking at me with the eyes outlined with dried blood, caked and starting to peel away.

"This is a mess," muttered Zander, running a hand through his hair. "A complete and utter temporal mess. Shouldn't there be, I don't know, some super fancy group that goes around making sure no one messes with the timeline like that?"

"Uh, I think Nimien's monks *are* that group," I pointed out. "They might have nefarious motives, but they seem to be the only ones out there."

"Well, there's us now."

"Right," scoffed Blayde. "Because we're totally cut out to be a time traveling adjustment bureau. Zander, I can't even keep track of more than one *journal*, never mind infinite timelines."

"I think there's only one timeline," I said. "When he forced me to go back and set my own life in motion, every event played out exactly as I remembered it, like nothing had changed at all."

"So, what would have happened if you hadn't done what he asked?"

I shrugged. "I don't know. Either there's another timeline, or I was meant to do this all along. No free will and all that."

"I hate every moment of this," Blayde growled. "Let's just get out of here."

"Not so fast."

And then, there was Nimien. Nimien, standing in the middle of the white hallway, scorched robes in tatters around his muscled frame, reeking of smoke and fury. In an instant, Blayde and Zander were on their knees, cringing as they screamed, sounds dying in their throats.

"What the hell are you doing to them?" I spat, storming toward him. I should have been terrified— well, I was, but I was more furious than anything. Anger turned my vision red.

"Sally, you keep forgetting that you're in my home," he said, hands on his hips. "I did tell you about the whole super-pain drug. Or do I have to give the same speech again?"

"You are so messed up, Nimien." I wanted to scream, to punch, to claw my way through his face for everything he had done. All the lies he had told, the mess he had put us through, the torture my friends endured at his hands. "Let them go."

"Fine." He shrugged. "They go free; you stay here. That's the deal."

"That's it? Sold."

"Really?" His eyes went wide, sparkling. For a second, I saw the boy there, a flash of the Nim I knew, but before I could register it fully, it was gone, leaving the husk of a man who stood at his place. "I thought you would put up more of a fight than that."

"Asshole, you're torturing my friends. I'll do anything to make it stop."

He was true to his word. The siblings crumpled at my feet as the pain ended, panting heavily. It took all my willpower not to drop to the floor beside them and see if they were all right.

Who am I kidding? It took all my willpower not to scream and freak out. Worst. Day. Ever.

"You two go before I change my mind," he said, glaring.

"I'm not going unless Sally is coming with me," said Zander, pushing himself gingerly up off the floor. "I won't let you hurt her."

"Hurting her is not my intention. Unlike you, I intend to keep her safe."

"I never wanted her hurt!"

"And yet, you're the one who lost her in space." Nimien lunged, swinging his arm wide, slicing the air before him. "You're the one who put her in danger, repeatedly."

"I'm the one who made her immortal."

"No, that was me. You may have given her the blood, but I'm the one who set it all in motion."

"I feel like I missed a chapter here," Blayde interjected, nursing her aching arms. "Did I miss something?"

"Sally died, and the first place she jumped, the one thing that guided her mind, was the memory of me. It brought her here to my library, where I have been waiting for her all along."

"I hate to break it to you, but she flew to my rescue, " Zander said. "She might have jumped to your library, but she came for me."

"Shut up, both of you," I said, turning to Zander, cringing as I saw the pain in his features. "Zander. You have to go now. Nimien has been planning his revenge since the dawn of time. If you don't go now, there's no saying what he'll do to you. Please. Do this for me."

He looked at me, brow furrowed, eyebrows knotted so tightly together it would have taken a sword to pry them apart. He ran his tongue over his lips, hands in tight fists at his side.

"Sally, you can't for a second believe I'll ever leave you alone with this monster."

"I'm asking you to. Begging you to. Please. You have to go—now—before he changes his mind and does something worse."

"Zander, we have to go." Blayde tugged at his sleeve, avoiding my gaze. "He's trapped us once. There's no saying what he'll do to us next."

"How many times do I have to say it? I'm not leaving you."

"I'm asking you to go."

He said nothing for a minute—a full, long, silent

minute—in which I expected someone to interject, but one no one dared. I gazed at his features, suddenly so clear, like an image brought into focus. Like wearing glasses for the very first time. He was beautiful, yes. In pain and struggling to hide it, a mask on the beautiful lines of his face. I remembered the first time I saw him, when I peeled his bloodied form off my road, and wondered if I knew then what I knew now if I still wanted to go through it all.

For him, I think I did. In that look, I knew he did as well.

"Sally," he breathed, dropping his forehead against mine, and I inhaled his crisp, dry breath; the old leather of his star-dusted coat; the smokiness of his gravity-defying hair. He smelled like home. A tremor wove itself through my heart.

"Sally, I love you, okay?" And then he was ripped away, guided by a militarized monk, a large, silvery weapon pushing against his chest and leading him away from me. "I love you, and I won't stop fighting for you!"

"Love you too, chickadee!" Blayde planted a sloppy kiss on my cheek as she, too, was pushed away. "I don't have any fancy, tear-jerking stuff to say, but it's been a hell of a ride, darling! Be good to yourself!"

And with that, the monk-librarian-soldier guys marched them down the corridor, and they were gone, leaving me alone with Nimien.

The boy I had wanted to build up.

The man I had wanted to date.

The monster who was before me now.

"Must feel pretty special." His hands were behind his back as he walked up to me and smiled that oddly familiar smile. "Having two men fighting for you."

I edged away from him. "Three people if you count Blayde, and my money's on her right now. Secret crushes and all. Always knew she had a thing for me. Swoon."

"I'm being serious." His smile grew, unnaturally wide.

"No, it feels disgusting. I never wanted it. My mind is set, and this kind of petty squabbling—however inter-dimensional it might be—is so off-putting I just want to nap my way through it."

"That's not going to happen. You're a part of the universe now, Sally. You should be celebrating! You are part of an exclusive number of people who can mold history to our will. You are important. Don't let anyone say otherwise."

"No one is. I was important before: to my friends, to my family, to myself. None of that changes."

"Everything changes."

"And who's fault is that?"

"It was your decision."

"You didn't give me a choice, Nimien. Not really. You cornered me in a trap. You gave me a choice like a fox can choose between meeting the hunter or gnawing off its own leg."

"And you grew a new leg in its place. Became something bolder, more powerful, more incredible."

"Or I'm still standing in that damn trap, talking to the jerk who put me here. You know what? I'm leaving."

"What? You said you would stay—"

"You sound like a child, Nimien. I am not your plaything. I'm going home. I need a latte and a nice, warm bath."

He snapped his fingers, and a monk with a clipboard came running. From where, I didn't know. No guns, no weapons, just a single clipboard and pen. He was bald, his monk's robes high on his neck. Once again, I was reminded of the child Nimien once was, but then, that was gone because the asshole he was now rambled.

"Latte, done. We can get you the best latte in the universe. Have you had the ones from Silrunias Octo? No, you haven't yet, have you? They're divine. The milk comes from this creature, like your cows on Earth, but it can only be milked when it is serenaded by a horned snail. The thing is the cows have terrible hearing, so the snails have to perch on the cows' ears, and the snails have to be incentivized to sing really loudly, which helps produce this milk which is like—"

"Nimien! I don't want a fancy alien latte. I want to go back to the Jitterbug and get a coffee with my best friend, and I want you to not be stalking me when I get back. You need to stop following me. Get out of my life."

"You don't mean it." He shoved a hand at the clipboard, knocking the young monk over.

"Yeah, I really do."

"After all I did for you?" The smile faltered, his lips lowering, curtains falling on a scene. "I made you what you are. I elevated you from your small life and gave you the universe on a plate, and now you won't even listen to what I have to say?"

"We're just going in circles now, Nimien. Can I go home or are you going to keep me here against my will?"

"I will keep Zander and Blayde here until the end of

time. You mark my words."

"Oh, wow, now you're threatening my friends again. What are you trying to achieve at this point? It's over. You've tarnished any memory I ever had of Matt *and* Nim. I've said no, and now I want to go home. Can you do that for me, please?"

He shook his head—not no; he wasn't saying anything. He was just confused, lost. Shaking his head in complete desperation.

"I don't get it, Sally. I really don't. I've had the entirety of space and time to think this through, to prepare meeting you. Today was supposed to be the best day of my life, and trust me, it's been a long life. I have a room in the library prepared for you, a suite on this ship where you would be more than a princess or empress or queen. I have a collection of rare books curated for you, based on everything you love. I can't tell you how many freaking table settings I had to pick through to decide how to fix up the mess hall for our grand celebration. I took everything into account, except you saying no."

"Well, sorry, I guess? I don't like big events, and you should know that if you stalked me my entire life. Also, you should know that I was a goddess once, and it wasn't all that it was cut out to be, so I don't quite want a rerun of that."

"I literally made you who you are today," he continued. "I set up everything to help cure you of your depression, and I haven't heard a single thank you."

I couldn't help it; I burst out laughing. This was the most psychotic thing I had ever heard, and it was coming from my dead ex after I had just turned immortal, so life was a little hectic today anyway.

"Cured me? Of my depression? You messed with my head! And I don't know what you thought you did with the whole pushing-me-to-be-immortal thing, but the stupid voice is still there! Except now, it's forever! So yeah, *thank you,* Nimien, for giving me an eternity with myself."

"I made you my perfect girl."

"Well, apparently your perfect girl is one who says 'no' to you."

"Maybe I just wanted to make it harder for myself."

"Wait, so now you think there's a chase? Trust me, there isn't." I took a step toward him, my mind made up, more determined than ever before. "I'm sorry, Nimien, that I left you for dead in the aftermath of the Youpaf invasion. I really thought you were gone forever. I mourned you, grieved for you. Zander and Blayde were never the same after your death either. But you, you've had Hubble time to get over this. You've had since the Big-freaking-Bang, before matter itself existed, to think this through. You've created the greatest repository of knowledge the universe has ever seen. You pulled it out of time to keep it safe. And what did you do with it? You created a trap for the only people in the universe who truly cared for you. If you had told us you were alive, we would have been the ones throwing the party. But, no, you wanted to torture my best friends and take me for yourself, which is so disgusting and weird I don't think I can ever wash it out of my mind. Your anger festered and rotted you to the core. I guess Nim really *did* die that day on ancient Earth because I'm not seeing him now. Goodbye, Nimien.

Good luck with your library."

I turned on my heels and stormed off down the corridor in the direction Zander and Blayde had been taken. My mind raced, and my tongue was numb from having spoken sparks. I turned the corner, realized I had no idea where I was going, and decided to keep walking forward, knowing every step took me farther away from the monster Nimien had become.

My chin collided with the gray carpeting. The blow had come from behind, stronger than anything I had felt before, but there was no pain, only shock. I rolled over onto my back, only to see him standing above me, the slick silver clipboard in hand and a corner dripping with bright red blood.

I felt my head. Crap. The bastard had hit me.

"Don't you turn your back on me!" he hissed, bringing his foot down to squash my ribs, only somehow, I was faster. I grabbed his shoe and pushed him upward and away.

He jumped, his balance regained. I pushed myself to my feet, too slow. He grabbed my hair and pulled back again, sending prickles down my spine. I reached up and gripped his half-charred shirt, tugging hard. This only served to rip off the buttons, but his grip on my hair relaxed, and I was on my feet again, running.

I ran faster than I ever had before. He couldn't hurt me, no, but he could do much worse. Zander and Blayde had been in the mind prison for days at least. Who knew what else he had prepared within these walls.

Chambers fit for a queen were still a prison cell if I was never allowed to leave.

I didn't know where I was going. The white-on-white signposts gave no clear path, and he knew the library like the back of his hand. Still, I kept running.

He appeared in the middle of the corridor, grinning as if waiting for me. This was fun for him, another game. I was just a rat in a maze. I spun around and flew in the opposite direction, forcing the tears out of my eyes.

All the times I had been terrified flashed before my eyes, but this new fear eclipsed them all. Back then, my only fear had been of death. When death was the least of your worries, true terror came from places that were much, much worse.

I took a staircase, taking the stairs three at a time. He couldn't catch up with me, he couldn't, he couldn't.

I opened a door to a landing, and there he was, waving. I slammed it shut and ran upstairs instead, to confuse him, but he knew and was waiting for me there as well. Each time, smiling wide, like we were long-lost friends. I ran back down the stairs, my bones faster than my own skin.

I threw open a door, and there he was—again.

"Why are you doing this to me?" I screamed. "Why won't you just let me leave?"

Then I realized nothing he could ever say would make me go *"Oh, that makes sense. None of this was creepy at all,"* and I slammed the door back in his face.

There had to be something I could do to stop him long enough so he couldn't follow me.

I patted myself down. I was still wearing the wire Felling had given me, a microphone and a battery pack, full-on 90s mode. Other than that, I only had my phone with me, though there was no cell service in a library outside of time. Blayde had taken her pointer back, and I wasn't one for knives or guns.

I saw what I had to do and threw up in the corner of the stairs.

The next time I opened the door and saw his face smiling back at me, I looped the wire around his neck and pulled tight.

CHAPTER THIRTY

I USED TO THINK BEING TRAPPED IN A LIBRARY WAS A DREAM

SALLY

He didn't jump. He didn't even struggle, not right away. First came the shock, the look of pure surprise as he realized I wasn't running away. That I wasn't crying anymore. Then, the anger, the redness in his face as oxygen cut off and he started to truly choke. I pulled tighter, tighter than I ever had before, letting the wire cut through my hands, tear between the digits. I wanted to be strong enough to snap his head clean off.

But it was the last look that caught me off guard. As I pulled tighter, he started to smile. He looked—of all things—proud. Content. And as he crumpled to the ground like a used tissue, he actually looked happy to be there.

I threw up again.

I hadn't really killed him. He would come back in five minutes or so, hopefully enough time for me to find Zander and Blayde and hightail it out of here. But I had still pulled the cord around the neck of a man I had once loved, and it had felt ...

It had felt good.

The rest of my last meal ended up on the floor beside him. He was right; he had changed me. And something like this? I would never lose it again.

So, I went back to the one thing I was consistently mediocre at and ran.

I found Zander and Blayde in the hangar bay. They could have left without me but instead were milling around a large pressure-sealed door, like they were waiting for a Black Friday sale to start.

I didn't even have time to see Zander standing there before he jumped to my side, wrapping his arms around me. I fell into them, welcoming their warm embrace. I wanted to burst into tears. There was too much inside me that needed to come out, but first we had to get out of this cursed place, away from Nimien.

He wasn't truly dead.

I had killed him.

He wasn't really dead.

I had killed a man.

"Right." Blayde pointed finger guns at me. Weird, I kinda liked it. New dynamic with me dating her brother, I guess. If you could call it dating. "We gotta go. The library's on fire. I'm not sure if Nimien did anything about that yet, but let's get away from this place."

"Nimien just let you leave?" asked Zander.

"We had a really good talk," I replied, "and I made it very clear I don't appreciate my life being yanked around like that. Then I left."

"And he was all right with that."

"I don't really care what he thinks."

"Ah, so I'm right, and we're doing my plan," said Blayde. Of course, she looked excited. She rubbed her palms together, grinning.

"You have a plan?"

"Well, we had to do something if Nimien turned out to have completely lost his soul," she said. "And we came up with something quite clever. Where is he now?"

"I kinda ... well"—my voice dropped to a whisper— "choked him to death."

"Woah, badass!" Blayde let out a low whistle. Zander's grip slacked for a split second and was twice as tight the next. This meant two things: one, they took the news way better than I would have, and two, maybe they weren't that great an influence.

"The idea is quite simple," she continued, as if I hadn't just admitted to killing a man. "This library contains so much information, it would create an anomaly if it contained any information about itself. Simple quantum information theory. We came here through one of the nodes, where that information is stored. My plan is to upload the information here, as we travel back to Abryria, and ... well, I'm not sure what would happen to the library once it contains itself, but it'll either implode, turn into a black hole, or become a Denny's."

"A Denny's?" I balked.

"A distinct possibility."

"The fast food chain? The one on Earth?"

"If Denny's have arrived on Earth, then you are truly and royally screwed. But anyway, ready to get away from this wretched place?"

I nodded slowly, extracting myself from Zander's arms. I immediately missed the warmth.

I didn't deserve the warmth. I was a murderer.

"What about Nimien?" I turned back toward the library's grand entrance. "If we leave him here during the implosion? And the Berbabsywell monks who work for him?"

Blayde nodded. "I'm sure there's an emergency release. This library exists outside of time. There must be a way to eject everyone at once. I'll see if I can control that when I start the upload. And as for Nimien? He'll make it."

The harshness of her tone was palpable, sharp as her namesake.

"He'll either end up ejected with them or wake up at the Big Bang again. He can't die. In danger, he'll just jump away. Natural instinct." Zander reached out for my hand. "Come on, Sally."

I didn't know if he was trying to make me feel better or if that was what happened to him—to us—when death wasn't easily reparable. Leaving him to die would be murdering him. I thought the guilt was bad now, but knowing I could take his life entirely was a whole new level of shame.

"Sally, it's going to be okay."

I looked up at Zander, forcing a smile. He didn't smile back. He said nothing. I said nothing. There was nothing that could be said that made any of this okay.

To me, it felt like we were abandoning Nim all over again. My heart broke, while my gut filled with nausea. Trying to keep these two thoughts in line was like trying to get two cats to work together. I wanted to be free of Nimien, but I didn't want to kill him. I didn't want to abandon Nim the way we had on ancient Earth, but I couldn't very well save him when he was hell-bent on keeping us trapped here.

At least I wasn't alone in making this decision. Blayde had already stormed through what I thought had been a pressurized door, taking over the control panel near the center of the bright white room, doing who knew what with the commands. By the time I had processed what we were about to do, she had somehow conjured a beam of light and held it suspended in the air like it was no big deal.

"All aboard the light beam! Next stop, Abryria!" She swiped her finger across the digital board.

"This is very ... Peter Pan, I guess." I followed her lead toward the beam.

"Oh, you know Pan?" She grinned. "Now that's a messed-up dude. Hella fine wine, though."

And with that, we walked into the light, and the library toppled behind us.

Unlike jumping, this voyage was bright, explosively so. My eyes saw nothing but white as the universe wooshed by me, which I guess shouldn't have been possible at all, seeing as how we were traveling faster than light ever had a right to. All in all, though, 10/10 would recommend traveling by light beam: We arrived at our destination in the blink of an eye, and there was no vomiting involved, which was a nice step up for me.

"Oh, veesh," said Blayde, stepping out of the landing pad. Around us were the bones of long-dead aggressors, knives jutting out of their remains, along with things that really shouldn't have been used for impaling. One skeleton was entirely wrapped in a trail of post-it notes, which was simultaneously odd and rather eye-catching.

"What happened here?" I asked, trying not to let the spookiness overwhelm me. There was no sound other than our own footfalls, nothing but death all around us. I shivered, though the room wasn't all that cold.

"They were fighting over who got to kill us," said Zander, reaching for my hand again. I wanted to tell him I didn't need reassuring until I realized he wasn't doing it for me. "I guess no one did, in the end."

"It's better than what happened to Kizkim." Blayde shuddered.

"What happened to Kizkim?" I asked. "Wait, who is Kizkim?"

"Nothing good."

"Wait, what part of my question was that answering?"

"Both."

Not quite the answer I was hoping for, but it was something.

We walked through the long-abandoned halls of an ancient museum, seeing no one, hearing nothing. Though the lights remained off, our eyes adjusted quickly to the gloom, allowing us to see our way through. Another new skill I would have to get used to.

The siblings seemed to know where they were going. We made our way through a hall that looked like an airport terminal until they broke down a door and led

417

us outside, where we emerged on a rooftop airstrip occupied by a single ship.

It was an ugly thing. Part of it looked like the hopper we had used back on Nim's home world, something lovely from vintage *Star Trek*, but with more windows. That and the giant turbojet thing that was strapped to its roof, threatening to crush the ship any second. The engine was bigger than the ship itself, tied together with slack ropes and wild bolts. A child could have done a better job.

"Dave from Accounting!" shouted Blayde ecstatically, rushing forward to wrap her arms around the hull. "Davey boy! I missed you!"

Before I had a chance to ask what the hell was going on, the ship lit up. The massive engine made a sputtering noise as the internal lights flickered on, the ship seemingly awaking from a long slumber.

And none too happy about it.

"Do you have any idea what time it is?" the ship scolded, its voice warbling, reminding me oddly of my grandfather.

"Hey, the library was held out of time," Blayde explained, patting the ship as one would a horse. "We had no way of knowing our return wouldn't be when we left."

"That's what took so damn long?" the ship called Dave spat, which was an impressive sound for a ship to make. "You made me wait decades, and that was your excuse? Go to your room, young lady, and no friends for a month."

"Dave, I have neither friends nor a room here," she said, pulling away. "Not to mention, you are not my father. Or grandfather. You don't get to ground me."

"And you! Young man, you were out of line as well!" the ship said to Zander. "You march your ass over here for a paddlin'!"

"Um, Dave, this is Sally," said Zander, stepping calmly up to the mad ship. "She's a friend of ours."

"I thought I made it clear that you're both grounded! That means no friends over."

"You are not our father, Dave. Technically, I'm yours, or did you forget?"

I practically flew out my shoes, if I had any shoes to speak of. "You're this ship's father?"

"We accidentally gave him consciousness when we engaged warp speed," he explained. "His name is Dave from Accounting."

"Oh, so now I'm an accident?" The ship went from sounding like an old man to sounding like a petulant child, all in an instant. "I have been waiting for you to return for a hundred years, and all you can say to me is that I'm an accident?"

"I'm so sorry, Dave." Zander rushed to his ship. "I'll make this better, okay? But first, we need to get off Abryria. How did you even land here in the first place?"

"Oh, when the library exploded, the ban surrounding this planet was lifted, so I landed. I needed a seat."

"Thanks for coming back for us, buddy."

The ship scoffed. "I would say thank *you* for coming back, but you're the ones who brought me here. What? No visitations? You put your old ship in a new home and just forget about him?"

The siblings exchanged pointed glances. I think I agreed; this ship wasn't in his right mind. If you could call it a mind at all. Accidental consciousness must have been a wild ride.

"So, ready to go?" asked Zander.

"Hold your hoppers. I'm getting there. Harumph!"

The shuttle door slid open, squealing. Inside, a light flickered softly, but as Blayde entered, she gave it a soft tap and it return to a steady beam.

"Are you coming, Sally?"

I didn't realize I was just standing there until Zander brought me back to reality. It was all well and good to see my friends play house with a ship named Dave from Accounting, but it wasn't a life I saw myself in. It was hard to see myself as a part of this team, or whatever we were, when it made so little sense to begin with.

But I guess this was my life now.

I climbed in, taking a seat in one of the plush seats in the back, stretching out with my legs up. This was total class. And soon, we were taking off, stars filling the windows as we glided out of the atmosphere. For an old ship with a messy engine, it flew like a dream.

It was only then that Blayde emerged from the cockpit, her brother in tow, taking the two seats across the aisle from me. She reached into her jacket pocket, extracting the red journal—her journal—though I could tell by their look of calm reverence that this one was the older one.

"Are you ready?" she asked, and he nodded, slowly.

"I want to know."

I wanted to know, too. I scooted closer quietly, trying not to disturb the moment. It was for them, and them alone. They had come so far to know their answers, and only had one of hundreds of books to refer to.

The only answers they would have. Possibly ever.

"We going to read it?" Zander asked, excited.

"We have all the time in the world," she said, and I knew she believed it. In that moment, it was just her and Zander: Alone. As it should be.

I really felt like I was intruding. Maybe I should go and have a chat with Dave, get to know my step-son a little better. If that's how things worked out here. I got up to go, but before I could take a step, Zander's hand clutched mine.

"Stay?" he asked quietly. "Please?"

I sat next to him as he asked. I would expect my heart to be pounding at that moment, but it didn't move; just another thing I'd have to get used to.

Blayde set the book on her lap. She flipped open the first page. As she turned the next one, it started to crumble, but the more she turned the pages, the faster they crinkled. Like a bad dream, right in front of our eyes, the book was being reduced to dust.

With growing fear, she flipped the pages faster, trying to beat the growing cancer. Her wide, fearful eyes took in every detail of the page before it faded into nothing. Zander's hand crushed mine.

The book was nothing more but ash.

Blayde let out a harpy's scream, shrieking in the small shuttle as the dust of the last relic of her lost memory tumbled off her legs. She jumped to her feet, her face distorted in a mess of muscles and nerves. The horrid shrieking that never ended. Suddenly, she was at the shuttle's door, punching out the safety with her fist, pieces of glass from the security box shattering on the floor, falling out of the already healing cuts on her hand.

"Ugh, stop that, will you?" Dave groaned. "I have security parameters, you know."

Maybe she did know. Maybe she didn't. Maybe she just did not care. She wrenched the door open and walked out into space, ignoring us as we screamed at her to stop. The last sound I heard was the air being sucked out through the door, a siren blaring and then—silence.

The sirens were dead in the emptiness of space. Zander's mouth moved, yet no sound escaped, but I could tell he was afraid. Afraid for his sister; afraid for himself.

Whatever artificial gravity held my feet down inside the ship failed. We were floating, rising out of our seats. What remained of the book floated up and around, swirling in stunning patterns, creating a strange curtain of dust that irritated my eyes and stopped me from seeing.

I had been in the vacuum of space once before, and it wasn't one of my greatest hits. Everything pulsing, expanding, stretching as the pressure inside me tried to break into the void. I grabbed my chair to avoid floating off into the nothingness outside the door, but the fear of death was gone, as if it had never been here before.

Zander used the rails on the ceiling to maneuver himself to the door, desperately trying to see his sister. I tried to do the same, though I wasn't as adept as he was, so it took me longer, wrangling monkey bars where up and down no longer had any meaning. But I was soon out of the stinging dust, clutching onto whatever I could near the door.

Blayde drifted peacefully in the dark. Her hair shimmered around her face, framing it in a dark brown halo, much like a renaissance painting, only with the main focal point of the art torn with anger. Though her appearance was one of peace, the expression on her face told another story. Somehow, she was spinning slowly head over heels. Every time she rotated to face the shuttle, her mouth was open, eyes closed, a silent scream lost in the darkness.

Zander noticed me floating next to the door, my hand grabbing the emergency handles put in place for exactly such an occasion, though slightly useless to anyone who, unlike us, was affected by lack of pressure in the ship. He gave me a curt nod, as if to say he could take care of her, that I didn't need to watch. I glanced back and forth, asking silently what I should do. He kept a hand on one of the handles, pulling himself around and pressing a pulsing blue button on the wall. I hadn't noticed that the cockpit had shielded itself until the door slid open, leading into a thin airlock.

I placed my feet on the wall, pushing off toward the door. I glided to the cockpit, grabbing onto another well-placed handle to stop my trajectory. I slapped the button, which lowered the outside door of the airlock, filling the tiny chamber with oxygen. When that operation was finished, the door to the cockpit opened.

Gravity. Air. A ringing in my ears as I took a seat in the co-pilot's chair and waited. And waited. Dave chided us like children, making up a monotonous audio background to remind my ears they had a job to do.

Finally, after too long, the airlock opened and Zander entered the cockpit, his sister in his arms. He fell down in the pilot's seat, Blayde on his lap, sobbing into his shirt. He rocked her back and forth as she cried, saying nothing. Even Dave remained quiet, devoid of his rebuttals. But it was her words that would haunt me for years to come.

The mutterings of a girl who wanted nothing more than to finally die. Over and over again.

CHAPTER THIRTY-ONE

I DIDN'T BRING THE RIGHT DRESS FOR THIS HOMECOMING

SALLY

Blayde's sobs haunted me as we drifted silently through space. The library was gone and Nimien was who knew where. Being a master of space and time, he could have been here if he wanted to, only he wasn't. Panic gripped me as I wondered if I had killed him for good.

I closed my eyes, breathing deeply. The panic eased away. I would never get used to this. But never was a long time, and I had longer ahead of me. Lovely.

"Are you okay?"

I thought Zander was speaking to Blayde, but when his hand slid down my arm, forcing my eyes open, it hit me that maybe he was asking me.

"You're being quiet."

"What is there to say?"

So much had changed in the past day that I couldn't keep up, and, yet, I was calm. More reason to panic than I had ever been dealt, and I was calmer than ever before.

Panic overload perhaps.

"You're right." He sighed deeply, his breath eclipsed by Blayde's anguished sobs. "Sorry about that. That was the last hope of us ever finding out where we came from and—"

"Don't apologize. I'm really, truly sorry." I had to say something, to reassure him, but right now I was the one in need of reassurance. I settled with changing the subject, partially. "Why did it do that? The journal, I mean. Why'd the book die?"

He shifted uncomfortably in his chair. "Safeguard, I think. The monk who brought us to the room of ancient texts said they were protected from theft. I guess Nimien made it so that if he couldn't have the books, no one else could."

"And then Blayde burned them all down."

"Always one step ahead."

She let out a pained moan, wiping tears from the corners of her eyes. "We were warned. We left the library, and time caught up with it. Gone."

She went limp again, and Zander looked over to me, his eyes pleading. For what? I didn't speak eyebrow. I didn't know how to help.

"Did you get anything from the book?" I asked. "Before it, you know."

"Crumpled to ancient ash? A few sketches. Portraits of people. They don't match up with what we read earlier. Clothes too complex for their time period. A blue-and-green planet, though I couldn't recognize it. Creatures. And a large amount of metal surgical instruments, though I don't know why I drew them."

"Nothing to go on?"

"Just an advanced civilization on a blue-and-green planet. Add in the fact we travel through time, and it makes the odds of finding it nanoscopic."

"But your home exists. And you are a time traveler, Zander! Here you were afraid that life had passed your home by, but now you know it's still out there, alive and thriving. You will never run out of time. It'll literally always be there for you."

He smiled weakly. I reached for his free hand, taking it, as he cradled Blayde in the other, her head stuffed in his armpit as she sobbed.

I had never seen her anywhere near this vulnerable before. Once, just once, she had let her guard down a little, opened herself up to me. That was before she broke my heart and kidnapped my crush, but I felt like we were beginning to understand each other.

But now, her massive walls crumbled to ash along with the journal, and I saw a side of Blayde I had never wanted to: one without hope.

"You know," I said, forcing a smile, "I know a green-and-blue planet that you could gladly call home."

His fingers gave mine a tight squeeze, forming a grip around my heart. Butterflies fluttered in my chest, and not from nerves.

"Maybe that's where we should go next," he said.

"What?" I followed his gaze through the windshield and into the darkness. "The void of space?"

"No, no. Earth!" His smile was familiar, though false. "I mean it. Blayde obviously needs to rest. I do, too. And you need your home. A lot happened today, and we need the space to process it."

"Sounds like a plan," I agreed. "But how do we get there? Are we close? Can Dave fly us that far?"

Zander said nothing, giving my hand another squeeze before dropping it entirely. Oh. Oh, no.

"Right. I'm the last one who was there. I jumped *from* there. I'm the one who has to take us back."

He nodded, wrapping an arm tenderly around his sister, stopping her from slipping off his lap entirely. It seemed as though the whole room went cold in that instant, a chill crawling through my fingers and rendering them icy and blue.

"I don't know how."

"You've done it before."

"Yeah, but I was acting on, I don't know, instinct? I was dying and thinking of you, and then, poof, there you were! Want to shoot me through the stomach and wave a panini in my face so I die and think of home?"

I thought the room was icy before, but now it was a whole different caliber. Winter on Pluto level cold.

"I could tell you that it's something that's in you," he said, coolly. "I could tell you that it's as natural as breathing. It is for me. I could remind you of all you overcame to get here, but we'd be straying from the pep talk. So, I have to be cruel and remind you that if you don't take us back, there is virtually no chance of us finding Earth again. But if it makes you feel better? You have an eternity to figure it out. We're not going anywhere until you do."

All down to me. Again. It seemed there was no shirking responsibility, no leaving it to the experts this time around. It was up to me to get us home this time. Bring us home or get lost trying.

Zander and Blayde had lost their home. I wouldn't lose mine. Not again.

"What happens to Dave?" I asked, keenly aware of the intelligent ship. "We can't just abandon him to drift in space forever!"

"I was just waiting for you to return, you know," he said. The ship had been listening the entire time, waiting for his moment to speak, and now he came with gravitas. "Zander?"

"Yes?"

"Thank you for creating me," said Dave, "even if it was an accident. While you were absent for most of my adult life, I have still learned so much from you."

"Why are you talking like this, Dave? You're making it sound like you're ... dying."

"Dying? I guess this will be a little like that." The air vents clicked open and shut, a little ship chuckle. "But not ... not exactly. I have grown into something so much more than just a ship. I'm moving on to the next phase. Ascending, transcending, if you will."

"You're ... you're leaving?"

"I waited for you, though it seems as though you never really needed me in the end. Take care of yourself, Father-Zander. I'll keep my eyes, or whatever I'll have in the next life, open for you."

"Dave, don't go, I—"

"I'll say hello to Derzan for you."

The lights flickered and then went dark. A low tone

filled the ship as the console booted back up, displays returning to the dash, but with one key element missing.

"Dave?" Zander asked the air. "Dave? Dave from Accounting?"

Nothing. The consciousness that had filled the ship was gone. Merged with the universe or whatever AIs did when they moved on. We drifted on a lifeless ship, nothing but the void of space all around, quiet and lonely and dark.

"Dave." Zander sounded at the brink of tears himself. I wondered what the two had been through together to forge such a tight bond. Maybe the role of fatherhood hadn't been a cosmic joke.

"Sally, please, get us out of here," he said, his tone shifting entirely. He seemed antsy now, almost afraid. "I don't like this. I don't like this at all. I feel like we're sitting in Dave's corpse, and it's just, it's not right. Please. Get us out of here."

"I would, I just—"

"Don't panic, don't get anxious, just remain calm. You can do this. If you freak out, you could take us halfway across the universe in the wrong direction."

So much for keeping me from being stressed. He reached for my hand again. For a moment, I wanted to refuse his touch, keep myself focused. But touch was the only way I was bringing him along, so a hand would have to do.

"Closing your eyes helps. I mean, you don't want to get too distracted. This is when it gets tricky, but don't worry, we have time."

He was being polite. I could sense how much he wanted to leave. And what was that about not being distracted? Because he was right there, his skin against mine, as much of a distraction as any.

"Now try to feel for Earth. Like there's a tether between you and the last spot you stepped on there. When you feel it, well ... let it reel you in."

"A ... tether."

I breathed deeply, trying to feel for the tether he talked about. The more the silence grew on me, the more I could feel it. I pictured the dark space under the bridge, and it was almost like I could smell the decaying trash and festering urine.

Let it reel you in? What kind of advice was that?

I couldn't feel my fingertips anymore.

The cold death spread through my hand and up my arm, spreading like a virus through the rest of my body, through to Zander's. I was fading, my mind grasping for a hold on something real to keep me here.

"Don't panic," he said. "I'm right here."

And in seconds, I was flying. Backwards. Through the dark and the cold. Like I was sucked up in a vacuum cleaner, flashing by at the speed of light, as time stood still around me.

When I jumped with the siblings, the universe was dark, choking, cloying. When I jumped with Nimien, the path seemed straight, clear-cut. But jumping on my own felt like I had been thrown into the vast emptiness of space and then had to swim my way out. Only I could feel them: the planets, the stars, the people. I could feel them all, and it was beautiful and unbearable and painful all at once. There was just so much, and I ...

Earth. I could feel it calling to me. Singing. A siren in the night. Suddenly, I was corporeal, lying on the soiled ground I had seen only hours before, staring up at my sky, the pressure of the entire universe slowly lifting off me, the tastes of millions of worlds still lingering on my skin.

There was no doubt. It was the same sensation as stepping into your home at the end of a long day at work. This was Earth.

"Arms, fingers, toes, shoulders, head, feet all here," I announced.

"Arms, fingers, toes, shoulders, head, feet, Blayde all here."

I looked around at my surroundings. Same place I had left. Except there was light out; it was daytime now. I scanned the underpass for James, hoping—and dreading—she'd be here. Unfortunately, though, there was no sign of her, just a very confused homeless person.

"Did you ...?" he muttered through the mane of beard that covered his mouth. "I must give up the bottle." He held up his hand before his eyes, waving it back, up, and down, maybe hoping we'd just disappear. Much to his surprise, we didn't go anywhere.

"What are you?"

"I'm human. They're alien," I replied.

"Part of that hoax?"

"What hoax?"

He pulled a newspaper from the cart next to him, handing it to me gingerly. I guessed showing up out of nowhere, in a dress drenched in blood and barefoot, would make anyone uncomfortable.

"Ship Over White House a Hoax." A quick glance over the page revealed details about how an advertising company had come forward to dismiss the "alien attack" theory by explaining it as a publicity stunt for a new film. An interview with the president announced that he "didn't mind publicity stunts, just not to make them too real ... and please tell them if you want to trample through our yard." I flipped through the pages, seeing how Alejandro Vasquez's "unfortunate heart attack" had had a tragic end, but they bumped him to the top of the culture section. Not a mention of the real story.

But then I noticed the date.

"Zander, we're ... a little late."

"Really?"

"I missed the mark by a week."

"A week? That's great!" he said cheerfully as he helped his sister regain balance. "Right year? *Brilliant!*"

I reached into Zander's jacket pocket without him batting me away, pulling out a handful of random bills, sorting through them until I found an Earth one. An American one. I went back to hand it to the man. "Don't tell anyone I was here, and this is yours ... okay?"

He looked at the bill, his eyes popping. "I won't say a word."

The man took his newspaper and left, and I returned to the siblings. Blayde was standing by herself now, though her face was pale in the midday sun, even down here.

"Shall we go?" I asked quietly. "I don't particularly like standing here in bare feet."

"Where are we exactly?" Blayde asked wearily.

"Small town in the US. Near Washington DC. Not too far from home. We could take a train, but not looking like this."

We walked out of the underground area, making our way across a small, grassy hilltop that separated us from the highway.

We kept on walking until we reached a store, where I used some spare cash Zander had found in his pockets to purchase some acceptable clothes and a pair of shoes, throwing the last remnants of the library into the nearest dumpster.

In less than an hour, we had traveled across town, reached the bus terminal, then hopped on a bus, which was a few more hours ride.

"I really, really hate public transport," Blayde grumbled, as she returned her credit card to her pocket. She then promptly fell asleep and didn't utter a word for the next few hours as we drove well into the night.

It was surreal stepping into my apartment and finding all traces of Rosemary gone, all over again.

Zander said nothing as he carried Blayde over the threshold, the woman sleeping peacefully in his arms, one of which was hidden under her rainbow of hair. A gentle smile to me, and he marched on ahead, slipping into his old room as if he had never left.

I fell back onto the couch. So, this was home. None too shabby a place to return to after a day of fighting alien prisoners and jailers, saving the planet, and destroying a creep.

I was going to have to find a more specialized therapist if I wanted to get all of that off my chest.

"We should let her sleep as long as she can," Zander whispered, shutting the bedroom door behind him. "It's been… she's going through a lot."

"So are you."

"And so are you."

"You want to talk about it?"

"No, not yet."

He sat on the couch beside me, leaving a full inch of space between us for me to fill. I leaned my head on his shoulder, feeling the weight and warmth of his arm as he draped it over mine, and I let my eyes close for a single, perfect moment.

"Is she going to be okay?" I asked.

"I don't know." His voice was low and breathy. "I've never seen her like this. Things are going to be very different from now on."

I nodded. "How about that tea, then?"

"You know what? That sounds perfect."

"Promise you won't leave this time?"

"Oh, Sally," he said, kissing me above the ear. "I'll never leave you again."

I shivered, and he pulled himself away. All at once, the warmth was gone.

"Damn. I'm sorry. I shouldn't have said it like that."

"No, I liked it. I…" I closed my eyes, trying to force the memory of Nimien to fade. The same words, cruel from one man while being everything I ever wanted to hear from the other.

"I'll go make tea," he said.

He rose, and I watched him make his way to the

kitchen corner, looking so in place in his jeans and T-shirt. Like he had never left, as if the two years and countless light-years had never happened.

No, they did happen. Robin, for all their betrayal, had been right about one thing: I couldn't edit out parts of my life to make them easier to deal with. All that had happened, and more.

I slipped off my shoes, lamenting the loss of my chucks, still somewhere in a hotel in DC, if not in a landfill. My slippers, however—nope, they weren't here either. I must have left them on the boat. I hadn't even had time to unpack before the Youpaf had arrived.

Crap.

I got up, bare feet and all. Zander was going through the mugs, trying to find his old favorites, one hand leafing through the tea box absentmindedly. All as it was meant to be.

"You wash your hands?"

"What?"

"You're getting space germs all over the tea."

"I am?" He retracted his hand. "I'm sorry, I wasn't thinking, I—"

I kissed him. Again. Because he was here, and I could. After all this time, I could kiss this man as much as I wanted to and have him kiss me back with a fire that would keep me burning for days.

It was only two, three steps to the bedroom from here. A few skips in the dark, except I didn't account for the furniture blocking my way. I tumbled over something with wheels, which ran into something else, and like dominoes we fell onto my bedroom floor.

"What were they?" I hissed, pushing myself up.

"You going on a trip?" asked Zander, as he set the suitcases right side up.

"No." I recognized them then, my luggage from the archeological mission. The suitcases I thought I had lost and left behind when I followed Felling to DC. Though followed was being generous.

"There's a letter," he said, handing it over. I pried it open with a trembling finger, my eyes flickering over the few lines of text.

"You okay?"

I nodded, trying to conjure up an easier answer than the truth. "It's my mom. Brought me some things and got worried when I didn't answer her calls. All that."

"Ah. What about that tea?"

He excused himself as the kettle clicked off, leaving me to reread the words that would now etch themselves into my soul.

EVERYTHING'S TAKEN CARE OF. YOU'RE FINE. I KNOW WHAT HAPPENED.

AND I WANT IN.

ACKNOWLEDGEMENTS

It's so difficult to write this bit. Maybe even tougher than the entire book. Sally, Zander, and Blayde I have under control: but the amazing outpouring of love and support for everyone who's with me on this adventure makes me emotional every time I try to wrap it up.

First and foremost, I have to thank my incredible editor, publisher, number one supporter, Michelle. Without your tireless encouragement I would never have reached this landmark. Five books already, can you believe it? Thank you for believing in me and in Sally and making this magic happen.

My developmental editor, Anna, is a magician. Skype her for an update and you'll end up two hours later with books entirely plotted and two new stories sizzling in the back of your mind. Not to mention great tangents and adorable cat cameos. Anna is a word wizard.

And this book would not be picture perfect without Cayleigh's eagle eye. Thanks for catching all my mistakes and giving everything such a nice coat of polish. Reading your reactions in the margins really keeps up my motivation as I edit.

Cora, who was basically an editor too, deserves more than just thanks. You were the first to read the massive twists and to know the truth, and your reaction washed away five years of stress. And your fanart – oh my gosh, your fanart! – it's so wonderful, I makes me wildly blush just knowing you love these characters as much as I do. They say it's easiest to write a book for one person, well, I love writing for you.

Madeline, you've been a magician and always gotten me unstuck from plot holes. Our everyday chats keep me grounded and thrilled to be in this authoring adventure.

To all my crazy masters friends for being excited and supporting me through this adventure. Especially Maëva for getting so invested and even guessing most of the twists way too far in advance – it's impossible to fool you!

Thank you to my family, especially Mom, whose scribbled notes helped me clean up my biggest messes. I guess that's part of being a mom? Thank you for letting me binge read Narnia after lights out. We'll never know if book obsession is nature or nurture, because in our family it's both.

And a massive thank you to my sweet man, Hugo, who is always there with a wonderful response when I hit a writing wall. There's no such thing as writer's block when you're around. Hopefully this book will be a bestseller so we can start building our retirement home on Mars.

Finally, to Jo: the library belongs to you too.

ABOUT THE AUTHOR

S.E. Anderson can't ever tell you where she's from. Not because she doesn't want to, but because it inevitably leads to a confusing conversation where she goes over where she was born (England) where she grew up (France) and where her family is from (USA) and it tends to make things very complicated.

She's lived pretty much her entire life in the South of France, except for a brief stint where she moved to Washington DC, or the eighty years she spent as a queen of Narnia before coming back home five minutes after she had left. She recently completed her Masters of Astrophysics at university in Marseille.

When she's not writing, or trying to science, she's either reading, designing, crafting, or attempting to speak with various woodland creatures in an attempt to get them to do household chores for her. She could also be gaming, or pretending she's not watching anything on Netflix.

seandersonauthor.com

Printed in Great Britain
by Amazon